PRAISE FOR
SEALED WITH A KISS SERIES

A TASTE FOR SCANDAL

"Very sweet and heartening. . . . The characters are likable and well written, the plot is delightful and keeps your attention, and the ending declaration of love is sigh worthy."   —Smexy Books Romance Reviews

"As satisfyingly sweet as one of the heroine's cakes, Knightley's delightful and charming romance is both tender and adorable."   —*RT Book Reviews*

"With endearing characters, eloquent writing, and a spoonful of charm, you've got the perfect recipe for a perfect read!"   —Under the Covers

MORE THAN A STRANGER

"This sweet treat of a romance will entrance you with its delicious humor, dollop of suspense, and delectable characters. It'll make your mouth water!"
    —*New York Times* bestselling author Sabrina Jeffries

"More than a romance—it's a witty and engaging love story that had me turning pages well into the night just so I could find out what would happen next. It's a truly captivating tale of two headstrong friends who become much more to each other than they could have imagined."   —Lydia Dare

continued . . .

Also by Erin Knightley

More Than a Stranger
A Taste for Scandal
Miss Mistletoe (Penguin Special)

ERIN KNIGHTLEY

Flirting with Fortune

A SEALED WITH A KISS NOVEL

A SIGNET ECLIPSE BOOK

SIGNET ECLIPSE
Published by the Penguin Group
Penguin Group (USA), 375 Hudson Street,
New York, New York 10014, USA

USA | Canada | UK | Ireland | Australia | New Zealand | India | South Africa | China

Penguin Books Ltd., Registered Offices: 80 Strand, London WC2R 0RL, England
For more information about the Penguin Group visit penguin.com.

First published by Signet Eclipse, an imprint of New American Library,
a division of Penguin Group (USA)

First Printing, September 2013

SIGNET ECLIPSE and logo are trademarks of Penguin Group (USA)

ISBN 978-0-451-41348-2

Printed in the United States of America
10 9 8 7 6 5 4 3 2 1

PUBLISHER'S NOTE
This is a work of fiction. Names, characters, places, and incidents either are the
product of the author's imagination or are used fictitiously, and any resemblance to actual persons, living or dead, business establishments, events, or
locales is entirely coincidental.
    The publisher does not have any control over and does not assume any re-
sponsibility for author or third-party Web sites or their content.

If you purchased this book without a cover you should be aware that this book
is stolen property. It was reported as "unsold and destroyed" to the publisher
and neither the author nor the publisher has received any payment for this
"stripped book."

ALWAYS LEARNING   PEARSON

For Papa, because you would have been so proud of me.

For Dad, because you have always been proud of me.

And for Kirk, because you are almost *as proud of me as I am of you.*

Acknowledgments

Whenever I have a story idea, it begins as a tiny seed, full of promise but without form. It's only thanks to the help of others that it grows and flourishes, becoming a book that I can be proud of. This book in particular would never have happened without the help of Heather Snow, Catherine Gayle, Olivia Kelly, and my wonderful critique group. Thank you all for sticking by me with my endless brainstorming and plotting, always there to lend an ear or a helpful suggestion.

A heartfelt thank-you to my fantastic editor, Kerry Donovan, and her team at New American Library— including the wonderful art department! I'm so lucky to have such gorgeous covers. As always, a big hug and lots of gratitude to my agent, Deidre Knight, and all the ladies at the Knight Agency.

Last, thank you to all my wonderful fans—nothing lifts my heart more than to know my stories make you smile. Please feel free to join me on my Facebook page or on Twitter—I'm always happy to say hello!

Chapter One

When one attends one of the most anticipated balls of the Season—even if it was only the Little Season—one is supposed to, well, attend the ball. But as Lady Beatrice Moore walked down Lady Churly's deserted portrait gallery, accompanied by nothing but the muted whisper of the distant orchestra and the slightest sense of accomplishment, Bea couldn't help the sigh of pleasure that escaped her.

She was in heaven.

Finally, she was away from the crowd, far from the eyes of fortune hunters who watched her as a hawk eyed a field mouse and beyond the earshot of the gossipmongers looking to snap up the latest *on-dit*. Bea was alone, with the soft glow of the turned-back lamps lining the hall and an entire wall full of some of the greatest masterpieces England had ever produced.

In no hurry now that she had escaped, she clasped her hands behind her back and strolled across the narrow hall, her slippers silent on the herringbone-patterned wood floors. This was why she had really agreed to come to this ball—well, one of two reasons, anyway. Lady Churly possessed the single largest collection of acclaimed painter Sir Frederick Tate's work: four spectacular portraits that were so much more than the sum of their subjects. His true genius had been in the play of light, particularly the incredibly lifelike shadows that always gave his pieces such moody brilliance. Dark yet full of life, each portrait was an absolute masterpiece.

Even more so now that he was gone.

She felt an odd sense of loss, thinking of his death. His work had made such an impact on her as a young artist—it was impossible to think that she could never meet the man who had somehow become her absentee mentor.

At least, as an artist, his legacy was preserved. She paused, studying a painting of a small boy standing in a library, a book in his hand. His dark hair fell across his forehead while challenging gray eyes stared directly at her. Impossibly, Beatrice felt as though she could see the spirit within him, almost pull the thoughts from his mind.

The tap of approaching footsteps broke through her study. Had someone followed her after all? No, the sound came from the opposite direction of the ballroom, presumably from the family's private rooms. She scowled, glancing around for someplace to slip out of view—not the easiest thing to do when one was draped in yards and yards of snowy white lutestring.

Even if it wasn't some fortune hunter trying to get her alone, or her mother come to chide her, the company was still most unwelcome. And really, she did not want to be caught snooping. Where was a decent potted palm when a person needed one, anyway? There were few places to hide, with only one viable option: behind one of the heavy gold curtains that fell in generous velvet waves from the high ceiling to the floor.

Feeling like a thief in the night, she gathered her skirts and slipped behind the nearest fabric panel, pressing her back against the freezing-cold glass of the window. She gritted her teeth against the chill as she flattened herself as much as she could. She almost grinned—who would have thought she would discover a situation where her small bosom was actually a *good* thing?

Whoever was out there certainly wasn't in any hurry. Judging by the heaviness of the tread and the harsh sound of the hard-soled shoes on the wood, she thought it must be a man. Beatrice willed him to move faster as the cold seeped through her and raised gooseflesh on her arms. Still, she didn't dare move a muscle. It was all so very undignified. She hadn't found herself in a position like this since she was a child. She was nineteen, no longer a silly girl listening at keyholes, for heaven's sake.

The footsteps slowed further as they drew closer and closer, and Bea held her breath when they stopped mere feet away.

And then, nothing. The man just stood there, unintentionally pinning her in place like a trapped mouse. She waited, her lungs burning more with every passing second. Blast it all, what was he doing? She quickly realized that it was a mistake to hold her breath. Now if she tried to release it, she would surely gasp with the need to draw air, giving herself away.

Move, for heaven's sake. Move!

Just when she thought her lungs would explode, he stepped away. As quietly as humanly possible, Beatrice released her breath and sucked in a fresh supply of air. No matter that it tasted of musty velvet and dust motes—it was the sweetest breath she had ever taken.

The intruder seemed to have stopped again, this time close to the opposite wall. Was it his plan to hold her hostage all night? Never mind that he had no idea she was even there—it was still annoying. Who was out there, anyway?

The old, familiar itch of curiosity flared to life deep

within her. She knew it well. It had gotten her into plenty of trouble with her siblings over the years. Of course, it had also resulted in her discovering all kinds of secrets—all of which she had kept to herself, of course. Her siblings might have called her a spy, but she had scruples.

She focused on possible answers: a butler or footman? But if it were a servant, why would he loiter in the portrait hall during a ball?

The only other option was that it was a family member, but Beatrice had taken care to locate each of them before sneaking away. They were all atwitter about a surprise guest who was to be revealed at midnight, and Lady Churly, her son, Captain Andrews, and her deceased husband's three children had been milling about all night, smiling knowingly and shaking their heads at anyone who begged to know the secret guest's identity.

Beatrice stiffened. That was it! This must be the person who had the *ton* holding its collective breath all night. Oh, how utterly delicious it would be to know his identity before anyone else. The fact that she even knew it was a man was a step above anyone else.

Restlessness welled up within her, making it nearly impossible to hold still. She bit down on her lip, trying to suppress the sensation as she willed her body to stay motionless. It was always like this. She simply couldn't stand not knowing what was going on around her. People could call her nosy and a snoop all they wanted—she *needed* to know things. It was the other reason she had come to the ball in the first place.

Without even making a conscious decision to do so, she started sliding sideways a quarter inch at a time. The edge of the drape was tantalizingly close, and if she could only make it over far enough to peek out, the burning curiosity would be satiated.

She barely breathed as she moved, pacing herself to about the speed of paint drying. At this rate, it would probably strike midnight before she could catch a glimpse of the mystery person in the room with her. For the thousandth time, she wondered who Lady Churly had secured for the ball. The woman was well respected and in all the best circles, so Beatrice knew it wouldn't be anyone scandalous or improper, which didn't leave much in the way of interesting people. She had pondered the topic all week—along with the rest of the *ton*, from what she had heard—and hadn't been able to come up with a single plausible candidate for the surprise guest.

Which annoyed her to no end.

Now was her chance. She could be the first to know who it was, a thought so tantalizing, she moved the slightest bit faster the last two inches toward freedom—more like the speed of grass growing. The gold velvet brushed across her hair, then her temple, and finally slid past her right eye.

Success!

The flash of triumph was immediately trumped by something else altogether as she focused on a man leaning against the opposite wall, his arms folded and amusement lifting the corners of his mouth. Her stomach flopped to the floor with an almost audible thump.

He was staring directly back at her.

Chapter Two

"So this is the lady who belongs to the scent of lilacs. How lovely of you to come out and join me."

He was amused.

She was not.

Never mind that the almost musical lilt of his Scottish-tinged accent sent a shiver down the back of Bea's already chilled neck. If he knew she was there, he should have had the decency to say as much. Embarrassment stiffened her spine—Lord, she must look a fool. With as much dignity as one in her position could muster, she extracted herself from the heavy drapes and shook out her skirts. "Yes, well, since you wouldn't leave like a proper gentleman, it seems as though I had little choice."

He lifted a dark eyebrow, tilting his head just enough so that a lock of midnight black hair fell across his temple. "I do beg your pardon. I should have left the moment I realized there was a debutant-shaped lump behind the curtains."

Well, when he said it like that. She lifted her chin regally. "Pardon granted, Mr. . . . ?"

She waited, but he didn't take the bait. Instead, he pushed away from the wall, closing the distance between them with measured, unhurried steps. He wasn't overly tall, but he had a certain presence about him, as if he could command an army, if so inclined. She couldn't have taken her eyes from him if she wanted to.

With every step he took, her heartbeat seemed to increase, until it fluttered like a caged bird beneath her breast. He wasn't traditionally handsome, not like her brother or even her brother-in-law. His appeal was much more intense than that. His jaw looked as sharp as if it were carved from granite and already possessed the slightest hint of dark stubble. His cheeks angled high, almost like a woman's, but his bold, masculine brow provided exactly enough counterbalance to give his features exquisite symmetry and depth. Such unique beauty made her fingers itch to take up her brushes and commit his visage to canvas.

Her gaze was too bold by half, but he didn't seem to mind her inspection. In fact, he watched her right back, his flint-colored eyes seeming to take in everything about her, leaving her feeling quite exposed. "Now, now, we haven'a been introduced. I wouldn'a want to break protocol at my very first ball. Unless, of course, it is your wish, Miss . . . ?"

Beatrice almost smiled. She'd as soon walk naked through the ballroom than tell him who she was. A lady did *not* get caught hiding behind curtains. "Yes, well . . . I suppose rules are rules."

She realized then the importance of what he had said: This was his first ball. There was no doubt in her mind that he was the mystery guest Lady Churly was so eager to present. Who was this man? He was five-and-twenty if he was a day, so why had he never been to a ball? Beatrice's curiosity rebelled with an almost physical force, but she firmly tamped it down. She was dying to know who he was, this man with the lyrical voice, compelling features, and unmistakable air of mystery, but not at the price of revealing her own identity.

"Indeed." He paused at exactly the proper distance away and folded his arms, considering her. "Although I suspect that you doona always play by the rules." He nodded to the curtains behind her.

This time she did smile. "My character exposed in two minutes or less. Alas, I cannot deny it. Following the rules will gain you naught but a stellar reputation and a tremendously boring life." Her older siblings, Evie and Richard, had taught her that much.

His answering smile was nearly as delicious as his accent, his perfectly bowed upper lip curving to reveal beautiful white teeth. Beatrice pressed her lips together. She hated the crooked front tooth that marred her own smile.

"Then you'd think me very tedious, indeed, I'm afraid," he said, mock regret weighting his tone. "I must admit, I am a rule follower to a fault."

She very nearly rolled her eyes. Any man with a face like that couldn't possibly be boring. "I don't believe you. If you were a rule follower, you would never have waited for me to emerge. Speaking alone with a strange female in a darkened gallery is not exactly perfect protocol."

His grin widened as he lifted a shoulder in a sort of half shrug. "Then it is a very good thing that you doona know my name. I'd hate to have it bandied about that I was anything less than a perfect gentleman upon my entrance into society."

"And if we encounter each other by chance?"

"Then I'll throw myself upon your mercy to protect my reputation. In fact, perhaps I should do so now. Pre-emptively, so as I know I'm safe."

She crossed her arms and nodded, unable to resist playing along. There was something about the ano-nymity of the moment that was almost intoxicating, like a first sip of champagne. "Very well—you may commence groveling."

He dipped his head gravely. "As you wish. Though I wonder how I should address you." He took in her elegant gown and the emeralds decorating her ears and neck. "Princess, perhaps?"

"I should think not," she said, wrinkling her nose. That was the very last thing she would wish to be called. Though she was the daughter of a marquis, she was no overly privileged, dreadfully coddled princess. "I value my freedom much too fervently for that."

"Clearly." Even in the low light, she could see the irony in his gaze. Which was a good thing, since it was deuced hard to detect it in the lilt of his accent. "*A stór*, then. It suits you, I think."

"A story? How on earth does that suit me?"

"Not 'a story,'" he said, pantomiming opening a book. "*A stór*. My treasure."

She sucked in a surprised breath, warmth infusing her whole body before flooding her face. His *treasure*? Her heart shuddered within her. There was something shockingly intimate about being called such a thing by a near-complete stranger.

Before she could think of a response, he chuckled. "As in *buried* treasure. Unearthed from the depths of the curtains. I dinna mean to imply anything else."

"Of course not," she replied, nodding as though her mind hadn't gone directly to that "something else." "You may call me whatever you wish. Now, on with the groveling, if you please—I'll be missed if I remain much longer." She hoped the soft strains of music from the ballroom disguised the breathlessness of her voice.

He stepped forward, bringing them closer than even the most liberal of hosts would have deemed proper. He put a hand to his heart and dipped his head to hers. Mischief lit his eyes, subtly challenging her. She blinked—why did he suddenly look so familiar?

"I beg you, *a stór*, from the very depths of me—could

you find it in your heart to have mercy on my depraved soul? Could you carry this encounter close to your breast, not to be revealed under threat of death, or worse—gossip?"

Good heavens, he was positively mesmerizing when he put his mind to it. The soft, lilting tones of his voice washed over her skin like warm silk, and she only just suppressed the shiver that flitted down her spine. Doing her best to sound lightly amused, she said, "Very well. You have my mercy. It was a pleasure *not* to meet you, sir. I do hope you enjoy the ball."

With a reluctance that surprised her, she started to turn.

"Perhaps," he said, drawing her attention to him once more, "you'd save a dance for me."

She lifted her brow. "Ah, but that would require an introduction, would it not?" Even so, the offer was absurdly tempting. The idea of being pulled into his arms was almost enough to make her forget that dancing wasn't her forte.

"An excellent point, to which I offer this solution: If by the end of the night, you wish to take me up on my offer, then I leave it to you to seek an introduction to me. Seeing how I now have assurance of your mercy, of course."

Beatrice drew back in surprise. "Seek an introduction to you? I do hate to disabuse you of whatever opinion you have formed of me in these past few minutes, but I am not a desperate woman. I assure you, I will be seeking an introduction to no one."

He didn't look the least bit disappointed, or the slightest bit offended. Instead, the corners of his eyes crinkled in an almost imperceptible smile. Dipping his head in the approximation of a bow, he said, "Your prerogative. However, I do feel it prudent to clarify that I was giving you the option of *not* being introduced, should you wish to remain anonymous. I assure you it was not meant to disparage your prospects. I, of course, shall respect your decision."

He certainly had a way with words. Was it the accent or his sentiment that muddled her brain and had her leaning the slightest bit forward? "Er, thank you." Already she was feeling like a ninny for having reacted as she did.

"You're welcome. And just so you know," he said, slipping a gloved hand beneath hers and lifting her fingers to his lips for a feather-soft kiss that had her holding her breath all over again, "I'll be keeping the last dance free."

As distractions went, she was a damn fine one.

Colin watched the girl as she sashayed out of sight, her white skirts swishing around her like a windswept cloud. Whoever she was, she was a damn sight better than the debutants he had expected to encounter tonight.

He drew in a deep breath and was treated to her lingering scent. She might have gotten away with her hiding place if it weren't for the hint of lilacs betraying her presence. It had stopped him cold, transporting him instantly back to his childhood home outside of Edinburgh. Even though he had left Scotland years ago, the smell of home was still arresting, particularly in the darkened gallery of his aunt's London home.

Her presence was unexpected, but he was glad for it. He had been incredibly on edge, dreading the stroke of midnight, when he would be thrust into England's high society once and for all. But at the moment she emerged from the drapes, his anxiety had ebbed and his spirits had lifted. The way she had looked at him . . . well, it was hard not to feel a boost of confidence. More important, she had given him something much more interesting to focus on—and damned enticing, at that. If a lady of the *ton* could sneak into private rooms and bury herself behind curtains, he had little to fear from high society.

Colin smiled. He didn't know what he was expecting to find behind the drapes, but she certainly wasn't it. If he were feeling fanciful—which he rarely was—he'd say she put him to mind of some sort of misplaced forest nymph. Exactly like the ones Gran had liked to go on about when he was young. Luminous blue eyes, hair of burnished moonbeams, and skin so pure as to almost look porcelain. He could easily imagine her at home in a midnight garden. And then there was that impertinent mouth. Colin shook his head, allowing a small chuckle at her cheek.

He sincerely hoped she would seek an introduction.

With the weight on his shoulders slightly lifted, he made his way toward the study where he was to meet his cousin. As he walked, he kept his gaze from the prized portraits lining the walls. They were well known to him—intimately so. Another time he might linger on them, but tonight he didn't want to face the tangled threads of nostalgia and resentment that he knew would unfurl within him at the sight of them.

The study was warm and welcoming, with an assortment of crystal decanters lining the sideboard and reflecting the low fire in the grate. Colin started to reach for the scotch but decided on wine instead. It was probably best to save the imbibing for *after* the ball. God knew he'd need it by then. He poured himself a glass and took a hearty draft.

"So is it as bad as all that already?" asked his cousin John as he strode into the room, his crimson coattails fluttering behind him. The man was the epitome of military elegance tonight, all sharp angles and efficient movements. He paused to shut the door before joining

Colin at the sideboard. "D'you mind pouring me a brandy?"

Nodding, Colin selected the appropriate bottle and splashed some of the amber liquid into a tumbler before handing it to John. "It depends on how you define 'bad.'" He walked over to the desk and leaned upon the corner. "If by bad you mean that my father, God rest his soul, has damned me into a marriage of necessity from beyond the grave, then, yes, it is as bad as all that."

John lowered his tall frame into one of the chairs facing the desk. "Yes, we know that," he said, waving his drink in the air by way of dismissal. "It is, after all, the entire purpose of this ball. And I am happy to report that, as promised, there are debutants aplenty filling the place. Not bad, considering the time of year."

It was quite a boon when John's mother, Constance, who was Colin's mother's sister, remarried a wealthy earl several years after the death of her first husband. However, in the dozen years since, Colin and his family had never had reason to call on their connection.

It was a damned nuisance that he had to now.

"I never doubted it—especially with your mother in charge of things. I merely despise the fact that I must look at them as if they are some sort of commodities to be purchased." Colin took another swig of the wine to wash away the distaste in his mouth, but it was no use.

"That, my good man, is where you need to adjust your frame of mind."

"Oh really?" Colin asked, crossing his arms. "Care to expound?"

"They are not commodities for you to purchase. *You* are the commodity for them to purchase. It is why they have dowries in the first place." John drained his glass and leaned forward to set it on the desk with a thump.

"I see," Colin said, his tone clearly indicating that he did not.

"Why do you think they dress them up like dolls and parade them around in front of us? They are all looking for the best match. You are a baronet now. There are women aplenty out there whose families would be more than happy to purchase that title from you via their dowries. It is not such a big ordeal; it's business."

Colin set his own glass down on the desk and pushed to his feet. "It may be business to you, my friend, but I find I canna look at it that way. The whole idea of it makes me ill. The only thing that makes it even halfway palatable is the conviction that I'll not lie about my situation if asked directly."

John leaned back in his chair and sighed. "I hate to be the bearer of bad news, but it is past time to get over your reservations and get on with the business of finding a wife. You have, what, four months before the bankers collect?"

Colin closed his eyes and nodded. Sixteen weeks before the world learned of his family's downfall—a mere three months to convince some young lady with a fat dowry to marry him and save his family from ruin. How utterly cliché. He tried to stifle the rising resentment he felt for his father. He had loved—still loved—the man who had been a genius and yet still had managed to make such horrid business decisions.

"Do try to remember what is at stake here," John said, coming to his feet. "Your brother, sister, and your grandmother are depending on you." He picked up the empty glasses and returned them to the sideboard. Turning back to Colin, he said, "The sooner you find yourself a bride, the sooner you can return to normal life." He headed toward the door, gesturing for Colin to join him. "Come. Let us weed through the merchandise, shall we?"

Colin gave a snort of laughter. "I thought *I* was the merchandise. Don't tell me you were feeding me a load of bullocks, just now."

"I? Never. Now polish up that title of yours and prepare to wear it on your sleeve; you have a wife to catch." Grinning broadly, he slapped a hand on Colin's back, propelling him through the doorway. "And with your secret weapon, tonight is sure to be a success."

Chapter Three

The entrance to the ballroom was elegant and sumptuous, with a great, arching doorway framed by intricately carved whitewashed wood. There were two matching columns on either side, both fluted, with a scrolled design at the top that was reminiscent of Greek architecture, providing a dramatic backdrop for anyone hoping to make a grand entrance.

These were not the sorts of details a casual attendee might notice.

But, after fifteen minutes of surreptitiously sneaking glances that way, Beatrice was fairly certain she was as well acquainted with the entryway design as the architect himself. And now that the clock hands were perilously close to meeting beneath the twelve, heralding the hour when her mystery man would reappear, she could hardly drag her gaze away. She breathed an impatient sigh and wrapped a hand around her middle. Newton, as it turned out, must have been mistaken with his whole "gravity theory" idea. Otherwise, how could her stomach feel as though it were hovering somewhere in the vicinity of the gilded ceiling?

"Darling, what has come over you? You haven't heard a word I've said."

Drat. Her mother was right—Bea had completely ignored whatever it was she was talking about. Lucky for her, Mama had only one topic of interest at these kinds of functions. Smiling vaguely, Bea gave a little flip of her hand, dismissing her mother's entirely true statement. "Don't be absurd—I've heard every word. Yes, there are many eligible gentlemen here tonight. No, I'm not overly inclined to dance with them. You know I'm as likely to tread on their boots as make a good impression."

Mama came as close to rolling her eyes as Beatrice had ever seen in public, briefly lifting her gray gaze heavenward. "Hyperbole does not become you. You are a perfectly adequate dancer—I hired the best instructors in London to ensure it. And *what* are you so interested in across the room?"

Beatrice snapped her gaze back, not even realizing it had wandered to the ballroom entryway once again. Oops. Well, there was no harm in the truth. "I'm merely anxious for the stroke of midnight, when we will finally discover the identity of the mystery guest."

Mama straightened, running a gloved hand down the burgundy silk of her gown. "Ah, the mystery guest. Well, let us hope he is an eligible gentleman so your interest can be for good."

It was Beatrice's turn to roll her eyes. With Papa's illness striking shortly after the start of her first Season, little attention had been paid to the endeavor of finding her a husband. At the time, there were much more important issues to attend to. But now, with her sisters, twins Carolyn and Jocelyn, set to make their debut in the spring, her mother was suddenly bound and determined to remedy the situation. It was why her parents had insisted they attend the Little Season. Normally, the family spent most of their time at Hertford Hall, their country estate, making the trek to London each spring. But no—if there was hope of avoiding having three daughters on the marriage mart at once, then Mama would do everything in her power to exploit it.

Never mind that London in the winter was positively dismal, lacking the sort of inspiration Bea craved when creating her paintings. Or that her elder sister, Evie, had had no fewer than five Seasons before her own marriage. Mama had decided that Bea must marry, and that was that.

"Good evening, Lady Granville, Lady Beatrice."

Beatrice's jaw tightened at the all too familiar voice of Mr. William Godfrey. Curse her luck—would the man be at every event they attended this month? Pasting a humorless smile upon her lips, she turned and dipped her head in a shallow greeting. "Mr. Godfrey."

He was dressed in clothes befitting of the youngest son of a viscount—sumptuous velvet jacket with an incredibly fussy cravat, buff pantaloons, and highly polished shoes—but Beatrice knew better than to be fooled by the display.

He was a gambler, a lush, and worst of all, a fortune hunter.

And it drove her mad that no one else seemed to have picked up on those facts. Although, to be fair, she knew of his gambling only because of her brother. But anyone with eyes and half a brain could see that he circled the daughters of wealthy men like a hungry, well-dressed vulture.

Beatrice didn't understand it. There were those whom the *ton* immediately identified as fortune hunters—men with well-known debts or bankrupt estates. But for some reason, they tended to have blinders when it came to others. Generally they were the rakishly good-looking type, with pretty manners and good backgrounds. Godfrey was one; Lord Andrew Gravell was another. Bea's fists clenched at the thought of that particular cur.

"Lady Beatrice, may I just say that you are looking particularly lovely this evening."

"Thank you." It was his favorite line, given every other time they met. Which, unfortunately, meant that he was about to follow up with the next line he delivered without fail. *I do so hope you'll do me the honor of dancing with me.*

Her eyes darted to the front of the ballroom as she tried to think of a way to curtail the question. She had more interesting things on her mind than dancing with Godfrey. But, of course, if she denied him, she'd have to sit out dancing the rest of the evening, and she'd never hear the end of it from her mother. "My goodness, am I parched—"

A stir at the front of the room drew her attention, and this time when she looked toward the entryway, the breath froze in her lungs, crystallizing like the icy early-winter mist hanging over the Thames.

It was him.

Without thinking, she started forward, wanting nothing more than to be closer to him. Well, that, and to learn at last who he really was.

"My lady?" Godfrey said at the same time her mother exclaimed her name softly. Beatrice turned long enough to offer an apologetic smile. "I'm sorry. Please excuse me," she called before allowing herself to be carried away by the building excitement of the crowd.

He looked different in the blazing candlelight of the ballroom, more aloof somehow. The hint of mischief was nowhere to be found, replaced by a passively pleasant expression directed at Lady Churly. Bea turned sideways to slip between Lord St. James and his spinster daughter, never taking her eyes from the man she had shared a secret encounter with. She slowed, her lips lifting in a tiny, private smile.

Secret encounter, indeed.

That made it all sound rather illicit. Anticipation rippled in her belly as she resumed her pace. Was it wrong to wish that he would look her way? To want their eyes to meet and to see his teasing grin once more?

Lady Churly clapped her gloved hands, her thin face alight with excitement. "Lords and ladies, gentlemen and misses, may I have your attention?"

She didn't have to ask. Everyone's full attention was riveted on her dark-haired mystery man, the hush unnatural in the huge space. He didn't look nearly as uncomfortable as Beatrice would have expected, knowing that this was his very first ball. Instead, he stood straight and tall, his hands resting loosely at his sides as he politely deferred to his host. Captain Andrews stepped up behind him and nodded in his direction. Bea tilted her head. Was he one of the captain's men?

"As you know," Lady Churly began, her voice slow and clear, "I am a great admirer of the late Sir Frederick Tate."

Tate? Beatrice's confusion at the mention of her idol brought her up short. What did he have to do with this?

"After the unfortunate and untimely passing of the master six months ago, a hole opened up in the hearts of many art lovers—my own heart included. Tonight, dear friends, I am honored to offer up a man who may help to bridge the gap."

Curiosity overwhelmed her initial surprise, and Beatrice brushed past a clump of awestruck debutants, all watching the dark stranger with rapt attention. Her own heart squeezed with the lingering sadness for Tate's passing.

As Beatrice stepped closer to the front of the crowd, Lady Churly held out her hand, beckoning for the man to stand beside her. "Without further ado, allow me to present my nephew, Sir Colin Tate—elder son and heir to the late Sir Frederick."

Beatrice rocked back on her heels, her breath leaving her lungs all at once. He was Tate's *son*? It was that moment that their eyes met, and his cool gray gaze sparked to life. So she did what any normal, rational young lady would do.

She turned and dashed off in the other direction.

It happened all at once.

His aunt introducing him, the collective gasp from the crowd, the collision of his gaze with that of the woman from the gallery, his sudden rush of pleasure at seeing her, then the all-consuming confusion as her eyes widened and she turned and fled in the other direction.

What the devil?

Colin's first instinct was to follow, but he immediately realized it was impossible on several levels—not the least of which was the tide of curious people surging forward like an ocean wave to meet him. He couldn't begin to imagine what had made the girl retreat like the blasted hounds of Hades were at her heels, but he didn't have the luxury of finding out just yet. His task for the evening had begun.

Straightening his shoulders, he turned to the first of the people that Aunt Constance wished to introduce him to, his smile as good as painted on. He knew his role well. John had spent an entire afternoon schooling him as to the best candidates—daughters of nobility and cits alike. He was leaning toward the merchants' daughters as default, since one, his becoming a barrister was less likely to be an issue, and two, his title would mean the most to them, therefore allowing him to bring something of value to the marriage.

"How very naughty of you, Constance, not to share

your relationship to Sir Frederick sooner." An older woman dripping in jewels and condescension eyed Colin as if he were a morsel to be eaten. Her gown was easily twice the cost of his monthly rent, with gold fibers woven among the cream fabric.

Aunt chuckled, completely unfazed by the overly direct statement. "Colin, allow me to introduce Lady Kimball."

"My lady," he murmured, bowing over her multi-ringed hand.

"So you're the son of the great Sir Frederick Tate," she said, her dark eyes sweeping up and down his form. She clearly was a woman used to indulging her desires and made no effort to hide her perusal. "Are you in town for his memorial exhibit, then?"

"Indeed." Colin dipped his head in assent, pushing away the flash of grief that seared his lungs. "It was exceedingly kind of the committee to invite me to be a part of it." And fortuitous, in a ghastly sort of way.

The woman's sly eyes seemed to miss nothing as she allowed a small grin. "Yes, well, since you didn't see fit to hold his funeral here, I think it entirely appropriate that you should attempt to make up for it now."

Colin clenched his jaw, biting back the retort that sprang to his lips. God forbid he go home to comfort his family and see to the burial rather than stay in London for the parade of insincere idiots who had seen his father as little more than a novelty. Father had lapped up the attention, but Colin knew the *ton* had no real respect for him, their shiny little plaything. "I'm so glad you approve."

Another matron stepped forward, her eyes bold and her color high. "Lady Churly, how could you keep such a delectable treat from us? You must introduce me."

The introductions went on and on, until Colin's head began to swim with all the Lord This and Lady

Thats. He'd been in the same place for nearly half an hour, an island in the midst of a shifting sea of multi-colored gowns and curious gazes. He was glancing longingly toward the terrace doors when Aunt Constance greeted yet another society matron.

"Lady Granville! Do please come meet my nephew."

Suppressing a sigh, Colin turned back to his aunt with a polite smile. Beside her were two women, one in deep burgundy and the other in a cloud of white. The tension fell away all at once as he looked down into the wide sapphire eyes of his little nymph.

She'd come to him after all.

Triumph heated his blood as his brittle smile transitioned to something he recognized as genuine and honest. He dutifully turned his gaze to his aunt as she made the introductions.

"Colin, allow me introduce to you the Marchioness of Granville and her daughter Lady Beatrice."

Good God, he knew exactly who she was: the Marquis of Granville's second-oldest daughter. Colin mentally flipped through the details of the family that he'd learned from John's lessons. Well-regarded family with an ungodly fortune, mostly from their vast estates, but also from the family's horse-breeding venture. There was a hazy bit of gossip about her brother, the heir, from the previous Season, but Colin couldn't recall the details just then. Lady Beatrice was nineteen years old, with twin sisters only a year behind her.

Most important of all, she was not on his short list.

Her family was too important, too powerful. His paltry title was child's play in comparison, and it would be an insult to even imagine the girl would be a good match for him. And yet, for the first time since entering the ballroom, he felt a spark of interest in a debutante. All he could think about was how endearing she'd been in the quiet of the gallery earlier and how she had intrigued him. He was so exquisitely aware of her just then, it was all he could do to properly acknowledge her mother first.

He forced himself to look to Lady Granville, who was taller than her daughter, with bluish gray eyes and blond hair shot with silver. He bowed. "A pleasure to make your acquaintance, my lady."

"And yours as well, Sir Colin."

He smiled his acknowledgment of the comment before allowing his gaze to slide to her daughter. Lady Beatrice's eyes glittered even more brilliantly than her jewels in the bright candlelight, and for a moment he savored the secret that hung between them like an invisible thread. "I'm delighted to meet you as well. Lady Beatrice, was it?"

She nodded, taking his slight teasing in stride. He liked that—clearly she wasn't at all the simpering miss the *ton* seemed to prize. "It is an honor to meet the son of one of the greatest painters to have ever lived. I hope you don't mind us seeking the introduction."

He almost laughed. The sentence was a bold challenge, acknowledging her part of the bargain. She wasn't afraid to swallow her pride after all, and he respected her all the more for it. "Not at all. In fact, I am honored in turn." He hadn't expected her to be the daughter of a marquis, for heaven's sake, when he had asked her to save him the dance, but he wasn't going to back down now. "And I wonder, do you have room on your dance card for a latecomer?"

She lifted a blond brow, her expression betraying a hint of mischief. "I'm afraid I do not, Sir Colin."

Colin's smile slipped the slightest amount as her words sank in. What was she playing at?

Leaning the slightest bit forward, she confided, "But I would sincerely love a turn about the terrace."

Chapter Four

Sir Frederick Tate's son.

Beatrice tried unsuccessfully to keep the giddy grin from her lips as Sir Colin escorted her toward the terrace doors. She could scarcely believe it—she was touching the sleeve of the man who was the direct descendant of an artistic legend. His son!

The moment she had realized who he was, she promptly abandoned all her intentions of not seeking an introduction and went off to locate her mother, who had been delighted at Beatrice's enthusiasm. But she decreed that they should wait until the crowd around him died down before approaching him and his aunt. The ensuing half hour had felt more like a half a day as Bea waited impatiently for the moment she could speak with him once more.

And now, instead of dancing in front of a roomful of people, they would be able to be alone again—or very nearly so, in any event. Completely by her design, of course. Normally at a function like this, the terrace would be filled to bursting with other people. But it was October, and Beatrice knew full well that it would likely be empty.

They paused by the door as a servant appeared with the wrap her mother had summoned, and when she was properly bundled, they stepped outside. Cold air immediately engulfed her. She gave a little shiver—half excitement, half chill.

"Are you certain you wish to remain, my lady? If you're cold, we can take a turn about the room, instead."

My lady. It's what she'd been called her whole life— rightly so—but for some reason the words wrinkled her nose. "Only an hour ago you called me *a stór*. Are we to be so formal now?"

He kept his eyes trained ahead, but pulled his arm— and by extension, her—closer to his side. She didn't resist in the slightest. "An hour ago I dinna know you were a lady. I'd never have been so familiar if I'd had any clue you were the daughter of a marquis."

"And I'd have never been so bold if I'd known you were the son of Britain's most celebrated painter."

He paused beside the stone balustrade and looked down at her, his eyes reflecting the dancing torchlight. With her fingers still resting on his arm, she could feel his muscles relax now that they were away from the crowd, farthest from the glass doors. The hint of mischievousness that had so enticed her in the gallery lifted the corners of his lips once more. "Well, then," he said, his voice low and intimate in the yawning darkness of the garden beyond, "I suppose we are very fortunate indeed to have had such an unorthodox non-introduction."

She lifted a single eyebrow. "Perhaps more providence than fortune. I shouldn't have even been there at all, but I so wanted to see your father's portraits." Realization dawned then. No wonder he had seemed so familiar when she met him—moments earlier she had been looking at a portrait of him! The very thought sent a shiver of delight through her.

What must it have been like, not only to be the son of a master, but to have been his subject as well? She smiled, hoping she didn't look as awestruck as she felt. "I imagine you were there for the same reason."

His jaw tightened the slightest bit. Blast—she hadn't intended to be so insensitive. It had been only six months since he'd lost his father. She pressed her eyes closed—for heaven's sake, she was still shaky about her father's illness last Season, and he was mostly recovered. "I truly am sorry for your loss. I imagine knowing that the whole country mourns with you does little to ease the pain."

He let out a harsh breath, the evidence of which rose in a cloud between them. "Thank you. It is . . . hard to think on him sometimes, but I need to move forward." He set his lips into a determined smile. "Tell me, are you so great an admirer of his, then? Was a glimpse of his work worth being discovered by an ill-mannered brute such as myself?"

She chuckled, relieved that he was smiling once more. "Hardly a brute. And, yes, seeing such incredible skill and talent would be worth all manner of punishments. I am a painter myself—not nearly so talented as he, of course—and seeing his work is nourishment for my soul."

"Ah, a painter," he said, nodding as if everything made sense to him now. "Are you a portrait painter, or are you fond of still life?"

"Whatever moves me. I've done a few portraits, but I think my favorites are landscape—particularly where man and nature meet. I think your father's earliest work is the most inspirational to me. I only wish I had the opportunity to see another of his early Scottish landscapes."

She'd surprised him, judging by the quick cocking of his head and the wrinkling of his brow. "You know of his early works, then? And you've seen one?"

"Indeed. I was absolutely enthralled when I saw his

portrait of Lord and Lady Hamilton several years back.
I'm embarrassed to tell you I may have become slightly
obsessed, and set out to learn as much as possible about
the man. As a gift for my sixteenth birthday, my father
arranged a showing at the Earl of Northup's personal
collection. Among the works were three portraits and
one small but magnificent landscape."

Sir Colin whistled low under his breath. "Father's
very first patron. I dinna think he allowed anyone into
his home anymore."

"He doesn't," she confirmed, biting her lip against
her satisfied smile. "But my father can be very persua-
sive when he chooses." It was far and away the sweetest thing anyone had ever done for her. There was no
doubt that Papa wanted the best for each of his children, but nothing else had better demonstrated to her
his desire for them to be happy as well.

"They were his favorite, you know," he said quietly,
looking out into the blackness beyond the balustrade.

"What were?"

"The landscapes." He turned to face her, the sharp
angles of his jaw somehow softened. "He loved them
most. He had incredible talent for portraits and realized early on that was how he could make his living,
but he never forgot his first love."

It was intoxicating, learning such intimate details of
Sir Frederick's life before fame from the man's own
son. She found herself leaning forward, close enough
to feel the heat of his body and smell the teasing hints
of his masculine scent. "I had no idea," she breathed.

The door rattled open and a pair of men stepped out
onto the terrace, bringing reality back with them. They
nodded as they walked past, apparently headed for the
mews. Sir Colin straightened, putting distance between
them. "Perhaps we should return before your mother
starts to worry."

Beatrice sighed, knowing he was right. "Yes, I suppose so. I must say, however, that I enjoyed our conversations very much this evening—both of them."

"As did I."

They should have started for the door, but neither of them moved. Beatrice looked up at him, her heart suddenly pounding in her ears as their gazes met and held. She expelled a slow breath, mindful of the fact that the cold air would betray her if she wasn't careful. "Sir Colin . . ."

"Colin, please."

"Colin, then," she said, savoring the return to more intimate terms. It gave her the courage to say the words that no proper debutant should. "When might I see you again?"

There—she'd said it. Exhilaration at her boldness heated her from the inside out, warming her chilled body. He'd have to be a simpleton not to catch her meaning. She really didn't want to come right out and ask him to call on her. She would do it, if it meant the only way to see him again, but she hoped she wouldn't have to. She swallowed. The very thought of Sir Frederick's son knocking on the black lacquered door of Granville House was enough to bring butterflies to her stomach.

His smile was small but genuine. "Then, you wouldn'a mind if I called on you, Lady Beatrice?"

They both knew that she had as good as asked him to say it, but she didn't particularly care, and he didn't seem to mind either. When a woman gets what she wants, there is no point in worrying about the method. Feeling playful, she nodded. "Yes."

"Yes, you'd mind?"

"Yes, *Lady* Beatrice would mind. Beatrice, however, would be delighted."

He gave a surprised laugh. "Well, then, it sounds as

though I can please only one. I suppose we'll have to wait until tomorrow to see whose wish is granted."

He had lost his bloody mind.

As he returned Beatrice to her mother, Colin's analytical brain outlined all the reasons he should have left well enough alone. She was a lady. Her father was a powerful marquis. He had absolutely nothing to offer her.

And yet, for once, he didn't give a damn about his difficult situation. Something about her brought out the carefree side of him, something he thought smothered years ago. Despite the worst possible timing, what harm could a single visit do? Fifteen minutes certainly wasn't going to disrupt his plans.

"Careful, man." John handed him a glass of champagne and smiled, nothing in his countenance betraying his warning tone. "That one may be a path to trouble. Her family is not only powerful, but also somewhat eccentric. Best stick to the list we came up with earlier."

Colin accepted the drink and nodded mildly in response. Nothing he didn't already know. He didn't need to ask to know that John wouldn't approve of the impulsive offer he had just made her. "Agreed."

"You've many a young lady's interest piqued. High time you get on with the dancing."

"Suggestions for my first dance?"

John's gaze swept the ballroom, a soldier surveying the battlefield. "Miss Briggs is looking right your way, cousin. Number two on the list, if I am not mistaken."

Miss Henrietta Briggs. Granddaughter of a prominent silk merchant who mushroomed some thirty years ago. Father active in the House of Commons and mother was the granddaughter of a viscount. The family made no bones of their desire to land a title for Henrietta. Dowry was quite respectable, but not indecently so. Her looks were rather unfortunate, and according to John, she had a tendency to chatter, which, combined with her origins, explained why she was as of yet unmarried.

Damn but he hated that he knew all of this about the girl.

Colin pushed aside his self-disgust, focusing on the image of his sweet sister, Cora, and his brother, Rhys. They needed him. Gran needed him. And as John said—this was business. Taking a bracing breath, he nodded for his cousin to lead the way, then smiled toward Miss Briggs and started toward her. She *wanted* a husband like him. Someone with a title and the favor of the Prince Regent. He just had to remember that.

But even as he approached, his mind wandered to the memory of his nymph emerging from the curtains, her eyes wide with surprise that he was waiting for her. No matter how ill conceived his offer to her may have been, he couldn't wait for the moment he could speak with her again.

Beatrice cursed her unfortunate luck. Clearly Mr. Godfrey was determined to dance with her this evening. She had managed to elude him twice, but she was in his sights again. So far tonight she had seen him dancing with the heiress Miss Briggs, the Earl of Kilmartin's youngest daughter, Lady Sarah, and the newly widowed Lady Brighton, whose husband had reportedly left a great fortune. And that was it. He had sat out several sets, despite the number of young ladies lingering near the dance floor, trying to hide their hopefulness at being asked to dance.

She could feel his determined gaze on the back of her neck like an unwanted insect, skittering across the fine hairs at her nape. She subtly increased her pace. As soon as she spotted him striding along the perimeter of the ballroom toward her, she'd taken off in the opposite direction, and now they both circled the dance floor in a sort of slow-motion game of cat-and-mouse. She scanned the room for a viable escape route, all the while nodding pleasantly and smiling vaguely to those she passed. She didn't want to get trapped into conversation, giving her pursuer a chance to catch up.

"If you're in need of rescue," a deep, teasing voice murmured at her ear, "I happen to know of someone who is sans white horse at the moment, but still very much a Knight in shining armor."

Bea grinned in relief, glad to have a suitable diversion. "I must say, Mr. Knight, your jacket looks more velvet than steel." At one-and-twenty, he was one of the youngest gentlemen present tonight. He knew full well how handsome he was, but somehow always came across as confident as opposed to arrogant or pretentious.

"True enough, my lady," he said, brushing a hand at the chocolate fabric, which was a shade darker than his amber eyes. "But armor is dreadfully gauche this Season, don't you think?"

Beatrice had little more than a passing acquaintance with the man, but with Mr. Godfrey bearing down on them, she seized the escape Mr. Knight offered, stepping close and bending her head toward his. "Oh, I'm not so sure about that. Perhaps you could start a trend."

She was blathering, but at least her tactic was working. Mr. Godfrey brushed past them without a word, his posture stiff. Beside her, Mr. Knight said something, and she turned her attention back to him. "I'm sorry. What was that?"

"I said, it looks as though your rescue was a success. Shall we dance, for good measure?"

Oh drat, she hadn't meant to encourage him. He was

a nice enough person, but he reminded her far and away too much of Richard when he was a young buck. Back when wild oats had been the only thing worth sowing. Besides, next to Colin, Mr. Knight looked more like a boy than a man—never mind that he was still two years her senior.

"Actually, I was just on my way to the retiring room for a bit of a rest. Perhaps later?"

He grinned and nodded, reaching forward and catching her hand before lifting it to his lips for a brief kiss. "I should be so fortunate."

She smiled as he spoke, but really her attention was leveled on her own hand, which rested limply in his. After the fireworks that the same gesture had elicited with Colin, it was a bit jarring to realize that she felt absolutely nothing now.

With a nod, she freed her hand and made a beeline for the corridor leading to the ladies' retiring room. Here, at least, she would have sanctuary. She slipped through the door, closed it behind her, and leaned against it gratefully. Perhaps she could hide in here until Mama was ready to return home at last. After all, it was impossible to imagine anything better happening tonight than meeting Colin.

She allowed her eyes to close, putting a hand to the side of her neck, feeling the pounding of her own pulse. She could spend ages trying to get the color of his eyes just right on canvas. Not gray, not brown, not dark or light. Like smoke rising from wood still too green to be burned. His face—now that, she could get exactly right. Bold slashes for his dark eyebrows, sharp angles for his high cheekbones, a decisive brushstroke for the perfect line of his jaw.

Now, if only there were a way to translate that accent to paints. She shivered just thinking about it. Even Sir Frederick couldn't have captured that particular delight, talented as he was. She really, really did hope Colin came to call on her tomorrow.

Blowing out a breath that sounded suspiciously like a sigh, she pushed away from the door and made her way to one of the mirrors hung above a large bureau. It was a pleasant space, with golden light shimmering from the low lamps interspersed along the floral-papered walls. The air was warm and lavender scented, helping to calm her nerves after her little escape.

A sniffle behind one of the screens brought her up short. With three sisters, Beatrice knew the watery sound of someone in tears. She held still, listening carefully over the low strains of music filtering through the closed door. There, from the very back of the room, came the soft hitching of someone trying not to sob. She put her hand to her heart—she hated when others were hurting.

Softly, so not to startle the poor girl, Beatrice whispered, "Is everything all right?"

The cessation of noise was so abrupt, Beatrice suspected the girl had stopped breathing altogether. She turned and stepped closer to the screen. "Can I get you something to drink, perhaps? Or a cool cloth for your face?"

"Beatrice? Is that you?"

Her eyebrows rose. "Yes. Who is that?"

Fabric rustled before a woman with silky brown curls peeked around the partition. Beatrice blinked in surprise. "Diana! Whatever is the matter?" She instinctively held out her arms, and Diana stepped into them. She pressed her wet cheeks against Bea's shoulder and shook with a quiet sob.

At a loss for what to say, Bea patted her back awkwardly, making the soft, soothing sounds she used to quiet her niece when Emma was fussy. She had barely seen Diana, the new Mrs. Rochester, since her marriage last summer. They had debuted together and had become fast friends, but they had lost touch by the end of the Season, after Bea's father had become ill. Beatrice hadn't even attended the wedding, since it was the same week as her brother, Richard's.

At last Diana pulled away, sheepishly wiping her tears with her already damp gloves. Beatrice leaned forward to retrieve a linen from the bureau and handed it to the soggy Diana.

"Thank you." She sniffled, dabbing her eyes and blowing her nose.

"Of course. Here now, let us sit down and be comfortable." She led her to the plush pink settee pushed against the back wall. Once they were seated, Bea patted Diana's arm. "Now, then, what on earth has you so upset?"

"I'm just such an idiot," she said, twisting the square of linen in her hand. "I'm only coming to realize exactly how much of a fool I truly am."

Bea clenched her jaw. She hated to hear someone speak so poorly of herself. She raised her eyebrows and said with great firmness, "You are not a fool, Diana Dow— I mean Rochester. You are a sweet, intelligent woman. I won't have you saying such things."

Diana flopped back against the cushions, expelling a humorless laugh. "What else would you call a girl who fell in love with a man who pretended to love her back, all in the name of obtaining her dowry?"

"Wronged, that's what." As she looked down at her friend's pained expression, a fury started to build within Beatrice's chest, pushing against her lungs and constricting her heart. Another lamb, fooled by a clever wolf. "Heinously so."

Diana pressed her lips together and nodded. "That too. I wish I hadn't been so terribly blind. And it's too late now. . . ." She trailed off, lifting the handkerchief to her nose as she sniffled.

Blowing out a helpless breath, Beatrice dropped back against the settee as well. Between the tears and the rumpled skirts, it hardly mattered at this point if she failed to maintain proper posture. How on earth had her night degraded from the excitement of earlier to sitting on a tufted settee in Lady Churly's retiring room, comforting a heartbroken newlywed?

She pursed her lips. It was a good question, actually. "So, did you only just discover the state of things tonight?"

Diana's sudden laugh bordered on hysterical. "That's one way to put it. It was fairly apparent before the honeymoon was even over, but it took me discovering him in . . . in the arms of another tonight for my humiliation to be complete."

Beatrice gasped, her hand flying to her lips. "Good heavens! Oh, Diana, I'm so very sorry. Are you"—she looked for a delicate way to put it—"er, certain it was your husband?"

"Well," she said, choking on fresh tears for a moment, "I was fairly certain it was him when he called me a silly cow and told me to go home without him—and for me not to expect him until sometime tomorrow."

Beatrice saw red at her friend's suffering. It didn't matter that the horrible words weren't directed to her. The fact that they were uttered at all, to any woman, made her furious enough to spit. "How dare he? Good Lord, the man doesn't deserve the air he breathes, let alone having someone as lovely as you for his wife."

Her friend's sigh was deep and long. When she looked up, her red-rimmed eyes held defeat. "I have no one to blame but myself. If I had paid more attention, then maybe I would have realized that his regard was for my dowry, not the woman attached to it."

Poor Diana. Her mother had passed away several

years earlier, and her father seemed to have little regard for his only daughter. He had offered a fantastic dowry with the hope of marrying her off as quickly as possible. It was heartbreaking to think that some of the young ladies entering society as innocents had no true champion for them. Love for her own family welled in Bea's chest. They may be annoying sometimes, but she could always count on them to have her best interests at heart.

"What can I do to help? Do you want to stay in one of our guest chambers tonight? I'm certain Mama wouldn't mind."

Diana shook her head. "No, but thank you. Mercy, I feel fool enough to have even told you in the first place. What must you think of me?"

"I think nothing different of you, my dear. Your husband's sins are not your own."

They both were quiet for a moment, two young ladies whose lives had diverged drastically after starting their first Seasons in nearly the exact same way. Beatrice thought of Mr. Godfrey and how another woman might not be as aware of his motives as she. If only someone could have warned Diana. What if someone had told her what to look for? It was just so heartbreaking that nobody was on her side when she needed it most.

Pushing off the cushions, Beatrice came to her feet, extending a hand to Diana. "Come, my dear. Let us get you tidied up."

As she watched her friend wet her cloth and press it to her eyes to try to wipe away the evidence of her devastation, Bea clenched her teeth against the desire to find Diana's cur of a husband and give him a piece of her mind. But it wouldn't help. There was little she could do to help Diana now.

Bea's gaze flicked away from Diana's reflection and

settled on her own. Would she have recognized Mr. Rochester for what he was if things had been different? She liked to think so. She was blessed with the ability to see things others overlooked. It's what made her a good painter, as well as a good spy.

She sighed, giving Diana a little squeeze. What was done was done—the only thing she could do now was be extra diligent for herself and those she loved.

And perhaps have Richard invite Mr. Rochester for a friendly match at Gentleman Jackson's. For the first time since hearing Diana's sniffle, Beatrice had to bite back a smile.

Chapter Five

"I'm fairly certain there is nothing in those tomes that will help you secure a wife."

"Yes," Colin said, craning his neck to smile at his aunt, "but there is plenty here to help me *maintain* one."

Aunt Constance's petite form floated through the library in a cloud of fine muslin and French perfume, distinctly out of place among the austere furniture and towering bookshelves. "Whatever do you mean, darling? The point of a well-dowered wife is to have one's financial situation taken care of."

He loved his aunt and was very grateful to her, but that was exactly the sort of attitude that drove him mad. "On the contrary. A well-dowered wife will save the estate—it is up to me to see to the financial security of the rest of my life. I chose my profession with exactly that in mind."

He'd always known of his father's ineptitude when it came to money. He pushed back against the memories from his childhood of hungry bellies and cold rooms. He'd lived it once—and no matter what, he wouldn't let that be his future. More important, he wouldn't let that be his siblings' future.

Constance waved a bejeweled hand through the air. "Oh, pish—why toil the rest of your life away? I'm af-

fording you exactly the opportunity to avoid all that."
She paused at his chair and tilted her head critically.
"You've very fine features. Not at all as rugged as your
Scottish father, thanks to your mother. And her temper-
ing effect on your accent works in your favor as well."

Colin allowed her the inspection, holding his tongue.
She had liked his father well enough, but it was certainly in spite of his Scottish origins. She never could
quite understand why her sister had fallen for the
thick-brogued, penniless artist from Edinburgh. Yes, he
had risen quite astonishingly and had certainly made a
name for himself, but Constance wasn't the least bit
surprised to learn the state of things upon his death.

Oddly, as much as his father had wronged him, Colin hated for others to think poorly of him. Closing the
law book, he leaned back in his chair and offered a
long-suffering smile. "Was there something you wanted,
dear Aunt?"

"A good lesson for you, Colin: A woman always
wants something." She winked and made her way to
the opposite chair. "I'm merely here to impart some
practical advice. Do strike while the iron is hot, my
dear, and be sure to call on all of the lovely young prospects you met last night. We mustn't give them a chance
to forget you, especially with the fleeting advantage of
novelty on your side."

"Sound advice. You'll be happy to know that I have
planned exactly that. Time is of the essence, after all."

"Indeed. Whom do you plan to visit?"

"Miss Briggs, Miss Graves, and Miss Paddington.
Perhaps Miss Trenton, if there's time."

"Mmm, I suggest you make time. There's enough
blunt between the four of them to save a struggling
country, let alone a single estate." Aunt Constance
straightened the glittering rings on her fingers before
regarding him once more. "Of course, if you'd like to

take your chances, there is always the Granville chit, with whom I saw you disappear outside last night."

Colin nodded, keeping his expression neutral. "Lady Beatrice expressed a great love for my father's work. She's a bit above my reach, I should think." It was the perfect opportunity to disclose to his aunt the fact that he had already decided to call on her. And yet he chose not to. Any good barrister knew that it was always best to hold one's cards close to the chest.

"Yes, she is. But if she shows interest in you as opposed to the other way around, I wouldn't rule it out entirely. With her father's connection, you could make King's Counsel in record time. Assuming, of course, you are dead set on carrying on with the business of becoming a barrister."

"You know I am."

"Well, then, as King's Counsel, you'd have quite the respectable income."

"Yes, I'm aware of that. However, I doubt a marquis would wish to sully his grand lines with the likes of me. The ink is barely dry on the creation of the baronetcy, as far as the *ton* is concerned. I'm practically a cit to them."

Aunt sat forward, a smug smile lifting the corners of her painted lips. "I very much doubt Granville would have a problem marrying his daughter off to a baronet after the wife his heir chose. They say she was a *baker*." The last was said with the whispered delight of one imparting the most shocking of news.

"No!" he exclaimed in mock horror. "And they dinna burn her at the stake?"

She huffed, sitting up straight once more. "You have no idea of the scandal such a thing can produce." She tapped a perfectly manicured fingernail against her lips, a tiny vee creasing the smooth skin of her brow. "And yet Raleigh has somehow managed to pull it off.

Rather vexing, really. He has this devil-may-care attitude that simply leaches the venom from the vipers of the *ton*."

"Quite a talent. Unfortunately, charming snakes has never been my forte. I'd best stick to those on the fringes of the beau monde. Those exactly like myself."

"Don't discount your charisma so easily. You've a bit of your father's shameless charm about you. Yes, he was tremendously talented, but he'd have never taken London by storm without it, and it can serve you just as well."

She was right about that. Father could have charmed the devil himself, if he put his mind to it. Too bad he hadn't a lick of common sense to go along with it. Colin glanced at the tall clock situated between the two front-facing windows. Finally, it was after one and he could get on with the task of the day. He stood and set the heavy law book on the nearest table. "Well, I'd best get to storming then. Wish me luck, Aunt."

A heady charge of anticipation rushed through him as he headed for the door. The only question was, should he call on Lady Beatrice first or last? He smiled.

Dessert must always come last.

"*Jane*—I never, ever thought to see you reading something like that."

Beatrice laughed when her sister-in-law started, dropping the journal in question as her hand went to her heart. "Jam and splash, but you startled me. You do know that normal people actually make sound when they walk?"

"Of course," Beatrice said, settling onto the opposite end of the sofa and reaching over to pull the paper into her own lap. "But I also know that the quieter the footsteps, the more information one can glean . . . like the fact that my very pragmatic sister-in-law has taken to reading the scandal sheets."

Jane's porcelain white skin tinged pink as she grinned sheepishly. "What? It's the best way for me to learn more about the people of the *ton*. I'm quite behind, thank you very much."

"Mmhmm. I rather think you've developed a taste for scandal these past few months." Beatrice was teasing, of course. Jane was still finding her way as a new countess. Thankfully, she hadn't given up on her former ways, for which Beatrice was exceedingly grateful—she had yet to taste biscuits more delicious than Jane's.

"No, though it is nice to know that there is always another scandal greater than the last to turn gossips' heads. Still, it's so undignified for me to be reading such drivel. I should have known you'd ferret me out."

"*Everyone* reads that drivel. And, yes, you should have known. Secrets are futile around me."

Jane chuckled, putting a hand to her middle. "Of that, I'll brook no argument. Behind Richard and my maid, you were the first to figure out our news."

A huge grin came to Beatrice's lips. "I kept it to myself though, didn't I? I might be nosy, but I do have scruples."

"For which I am grateful." Jane's lips relaxed into a soft, genuine smile as she leaned forward to retrieve her teacup from the sofa table. "Do tell me. What did your nosiness discover last night? I don't know why I read that scandal sheet when I know you'll always come home with the best gossip. I wish I had been feeling well enough to attend with you yesterday."

Beatrice's nosiness hadn't so much discovered anything last night as get *her* discovered. Butterflies flitted through her stomach as she thought of Colin's watchful eyes and mischievous grin when she emerged from the curtains. Would he come to see her today? She couldn't have been plainer in her desires, but still, it was impossible to say whether he would follow through.

"Good heavens, *what* are you thinking about?" With her teacup frozen inches from her lips, Jane's dark eyebrows lifted, a spark of interest lighting her hazel eyes.

Beatrice grinned, lifting her shoulders in feigned innocence. "Only about how lovely the evening was."

Jane set her untouched tea back on its saucer. "I don't believe you for one second, Beatrice Moore."

"Well, if the scandal sheets won't tell you, then I'm certainly not going to."

Jane narrowed her eyes at her as if attempting to divine her secrets. "This involves a man. Yes, I'm sure of it."

"Oh? And what leads you to that conclusion?"

"There are certain looks that can be caused only by a devilishly handsome man and that, my dear, was one of them."

There was no stopping the grin at that. Oh, how right she was. Before Beatrice could formulate a response, the soft murmur of voices arose from the corridor, and her younger twin sisters, Jocelyn and Carolyn, came in to join them.

"There you are, Beatrice," Jocelyn said, pausing to bid Jane good afternoon before taking a seat on the sofa across from them. "We thought you might be in your studio today, but I suppose the grayness of the day isn't the most inspiring thing in the world."

"It's useless to me. I didn't even feel like sketching in this gloominess." That, and the fact that she was so full of hopeful excitement about seeing Colin again, she couldn't have concentrated on a painting to save her life.

"Good—the better to concentrate on telling us all

about last night, *without* Mama around to tighten your lips."

"You're just in time," Jane said, sending Beatrice a surprisingly wicked grin. "Beatrice was just about to tell us about a very special gentleman she met last night."

And to think, Beatrice would have said her sister-in-law was the reserved one of the group. She rounded her eyes at Jane in admonishment, but Jane only grinned back, utterly unabashed. Clearly, she knew that Beatrice would tell them about the night anyway. Half the fun of having sisters was being able to share with them.

"Very well." She proceeded to regale them with tidbits and gossip, saving the best part—full descriptions and commentary on Colin—for last. Of course, the version she told them started with the ballroom introduction; some things were too delicious to share.

The only other part of the evening she kept to herself was the encounter with Diana. For her friend's sake, she didn't share her humiliation. It was too private a moment, one she wouldn't betray.

But looking at her sweet, innocent sisters now as they drank in the stories from the ballroom with the excitement of those so close to finally being able to experience it for themselves—their debuts were only a handful of months away—it made her blood boil to think of some depraved fortune hunter duping one of them.

Yes, she would be there to help guide them, but what of all the young debutants whose families weren't as diligent? Or those whose parents wanted nothing more than to marry them off to the first bidder and be done with the hassle? The thought weighed heavy in her heart.

"Do you think he'll come?"

Jocelyn's question abruptly changed the direction of Beatrice's thoughts. She glanced to the clock. They were square in the middle of the afternoon, the acceptable time for a gentleman to come calling. Swallowing back the rush of nerves, she raised her shoulders. "I've no idea, Jocelyn, but we'll know soon enough."

Coming to her feet, Carolyn pulled aside the lacy drapes, revealing water-streaked windowpanes as she looked down on St. James's Square. "I wouldn't blame him if he didn't come. It's raining buckets out there."

"He's Scottish, Carolyn—I doubt a little cold rain would get between him and his woman."

"Jocelyn!" Beatrice tossed a pillow at her sister, who laughed and tossed it back. Even Jane chuckled at the audacious statement, though she had the decency to hide it behind her hand. "He is only half Scot, I am not his woman, and you are beyond outrageous."

"Keeps things interesting," she replied, completely unrepentant.

"I think that's my cue for this old married lady to make her escape," Jane said, shaking her head at the lot of them. "I do hope your gentleman comes to see you, Beatrice. And if he does, I expect a full report."

As she left, Jocelyn picked up the discarded scandal sheet, flipping straight to the cartoons that always filled the back page. Beatrice did the same thing whenever she read one—there was something about the illustrations that begged for attention.

"Oh my," Carolyn exclaimed, dropping the drape and jumping back from the window. "A carriage just arrived. It must be him!"

Jocelyn and Beatrice exchanged glances before jumping up from the sofa and hurrying to Carolyn's side for a glimpse outside. Jocelyn started to lift the curtain, but Beatrice swatted at her hand. "No! Don't be obvious—he'll see you."

"All right, all right. God forbid he look up into the pouring rain to our exact window and see the vague outline of a person within."

Beatrice did not acknowledge her sister's cheek. She was too busy trying to tamp down on the wave of nervousness that swept through her like a rolling fog, swift and thick. Yes, she was excited about the fact that Colin was Sir Frederick's son, but it was so much more than that. Only the man himself could be responsible for the giddy unrest within her.

Taking a deep breath, she inched aside the edge of the curtain and peeked onto the street below. A shiny black carriage waited at the curb, its canopy pulled up against the rain. The matched pair of grays in front of it tossed their heads as a man emerged from within.

She squinted, but it was impossible to see his face from her vantage point. As a servant secured the horses, the man turned toward the house, one gloved hand holding the brim of his tall hat. Was it Colin? The build looked right, as did the— "Oh, blast."

"What?" the twins asked in unison, diverting their attention to her.

"It's not him."

Carolyn's face fell. "What? How can you be sure? All I can see is a wavy dark figure next to a wavy dark carriage. I'd be hard-pressed to tell you if the carriage is hooked to horses or elephants."

Drat her dratted luck. "It's in the way he moves." She blew out an annoyed breath, turning away from the window and stalking back to the couch. Colin had a certain fluidity in the way he carried himself and a confidence that wasn't conceited. Nothing showy, simply sure.

The man below was a peacock. Even in the rain, he sauntered toward the door, smugness wrapped around him like a cloak.

"I swear, Bea, you have gone daft." Carolyn peeked outside once more before shaking her head. "There is no way to tell from two floors up who he is or isn't."

"Care to make a wager on that?" Beatrice's voice was more sarcastic than she intended, but she suspected she knew exactly who was outside: Mr. Godfrey.

Jocelyn raised a pale brow, then turned her attention to her twin. "No, you wouldn't, Caro. She's got that look about her when she knows something the rest of us are too slow to catch on to."

Why did he not simply give up the hunt? She didn't want to be stuck with him now, not when Colin could come at any moment. Beatrice turned to her sisters suddenly, her eyes beseeching. "Oh please, *please* come with me when Mama calls me to the drawing room. I do not want to suffer that man alone, and I know Mama wouldn't turn him away." Why should she? Beatrice had never addressed her concerns about Godfrey with her mother. She had never thought it necessary—her cold shoulder with the man was practically frozen.

Carolyn regarded her with her wide, brilliant blue eyes. "Good heavens, don't tell me you, of all people, are scared of a man. If that's the case, then where's the hope for the rest of us less stalwart females?"

"Oh, shush—being *afraid of* and being *repelled by* are two very different things. Now please, be sisterly and support me in my time of need."

Jocelyn snorted. "Now look who's being dramatic."

"Think of it this way—you are always looking for all the gossip about the gentlemen of the *ton*. Well," she said, putting her hands palm up, "here's your chance."

At least now she had their attention. The soft tap of approaching footsteps had her on her feet. "He's the handsome third son of the Viscount Ashworth." She leaned in closer and lowered her voice, desperate to pique their interest. "I believe he has a secret gambling problem, mounting debts, and he is on the hunt for a wife wealthy enough to set him up for life. Gossip doesn't get any better than this."

The footsteps paused at the same moment someone scratched on the door.

"Well?" she whispered, looking back and forth between them. Surely they wouldn't abandon her. Neither one of them was giving her any tells, their faces both impressively blank as they exchanged looks. Honestly, communicating without any outward signs would be *so* useful.

Jocelyn grinned and craned her neck toward the door. "Enter!"

A maid popped her head in and curtsied briefly. "Begging your pardon, my ladies. Lady Beatrice, Lady Granville wishes for you to join her in the drawing room to greet Mr. Godfrey."

"Thank you, Emily. I'll be right down."

The girl bobbed another quick curtsy and started to close the door.

"Emily," Jocelyn called, halting the maid in her tracks, "please let them know to bring enough tea for five." She waited until Emily withdrew to turn to Beatrice, hands on hips. "Before you thank me, just remember that you owe us."

Even so, Beatrice blew out a relieved breath. Holding her hands out to her sisters, she smiled. "Whatever you say, my dears, just so long as you don't leave my side."

Chapter Six

Well, of course—Granville House would be the largest house on the block.

Colin shook his head, sending raindrops flying from the brim of his hat. As if he needed a reminder that he had no business calling on someone like Lady Beatrice. But he was here now—practically at her invitation—and he sure as hell wasn't going to stand around in the pouring rain and dither on the subject.

He dashed the last few yards and was lifting his hand toward the knocker when the door whooshed open. An austere, balding butler offered him a remarkably blank look. "Yes?"

Taken off guard, Colin fumbled inside his jacket for his calling card. "Good afternoon," he said, locating the card at last and handing it over. "I'm Sir Colin Tate and—"

"Very good, sir," the man said, interrupting him. Then he stepped back to allow Colin entrance. "If you will wait here, I will let her ladyship know you have arrived."

Well, that went much more easily than anticipated. Had Beatrice warned the butler that Colin would make an appearance? She must have, because none of the other butlers today had made things nearly so simple. As the man headed up the great marble staircase, a footman stepped forward to help him out of his dripping-wet overcoat and take his hat.

Colin nodded his thanks before stomping his feet a few times to shake off the excess moisture from his boots. Duly relieved of as much rainwater as he could manage, he glanced around the entry hall, taking in the cavernous space. And here he had thought his aunt's house grand. Opulence extended in every direction, from the black-and-white marble floors to the velvet-covered walls, and of course, the mural on the ceiling—all the hallmarks of a family with exceedingly good taste and a budget to match.

The butler reappeared, descending the stairs with measured steps. "If you'll follow me, please."

By the time they stepped onto the landing, the soft sound of feminine voices reached Colin's ears. Her sisters, perhaps? The low tones of a male voice interjected, and Colin slowed, taking stock of the situation. Was it Beatrice's brother? Her father? He didn't know if he was quite ready to meet either of them.

The butler paused outside of the door and murmured, "Mr. William Godfrey has called upon the family as well."

Colin's jaw tightened. He really did not want to make small talk with one of Beatrice's beaux, for God's sake. Especially half-drowned and feeling like a damn fraud for having come in the first place. But with no other choice, he followed behind the butler as the man opened the door and announced, "Sir Colin Tate."

Five pairs of eyes turned in his direction, but there was only one gaze he had any interest in. Framed on either side by a matching blond sister, Beatrice smiled at him from her place on the sofa. "Sir Colin, I'm so very glad you decided to join us today."

She set down her teacup and came to her feet as he

stepped toward the conversation area. She was exceedingly lovely in her simple green-and-white morning gown, her hair loosely arranged atop her head. Though the dim day offered little in the way of flattering lighting, she looked sweet and fresh and almost . . . relieved? The light must be playing tricks on him. "Lady Beatrice, it is a pleasure to see you once more. And Lady Granville, too, of course."

Her mother smiled and nodded from her place in front of the tea service. "May I offer you some tea, Sir Colin?"

"Yes, thank you. Just the thing to take the chill from the day. No sugar or milk, please."

Beatrice grinned as his gaze naturally fell back to her. "Allow me to introduce you to my sisters Lady Jocelyn"—the blond head on the right bobbed—"and Lady Carolyn"—the one on the left followed suit. "They will both be making their debuts in the spring."

If he'd met them in the street, he never would have known that the twins were younger than Beatrice. Their direct gazes, surprisingly voluptuous figures, and broad smiles were no doubt going to keep Lady Granville on her toes next Season. "Lovely to meet you both."

As strange as it was to think, the pair of them were almost too pretty. He much preferred Beatrice's loveliness, where her sweet but imperfect features made her eminently more approachable. Her slender figure, her wide-set eyes and slightly pointed chin, the way she covered her mouth when she smiled—all of these were endearing to him. His father sought perfection; Colin preferred character.

She glanced toward the gentleman on the couch, keeping her lips together in something slightly more friendly than a grimace. "Have you met Mr. Godfrey?"

"Oh, we haven't *formally* met," Godfrey answered

before Colin could respond. "But I witnessed your induction into society last night. Quite a to-do."

There was no mistaking the thinly veiled disgust in the other man's eyes, even as his voice was all that was pleasant and cordial. Colin dipped his head in a shallow greeting. "Pleased to make your acquaintance, sir."

Lady Granville smiled as she handed him a delicate gold-rimmed teacup filled with fragrantly steaming tea. "Mr. Godfrey is the son of the Viscount Ashworth and was just telling us about his latest trip to their country estate."

"Yes, for the harvest. Father wishes for me to become more involved in the running of the estate, but I don't see the need when we have a perfectly good estate manager." His lips turned up in a sort of condescending amusement as he eyed Colin from the tips of his damp hair to the bottom of his rain-spotted boots. "Men such as yourself may not mind the elements, but I am relieved to be back in the bosom of the city."

Ah, so Godfrey was an ass. Now that he had a better handle on the man, Colin took a calm sip of his tea before responding. "A bit of rain was no match for the pleasure of enjoying Lady Granville's and her daughters' company."

Beatrice's eyes flashed with gratification as she reseated herself between her sisters. He couldn't say what made him think it, but he was almost positive her reaction was to his subtle put-down and not the pretty compliment to her and her family.

"Yes, of course," Godfrey returned, his eyes narrowing the slightest amount. "I simply prefer to use civilized conveyance when the weather is so dreadfully inclement. Wouldn't want to sully my hostess's fine furniture with damp clothing, after all."

"Oh, don't be silly, Mr. Godfrey." Lady Granville offered them both a steely, determined smile. "We're in

England, after all. If our furniture couldn't hold up to a few drops of rain, it'd be positively unpatriotic."

Colin chuckled. "Well said, my lady. Before I left Scotland, I thought we had the corner on dreadful weather."

"I've heard Scotland has the corner on all manner of dreadful things," Godfrey remarked, leaning forward to set his empty teacup on the sofa table. "You must be so relieved to have an aunt here to take you in."

Right—more of a bastard than an ass. Colin opened his mouth to retort, but Jocelyn cut him off.

"I always thought Scotland was romantic. If Romeo and Juliet would have had a Gretna Green to run off to, that play would have had a *much* happier ending."

Lady Granville nearly choked on her tea as Beatrice widened her eyes at her sister. Setting down her cup, Lady Granville offered a forced chuckle. "Jocelyn, *we* know you are only teasing when you say such a thing, but our guests may not. Please," she said, turning back to offer Colin and Godfrey apologetic smiles, "pay her comment no mind."

Godfrey gave the girl a little sideways look before smiling at Beatrice. "Yes, of course."

Colin rather liked the girl—she reminded him of his own sister. "No mind paid. Although, if I had, I would be inclined to say that Lady Jocelyn has a point."

He'd defended her sister.

Beatrice pressed her lips together, stifling the silly grin that threatened to emerge. He'd managed to handle Mr. Godfrey's subtle rudeness quite well since the moment he arrived, and now he'd championed Jocelyn. She tossed a displeased look in Godfrey's direction. The man should have taken his leave when Colin arrived. He'd already been here a quarter hour, so it wasn't as though Colin's visit was cutting anything short.

Sitting forward slightly, Beatrice turned the whole of her attention to the dark Scotsman—or should she say half Scotsman? "I'd love to hear more about Scotland, Sir Colin. None of us has ever been, but the paintings I've seen are quite majestic."

His charcoal eyes warmed as he smiled at her, a lock of damp black hair falling across his forehead. "It's rugged, and mountainous, and almost unbearable in its beauty. In the spring, when lilacs scent the air and heather blankets the fields, it is almost magical. My family's estate is on the edge of a forest at the foot of a steep hill, and my gran swears she can hear the faerie wings on many a quiet night."

Carolyn sighed. "It really does sound romantic. Not Gretna Green romantic, but inspiring-in-its-loveliness romantic."

Beatrice saw her mother press her eyes closed for the space of a second. The twins would do well to purge the words "Gretna Green" from their vocabulary. "Yes, very inspiring, Sir Colin. Is your family still in Scotland?"

"Yes. My stepbrother and stepsister live there with our grandmother."

"My, how they must miss you, especially so soon after your father's passing," Mr. Godfrey interjected, shaking his head. "I hope you won't be gone from them long."

The man's jealousy—which was completely unfounded—was beginning to grate on Beatrice's nerves. Did he think he was helping his case by acting the cad toward Colin? Yes, she realized there were some who looked down on him and his freshly created title, but that was rubbish, as far as she was concerned. If he treated Colin this way, how would he react to Jane and her background?

Colin, at least, seemed to take the statement in stride. "They are happy that I could be here for the memorial exhibit. It was too much of a journey for Gran, but I know she is comforted that I am here now."

Mama tilted her head, sympathy clouding her eyes. "It really is lovely that you could be here for the exhibit. I know that many, especially our resident artist, Lady Beatrice, are eager to attend."

Colin opened his mouth to respond, but Mr. Godfrey jumped in. "Perhaps you would allow me to escort you. I know how fond you are of the arts, Lady Beatrice." He offered a calculated smile that probably softened most females, but only made her grind her teeth.

"I didn't realize you were an artist, Lady Beatrice," Colin said, taking her by surprise. He most certainly *did* know that she was a painter. She liked where he was going with this.

Blinking innocently, she tilted her head and smiled. "Why, yes! I am not only a painter myself, but a most fervent admirer of your father."

His face revealed nothing, but his eyes betrayed his delight in her playing along. "Well, if that is the case, perhaps I can interest you in a private tour of the exhibit before it opens to the public."

Rescuing her from Godfrey's invitation *and* offering her the opportunity of a lifetime? If her mother wouldn't faint on the spot, she could have kissed the man.

"Thank you, Sir Colin. I am honored to accept your generous invitation."

"I'm afraid you may have permanently endeared yourself to my sisters."

Colin gave her a brief grin before accepting his hat from a footman, who then retreated to his post beside the door. Based on his calls to the women on his list earlier, she shouldn't have accompanied him on his way out, but it seemed that little stood between her and something she wanted. He rather liked that about her. And he was exceedingly glad for a moment of semiprivacy with her, however brief.

"Well, if she was going to defend Scotland, it was the least I could do. Patriotic duty, et cetera, et cetera."

She tilted her head a bit, her bright blue gaze never leaving his. "You may discount your kindness, but I'm not going to let you get away without a proper thank-you."

A *proper* thank-you? Her voice was quiet, her eyes focused solely on him, and for a fleeting moment, he had a vision of her rising on her toes and brushing her lips to his. He swallowed, his blood heating at the thought. "Think nothing of it."

"I think *much* of it," she insisted, holding out her hand to him. "And I thank you."

He reached forward, gathering her slender fingers in his hand. There it was again—that tingle of awareness that slipped over his skin whenever he touched her, even through the fabric of their gloves.

He lifted her hand to his lips, inhaling her lilac scent along with the subtle hints of linseed oil. He paused just shy of his mouth and murmured, "You are most welcome, my lady."

He pressed a kiss to the back of her hand, and she tightened her fingers for a moment, a gesture that no one but he would notice.

"I bid you good day, sir. I'm very much looking forward to our tour."

Reluctantly releasing her, he stepped back and set his hat over his still-damp hair. "As am I, my lady."

With a slight bow, he turned and headed for the door, keeping his expression neutral for the servant's sake.

As ill-advised as it might be, he already knew he would do anything in his power to ensure that the private tour at the gallery with Beatrice was exactly that: private.

Chapter Seven

Stepping into the airy rooms that housed his father's memorial exhibit, Colin was suddenly very glad that he had decided to arrive early. The emotions that assailed him were not completely unexpected, but somehow they still came as a surprise. He turned in a circle, taking in the more than twenty pieces that had been brought together for the event.

No matter what his father had done wrong in his life, he had done his paintings exceedingly right. Colin breathed in a deep lungful of air, pushing against the steel band that seemed to have wrapped around his ribs. It was an odd sort of blissful agony to see the paintings, as bright and vibrant as ever despite the fact Father was gone.

He breathed out, exhaling the pain and regret away with it. This was to be a good day. All he had thought about since the moment he awoke was seeing Beatrice again, with no one between them but a single chaperone. Certainly not that jackass Godfrey. Seeing the man's face when Beatrice accepted Colin's invitation had been worth the impromptu proposal a thousand times over—and even that didn't compare to the thrill of Beatrice's acceptance.

For some reason, he loved the idea of a little more stolen time with her.

And though the gallery wasn't nearly as intimate as his aunt's portrait hall, it was a vast improvement over Beatrice's crowded drawing room. The space was quiet and bright, two feats he would not have thought possible in this part of London. The plain white of the walls left nothing to distract the viewer's attention from the highlighted masterpieces. Coming from so many different collections, the frames were a bit of a mishmash, some glinting gold, others silver, and a few polished wood ones mixed in. He rather liked the eclectic feel of the groupings.

He wandered forward, his footsteps echoing in the open space, which was devoid of all but a handful of potted plants and a few strategically placed benches. He could almost feel his father's presence in the starkness of the room. When he worked, Father wanted nothing cluttering his creative space. His studio was always clean and orderly, in complete contrast to the house itself.

"Sir Colin?"

Colin glanced to the door and smiled, warmth infusing the emptiness inside his heart. God, but she was lovely.

"My lady. I'm honored you could join me today." He strode forward to greet her properly and was treated to the whispered hint of lilac.

She looked perfectly divine today, in her simple muslin gown and light green spencer jacket. An easy smile curled her lips as she slipped off the jacket, the movement highlighting the delicate rise of her collarbone. "I'm beyond delighted to be here."

Without the ball gown or opulent furnishings, she was completely approachable—almost the total opposite of what he would expect of the daughter of a marquis. In the diffused daylight streaming in from the open windows, he realized her dark blue eyes held the slightest suggestion of green toward the pupil.

She gestured to a mousy young woman behind her whose presence he'd hardly registered. "Is there a place for my maid to rest while we look around?"

"Yes, of course," he said, leading them to one of the benches in the corridor outside the gallery. The girl promptly pulled a book from a pocket of her coat and settled in to read. He couldn't have asked for a more perfect chaperone.

"I would have thought you might have brought one or both of your sisters today."

"Oh no—they would never have been able to resist chattering, which would have ruined the whole experience. I love them, but I do not want to be listening to their commentary while viewing such dignified works."

"And your parents didn't mind letting you join me with only a maid?"

She shook her head. "I convinced them it was more or less just another visit to a museum or gallery. They knew the committee staff would be here as well."

It was a gift horse, really, and Colin didn't intend to look it in the mouth.

Offering his elbow, he led Beatrice back to the exhibit. "I was just getting my bearings when you arrived. Mr. Swanson informed me that all but two of the pieces are in place. One from Wales, which is en route as we speak, and the royal portrait of King George, which will arrive shortly before the exhibit's official opening."

"What an honor for you and your family that the prince has agreed to lend the painting. You must be very proud."

He was, actually. Regardless of anything else, his father had come from nothing and had succeeded in earning not only royal favor, but the baronetcy as well. He knew that the title was perhaps not of major significance to someone of Beatrice's status, but he appreciated her sentiment. "I am. Thank you."

Her smile was unstudied and natural, revealing a quarter-turned front tooth that somehow suited her, as if it were rebelling against the straight and narrow. "I cannot tell you how much I have looked forward to this afternoon. It may have been only a few days, but it felt much longer. I fear my family may never allow me to utter the name 'Sir Frederick' at the breakfast table again."

He'd been looking forward to it, too, though his reasons had nothing to do with his father and everything to do with the lady beside him. It had been a long week. A very, very long week. In addition to his all too brief visit with Beatrice, he had called on just about every eligible female on his list, making an effort to get to know each of them a bit. If he could have found one, just one, that seemed to be an even halfway decent fit, he would have considered it a success. But so far, none of them had seemed right.

The only bright spot had been the promise of seeing his little *stór* again. It was refreshing to know that she was outside of his reach and he therefore had no need to be on his guard or feel as though he were some sort of hunter stalking an unsuspecting prey. The smile came easily to his lips as he looked down at her. "Well, then, I hope the day lives up to your expectations. Believe it or not, I'm not the best guide when it comes to the works themselves. I know little about the mechanics of painting."

"I didn't expect you to. Techniques I understand—it's the master himself I'd love to hear more about. Feel free to impart any juicy bits of gossip you may have along the way," she said, tossing a teasing look his way before releasing his arm and turning to take in the room. "Truly, just being here is one of the greatest treats I could imagine."

He clasped his hands behind him, watching her as her gaze flitted from one portrait to the next. The oddest sense of pride wended its way through his bones, making him stand straighter. There were few things that he had to offer anyone, but it felt damn good to know that he could give her this. In fact, no one else could offer her the sort of insight into his father that he possessed. In this small thing, they were perfectly matched. "Perhaps we should start at the beginning," he said, sweeping his hand to the back corner of the room.

"Do they have some of his landscapes after all?"

"Sadly, no. Even if the committee had been interested in them, I don't know of a single owner who would be willing to loan their piece. Several went to friends in and around Edinburgh, and you already know how Lord Northup feels about sharing."

She chuckled. "Indeed. I remember wondering if he stocked crocodiles in that moat of his. Though I suppose the castle is intimidating enough in and of itself."

"What, he dinna welcome you with open arms?"

"Hardly. Although, I suppose I should be grateful that no arrows were trained on us nor boiling oil at the ready."

"That you know of, anyway."

This time she put a hand to her lips as she laughed out loud. "So true. We could have had an army of archers trained on us from those arrow slits and we'd have never known."

"Northup was just odd enough to do it, too. Any man who wishes to have his portrait painted in a full suit of armor while holding his small dog and being fanned by his servant has more than a little madness running through his veins."

Her eyes widened at this piece of gossip. "No! However did your father convince him to forgo such a splendid pose? If I remember correctly, there was no armor or servants, and he was instead astride a rather magnificent black stallion. That much I know for sure, since Papa commented on the impressive stature of the beast."

Colin nodded, maintaining a perfectly straight face. "I believe it was an argument of the earl's magnificent figure being obscured by the armor."

"Oh, well, I can see how that would be a perfectly valid argument."

"Once the armor was overruled, Northup decided the dog and servant simply wouldn't make sense."

"Yes—clearly the armor would have been the linchpin in the whole look." Merriment sparkled in her eyes as she shook her head. "Well, thank heavens for his reasoning, however odd. It wouldn't do for his descendants to be able to pinpoint the exact moment in their lineage when the madness broke forth."

"So true. They should be left to wonder when it hit the family like the rest of us. And more important," he said, pausing in front of the earliest piece in the collection, "Northup's old friend Lord Pruitt would never have seen my father's genius and hired him to paint this."

Stepping close to the painting, Lady Beatrice let out a breathy sigh of contentment. The sound seemed to go right through him, weaving around his shoulders and tugging him to her. Without looking away, she shook her head. "So marvelous. I can almost feel the warmth of the fire behind him."

Colin could feel the warmth, too, but it had nothing to do with the painting. He studied her perfect profile, the delicate curve of her ear, the long line of her neck. For the first time in his entire life, he wished he had even an ounce of his father's talent so that he could somehow capture her image on paper.

He averted his gaze just in time when she looked over at him. "I suppose Lord Pruitt appreciated a more classic portrait."

"If by classic you mean a full Greek toga, complete with sandals and the hand of Zeus reaching down from the heavens, then yes."

Her peals of laughter washed over him, freeing his own. "Truly?"

"No, not truly. Lord Pruitt was happy to have as standard of a pose as possible. Father had to cajole him into allowing the use of props in the background. If I remember correctly, he convinced the man that fire would evoke a tone of power and dominance and the mountains beyond a certain permanence."

Tilting her head to the side, she said, "I suppose that's true. I wouldn't have thought of it, but all of those elements combine to create a very compelling, almost authoritative painting."

"It was utter rubbish. He just thought portraits were boring if there wasn't enough visual interest added above and beyond the subject. And, as you know, he reveled in the play of light, so fire fascinated him."

His eyes had strayed from the painting again, taking in the neatly arranged curls of her upswept hair. The afternoon light glinted on the golden strands, shining with every movement she made. Apparently, Father wasn't the only one who reveled in the play of light.

"I don't believe you."

He blinked, raising a brow as she met his gaze. "What is it you're not believing?"

She moved toward the next painting, depicting Lady St. Clair in a flowing white gown, a mirror on the wall behind her reflecting the room at large. "That he didn't care about the symbolism in his portraits. Even if he didn't consciously add them, they are there nonetheless. All of his portraits—well, the ones I have seen, anyway—are rich with subtle symbolism."

"So subtle, he dinna know he was using them?" He crossed his arms, patent disbelief clear in his tone. He was teasing her, the vaulted daughter of a marquis, without any thought of her station or rank. It was nice, very nice, to feel so at ease with her.

"Yes, that's it exactly. Mark of a true genius, don't you agree?" She winked at him before returning her gaze to the painting. "Look at the use of the mirror in this one. First of all, how incredible is his technique here, giving us every angle of the space? But what is he really saying? I think he was adding commentary as to the lady's reflective nature. She looks very thoughtful, does she not?"

"I suppose. But if I were to hazard a guess, my lady, I'd imagine he liked the challenge of painting the whole of the woman."

She rolled her eyes, clearly not impressed with his interpretation. "Do you always look at everything so literally? Perhaps it's not your father who doesn't appreciate symbolism, but you yourself?"

"No mystery in that. A barrister has little use for symbolism in life."

"Barrister?" He had her attention now. "I had no idea you were a man of the law. Do you practice in Edinburgh?"

"London, actually. And I'm not quite practicing yet—I've still a year left to go at the Inns of Court." If he could secure the funding. He had no idea that the money his father had been sending all this time had been borrowed funds.

"London?" she exclaimed, her hands going to her

hips. "For heaven's sake, I thought you were merely visiting with your aunt. You've been in London for two years and your very first ball was this week?"

Her accusatory glare made him smile. As if he had purposely prevented their worlds from intersecting sooner. "Not exactly on my list of things to do, *a stór*."

A stór.

A shimmery thrill raced down Beatrice's back. She hadn't realized she'd been waiting to hear the endearment from his lips again. She'd never thought much of a Scottish accent, but the marriage of Scottish and English tones on his tongue was like mixing two uninspired pigments and coming up with a completely unique, perfectly gorgeous color. She swallowed, trying to come up with something clever to say when all she could think about was the look in his smoky eyes the first time he called her that. "Well, we'll certainly have to remedy that."

Judging by the look of sudden interest on his face, she probably hadn't hidden her reaction as well as she hoped. His lips parted, the teasing smile transforming to something more intimate. "Is that so? And why should it matter to you if I'm attending balls or not?"

A good question. She looked away from his ensnaring gaze as she moved to the next painting, trying her best to maintain a casualness that she didn't feel. "Well, we never did have that dance. You need to make good on your promise, like a proper gentleman."

"Who said I was a proper gentleman?" He leaned a shoulder against the wall beside the painting, his body as lithe and lean as one of the great cats she'd seen in the Tower Menagerie. She had a sudden image of painting his portrait in just that position but stripped bare to the waist.

Heat swamped her cheeks, and she hastily dropped

her gaze to the floor. Lord have mercy, where had *that* thought come from? She drew a deep breath, trying to get herself under control. She wasn't a blusher, and she certainly wasn't shy. Gathering her scattered wits, she put a hand to her hip and met his gaze head-on. "*You* did—when you decided to attend that first ball."

"Ah, is that how it works? I'd argue the point," he said, a bit of mischief lifting a single dark brow, "but it wouldn'a be very gentlemanly of me. Now, as for the dance, it was your decision to take a stroll outside over my offer to dance. You canna expect me to leave the door open indefinitely for that particular delight."

"Of course I can. It's one of the few perks of being a female. We may make unreasonable demands upon men until our hearts are content. Of course, it's up to them as to whether or not they choose to indulge us."

"And that, I suppose, separates the men from the gentlemen?"

"No, that separates the gentlemen from the rakes."

"So my choice is to honor a lady's wishes or be labeled a rake?"

"More or less. And truly, you are entirely too generous to be a rake—otherwise I would never have had the chance to be here. Therefore," she said, grinning as she presented her victorious argument, "your offer to dance still stands. And I accept."

"Do you now?" He pushed away from the wall and took a slow, languid step toward her. "Well, far be it from me to keep a lady waiting."

A spark flared to life within her as he extended his gloveless hand. He couldn't mean to dance now. Could he? She considered the slight upward curl of his lips and the genuine amusement crinkling the corners of his eyes.

He most definitely did.

She swallowed, dropping her gaze to his boldly offered hand. Did she know that accepting his offer was highly imprudent, given that her maid was right outside the door and at least three men were at work in the front room? Absolutely. Did she care?

Not particularly.

Not while he was looking at her with those charcoal gray eyes, daring her to accept his teasing offer. The spark grew to an effervescent burn as she took a step closer, lifted her chin, and slid her hand into his. The soft, supple leather of her kid gloves did nothing to shield the heat of his skin or the strength of his grip as his fingers closed around hers.

"You really don't play by the rules, do you?"

She allowed him to draw her a step closer to him, all the while savoring that unmistakable thrill of being just the slightest bit wicked. "No. But you knew that. Isn't that why you asked me to dance in the first place?"

"Perhaps," he said, giving a quiet chuckle, "which is very interesting, since I like rules. I follow them by nature."

Beatrice lifted their joined hands. "Could have fooled me."

He chuckled, tugging her forward. "You, my lady, must be a bad influence on me."

With that, he snagged her other hand in his and swung them both around in a dizzying circle. It was such an unexpected move, she gave a little squeak, tightening her grip. "What are you doing?" she half gasped, half laughed. It was the sort of thing she might have done in the meadow by the lake at their estate in Aylesbury, when the flowers were blooming and there was no one around to see. Certainly not something she would have done in the middle of the stark white walls of a London gallery filled with priceless paintings.

"Dancing, of course," he said, releasing one hand to

swing her out before changing directions and rejoining hands. "Don't you just love a good Scottish reel?"

She giggled as he spun them around, her skirts swirling out with the movement as the paintings whooshed by in a blur of muted color. It was by far the most fun she'd had in months—years, perhaps. In a move so fast her head was spinning, he brought them both to an abrupt stop, facing one of the portraits.

"As you can see, Father decided to use a brilliant sunset as the backdrop for Lady Westmoreland's portrait."

She gaped at him, at a complete loss as to his sudden shift of demeanor. He sounded like a bored guide at a museum, not even a hitch in his breathing while she huffed like a racehorse to regain her breath.

"Is everything all right in here, Sir Colin?"

"Yes, of course, Mr. Swanson. Thank you for your concern." Colin's smile was utterly polite and disengaged as he nodded to the man standing in the doorway.

Sucking in a breath, Beatrice followed suit, offering her own bland smile even as her heart pounded wildly within her chest. How on earth had she missed the approach of the gallery worker? She was more perceptive than most spies, or so her brother-in-law, Benedict, had once teased. She never missed what was going on around her.

His brow creased in confusion, Mr. Swanson nonetheless dipped his head and retreated back to the front room. Letting go of the pent-up air in her lungs, Beatrice turned widened eyes to Colin. "Thank you so much. Can you imagine if he would have caught us?"

He shrugged, the motion drawing her attention to the strong line of his shoulders, encased in a simple black jacket that suited him perfectly. "I see far too many cases where people break the rules without paying close enough attention to the possibility of being caught. In fact, it is exactly what keeps the courts full and barristers in demand." He paused and gave a little tip of his chin. "And you're welcome."

She lifted a brow imperiously, a gesture passed down from Mama. "Learned a thing or two about getting away with murder, did you?"

"Murder, theft, dancing with a beautiful lady—only the most grievous of crimes."

The compliment caught her by surprise and sent an immediate flush of pleasure through her. He thought her beautiful? She turned the compliment over in her mind, inspecting it as one might a stumbled-upon treasure. Her sisters were beautiful. Her mother was beautiful. Even her sister-in-law was gorgeous. Beatrice had always been the passably attractive one in the bunch. The one whose eyes weren't quite as blue, whose hair wasn't quite as blond, whose teeth weren't quite as straight, and whose bosom was more a hint than a reality.

She would say that he was just making a pretty statement, with no real meaning behind it, but he struck her as a man of honesty. He was nothing like the hordes of men who paid her empty praise and waxed poetic about her beauty and charm. Those men had agendas, and heaven knew they wouldn't look twice at her if she were separated from her ever-present dowry.

But Colin seemed different somehow. She got the impression that if it wasn't true—in his mind, at least—then he probably wouldn't say it. She tucked the comment away and nodded gravely. "All the worst crimes, punishable by death or marriage, no?"

"Precisely."

They grinned at each other a moment, her heart still elevated from their romp. The afternoon sun bathed half his face in slanted light, illuminating his sculpted jaw and cheekbones, and she wished that she had her paints with her. He looked like a fallen angel, half human and half heavenly creature. As he turned his attention back to the priceless masterpieces lining the walls and continued with his thoroughly interrupted tour, Beatrice realized that something rather shocking had happened in the course of their time at the gallery.

Here she was, surrounded by some of the most exciting and expertly executed works ever created, and somehow the one thing that seemed to hold her attention was the least known of all the painter's accomplishments.

His son.

Chapter Eight

Beatrice was late, and she knew it. With the daylight fast fading to a dull gray twilight, she tightened her hold on her reticule and hurried forward, urging her maid, Rose, to keep up. The carriage would be waiting at the end of the street as ordered, but first they'd have to make their way through the growing crowd.

Whoever had decided that Bond Street was perfectly appropriate for ladies for half a day, at which time it suddenly transformed into a forbidden street acceptable only for the club-going gentlemen of the *ton*, clearly had never been caught up in a newly arrived shipment containing a gorgeous selection of red sable brushes imported directly from Italy.

But no one had consulted her on the issue, and the window for making it to the end of the street by five and then home before her family sent out a search party was fast closing. Already the pavement was emptying of swishing skirts and harried servants, replaced by the sure-footed thump of Hessian boots and the low rumble of male laughter.

Of course, even if she was late, it would be worth it. She could hardly wait to try out the new brushes she'd finally decided on. Viewing Sir Frederick's incredible collection had redoubled her passion for capturing the world around her on canvas. She wanted to stretch her abilities, experimenting more with light and darkness to bring true depth to her paintings.

A silly grin came to her lips, and she pressed them together to keep from looking a fool in the middle of Bond Street. She couldn't help it—every time she thought of Sir Frederick's paintings, her mind inevitably slid toward thoughts of Colin and the magical afternoon they had spent. Was there any other man on the planet like him? With his cool, logical side underscored by unexpected whimsy and kindness, one never knew what he would say or do next.

Ahead of her, a trio of young bucks walked abreast of one another, completely unmindful of the fact they were blocking the way of anyone who might wish to pass them. Beatrice slowed, glaring at their dark greatcoats as they lumbered along, offering jovial jabs and slaps on one another's backs as they walked, their voices gratingly loud.

Oh, for heaven's sake. At this rate, she was sure to be here when the bells tolled the hour. She started to speed up, to attempt to slip between them and the storefronts on the right, when she suddenly realized she knew them.

On the outside was Lord Bridgemont, the young heir to the Earl of Marks, in the middle was Mr. Bickett, if she wasn't mistaken, and on the left was Mr. Knight. It was jarring to see them so completely uninhibited. One would think they would at least wait until they were inside their club to engage in such behavior. They laughed in unison, the bawdy sort of sound that could only mean that they were speaking of the sort of things not meant for young ladies' ears.

Which, of course, meant that she wanted to hear what they were saying.

Softening her footsteps, she steadily closed the distance between them, straining to filter out the sounds of the traffic. Keeping her head down and counting on her small stature to provide some amount of inconspicuousness, she advanced until she was only a few steps behind them and could clearly make out their words.

"You really should go to the Carlisle ball t'night, Knight." Mr. Bickett paused, then promptly tilted his head back and laughed. "T'night, Knight!"

"S'right, Knight—you should spend the night with him," added Bridgemont, and the three of them laughed all over again. The stagnant odor of spirits trailed in their wake, making Beatrice wrinkle her nose.

"You're on your own, m'afraid. I've got my pockets lined with my father's blunt, and I intend to spend every penny at the legendary Madam V's tonight. I'll leave you to your horse-faced heiresses—be sure to dance with one for me."

Mr. Bickett groaned, shaking his head. "S'hardly worth it. Might as well hold out for the new crop come spring. God knows only the dregs are left now. 'Course, I'm still bitter over Rochester bagging that Dowling chit right out from under me. Now he's free to tup his mistress, and I'm still trying to find a dowry attached to a female I can stand to look at for more than five minutes."

"Don't worry about that," Mr. Knight said, elbowing his friend. "You can always look at the pretty ones while dancing with the rich ones." More laughter and back-slapping.

Beatrice came to an abrupt halt, her heart pounding painfully in her chest. Of all the disgusting, vile, awful . . . She made a sound perilously close to a growl as she glared after the men. Rose came to stand beside her, worry clouding her dark eyes as she waited for Beatrice to move.

Clenching her jaw, Beatrice lifted her chin and

started forward again. Her steps were heavy for once, her half boots connecting solidly with the pavement. It was all too much to bear. For Bickett to speak of Diana so callously, to actually *envy* her horrible husband, it was just so *wrong*.

She needed to get home. As anger built like trapped steam within her, propelling her forward, she felt compelled by the need to *do* something, to help protect the unsuspecting young women of the *ton* from such greedy scoundrels. Someone had to warn them of the nefarious intentions of single-minded fortune hunters like Bickett—and Godfrey for that matter. And Rochester and heaven knew how many others.

As if of its own volition, her right hand tingled with the need to pick up her tools and express her emotions in her artwork. An idea began to form in the back of her head, one that was risky and ill-advised and somewhat mad.

As far as she was concerned—it was perfect.

"Bonjour, monsieur."

Beatrice smiled brightly as she strode to the counter of the artist supply shop, behind which she knew her quarry would be. The space was well lit by the huge front window, even with another cloudy day outside. At least it had stopped raining. Otherwise, her mother would never have let her out of the house with so vague an explanation.

Just as she expected, Monsieur Allard sat hunched on a stool at his worktable, his white hair poking from beneath his black cap. When she stopped just shy of the counter, he looked up, his curmudgeonly expression steadfastly in place. His great, crooked nose held up a pair of ancient spectacles, magnifying his eyes oddly.

"Mademoiselle. Back already, I see."

It wasn't so much a greeting as an unenthusiastic

acknowledgment of her presence. Her grin widened—
it was no less than she expected. *"Oui. Ça va?"*

His gaze returned to the half-finished engraving on
the worktable in front of him. "This is London, my
lady, and you are English. There is no place for *français*
here today." His heavily accented words were gruff,
but not unkind.

Beatrice gave a small shrug. "As you wish, monsieur." She clasped her hands and waited, allowing her
gaze to wander around the plethora of supplies behind
the counter. Easels, a huge selection of brushes of
nearly any size, an array of canvases, and pigments
enough to create every color known to man. It was the
sort of place women were not generally allowed, but
she spent enough money here for him to overlook that
fact. Yes, she could send a footman in her stead, but no
one else would know quite what she would want.

And no one else could possibly be trusted with her
task.

"Is there something I could help you find today?"
He was long-suffering, as usual, but she knew that,
deep down, he did actually like her. He always saved
the best of each shipment for her, as he'd proven two
days earlier when the red sable brushes had arrived.

Which was why she had decided to try to enlist his
help in her unorthodox plan, "try" being the operative
word. As good a customer as she was, she wanted to
think that he would agree to help her, but the truth
was, she couldn't be sure of such an eventuality.

She placed her gloved hands on the utilitarian counter and leaned forward the slightest bit. "I think not,
actually. As it turns out, *you* are the person I'm here to
see today."

That earned her little more than a flicker of his eyes
before he returned his attention to his work. "Perhaps
you will wish to come back when I am less busy, *non*?"

Definitely not. There wasn't a soul in the shop other than the two of them since she'd convinced her maid to pop in the small bookstore next door and choose a new book. And besides that, it had taken quite a bit of nerve to come here today, with the carefully rendered drawing tucked in the crook of her arm for safekeeping. "Never fear. I'll take only a moment of your time."

He grunted in acknowledgment, somehow infusing incredulity into the inarticulate sound.

"Tell me, monsieur, do you ever break the rules?"

His hands paused for a second or two before he resumed his task. "I am a Frenchman living in London, my lady. A man in my position admits to no wrongdoings."

"I don't mean anything nefarious. I merely wondered if you have ever tried something . . . a bit outside of the accepted norm."

He sighed, setting down his carving tools beside the small steel plate. She could see what he was working on now: a fashion plate of a stylish morning gown.

"And what is the norm? I wonder. I suspect my normal and your normal are quite different."

"True," she allowed with a bob of her head. Her eyes landed on the small, framed print hanging on the wall directly over his workspace. Rendered in the limited medium of lines and crosshatchings, it was a masterful portrayal of a laughing young woman looking playfully over her shoulder. It was the sort of piece that would have taken hours upon hours of careful, delicate work. Every time she visited the shop, the young woman's portrait drew her notice. And she had a pretty good idea of who the lady must be.

It was time to test her theory. Changing tactics, Bea met his skeptical gaze head-on. "Are you married, monsieur?"

His bushy brows snapped together, eyes narrowing. "I used to be."

It was exactly as she thought. "Did you love your wife?"

An Englishman might have kicked her out of the shop right then and there. In fact, many Frenchmen would have as well, and she braced for the possibility of his anger. But one look at his softening expression, and she knew her hunch was correct.

"Ah, yes. Very much."

"I thought that might have been the case," she said, her tone soft and sincere. "It's why I hope you'll help me now."

He crossed his arms, his stubby, callused fingers fanning out across the coarse gray wool of his chunky knit sweater. "And what is it you think old Georges can do to help the daughter of a marquis?"

Beatrice bit her lip, hoping she was making the right decision coming to him. "First, I think this is something that can help both of us. Second, well, perhaps you should take a look at this."

She pulled out the rolled sheet of paper and handed it to him. He didn't know it yet, but she *would* get him to help her. She had to—her entire plan to help the unsuspecting ladies of the *ton* depended on it. She watched as he untied the ribbon and unfurled the paper.

The seconds stretched on as she waited for some sort of reaction from the old man. Nothing. She curled her hands at her sides to keep from fidgeting. Her gaze flicked to the image, studying it with fresh eyes. Her idea had turned out better than she had even hoped. Apparently, anger fueled the arts as effectively as passion. It was slightly brilliant, if she did say so herself.

If Monsieur Allard agreed to help.

His head remained bent over the page, his countenance giving away nothing as the low sounds from the busy street outside filled the silence. At last, he looked up at her, his magnified eyes unusually bright behind their lenses. "Very interesting, mademoiselle. Am I to assume you have plans for this piece?"

"I hope to. Anonymously, of course. And only with your help."

He grunted, a noncommittal sound that could have either meant she was mad, or she had his interest. She decided to go with the latter. "I'll pay you, of course. For your time and talents, as well as your trouble."

He sat back in his chair, studying her as if gauging her mettle. She lifted her chin, a gesture she found herself doing whenever she wished she weren't so small. Long seconds ticked by, but still he didn't say a word. Anxiousness tugged at her belly, and she couldn't keep quiet another second. "What do you think?"

"I think," he said, coming to his feet and turning to face her fully, "that you will either get us both in much trouble . . ." He trailed off, tilting his head as he considered her.

"Or?" she prompted.

"Or make us the talk of the town."

She grinned, confidence that he would help her flooding her chest. "Let us hope," she said, leaning forward with a bit of mischief, "that it will be the latter."

Chapter Nine

"Christ Almighty, have you seen this thing?"
John strode into the breakfast room waving a small publication of some sort. Colin's mind had been so far away at that moment, immersed in his plans for the day, that it took him a moment to realize what his cousin was holding.

A ladies' fashion magazine.

Colin raised an eyebrow. "No, actually. Though I am riveted to hear why you have seen it." He set down his coffee and reached for the rag, holding it between two fingers as if the vapidness contained within was somehow catching.

"You're lucky I did. My stepsister was positively agog over the thing." His cousin began to pace the length of the breakfast room, turning sharply at the end of each circuit. "Go on; read it."

Colin looked down at the rather hideous fashion plate that was illustrated on most of the page. With a shrug, he read the caption. *"Fashionable morning and evening dresses for November."*

Stalking back toward where Colin sat, John snatched the magazine from his hand and flipped it around. "Try again."

Damn but the man was in a snit. Colin sighed and

refocused on the page before him, turning it to catch the dim light filtering into the room from the dreary morning outside. *"Dear Gently Bred Lady."* He paused, raising an eyebrow to his cousin. "Clearly meant for the two of us."

John rolled his hand in a "keep going" gesture, and Colin returned his attention to the page. " 'It has come to my attention that there are some things for which a young debutant may not be adequately prepared. I should know—I myself have been one. I know exactly what it feels like to have the admiring eyes of a handsome gentleman bring a blush to one's cheek and the elation of being asked to dance by a long-admired suitor. In that moment, an innocent young miss can easily be misled by a man whose intentions are not as they seem.

" 'I speak of the type of person known as a fortune hunter.' "

Colin's gaze jerked up. "Bloody hell."

"It gets better," John said, resuming his pacing.

Returning to the letter, Colin forged on. " 'A fortune hunter has no care for the lady herself, only the promise of the money she is attached to. If he succeeds in marrying a hapless young lady of fortune, the lady herself is no longer of interest. His fortune secured, he'll carelessly set aside his wife and carry on with whatever behavior landed him in need of funds in the first place. So, in hopes of rescuing the innocent from this sort of fate, I offer up my thoughts on how to recognize a fortune hunter.

" 'The simplest method for determining a man's motives is observing whom he asks to dance. If he focuses solely on ladies of notable dowry, then he is likely to be a fortune hunter and therefore should be avoided.' " It was signed *The Daring Debutant.*

Well, this was just bloody great. It was hard enough

feeling as though he were some sort of predator by looking to marry a woman with a decent dowry. Now he'd have to contend with newly suspicious females watching his every move.

"And the *pièce de résistance*," John said, interrupting Colin's wandering thoughts. "The blasted cartoon."

Colin directed his attention to the engraving below the letter. He blinked suddenly, his eyes widening in disbelief. The setting was a strikingly familiar ballroom, with elegant twin pillars framing the arching doorway. He jerked his gaze to the doorway of the breakfast room, which sported a similar, if less elaborate, motif.

"I see you recognize the background."

"Your mother's ballroom? That's a bloody bold move."

"An apt description. Though I'm certain Josephine would have never brought it to me if she hadn't recognized our own ballroom, so I suppose we should be grateful. Tell me what else you see."

Shaking his head, Colin lifted the page for a better look. Standing to one side was a man dressed in the style popular with those of the Bond Street Beau set. He was leering at three ladies, each with progressively smaller stacks of gold spilling from satchels at their feet. The fop had his hand extended to the lady with the largest stack and the caption above his head read, "Would your dowry—I mean, would *you*—care to dance?"

"I see a fortune hunter sizing up three ladies based on their dowries." He tossed the magazine on the table, more in disgust of himself than anything else. "It's a wonder my name isn't sprawled across the poor bastard's face."

John leaned over to retrieve the damnable thing and thumped the cartoon with the back of his knuckle. "Not your name, my friend. Godfrey's."

"What?" Colin sat up straight, snatching the thing from John's fingers for a closer look. Surely the artist wouldn't be so brazen. "I don't see his name anywhere."

"That's because you are unfamiliar with the people of the *ton*. If you had spent every last social minute with these people as I have, you would see that Godfrey is as good as labeled. See that distinctive waistcoat? It was what he wore to Mother's ball. Combine that with the overly dramatic version of his hairstyle and the spot-on expression on his face, and there is no way that's not him."

The page crumpled in Colin's hands before he realized what he was doing. Carefully releasing his grip, he laid the rumpled magazine on the table before crossing his arms and facing his cousin. "Who would do such a thing? Granted, the man is an ass, but how could someone make a mockery of another in such a public forum? It's not as though he's a bloody political figure."

"Not uncommon, I'm afraid. The scandal sheets regularly call out 'Lady D' and 'Lord H,' as if everyone doesn't know exactly who they are referring to. It's something of a game in this society."

"Bloody hell," Colin breathed, running a hand through his hair. "Seems as though I am taking a greater risk with my reputation than I realized."

Not that it really mattered. If he didn't find a wife with a hefty dowry in three months' time, the world would learn of his father's spectacular business failure and the family reputation would be in tatters anyway. No one wanted to be associated with the utterly bankrupt family of an eccentric painter. Colin harbored no illusions that his father was some sort of national hero. The moment they caught wind of the fact he had died in debt up to his nose, the condemnation would come.

And Colin should know.

That was exactly the way he had felt about his father when the solicitors had shown up at his doorstep last month to inform him that his father had mortgaged everything he had in the world, including the estate and everything in it, against the engraving business he'd started last year. The same business, incidentally, that Colin had vehemently advised against. And the same one that, according to the representatives for Father's investors, had never even turned a half penny's profit.

Resentment built deep in his stomach, spilling out into his blood and pumping through his body with every beat of his heart. Father had mortgaged the estate— Colin's entire inheritance and the only home his siblings had ever known—without ever even telling him. He had told him the money had come from eager investors. Never did he admit that the investors were eager thanks to the massive amount of collateral he'd put up.

John laid a reassuring hand on his shoulder. "Nothing ventured, nothing gained. You've little other choice, no?"

"No."

"Then carry on as you must. I just thought it best to share with you what you are up against. An invisible foe is much more dangerous than the one you can see. At least now you know to be on the alert. Have a care with how you are perceived."

Colin nodded. "Agreed. Thanks for sharing, cousin. It's always better to be prepared." If he'd learned nothing else in his past two years at the Inns of Court, he'd certainly learned that. A barrister was only as good as the information he gathered. Well, that and his ability to argue his point the way a dog chewed on a bone.

As his cousin headed to the sideboard to fill his plate

for breakfast, Colin considered the letter and accompanying cartoon. The words of warning would no doubt resonate with the young ladies who read it. It had a distinctly empowering feel to it, as if the author had decided it was high time women took responsibility for their own fates. It was both bold and clever to print such a thing in a fashion magazine—after all, how many men would ever see it?

Colin leaned back in his chair, considering what, if any, changes should be made to his approach to finding a wife. This article may very well be intended as a guide to females on how to avoid fortune hunters, but it could also be used for exactly the opposite purpose. Did he not know what they would be looking for now? He could use this knowledge to his benefit.

He picked up the magazine and scanned the letter once more. A fortune hunter danced only with women of a certain worth? Fine. He'd go out of his way to dance with any woman he found interesting. Actually, he quite liked that strategy. It felt much more natural to enjoy a lady based on her own merit, anyway.

Unbidden, an image of Lady Beatrice flashed into his mind. Some of the stiffness drained from his shoulders, and he smiled absently. Their tour had been every bit as enjoyable as he'd imagined it would be. She was so much more than he ever expected a privileged daughter of the nobility could be. How many other debutants could have inspired him to dance a Scottish reel in the middle of a gallery? And more to the point, how many other debutants would have taken him up on the offer?

"What are you over there grinning like an idiot about? Nothing good can come from that blasted letter, my friend."

Colin raised an eyebrow to his cousin as he set down his plate and pulled out a chair. "On the contrary. This letter did little more than arm us with the knowledge we need to avoid raising suspicions."

John slowed in the process of laying his napkin in his lap. Colin could practically see the man's military brain going to work. "By Jove, you're right, old man. Don't know why I didn't think of it before."

"Too much time away from the battlefield can make any man go soft. Mustn't blame yourself." He grinned at the sarcastic expression John threw him before picking up his fork.

"No, I think it is the lack of stimulating conversation around here. Regardless, you have your battle plan. Dance with a variety of ladies. The trick of it is having a care not to lead on any of the unsuitables."

"Agreed." The last thing he wanted to do was hurt some girl's feelings. He had to be charming and agreeable with the ladies he considered prospects and cordial but impersonal to those who weren't.

Of course, if he adhered strictly to that plan, it would mean no more ill-advised romps with the enchanting Lady Beatrice. He smiled wryly. So far, he had shown a complete lack of judgment when it came to his *stór*.

And he wasn't sorry for it.

It was a bloody rotten time for him, and if there was one person in the mess of it who made him feel like an equal, as though he actually had something of true worth to offer her, then he wouldn't apologize for whatever small amount of time he could spend with her. There was literally no one else in London, or on the planet, for that matter, who could offer her what he could, and he planned to enjoy that.

Tonight at the Westmoreland ball, he would dance every set, with any young lady who took his fancy. He had only two goals for the evening: to further charm prospective brides and to dance a proper dance with Lady Beatrice.

*				*				*

Beatrice had been expecting the knock for so long, it was a relief when it finally came. "Enter," she said, setting down her paintbrush and turning to greet her sisters.

Just as she expected, Jocelyn and Carolyn let themselves in, their blue eyes bright with the anticipation of sharing their discovery. Beatrice had known they would come and had painted with half an ear to the stairway since the time she heard the knock on the servants' door exactly two floors below her studio almost an hour earlier.

It was Tuesday, after all: delivery day.

"Oh my word, Bea, you will never believe what they printed in *A Proper Young Lady's Fashion Companion* this week." Carolyn was ahead of her sister by half a foot, holding out the periodical in question. They hadn't even taken the time to properly dress, each wearing wrappers over their night rails with their hair simply braided.

Good. Beatrice liked to think that girls all over the city were just as excited.

Schooling her features into an expression of pure innocence, she wiped her hands on the bottom of her apron and regarded them with false curiosity. "What is it? Something new from France?"

Jocelyn plopped onto the studio's only piece of furniture, a slightly worse-for-the-wear chintz sofa, and shook her head. "Much more scandalous than that. Oh, it's brilliant. Wait until you see."

Carolyn handed over the magazine before joining her twin on the sofa. If either of them noticed that Beatrice's fingers trembled or that her breath wasn't quite even, they didn't let on in the least.

Drawing a quiet breath, she turned under the pretense of holding it to the meager light from the cloudy day and looked down at the printed page. Her heart gave a little leap. There it was, in black and white. Her words, her art, her labor of love for her fellow females, published in a legitimate magazine for all to see. The surge of pride was so powerful, so consuming, she actually felt the prickle of tears behind her eyes.

"Can you believe it?" Carolyn asked, nudging the bottom of Beatrice's skirts with her foot when she didn't say anything. "It says the author is a former debutant." The implied scandal of such a thing hung heavy in her breathless tone.

"How utterly remarkable," Beatrice murmured, infusing a healthy dose of incredulity into her response. She couldn't seem to take her eyes off the etching, the product of her own hands. Almost, anyway. Monsieur Allard had done a superb job of transcribing her drawing into an etching. She ran a finger over the crosshatched shading of the imposing columns in the background. It had turned out perfectly, and all she wanted to do was hug it to her chest and proclaim to the world that it was her handiwork.

But of course she could not.

If anyone knew that she had written the letter and submitted the drawing, her reputation would be utterly ruined. No one would ever see the good in what she did, only the breaking of unspoken rules.

"I wonder who wrote it," Jocelyn mused, pulling her legs in to her chest and resting her chin on her knees. "Do you think it is true that it was written by a debutant? Who's to say it wasn't some dried-up old journalist trying to ruffle feathers or create a story where there is none?"

Carolyn's eyes rounded. "Do you think someone would do such a thing?"

Beatrice bit her lip against the need to defend herself and the validity of her work. Instead, she gave a casual shake of her head. "No, I don't think it could be a journalist." She came to sit between her sisters on the sofa and pointed to the engraving. "See the background? That's Lady Churly's ballroom. See the fluted columns?" she said, sliding her finger across the drawing.

Jocelyn snatched the paper back and pored over it with renewed fervor. "How very, very bold. If the setting is real, then . . ." She paused, tilting her head as she regarded the image through squinted eyes. "Oh my goodness gracious, I think that's Mr. Godfrey!"

"No!" Carolyn exclaimed, leaning over the page for a closer look.

"Of course not," Beatrice said, rolling her eyes as she pulled the magazine out of her sister's hands. "None of these people is real. They are just figments of the author's imagination."

She looked down at the etching, shaking her head at the absurdity of the claim. But . . . A trickle of dread slid down her spine as she stared at the picture. Oh heavens. She bit the inside of her lip hard as she took in the man's clothes, his smug expression, his Corinthian hair.

"I think Jocelyn's right," Carolyn said, craning her neck as she inspected the image. "It looks quite a bit like Mr. Godfrey. How utterly scandalous!"

"And mean," added Jocelyn

Beatrice couldn't seem to draw a proper breath. She hadn't *intended* to portray him, despite the fact she knew full well he was a fortune hunter. She swallowed, trying to loosen the tightness holding her throat closed.

"I don't know," she said, the flippant tone she strove for falling just short of her reach. "Any number of gentlemen would resemble such a characterized drawing."

Pulling the magazine back into her lap, Carolyn shook her head. "I don't know. I spent only a few minutes with the man, but I have to say, something about this drawing just seems to capture his personality."

"You mean like the arrogant expression?" Jocelyn said, raising a collusive brow. "Yes, I'd say that was rather spot-on."

"Exactly," her twin replied, giving a guilty little grin.

It was nothing compared to the guilt wrapping itself around Beatrice's heart. "Come spring, you two will see exactly how common such an expression is among men of the *ton*. Perhaps you were right, Jocelyn. Perhaps it was just a journalist's rendition."

"Not if what you say about this being Lady Churly's ballroom is true. There is no way they would have allowed a journalist inside. No, if this is an accurate drawing of the ball, then it stands to reason that this really is Mr. Godfrey."

"Poor man," Carolyn said, shaking her head. "Truly, Mr. Godfrey was not my idea of a perfect gentleman, but I have to admit this makes me feel a bit sorry for the man. What if he's not really a fortune hunter?"

Beatrice put an icy hand to her chest. She might have been guilty of inadvertently calling the man out, but at least she was beyond certain that he was indeed a fortune hunter.

Perhaps this would be a good thing if she managed to save some poor girl from his clutches. "He is," she said with authority, nodding her head for good measure. "Believe me. I have seen him in action enough to know the truth of it."

"In action?" Jocelyn raised a pale brow. "What, does he go around with a ledger, tallying each lady's worth?"

"Practically, yes. He does exactly what the author said he does: dancing only with those whose dowry heft is well known."

"Hardly enough to convict a man."

Beatrice scowled at Jocelyn. She already felt bad enough—she didn't need her sister doubting her judgment. "Trust me, the man has eyes only for money. The author did the right thing by pointing out how a lady may recognize a fortune hunter like him. The better armed a lady is, the better able to protect herself."

Carolyn tucked her feet beneath the voluminous white fabric of her night rail and shrugged. "If you say so. What do you think will happen to him? Do you think he'll read it?"

Heavens, she hoped he never would. "I should think not," Beatrice said, flipping the magazine closed and gesturing to the title. "It's a ladies' fashion magazine, after all. I sincerely hope that gentlemen are not reading this sort of thing."

"Well, not normally, of course," Jocelyn said. "But this is positively scandalous. I wouldn't be surprised if the whole of the *ton* has read it by the end of the week."

Butterflies took flight within Beatrice's belly at this pronouncement. The thought of thousands of eyes reading her letter was daunting enough; to think of Mr. Godfrey recognizing himself . . .

"Don't be silly. It's not as though it was printed in the *Times*, for heaven's sake. It likely won't leave the bedchambers of any of the young ladies for which it was intended."

Jocelyn leaned against the arm of the sofa, tilting her head thoughtfully. "Oh, I bet it will. I only wish I could go to the Westmoreland ball to witness the reaction for myself."

A sudden rush of nerves whisked through Beatrice's veins. By eight o'clock that night, she would know exactly what the *ton* thought about the letter—and by extension, her.

Chapter Ten

Beatrice was not, by nature, an anxious person. In fact, she was generally actively *not* anxious, remaining more or less calm in all sorts of situations. But standing at the doorway to the Westmorelands' surprisingly crowded ball, she had only one thought: whether she could make it to the ladies' retiring room before she cast up her accounts all over the eggshell-hued marble floors.

She took a deep breath, trying her best to ignore the cloying scent of a hundred perfumes mixed with beeswax and freshly polished wood. For heaven's sake, she was made of sterner stuff than this. Just because she may or may not have baldly called a gentleman out for being a fortune hunter in a widely distributed magazine with a highly scandalous letter meant to help, not hurt anyone, did not mean that she could fall to pieces over it.

Besides—if she wished to slip through the crowd unnoticed in order to eavesdrop on gossip, she'd best keep her dinner where it was.

The good news was, a problem with the carriage had delayed their departure, so they were more than fashionably late, which meant that no one announced their arrival.

"Are you quite all right, my dear?" Mama's voice was little more than a whisper in Beatrice's ear. "You look rather pale."

"Yes, of course," she murmured back, keeping a forced smile on her lips. "Although," she said, inspiration striking, "I think I will visit the retiring room to freshen up after our ordeal with the carriage."

"Shall I join you?"

Beatrice tried to relax, stretching her lips into a broader smile. "No, no, I'll be only a moment. And look, Lady Wembley has already spotted you." She waved at the lady in question, and Mama nodded and went to speak with her friend.

There—she felt slightly better already. Adopting a bland expression, she slipped into the crowd, doing her best to meld with her surroundings. She really was headed to the retiring room—often the best gossip could be had there—but more than anything, she wanted a chance to observe as nonchalantly as possible. It'd be easier if she could have worn a plainer gown, but her mother had insisted Beatrice don the new one that had been delivered the day before. Shimmery metallic threads did tend to make one feel conspicuous, but with any luck no one would—

Seemingly out of nowhere, Mr. Godfrey stepped directly in her path. *Drat, drat, drat.*

"Lady Beatrice," he purred, his light brown eyes pinning her with unsettling intensity. "I was beginning to despair of seeing you this evening."

Her stomach clenched, and she would have taken a step back were the space available. Curse her blasted luck—of course he would be the very first person she ran into. She eyed him warily, guilt marching up her spine while she tried to divine if he knew anything of the letter.

If he did, he gave nothing away. His inflection was

exactly the same, his posture ever straight and his gaze entirely too direct. Nothing about him spoke of affront or anger, merely his normal, all too arrogant self.

She swallowed past the lump of self-reproach that clogged her throat and offered him a weak smile. "Good evening, Mr. Godfrey. I'm afraid you have caught me on my way—"

"Yes, yes, I can see that you are quite on a mission. I don't wish to keep you, my lady—I merely wished to add my name to your dance card *before* it fills up."

No polite question this time—instead he held out his hand as if it were a foregone conclusion that a dance would be his tonight. Beatrice looked down to the small card attached to her wrist with a slender green ribbon and sighed. It was as good a penance as anything. And perhaps, if she were very lucky, he would be so busy with his usual tactic of dancing with the wealthiest women, he wouldn't have time to hear any gossip.

Holding out the card and pencil, she smiled a bit too brightly. "But of course."

He bent over the card and scribbled his name beside one of the two dozen dances listed out. When he was done, he looked up to her with a triumphant smile. "Thank you, Lady Beatrice. I look forward to our dance with much anticipation."

That made one of them.

She dipped her head in acknowledgment before turning and escaping into the crowd. Sneaking a look at the card, she groaned. Of course he would claim one of the waltzes. Oh, well—tattlers couldn't be choosers.

She had gone all of a dozen steps when a hand closed around her arm. Before she had the chance to get annoyed at being waylaid again, Miss Sophie Wembley hooked her arm around Beatrice's elbow and grinned, her dark eyes positively glittering with excitement.

"Finally—I'm so glad I found you. Did you see it? Tell me you saw it. Of course you did—you see everything."

Beatrice grinned despite herself. Sophie was absolutely irrepressible. "The letter?"

Sophie nodded and started forward, dragging Beatrice in exactly the direction she was headed in the first place. Sophie's normally riotous curls had been brought to heel tonight, pulled up into a tight bun at the top of her head, but a few black curls had managed to escape and were now floating like silk streamers behind her as she rushed forward.

The moment she pushed through the door to the retiring room, she turned on Beatrice. "Tell me what you know. Assuming you know something, because you probably do. You *always* do."

Drat—she hadn't expected anyone to come right out and ask like that. Beatrice tried to think of a way to respond without lying to her friend. They had been slow to befriend each other initially, but with them both being middle sisters, they had eventually built on that common ground.

They also had their own talents, Bea with her paints and Sophie with her music. She was no savant like Charity, Beatrice's longtime family friend and near-genius pianoforte player, but Sophie was still quite talented on her oboe. Her mother had chosen the odd instrument under the mistaken notion that the more unusual the instrument, the more memorable the musician, but Sophie had embraced the small, high-pitched woodwind and somehow made the thing sing.

Beatrice opened her mouth, fully prepared to sidestep the question, but a shuffling noise alerted her to the presence of someone else in the room. Cutting a glance to Sophie, she shrugged. "I know what I read, same as you."

Miss Marianne Harmon, Lord Wexley's youngest daughter, stepped from around the screen and eyed them both. "You must be speaking of the letter printed in *A Proper Young Lady's Fashion Companion* today." She paused in front of the mirror to pat her hair—as if a single strand would dare disobey her and fall out of place—and smiled at her own reflection. "Pray, don't let me interrupt your conversation."

Since Beatrice was technically related to Marianne, she refrained from making the face she wanted to. Third cousin might sound distant, but Mama would likely hear of it by the end of the night, and Lord knew Beatrice already had enough potential trouble on her plate. Instead, she gave a one-shouldered shrug. "No conversation, really. Neither one of us knows anything above what we read in the magazine."

Family or not, Beatrice had no problem lying to Marianne. The woman possessed a remarkable ability to retain information and mold it to her benefit when the time was right, and Bea wasn't about to provide her with any fodder.

"Well, it hardly matters. It was just a silly thing, obviously written by someone who hasn't the sense God gave her. Why else would she—if indeed it is a she—stoop to publishing such a thing?"

"Oh, I thought it was brilliant," Sophie chimed in, a broad grin lighting her features. "I never thought of such a thing before. Not that I'd need to, of course. Heaven knows no fortune hunter would ever have a use for me."

She had a way of saying things no one else would get away with and somehow come across as charming. At least Beatrice thought so—Marianne's raised brow seemed to indicate she thought otherwise. "Yes, well, I think it reeks of bitterness. Perhaps the author was tired of not being asked to dance and she decided to paint all men of discerning taste in a negative light in order to force their hands."

"Quite a bit of effort to go through merely to win a dance partner, don't you think?" Beatrice had intended to keep her mouth shut, but Marianne's theory was completely ridiculous, and she didn't want her to go spreading that sort of discrediting speculation around. "I think the author wished to help the innocent young women preparing to make their debuts next year."

Marianne made a delicate sound of disbelief. "Don't be so gullible, Beatrice. No one does something like that without hope for personal gain." She gave her cheeks a little pinch and turned away from the mirror. "I'll leave you to your gossip."

With a condescending smile, she glided from the room, her golden gown swishing behind her with the exaggerated sway of her hips. Beatrice rolled her eyes and turned back to Sophie. "Good riddance."

Her friend giggled, completely without rancor for the high-and-mighty Marianne. "Don't mind her. She's just miffed that something else other than her legendary beauty and divine pianoforte talent has captured the attention of all present."

"All present? You mean you and me?"

"No, silly—I mean everyone. Haven't you heard the whispers and conjecture going on out there? Everyone is positively rapt to know who the author is. And not only that," she said, leaning in conspiratorially, "they're all atwitter about the identity of the fortune hunter."

"The fortune hunter?" Beatrice squeaked. "I don't know what you're talking about—the letter spoke in very general terms."

Sophie clasped Beatrice's hand in earnest. "The letter, yes. The drawing, well, that remains to be seen, doesn't it? Surely you saw the resemblance. I mean, if I did, it's impossible to believe that you did not. Did you?"

Well, then—good thing they were in the retiring room. Her stomach rebelled all over again, with a surge of guilty nerves racing through her. "Well," she hedged, "I think it could be any number of gentlemen, or more likely, just a conglomeration of several into one."

"I can scarce believe you can't see it. Honestly, if it's not Mr. Godfrey, I'll eat my slippers."

Curses. That was exactly what she was afraid of. Although, if anyone was going to have her foot in her mouth, it would doubtless be Beatrice.

Oblivious to her distress, Sophie spun an escaped curl around her finger. "The author is one brave, bold soul."

Beatrice glanced at her friend in the mirror, surprised by the unknowing compliment. A bit of the anxiousness ebbed away at the kind words. "She is a bit brave, isn't she?"

"A bit? A good deal more than that, I should think. I'd never have it in me to be so brilliant."

The knot in Beatrice's stomach further unraveled and she smiled hugely at her friend. "Of course you do—more so, I should think."

"Now, that's a load of hogwash, and we both know it." She winked at Beatrice's reflection, her cheeks blushing merrily. "But I'm glad someone does. The letter may not be useful to me, but if it helps even one girl avoid the fortune hunter's snare, then I say bravo."

Beatrice very nearly hugged her. She was right—even if her drawing caused Mr. Godfrey a bit of discomfort, it very well might be helping to save a fellow debutant from poor Diana's fate. Even if it were only one less girl duped by a fortune hunter, it would be well worth the risk and minor scandal for Mr. Godfrey.

All guilt aside, he *was* exactly the sort she was warning against.

Sophie pursed her lips, her finger still twirling the same dark curl. "Do you think she is here now? The author, I mean. She was at Lady Churly's, so it stands to reason she'd be here, don't you think?"

That was a question she could answer with absolute honesty. "As a matter of fact, I do."

The Westmoreland ball was proving to be quite a bit more entertaining than the last one Colin had attended. Here, he gladly released himself from the need to write his name on the dance cards of only the ladies on his list of suitable wives. So far, he had claimed dances with half a dozen young ladies of varying stations and backgrounds.

Unfortunately, he had yet to find the lady for whom he had reserved two waltzes, just in case one of hers was already claimed. Taking another sip of champagne, he scanned the room for the golden-haired nymph who had assured him that she would be there.

"Looking for someone?" Aunt Constance nodded in greeting, causing the ostrich feather affixed to the front of her emerald green turban to sway regally.

He offered her a bland smile, unwilling to reveal that that was exactly what he had been doing. "Taking it all in. Are you enjoying yourself this evening, Aunt?"

"One never enjoys oneself at a society ball, dear boy. One merely tolerates the evening as best one can."

Every now and again, her dry humor made an appearance. Colin chuckled, clinking his glass to hers. "Well, then, here is to enduring the evening in style."

She chuckled and took a sip, glancing out over the attendants as if she were surveying her kingdom. "Of course, it's always slightly more entertaining when the *ton* is abuzz about something. Just look at the number of people here tonight. That dreadful letter has created quite a bit of interest for the Little Season."

"Don't I know it," he said, the words low to prevent them from traveling. Just another reminder to stay vigilant. He must not give the *ton* any reason to doubt his family's standing. If someone asked a direct question about his finances, he refused to lie about it, which made keeping up appearances all the more vital.

As he started to lift his goblet, something made him look to the right, as if an unseen hand turned him by the chin.

And that was when he saw her.

He froze, his glass halfway to his lips, as his gaze locked on Lady Beatrice's small form slipping through the crowd. Her dark blond hair was studded with tiny jewels that flashed with every step she took. Her gown, a pale blue creation that shimmered in the candlelight as if shot with slivers of silver, suited her perfectly. She looked ethereal, and beautiful, and completely enchanting.

He lowered his glass and took a steadying breath. "Will you excuse me, Aunt? I've still a few dances free for the night, and I'd best get to filling them before it's too late."

She waved him away with her free hand. "Go, go. I wouldn't want you to miss anything on my account."

He wove his way through the crowd, but it was slow going. Damn, he'd never catch up to her in this crush. As he stepped around a pair of matrons chatting behind opened fans, he lost her completely. He paused, scanning the vicinity for another glimpse of her, and saw that she had stopped by the refreshment table.

He hurried in that direction, arriving just as she turned away from the table, lemonade in hand. Her lips parted in surprise before she broke into a pleased grin.

"Well, if it isn't Sir Colin Tate."

It was hard not to think of the last time he had seen her, when they had indulged in their illicit, impromptu dance. He offered her a perfectly polite smile, even as he allowed his eyes to convey his pleasure at seeing her again. "Lady Beatrice, lovely to see you here."

Her eyes, dark, glittering sapphires in the warm glow of the chandelier above her, offered nothing but delight as she took a small step closer. "And you, sir. Allow me to introduce my friend Miss Sophie Wembley."

It had totally escaped his attention that the lady beside them was turned toward the conversation as well. At mention of her name, the girl beamed up at him with a broad smile. He bowed and said, "A pleasure to make your acquaintance, Miss Wembley."

She gave a small curtsy and giggled. "We've been introduced, actually. Last week at your aunt's ball, in fact. But with the scores of people clambering for an introduction to the great Sir Frederick Tate's son, it's little wonder you don't remember. But it's ever so nice to meet you again."

Colin tried not to cringe. There was no accusation in her words at all, but he should have remembered meeting the girl. She definitely wasn't on his list, but that was no excuse. "I must have been terribly overwhelmed not to remember one as lovely as you. Perhaps you will allow me to make amends, and dance with me tonight? Actually, a man could do no better than to be granted dances by the both of you."

Miss Wembley shook her head, her brown eyes sparkling affably. "I hadn't taken you for the charmer, Sir Colin, but I am happy to find you are. I know you are just being polite, but I would be delighted to share a dance with you." She offered up her dance card, and he chose a quadrille toward the end of the evening.

"Thank you, Miss Wembley. Hopefully you won't mind dancing with a half-Scottish barrister baronet with less than impressive rhythm."

"You've wonderful rhythm," Lady Beatrice said, her lips tilted up with a nearly imperceptible hint of mischief. No one standing around them would have any idea she was referring to a rogue Scottish reel in the middle of a staid portrait gallery.

He loved that about her. Playfulness in the midst of all this proper society nonsense. Keeping his expression utterly bland, he nodded. "Why, thank you, Lady Beatrice. The same could be said about you. I wonder, do you have room on your dance card for one more?"

"Hmm," she murmured, producing her card and frowning down at it. "It appears all I have left is the next waltz. Will that do?"

This time he did grin, imagining what it would be like to hold her in his arms. "I think I can handle that." He accepted the card and the little pencil from her, then looked for the open spot. He blinked, confusion knitting his brow. Every spot was empty save for a single dance, which appeared to be claimed by Godfrey. He glanced back up at her, and she gave him a completely innocent smile.

It was all he could do to keep a straight face as he returned his attention to the card and filled in his name in the appropriate slot. Breaking the rules again, his little *stór*. He loved that about her. She was daring without being reckless, bold but not brazen.

When he was finished, he bowed to both girls. "Miss Wembley, I look forward to our dance later this evening. Lady Beatrice," he said, lowering his voice, "I'm sure this dance will be as delightful as our last."

Chapter Eleven

Sometimes a lady had to do what a lady had to do to get what she wanted. And by Jove, she wasn't sorry for it. He was just so blasted handsome, in his unconventional way. His lean build was perfectly accentuated in his plain black jacket and deep charcoal waistcoat that was almost the exact color of his eyes.

With plenty of time until their dance, Beatrice strolled along the perimeter of the ballroom, keeping an ear out for conversation related to the article. Sophie had been snagged by her mother, and Beatrice wanted to do a little reconnaissance now that she was alone. The trick to blending was skirting around pods of conversation without pause so people didn't think she was eavesdropping.

Already she had heard the whispers, young ladies bandying about words like "magazine," "fortune hunter," and "dowry." It seemed as though, with a few exceptions, the chatter was more or less positive, thank goodness. If nothing else, it had certainly raised awareness. What more could she ask for, really?

The corridor leading to the retiring room came up on her right, and as she glanced down the empty passageway, she came up short.

Something was different. She glanced up and down

the corridor until she saw it: A door, about halfway down, was slightly ajar, with the subtle glow of firelight flickering from within.

Her inquisitiveness flared to life, that old familiar need to know what was going on around her. She glanced to the clock; she had minutes still before she needed to meet Colin. Looking around to make sure no one was watching, she casually rounded the corner and headed toward the door. As the sounds of the ball receded, she could hear the murmur of voices up ahead. Instinctively, she slowed, quieting her already muted footsteps and calming the rustling fabric of her gown. The voices were male and they were speaking in tones just hushed enough to justify her curiosity. Normal conversations rarely interested her, but the moment voices were dropped and two heads were put together, she knew something interesting was going on.

She stepped closer, moving her head back and forth in an effort to see through the crack where the door wasn't quite closed. She could see the multicolored spines of rows upon rows of books as she moved—so this was the library, then. She stepped further sideways. There! She finally caught a flash of a burgundy jacket and the deep forest sleeve of another man beside him. Hadn't Mr. Godfrey been wearing that shade of burgundy? She crept forward a few more steps, adjusting her angle until—aha! It was him. His movements were agitated, almost jittery as he shoved a hand through his hair.

Her triumph turned to worry as a wisp of unease floated through her, like a drop of paint in a glass of water, slowly spreading outward from her chest. She took a quiet step forward, straining to hear what they were talking about. Blast the noise from the ball; it was making it impossible to catch actual words. Had he discovered his infamy? What would he do if he had? She took a calming breath, reminding herself that there was no way for him to know that she had written the letter and drawn the cartoon.

Music rose above the low roar of the crowd from down the corridor, and she pressed her lips together in frustration. The waltz would be starting in a minute or two. Of course—just when things were proving to be interesting. Her curiosity almost always won, but in this case, nothing was going to keep her from her waltz with Sir Colin. Taking one last look at Godfrey, she backed away, turned on her heel, and hurried to the ballroom.

Perhaps she could glean some small bit of information from Godfrey during their dance. He'd chosen the second waltz, so she had a good half hour to cool her heels until she could speak with him.

As she emerged from the corridor into the bright candlelight of the ballroom, Beatrice rose on her toes and looked around. She didn't see Sir Colin anywhere. His black jacket was fairly distinctive among the fussy colors of the rest of the *ton*. When she spotted him, all thoughts of Godfrey and the magazine and even the heat of the room seemed to fall away with the lift of a single corner of his mouth.

He was looking right at her, moving toward her with a purposeful stride. All those around him seemed to fade into the background while he remained in stark relief, crisp and perfectly clear.

Oh my.

She blinked, mentally framing the image. That's how she would paint him. Colin, bold and sharply detailed in the dead center, with the rest of the world soft and indistinct behind him. The painter's son, lacking the artist's touch, but blessed with looks that positively begged to be painted.

Lord, he was gorgeous. His gaze didn't falter from hers, the whole of his attention settled on her and her alone. She swallowed, trying to remember how on earth to breathe properly when a herd of butterflies had suddenly overtaken her stomach.

He stopped directly in front of her and offered a languid bow. "My lady," he said, his accent somehow transforming the words into a caress, "I believe this dance is mine."

She nodded, words seeming quite beyond her in that moment. He extended his hand, a completely proper and acceptable gesture, and yet the intensity in his smoky gaze seemed to make the simple task of accepting his hand seem like a declaration of something . . . more. Licking her suddenly dry lips, she placed her hand in his.

He smiled, giving her a wink so subtle, she almost doubted she had seen it at all. "Let's see how we do at a proper dance, shall we?"

His teasing grin quieted her rioting nerves, and she offered him one of her own. "I should warn you again, sir, that I am not the most accomplished dancer in the world. If I trod on your foot, you cannot say I didn't warn you."

"It will be worth it, my lady, if that is the price of having you to myself for a moment."

So much for calmed nerves. The honesty in his voice matched the sincerity in his eyes, even if his lips were still curled in his charming smile. Good heavens—was a single sentence really all it took to turn her to putty in this man's arms?

Apparently, it was.

His fingers tightened on hers as he led her onto the dance floor. They took up the proper position, a perfectly respectable distance between them to the casual observer. What the others in the room couldn't see was the tingling nerves of her back where his hands rested against her skin.

"Do you know," he murmured, holding his position as they waited for the start of the dance, "as beautiful as you are in daylight, I think I prefer you in the candlelight?"

"You do?" she squeaked, taken off guard by the unexpected statement.

"I do. Sunlight makes your eyes sparkle, but candlelight illuminates the fire within. It's more true to your personality."

Before she could utter a word in response, the music started and he swung them into motion. For once she didn't focus on counting out the steps in her head. How could she? Her mind whirled faster than even their bodies as she basked in the compliment. Did he think her fiery then? That thought made her feel the slightest bit reckless and a great deal more bold.

His steps were smooth, his rhythm sure. Somehow, her body just seemed to follow his, to give up to the authority of his lead. He wasn't the most graceful dancer in the world, but he moved with a certain confidence that suited her much more than an exceedingly polished partner might. She didn't need someone whose elegant moves would make her look clumsy— she needed someone who knew how to lead. She wouldn't have thought a man of his background would have such command of the waltz, but here they were, gliding along with the dozens of other couples as if he'd done such a thing his whole life.

"And here I thought your specialty would be the Scottish reel. Who taught you to dance so well? From what I know, Sir Frederick attended many a ball, but never danced."

"You can thank my aunt for that. My mother died when I was five years old, and no matter how accomplished my father was, Aunt Constance always feared that he was raising her sister's only son to be some sort of Scottish brute. It dinna help that my father moved us back to Scotland shortly thereafter. Determined to bring culture to her nephew, she arranged for private tutors for my education, elocution, and etiquette."

"So she's the one responsible for that singular accent of yours."

He raised a dark brow, amusement flickering in his gaze. "Singular accent? I've heard it called many a name, but that is a first."

"Why would anyone call it names? Your accent is"— *divine, intoxicating, toe-curling*—"lovely."

She'd pleased him. He dipped his head in acknowledgment of the compliment, tucking his chin in a way that was almost bashful. "Why, thank you, my lady. I think the problem is I doona quite fit any molds. Most Scots find my way of speaking annoyingly English, and most Englishmen find it dreadfully Scottish."

"Well, then, most Scots and Englishmen are idiots."

He laughed out loud at this, drawing the attention of several of the couples around them. He ignored them as he smiled down at her, his fingers giving her a little squeeze. "I'm inclined to agree, my lady."

"I hate it when you call me that."

She'd said the words almost to herself, but clearly he heard them. " 'My lady'?"

She nodded. She would never have said such a thing to anyone else, but he thought her fiery, did he not? She allowed the space between them to close just the slightest amount, her heart pounding all the while. "It's what servants and strangers call me, and even formal acquaintances. I don't think of you that way."

His eyes met hers, his gaze seeking. "Doona you, now?"

"How could I? You've unearthed me from the curtains, braved the elements to sit in my drawing room and defend my sister, and danced the Scottish reel with me among your father's most priceless works of art. If that doesn't do away with the 'my lady' nonsense, I don't know what would."

"Well, is that all?" he said, the corner of his mouth lifting in a lopsided grin.

"No," she admitted, focusing on his shoulder for a moment before looking up at him from beneath her lashes. "You shared your father with me. You, Colin, made my dreams come true."

Colin could hardly think straight with the way she watched him, as if he were some sort of knight in shining armor. He was allowing himself to be caught up in the liquid fire of her gaze, and he really needed to remember that this was just a simple dance with an off-limits woman. "I wouldn'a go as far as all that, surely. Perhaps you could say I made your day?"

She looked up at him with those huge blue eyes, which were a thousand times more brilliant than the sparkling aquamarine necklace hugging her slender throat. Damn, he really needed to watch himself. Two weeks among the *ton* and he was turning into a bloody poet.

"You made my *life*. No one on earth could have crafted a more intimate portrait of Sir Frederick, sharing all those little things that made him who he was, over and above his mastery of painting."

He couldn't deny the truth of that. As much heartache and trouble as his father had brought to Colin's life over the years, he had still loved the man. It felt good to share the harmless, interesting little bits about him with Lady Beatrice—someone who had genuine respect and admiration for the man.

Instead of denying her sentiment, he merely cocked a brow, allowing a bit of levity to show in his eyes.

"You, Lady Beatrice, need to reach for higher goals in life."

She rolled her eyes at him, unoffended. "So you say. I'm content with them, thank you very much. And I meant it when I said no more 'my ladying' me, if you please. Lady Beatrice in public because we have to, but when next we find ourselves alone, I expect you to drop the 'lady' altogether."

His mind skipped right past her request—demand?—and landed on the fact that she clearly intended to spend more time with him.

Alone.

Swallowing the surge of satisfaction that spread through his chest, he gave a brief nod. Yes, he knew very well that he should be distancing himself from the addictive woman in his arms. But that was the thing about vices—the fact that they should be avoided only made them that much more enticing.

As if his little *stór* needed any help in that department.

He tightened his grip on her, sliding his hand across her back as he led them across the dance floor. Neither one of them was an excellent dancer, but they were a good match for each other.

This was what he liked best about Beatrice. She made him feel like a normal gentleman, enjoying being with a normal lady. No thoughts of what she could do for him, only what he could do for her. The self-disgust of being a fortune hunter slipped away, like the hood of a dark cloak falling back. *She* had sought him out, had she not? In every instance, in fact. She had sought the introduction, invited him to call on her, and even asked him to waltz, in a roundabout way.

"Well?"

He glanced back down at her. "As you wish."

"That's more like it. Now, I'd like for you to do something for me. Please," she added belatedly.

He didn't even pause to think. "Anything."

The music came to a close then, and he reluctantly pulled away. Beatrice curtsied as he bowed, and he held out his arm to escort her off the dance floor.

"I'd like for you to meet me in Green Park on Monday. Around noon?"

There she went, seeking out his company again. It was the sort of thing that could easily go to a man's head. "I'll be there." He cut a sideways glance at her and lowered his voice to a conspiratorial whisper. "You do realize that at some point I should probably be the one to suggest a meeting?"

Beatrice raised a single golden brow, her eyes alight with mischief. "Yes, but what is the fun in that?"

"Do you truly think it was Mr. Godfrey?"

The whispered question brought Beatrice up short. She glanced around casually, as if looking for someone she knew, but really she was trying to overhear what the response would be.

Lady Chester and Mrs. Langford had their heads bent toward each other, their fans lifted strategically to shield their mouths. "It did rather look like him, but it doesn't make sense. His father is a viscount, after all. And a wealthy one at that," Mrs. Langford replied, her trilling voice carrying over the din.

"But didn't I hear somewhere that his father wishes for him to *work*?"

Beatrice almost rolled her eyes. Yes, working would be so much more scandalous than marrying a person he had no affection for in a bid to get his hands on her dowry.

"Shhh, he's coming."

The hushed admonishment had Beatrice's stomach

sinking. There were a good ten minutes before their dance was at hand. Perhaps he was just passing by. She tried her best to blend into the clump of matrons loitering in the area. *Please don't let him want to speak to me. Please don't let him want to—*

"Lady Beatrice, I'm so glad that I found you."

Drat. She turned, raising her brows. "Oh? Is it time for our dance already, Mr. Godfrey?"

He looked quite a bit worse for the wear since she had seen him earlier in the evening, with his pale skin looking waxen and his hair finger-combed to the side. "That's just it," he said, his spirit-laced breath assailing her. "I've had some unexpected business come up. I do hope you'll forgive me if I miss our dance."

Beatrice bit the inside of her lip. Her emotions couldn't seem to figure out whether to be joyful at the news or to swamp her with guilt. "Well, I can certainly understand if you have more pressing matters to attend to. Thank you for letting me know."

He offered a slightly off-kilter bow. "Of course, my lady. And I do hope you'll save a dance for me next time."

"Absolutely," she assured him, nodding for emphasis—too much emphasis. Apparently, the guilt won out. Although there was a *smidge* of happiness, as well. "Good evening to you, sir."

With a nod, he turned and bobbed his way through the crowd, his body adopting the sort of loose-limbed movements of one well and truly in his cups. So had he discovered his likeness in the drawing? It was hard to tell. She didn't detect any anger in him, just . . . distress. Worry. But what else could have caused the change in mood?

She supposed she was going to have to make a greater effort to be nice to the man now. If he was suffering any ill effects from the inadvertent likeness in the letter, then it was the least she could do. As she watched him disappear around the bend, another face in the crowd caught her attention—Diana. Beatrice hurried toward her, anxious to hear how she was doing. She needn't have rushed—her friend stayed where she was, planted beside a potted tree near the wall as she scanned the assembly. When Diana saw her, her face brightened and she lifted a hand in greeting. "I was hoping I'd see you here tonight."

"Were you?" Beatrice replied, innocence coloring her tone. Diana was the only person Beatrice could think of who might suspect the truth of the letter. "Well, I'm always delighted to see you. Shall we take a turn about the room?"

Her friend glanced around the crowded hall. "Perhaps somewhere more private?"

Nodding, Beatrice linked arms with her and started forward. "I stumbled upon the library earlier. Why don't we try there?"

It took only a few minutes to return to the room, and Beatrice was happy to see that a fire still burned in the grate. Lighting a few candles with it, she turned to Diana and smiled. "You look much improved from when last I saw you."

She smiled, not hugely, but it seemed completely genuine. "Well, a few things have transpired, giving me reason for a bit of happiness."

"Such as?"

"A certain letter in a magazine, for starters." She drew a finger across the spines of the books at her shoulder as she strolled the perimeter.

"It does seem to be the talk of the evening, does it not?" Beatrice would admit nothing to no one, but it didn't mean she wouldn't allow her friend to draw her own conclusions. After all, if it weren't for Diana, Beatrice would have never printed such a thing.

"Indeed." She looked a bit of the old Diana, with her eyes bright and her head held high. "It rather begs the question: What inspired the author to publish such a thing? And it occurred to me that perhaps her own misfortune prompted her to help others avoid her fate."

"It's possible."

"Or perhaps," she said, pausing to send an entirely too knowing look in Beatrice's direction, "it was the author's friend who suffered the misfortune, and that was what inspired the letter."

Beatrice leaned against a stout writing table placed beneath the shuttered window. "We may never know." She couldn't contain an impish grin. It made her exceedingly happy that Diana approved of her tactics. It was far too late for Beatrice to help her, but clearly she had brought her friend some amount of satisfaction.

"More's the pity. I do hope, however, that we haven't heard the last of the Daring Debutant."

Chapter Twelve

The bell above the shop door chimed as Beatrice let herself into the warmth of the art supply store, her smile already overtaking her attempt at a professional facade. Diana's reaction at the ball earlier that week had been so encouraging, she had been thinking over her statement for days. Would the publisher want more? Would the readers?

"Bonjour, Monsieur Allard."

He grunted in response, not bothering to look up from his etching. A long, coiled ribbon of steel curled off of the plate as his hands worked in a smooth, continuous arc. "Well, if it isn't the little troublemaker," he said without heat, his heavy accent making the words sound almost complimentary.

"Indeed, it is," she replied with a grin. "I'm here to see my coconspirator."

He chuckled at this, shaking his head even as his hands remained steady. "I conspire with no one, my lady." He finished the long peel, brushed it aside, and swiveled in his chair to face her. "What is it that you want now? I wonder. Pigments? Brushes? A selection of canvases, perhaps?"

"As you well know, I am stocked for at least the rest of the month. I'm here because I am dying to know if you have heard anything from your publisher. Are they pleased?"

He took off his spectacles and rubbed them with a soft white cloth from his worktable. "They are, I think. At least I imagine so, since they have asked for another submission for their next publication."

"They did?" Beatrice resisted the urge to do a highly undignified little dance. If that wasn't success, then she didn't know what was.

"They did." He reseated his spectacles on his great nose and stood, stretching his back. "Apparently, they have already received many requests for another installment, as well as an increase in subscriptions."

Excellent. There was no surer way to affirm that her words had resonated, and, hopefully, that they would be helpful. She still felt rather rotten about Mr. Godfrey, but with any luck, whispers would quickly subside, and the gist of the article would be what would linger. "I can't believe it. I wish you had sent word! I wanted to do another engraving, but I thought I would speak with you first." Already, she was thinking of the advice she could give in the next letter.

"I'm not so sure it would be wise, mademoiselle."

Her excitement fell like a dropped ball. "Not wise? Why ever not? It is helping people."

"You've said your piece, have you not? I fear that if you push your luck, it may then push back. *Comprenez-vous?*"

"Don't be silly, monsieur. We are not talking about national security here. Offering up more advice can only be a good thing."

"Then why not do so under your own name?"

She opened her mouth to argue, then snapped it shut. Very well. So he had a small point there. "You know full well a female of my standing must take care with her reputation. Writing anonymously serves my purpose while protecting my good name. But remember, monsieur—rules must sometimes be broken for the greater good."

He grunted, turning his back on her and returning to his chair.

"Please say that you will help me again. Your work was spectacular—without it, the letter wouldn't have had nearly the impact it did."

"Pretty words from a pretty girl are all well and good, but they will not work on old Georges."

She wrinkled her nose at him. Why was he suddenly being so stubborn? "Please, Monsieur Allard? There is more good to be done. You would not send a soldier into battle unarmed, would you?"

He flicked a glance her way before picking up his tools. "Of course not. I don't see what—"

"Sending young, unprepared girls into the marriage mart is not so different. The consequences last a lifetime, do they not? And though the scars may not be as visible, they can certainly cut just as deep."

"So much passion for people you may not even know."

Diana's tear-streaked face flitted through her mind, strengthening her resolve. Betrayal by a person one thought to love could be the cruelest fate of all. "I believe we call that compassion for our fellow man. Or woman, as the case may be. It's part of the human condition, I'm afraid."

The old man sighed, rubbing a hand over his bushy white eyebrows. "I am convinced that if you had been born a man, you could have quite the career as a man of law. Argue, argue, argue."

"And win?" she asked with a pleading smile.

His gaze rose briefly to the etching on the wall above him, where the pretty young woman smiled encouragingly at him. "*Oui*, and win."

Her smile grew to a full-fledged grin. "You, monsieur, are a gem. When is the submission due?"

"Two weeks. Just be sure to give me two days this time for the engraving, *d'accord*?"

She nodded, wishing he was close enough to kiss his cheeks. "*Oui, d'accord.*"

Slogging through the wet grass of Green Park, the smell of damp earth and soggy wool filling his nostrils, Colin rubbed the light, misty rain from his eyes and scanned the landscape for Beatrice. The chances of her actually being here were slim, but they hadn't specified rain or shine. He didn't want to look too closely at his motivations, but he knew that if there was a chance for seeing her, he'd gladly take it.

He'd already done his prerequisite visits to proper wife candidates today—all of which served not only to depress him, but to make him wonder if the problem was with him and not the dozens of young women who either seemed too boring, too garish, too talkative, or too impossible to imagine living with for the rest of his life. The thought of spending time with Beatrice seemed like breaking out of prison. She was like a pop of crimson red in a box of pastels.

He turned right and headed down Constitution Hill. The wind blew, and he turned his face away from it, tilting his hat to shield him better. Turned as he was, he caught sight of two young women huddled beneath one of the larger trees. He smiled, thoughts of the miserable day falling away as Beatrice looked up and waved, a wide grin on her face.

How on earth did she manage to look so remarkably charming when he felt like a half-drowned rat? He picked up his pace, eager to speak with her again. "Good afternoon, Lady Beatrice," he said when he finally reached them, nodding in greeting to her and her

maid. The mousy servant ducked her head and stepped
back a few paces, wordlessly offering Colin and Beatrice some privacy.

"Isn't it lovely?" Beatrice teased, looking every bit as
delighted to see him as he was to see her. His head
buzzed a bit with the knowledge, warming his blood
and making it impossible not to grin at her.

"I can't imagine why so few are out to enjoy the fine
weather. We practically have the park to ourselves."
Which suited him perfectly. Even after several weeks
among the *ton*, he still had trouble adjusting to the con-
cept of prying eyes constantly being turned in his direction. In *everyone's* direction, really—the whole
bloody beau monde seemed to make a career out of
seeing and being seen.

He craved the privacy and anonymity he had enjoyed at the Inn.

Although, if he were still at Lincoln's Inn, he would
have never met Beatrice, something that seemed remarkably distasteful. It was like imagining never having seen a proper sunset, or the heather fields near his
estate, or the crashing waves of the ocean. She was almost a force of nature to him, and he couldn't bring
himself to wish things had happened differently.

"Perhaps we should have been so clever as those
who stayed indoors. I had such grand hopes of painting in the park with you, but clearly the weather had
other ideas." She looked utterly adorable with the rain
misting on her upturned face, clinging to her eyelashes
and causing the fine hairs around her temples to curl
into delicate corkscrews.

Two completely inane thoughts came to him as he
smiled at her like some sort of besotted fool. First, he'd
had no idea her eyelashes were quite so long. And second, it was utterly absurd that he should even notice a

woman's eyelashes—he wasn't entirely certain if he had ever noticed his own lashes, for heaven's sake.

Even with that thought bouncing around in the suddenly empty chamber of his head, he couldn't stop himself from bantering with her a bit. "What, you mean you let a little thing like rain get in the way of painting? Not very dedicated to the arts, I see."

She scrunched her nose at him, making a face that he couldn't help but laugh at. "Oddly enough, oil paints and rain are not the best of companions. Although, we could always start a new movement. 'Smears on Canvas' could change the art world forever."

He couldn't imagine any other lady of the *ton* having braved the elements to come to the park at all, let alone to meet a nobody like him. He didn't want to cut the day short, but he could hardly keep her out in this mess. "Hmm, perhaps not. We aren't far from my father's studio. Perhaps we could move there for a dry place for you to work."

She gaped at him. "Your father had a studio nearby, and you are just now telling me this?"

"No great secret, really. He had intended to take on a few apprentices to help increase his production, but found that he didn't like handing over any part of his art to others. He didn't mind sharing his techniques, but once he started a portrait, it was his until the very last stroke." No matter how much time it took. When Father was in the midst of one of his paintings, the rest of the world faded to gray, with the only color found in the bristles of his brush and the vision in his mind.

"Well, then," she said, putting her hands to her hips and raising an imperious eyebrow, "*if* you can get us there within the next quarter hour, I *might* consider forgiving you for this tragic oversight."

Her tone was grave as she looked down her nose at

him—an impressive feat, considering her diminutive height—but her eyes sparkled merrily with a light all their own. They reminded him of the deep-water lake not far from his estate, on those rare, brilliantly sunny days that made the water look as though fire kissed its rippling surface.

And there he went again. Yanking his mind away from its poetic turn, he gave her a smart salute that would have made his cousin John proud. "Yes, my lady. At once, my lady."

She rolled her eyes at his cheek. "Very good—though enough with the 'my lady' business. And you gave in entirely too easily, by the way. I was completely prepared to beg, if necessary."

"It's not too late. Since I've already thrown myself upon your mercy, I'd be more than happy to turn the tables."

"No, no, I think I shall save it for another occasion. One never knows when one will have need of that sort of thing. Now, then," she said, tucking her hand into the crook of his elbow, "let us be off. I'm assuming it's walking distance?"

He nodded, enjoying the weight of her hand on his arm. It was a shame his greatcoat shielded him from her heat. "If you don't mind another five or ten minutes in the rain."

"Oh, pish—I'm much hardier than I appear, I assure you. I am a country girl, first and foremost."

They started forward, their gaits in easy synchronization, as if they'd been walking together like this for years. He gave her a sideways glance, sizing up her petite form. "I'll admit—you look as though a strong wind could carry you away. I have a hard time picturing you traipsing through the countryside in all types of inclement weather."

"My eldest sister, Evie, is much more of the traipsing

type, although more often than not she's on horseback. But I do get out quite a bit. The rolling hills of our estate call to me like a siren. I've painted dozens upon dozens of landscapes, all perfectly bucolic and safe. One of these days I'll have the opportunity to visit a truly rugged landscape and really stretch my repertoire."

"You mean you doona find Green Park a challenge?" He guided them around a puddle and onto the main path leading to the street.

She shrugged. "One must make do with what one has to work with. I suppose I should be happy that London has this and Hyde Park. I'd be lost without some small bit of nature around me."

"I don't know about that. Have you ever attempted to paint the buildings of London? You may find architecture just as inspiring as nature."

"From time to time I try the view from my studio in Granville House, but straight lines and orderly shingles hold little interest for me."

Now, there was where they differed. After a lifetime lacking structure, he found comfort in all things logical. "Really? I adore straight and orderly. I like for things to be neat and methodical."

"Good heavens, then you may wish to part ways with me now. Nothing about me is orderly." Her fingers gripped his arm just the slightest bit tighter as she spoke.

"Fair warning, then? I should probably take heed. After all, five minutes into our first meeting, you already had me breaking rules. Such a terrible influence."

"I know, I know. Mama has tried her best with me, but I shall never follow anyone's path but my own."

"Thank God," he murmured.

She paused, and he turned to see what was the matter. Instead of the scowl he half expected, she was looking at him with honest confusion. "Are you saying you think that's a *good* thing? What happened to Mr. Straight and Narrow?"

"I doona know if it is a good thing or not. I only know that you are perfect exactly as you are."

He hadn't realized how that would sound until the words were out of his mouth, and it was too late to call them back. He snapped his gaze to meet hers, cautiously analyzing her reaction. Her jaw dropped in complete disbelief, and she leveled those enormous blue eyes on him, pinning him where he stood. "Do you mean that?"

He bit the inside of his lip, debating whether to deny it. Instead, he told her the truth. "Yes. I never lie, Beatrice."

The slightest hint of pleasure stole over her expression, and she started forward once more. "A barrister who only tells the truth? Surely that's against the rules."

"Ah, well—there is an art to telling the truth. If I doona tell you everything, I have still been honest in what I have said. The trick is to always ask the right questions." Why was he telling her that? Yes, he was teasing, but it was exactly the truth of his situation with the estate. If anyone *asked*, he had vowed he wouldn't lie. But so far, no one had come out and addressed his finances, and he sure as hell had no intention to bring it up.

She pursed her lips, her brow knitted in a soft vee. "I'm not sure that's any better than lying."

"So you've come right out and told people your deepest and darkest secrets without being asked, then?"

"Gads, of course not. Not," she added, cutting a playful gaze to him, "that I have many secrets. Mostly I have *other* people's secrets."

His brow furrowed as he turned right down his father's old street. "Other people's secrets? What, are you some sort of spy or something?" He grinned at the thought, picturing her stealing through the night in all black, peeking in windows and listening at keyholes. "Come to think of it, I wouldn'a be too surprised if you were. I did catch you red-handed behind my aunt's curtains, after all."

She admonished him with a swat of his arm. "Not something you are supposed to mention, thank you very much. And I wasn't spying; I was *hiding*. From you, I might add."

"Let us hope," he said as he stopped in front of the unmarked wood door and withdrew his key ring, "that you'll never have need for that again."

"Hardly. If anything you'll have to shoo me away."

Chapter Thirteen

Yes, those words had actually left her mouth.

Yes, her parents would personally drag her home and lock her within her bedchamber if they knew, tossing the key in the rubbish bin. And, yes, they were shockingly forward, even for her.

But she didn't regret them.

They were true, after all. And hadn't he just said that he always told the truth? Well, so could she.

And the truth was, she felt alive when she was with him—exuberant in a way no other man of the *ton* had made her feel. Not self-conscious, not hunted for her dowry, not seen as the daughter of a peer—just Beatrice, lover of art and slightly awful dancer.

She pressed her lips together in a shy smile before brushing past him and up the stairs leading to the rooms above. Her half boots clicked hollowly against the aged wood steps, and the air smelled of disuse. She paused at the small landing and waited for the others to catch up. Rose was right behind her, her dark eyes wide with worry. "I don't know as we should be here, my lady."

"Nonsense, Rose. Would you rather be in the rain?"

"No, my lady, but—"

"And it's not as though visiting an artist's studio is

inappropriate. I've visited Monsieur Allard perhaps a dozen times."

Her maid bit her lip uneasily, but nodded. "I suppose so. Still—"

"There's nothing to worry about. I promise."

"Is everything all right?" Colin asked as he mounted the last step.

Beatrice smiled, determined not to let anything get in the way of this once-in-a-lifetime opportunity. "Right as rain." She ignored Rose's frown—she'd be happy once she had a quiet place to sit and her book in her hands. The maid's love of reading made for easy bribing, and Beatrice had presented her with a brand-new copy of *Rob Roy* this morning.

He hesitated for a moment, then nodded and reached for the tarnished brass knob before them. The door swung open on rusty hinges, and as the room was revealed to her, Beatrice gasped, her hand going to her heart.

"Oh, my, it's gorgeous." She turned to face him, shaking her head in wonder. "I can't believe this was only minutes from my home all this time!"

He smiled and spread his arm out, inviting her to go inside. She stepped through the threshold, hardly able to take it all in. The faint smell of mineral spirits clung to the space like a memory, despite the dankness.

Behind her, Colin directed Rose to a small parlor off the main room, where a single sofa was stationed in front of the back windows, facing out on the alley behind them.

Beatrice hardly paid them more than a passing glance. Her gaze—her whole heart, really—was riveted on the wide-open studio that encompassed the entire front half of the floor. The centerpiece of the room was a huge, arching Venetian window that took up nearly half the front wall. It had seemed unimpressive from the street, but from where Beatrice stood, it was spectacular. The bottom of the window rested mere inches from the broad-planked floor, and it spanned in a great arc from one side of the room to the other, almost touching the ceiling at its center.

With the miserable day outside, the space was still nicely lit, but she could just imagine the place flooded with light on a sunny day. Several easels stood empty around the room, their spindly legs coated in a rainbow of paint drippings. Various brushes, scrapers, palettes, and rags were stored on racks and tables throughout the space. Mixing cups sat by a paint-splattered sink, and a utilitarian pitcher showed the frequent touches of a paint-covered hand.

Something magical shimmied through her, raising gooseflesh on her arms. These were the tools of Sir Frederick's masterpieces. Which works had rested in this very room, painted by these brushes, supported by these easels, and lit by these windows? She walked through the space, reverently, imagining half-finished canvases lining the plaster walls.

She turned to Colin, who leaned against the doorway watching her, his dark greatcoat still pulled tight around him to ward off the chill of the unheated room. "What happened to the unfinished portraits?"

He gave a one-shouldered shrug, then pushed away from the wall to join her in the center of the mostly empty space. "We dinna find any."

She blinked. "None?"

Shaking his head, he said, "Not a one. My sister was certain he was working on something in his studio in Scotland, but there was nothing there, either."

"How odd," she murmured, glancing around once more. She had half a dozen unfinished paintings in her own studio at any one time. She rarely concentrated solely on one until it was finished, instead preferring to work on the piece that most moved her. And then there were the ones that just didn't feel right, which she set aside indefinitely.

Sadness crept into her euphoria. The world would never again have a Tate masterpiece. She had just assumed there would be some unseen pieces somewhere, languishing in various stages of completion.

"My father was odd." The words weren't spoken with animosity, but quiet truth.

"Was he? Not terribly surprising, I suppose. Genius often is." If she had to choose between being average and normal or being brilliant and odd, she'd go with brilliant any day of the week. "I wish I could have seen him at work. Actually," she said, trailing a finger down the side of one of the easels, "Father had written to him to engage his services more than a year ago, but Sir Frederick declared that he was much too busy and that it might be years before he would be available to us."

"Really?" His eyebrows rose in surprise. He pressed his lips together, not quite in displeasure, but something close. She looked away, realizing that such a mention might be painful for him. Who could have known his father's life was measured in months at the time, not years? "Well, I wish I could see *you* work."

Her gaze snapped back to his. His voice was low and sweet, his eyes unclouded. Thank goodness—she hadn't ruined the mood after all. "You're teasing me," she half asked, half accused.

"Never." He broke out in a half smile and gave a small shrug. "All right, sometimes, but certainly not now. Anyone who displays such passion when speaking of art must be equally as passionate in the execution."

"Oh, I am. But I assure you, it's not pretty. I don't remember to smile, or have proper posture, or even to have my mouth closed." She cringed a bit—that did not come out the way she'd intended. He was probably picturing her as some sort of trained sloth with a paintbrush.

"And how do you know that's not pretty? I think many men would appreciate a woman at her most natural. Certainly any Scot would," he said with a devilish wink.

"You say that, but when it comes down to it, I'm not so sure. Why else would only the prettiest of countenance *and* manners be called Incomparables and diamonds of the first water? Those with large dowries are also sought, but it is the ones possessing beauty and comportment that gentlemen really want."

"Such an expert on the wants of men, especially for one still in her debut year." He walked toward her, tilting his head as he sized her up. He'd taken off his hat, and his damp hair rebelled against his normally neat style. It swept across his forehead like a raven's wing, stark against his pale skin. She loved the contrast, loved the way it made his eyes seem almost pewter while the pale pink of his lips stood out.

She swallowed as he stepped closer and closer, stalking her just as he had the night they'd met in his aunt's gallery. "I'm very perceptive. And one needn't be out long to see how things are in our set."

"Well, I think we need to put your perceptiveness to the test," he said, giving her a subtle wink as he brushed by her close enough for her to catch a hint of his clean, masculine scent. She turned like a sunflower tracking the sun, suddenly a little light-headed.

"You do?"

He grabbed one of the blank canvases stacked against the wall and lifted it to his chest. "I do." He returned to where she stood and set the canvas on the easel closest to the window. "Now, would you be wanting to paint with my father's brushes or your own?"

Sir Frederick's brushes? A thrill raced from her heart straight to her toes and back. "Oh my goodness. I couldn't possibly." But even as she said it, her fingers curled at her sides, anxious to hold them in her hand.

"Of course you can. What good are they doing, cluttering up the place? Might as well give them a go before the lease runs out and we sell the lot of them."

She gasped. "You can't just *sell* his brushes! They were likely as much a part of him as his own hands."

"Then give them life again." He said it so simply, as if it were no more an issue than choosing what gloves to wear or what to have for breakfast.

It was entirely too much temptation for her to resist, especially when he was so matter-of-fact about them. "Are you absolutely certain?"

"Utterly."

A shiver of excitement raced down her spine, and she couldn't help the huge smile that came to her lips. "All right then. What shall I paint?"

"Whatever you want. Since you doona like straight lines, I'm not sure what might inspire you. Shall I put together a still life?"

A bit of the giddiness spilled over, obscuring her need for propriety. "Yes," she said, crossing her arms as she eyed him. "You. Now stand still."

He laughed. "You canna be serious. Why don't you choose something interesting?"

She pursed her lips as she inspected him—in the name of art, of course. His angular cheekbones, the authoritative brow, those expressive lips—all of it begged to be captured on canvas. Actually, it begged to be captured in sculpture, but that was entirely beyond her skills.

"I am serious. Your features are strong and unusual. I think they would be a challenge to get just right on canvas." The night of their first meeting came to mind, making her smile. "Though I don't believe I'd be the first to try. That was you in the painting in your aunt's gallery, wasn't it? The young boy with the defiant eyes?"

His expression shifted, as if the mists of nostalgia softened his gaze and gentled the sharpness of his features. "You really are perceptive. I was five. It was shortly after my mother's death, and my father thought it would be a nice gesture for Aunt Constance."

"Well, I'm very glad he did it. Now I feel as though I've seen a bit of you as a boy. He captured your spirit quite well, I think."

He nodded absently, his gaze flitting around to the supplies situated near the easel. Pulling off his gloves, he stuffed them into the pockets of his greatcoat. Her gaze went immediately to his bare hands, which seemed strong and capable, especially for a barrister. Must be the wild Scot in his blood.

"Well, then," he said, selecting a brush from a tin cup beside the easel, "let us see if you can do the same."

He held it up like a delectable bonbon, the same challenge she'd seen in the boy's eyes now lighting the man's. Throwing down the gauntlet, was he? She pressed her lips together, eyeing the brush as if it were the apple in Eden. Taking a breath, she removed her own gloves and reached for the prize.

The moment her fingers touched the smooth wood of the handle, his hand settled over hers, holding it in place. Fire swept up her arm, down her back, and straight through her belly at the touch of his skin against hers.

Her gaze flew up to meet his, but she couldn't have said a word if her life depended on it. His eyes darkened, from flint to coal, just enough for her to know without a doubt that he had felt it, too. He swallowed, but he didn't release his hold.

"First," he said, his voice quiet in the thickness of the moment, "you must solemnly promise that you will ignore my father's techniques and paint me using only your own style."

His hand still held hers, making it impossible to think. His fingers were warmer than they should have been, his skin softer, his grip firmer. Wetting her lips, she nodded, two shallow bobs of her head agreeing to whatever he wanted in the world just then.

He released her, surrendering his hold on the brush, her hand, and her wits all at once. She drew a steadying breath, trying to calm her thundering pulse. Had anyone's touch ever affected her like that? Surely not. Though really, how many men had she touched skin to skin like that? None, unless one counted her family members. Richard and Great-uncle Percival hardly counted when compared to the likes of Colin.

"Well, then," she said, rallying her wits, "I should start with a drawing first, then move to paints when the pose is just right." Unwilling to part with her prize, she tucked the slender brush behind her ear, just as she sometimes did with pencils when she was distracted.

"All right, then. How would you like me to pose?"

Lord have mercy, what a question. Beatrice bit the inside of her lip, trying to push past the completely inappropriate image of him leaning against the curving window casing, his hair tousled, thanks to the rain, and his shirt tossed over the chair beside him.

Papa would probably send her to a convent if he knew the sort of thoughts racing through Beatrice's head just then. But she was an artist, was she not? She had observed and studied many a male form, in much, if not all, of its glory. She knew what positions put a person at his best advantage, and with Colin's surprisingly fit form, she just knew the play of light over both his angular face and well-proportioned upper body would be divine.

She also knew she could never bring herself to actually do such a thing.

She might be brave, but she wasn't reckless. Well, sometimes she was, but she certainly had never asked a man to take off his shirt, and she wasn't about to start now—especially with her maid in the next room and no closed doors between them. That didn't stop the torrent of butterflies from whirling within her belly at the very thought.

Still, the pose was a good idea, even if the bare chest wasn't. "I think perhaps you should be leaning against the window, looking out at the rooftops beyond."

He lifted a dark brow, amusement clearing the lingering darkness from his eyes. "Are we going for 'gazing longingly in the distance,' then? Because I have a fantastic pining expression."

Stepping to the window, he draped himself across it like a lovesick maiden and gazed out, his eyebrows lifted and knitted as though hope itself resided in the rooftops beyond the glass.

She smacked his shoulder lightly. "Oh stop. You shouldn't tease me."

He dropped his ridiculous expression and chuckled. "Yes, I know. I never tease anyone, actually. I doona know why I canna seem to stop myself when you're near."

What a thing to say. It didn't sound like a compliment, but it certainly felt like one. "Perhaps that means I put you at ease."

"Perhaps. Or perhaps I've let myself become too familiar around you. It's a social sin that I should feel much more concerned about than I am." His expression bordered on boyish, especially with his tousled hair. Lord but she loved the rumpled version of the man. He was always so proper, she felt as though she were seeing him in a way few ever did.

"Hold that."

His brows dipped together as he blinked in confusion. "Hold what?"

"That," she said, waving her hands around to encompass his position. "Your pose, your expression, whatever you were thinking about just then."

He went stiff, doing exactly as she said. She rolled her eyes. "No, don't go rigid. Just relax. Breathe. Be still, not frozen."

He loosened up a bit, and she smiled. "Yes, that's better. Give me a moment. I'll be right back."

She scurried around the room, rooting out a wide notebook with blank pages and a pencil. She dragged a tall stool over to a spot just in front of him and sat down. "All right. Now, turn your head a bit to the right and look out as if there is something interesting right outside the window."

"That's requiring quite a bit of imagination from a barrister in training."

She widened her eyes meaningfully at him, and he sighed and obeyed. "Excellent. Now tip your head down a bit . . . a little more. That's good. Now relax your left arm and lean a bit onto the casing. There— perfect." The daylight illuminated half his face, sending the other half into soft shadow. It made the scale of grays and whites that much more dramatic, highlighting all the angles and planes that she loved so well.

She set to work on the drawing, sketching in his general outline, the shape of the window, and the lines of his limbs. It was quick work, and she glanced up repeatedly as she went about it. After only a few minutes, she looked up to find him watching her. "Colin," she admonished, pointing her pencil at him, "look outside."

"Sorry," he murmured, not appearing the least bit chastised. He averted his gaze to the window again, and she went back to work.

Less than a minute later, she glanced up and found herself caught in his gaze once more. "Ahem," she prompted.

"Such a taskmaster," he teased, shaking his head, "especially when the view inside is vastly preferable to anything outside."

She bit her upper lip, fighting against the pleased smile that threatened to encourage him. "Now you sound like my brother. Richard is forever saying things like that."

That won her exactly what she had intended. With a mild scowl—who wants to be compared to a woman's brother, after all—he turned to look back outside.

"Now the angle is all wrong. Chin down, please. No, more to the right. No, that's not quite right either. Just a moment," she said, standing up and setting her notebook on the stool.

Stepping up to him, she reached out to adjust his angle, but realized all at once that her hands were gloveless and he was no family member to be casually arranged to her liking. She froze, her hand only inches away from his chin. "I'm sorry. I shouldn't—"

She started to drop her hand, but he smiled and caught her by the elbow. "No, it's fine. My father did this a thousand times. Consider me your still life, to be adjusted at will."

She drew a slow breath, trying not to betray her wildly pounding heart. This was art, after all. Arranging one's subject was to be expected. When she nodded, he released his gentle hold and lifted his head, inviting her to do with him what she would.

Wetting her suddenly dry lips, she slipped her hand beneath his chin, touching the surprisingly smooth skin stretched across his angular jaw. He watched her, his eyes tracking hers even as she tilted his chin in just the right angle. He responded to the lightest of touches, moving easily with her direction.

"There," she breathed, not quite able to find her voice. "I think that's good."

"Are you certain?"

Beatrice nodded, the movement slightly jerky under the weight of his gaze. She should step back, she knew she should, but something in his smoky eyes held her rooted in place, her skirts brushing his legs. With the way he leaned against the casing, the difference in their heights wasn't as great as it might have been, making him seem all the more accessible.

"You wouldn'a rather have my chin tilted down a bit more?" He lowered his head, pressing his jaw more firmly into her hand and closing the distance between him and her upturned face.

Her pulse thundered in her ears, drowning out reason and thought, narrowing her world to the warmth of his skin against her fingers and the incredibly intoxicating scent of his breath as it caressed her cheek. When she didn't move, he reached up and slid his fingers over hers, flattening her palm against the curve of his jaw.

His eyes never left hers, and she watched as they darkened and his pupils widened, drawing her toward him without even moving a muscle. She swayed forward, drawn by his heat, and his scent, and the intensity of his gaze. Even as he bent toward her, she lifted her face to him, seeking, eager, driven by a need she never knew she possessed.

And then his lips touched hers.

Chapter Fourteen

The scent of lilac and fresh rain washed over him as Colin gave in to the overwhelming need to kiss her, letting his lips press against hers with a gentleness that belied the driving desire that raced through his body. She smelled of home, and innocence, and happiness, all wrapped up in the sweetest of packages.

He held his body rigidly still, forcing himself not to swallow her up in his arms, letting her have the control. After a long, perfect moment, she pulled away, peering up at him through her golden lashes with wide-eyed wonder.

She didn't say a word, just looked at him with those huge blue eyes as her chest rose and fell with each rapid breath. His own breathing refused to be calmed— he could hardly believe he had just kissed her!

Her tongue darted out and swept across her beautiful lips, bringing his attention to them once more. He could feel the warmth of her body only inches from him, a siren call that begged him to pull her to him and kiss her properly, to tangle his tongue with hers and wrap his arms around her.

God, he needed space, or he would do just that. She was an innocent, and she sure as hell didn't need the likes of him corrupting her.

He started to straighten, moving slowly so not to upset her.

"Wait," she said, her voice little more than a whisper.

He immediately froze, arrested by the look in her eyes as much as the tone of her voice.

"It's just . . ." She trailed off, looking unsure of what to say. Swallowing, she drew a deep breath, rose up on her toes, and pressed her mouth full across his.

He was so surprised, he didn't react at first. But when her hands stole up around his neck, pulling him even closer to her, he gave in to the kiss. It was exactly what he wanted, what his body craved, and he couldn't stop his own arms from encircling her slender waist. She was somehow bold and tentative all at once—a little bit wicked and a lot tempting.

Her lips parted, and he slipped his tongue into her mouth. She responded at once, sliding hers over his in a dance that made his heart hammer. He heard nothing but her soft moan, felt nothing but her body against his, tasted nothing but her sweet mouth. She inhabited his every sense, and he loved it.

When at last the kiss ended, he was near light-headed with the pounding of his poor heart and his desire for her. Her cheeks were flushed and her lips slightly swollen as she stepped back. "Now *that* was a proper first kiss."

He broke into a broad grin, shaking his head at her. No one could ever master her perfect mix of frank adorableness. "I'd say that was a good deal more than proper. I feel as though I should apologize for taking advantage of you, but I'm fairly certain you have the advantage here."

"Exactly the way I like it." Her eyes shone with impish delight, and he resisted the urge to tuck her beneath his chin, hugging her to him. "Now, then, about that pose."

The world was still as it was before the kiss—he was sure of it—but for him, everything somehow felt different. Beatrice didn't just respect him, didn't simply admire his father and enjoy the company of the man's son. No, clearly she saw him, Colin, and liked him as much as he did her. No one kissed like that without the hot simmer of attraction burning deep inside them. That thought brought a rather pleased smile to his lips.

He leaned back against the window and spread his arms. "Care to adjust my position?"

Her laughter was sweet and merry. "Indeed I would, but I think perhaps I should refrain. And truly, it's getting quite late. I should probably be getting home."

"Of course." As she gathered up the notebook and pencil, he went to the easel and plucked a handful of brushes out of one of the cups. "Here. Take these with you. Perhaps they will give you some inspiration as you work this week."

Her gaze settled on his offering before rising up to meet his. "You are too kind to me." She accepted the offering, tucking the handful of brushes against her chest, along with the folded piece of paper that contained her sketch. "Although I hardly think I shall be in want of inspiration this week."

With a wink, she turned, collected her maid, and made good her retreat. He stood in the window, watching as they emerged onto the street below and headed toward St. James's Square. Just before she disappeared around the corner, she turned around, touched her fingertips to her lips, and offered up a small wave.

And with that, he was lost.

"What has you smiling so brightly this afternoon? You look like the cat that got the cream."

Jane eyed Beatrice over her teacup as she took a dainty sip. Her eyes were more green than brown just then, which meant Beatrice had clearly piqued her interest.

"Sir Colin gave her a bunch of his father's paintbrushes," Jocelyn said around a bite of ginger biscuit, rolling her eyes in the process. "One wonders if he has ever heard of flowers before."

Beatrice glared at her sister, despite the fact she provided the perfect excuse for Beatrice's overbright smile and warm, sure-to-be-rosy cheeks. "Anyone can give a lady flowers. It takes a very special man to come up with something much more personal."

Jane bit back a grin, her porcelain skin blushing a pretty shade of pink. "Indeed." When she realized all three of her sisters-in-law were looking at her with interest, she cleared her throat. "Well, Beatrice is right. Flowers and poems are all well and good, but it's the more unique gifts that stand out during courtship."

"Courtship?"

Beatrice turned, internally groaning at her brother's dreadful timing. Looking sharp in his deep blue jacket and gray breeches, he strode into the room and sat beside his wife. "Who is courting whom and why have I not yet heard?"

"Perhaps," Jane said, sliding her hand through the crook of his arm, "because you've had other things on your mind lately."

His gaze softened as he glanced to Jane's still-flat belly. "Excellent point." He leaned over and kissed her square on the lips, ignoring the twins' groan. Beatrice couldn't help but smile, however. Their happiness was a long time coming, and it did her heart good to see them so in love.

Richard returned his attention to the room at large. "Right then. Well, I'm here and present now. All I need is the name and direction of the scoundrel who thinks to court my sister, and I'll be off."

"You'll do no such thing," Bea said, rolling her eyes at his threats. "And honestly, I'm not even being properly courted yet. We're merely . . . enjoying shared interests." For some reason, the words brought to mind their incredible kiss, and without her consent, her cheeks heated with a blush.

Her brother's brows rose, and he exchanged a quick glance with Jane. "That's it—tell me his name now so I can get the headstone carved in time for the burial."

"Oh, for heaven's sake—stop teasing. Sir Colin has been a perfect gentleman. It's I who gets flustered every time I think of who his father was."

"So you're thinking of his father now?" Carolyn asked, setting down her teacup. Jocelyn chuckled, earning them both a glare from Beatrice. Carolyn patted Beatrice's knee, smiling sweetly. "I'm only teasing. And it sounds as though the brushes truly were a lovely gesture."

"Brushes?" Richard asked.

"He gave her a bouquet of his father's paintbrushes," Jane supplied, ever so helpfully.

"Sir Colin Tate, then. One 'L,' two 'T's'?" He pantomimed spelling the name out on an invisible pad of paper.

Beatrice raised a haughty brow. "You forget, I think, that I know all about the certain bouquet—or should I say basket?—you sent to Jane. Or didn't you know? Cook does so like to chat when she's cooking."

"Right then," he said, winking to her as he reached for a chocolate biscuit and took a bite. "Though I'm not entirely certain you are helping your cause by pointing that particular similarity out. Am I to assume Sir Colin's intentions toward you are the same as mine were toward Jane?"

"Good heavens, I should hope not. I think you'll

find Sir Colin to be quite the gentleman." Except when she pushed the issue, in which case he could be deliciously ungentlemanly.

"And are the brushes a declaration of intent?"

"No, nothing like that. He knows how much I admire his father and decided to pass them on to a fellow artist."

"Mmhmm." Richard took another bite of his biscuit. "Darling, these are excellent, as usual," he said, smiling to Jane. He then turned his attention back to Beatrice, tilting his head just so, with a decidedly wicked gleam in his eye. "Perhaps I'll take a batch when I go to visit Sir Gift Giver."

Beatrice collapsed back against the sofa, scowling at her brother. She did *not* want him sticking his nose into things. One, she didn't want to cause Colin undue worry, and two, she didn't want to scare him away.

Especially when she was having a hard time thinking of anything other than his perfect kiss. A wisp of pleasure danced through her at the memory. She wanted *more* of that, not less. "Richard, if you embarrass me, so help me, I will make you regret it. Sir Colin is a *nice* man and deserves respect."

Richard's smile was overly sweet as he blinked his light blue eyes innocently. "Me, embarrass you? I wouldn't dare."

Drat her brother and his stupid newfound sense of responsibility. At least her brother-in-law was back in Aylesbury with Evie. She could just imagine Benedict and Richard showing up on Colin's doorstep together. "Fine. Do what you must. Just know that of the two of you, you're the one who has to sleep in the same house as me."

"Put away the stinger, Bea—I promise to be nice . . . enough."

* * *

Colin stared down at the heavy, cream-colored calling card, trying to remember where he'd heard the name before. "The Earl of Raleigh," he muttered, turning it over in his head. Damned if he could place it. "Thank you, Simmons. Please see him in."

Aunt Constance's butler bowed his head and retreated, his impassive expression not helpful in the least. Colin closed the law book he had been reading and came to his feet. He was absolutely certain he had heard the name before, but for some reason he couldn't recall where. And he certainly couldn't figure what an earl would want with him.

Footsteps echoed down the corridor and the butler reappeared. "The Earl of Raleigh."

One look at the man and Colin knew exactly who he was. "Lady Beatrice's brother, I presume?"

Raleigh tilted his head, raising a single brow in exactly the way his sister did. "Does my reputation precede me, then?"

"No, but your looks certainly do." Colin gestured to the chairs situated closest to the fire. "Can I offer you a seat?"

At Raleigh's nod, they made their way to the little seating area. Colin paused by the sideboard. "Care for something to drink?"

"A good scotch, if you have it."

"Ah, a man after my own heart. Or tastes, at least." He poured two glasses before handing one to his guest and taking his seat. The afternoon sun slanted through the room's three windows, lightening the tone of the normally austere library. Beatrice's blond brother seemed to fit right in, with an easy smile, slightly mussed hair, and an insouciant air about him that Colin was certain put most people at ease.

Not him.

Especially when he had no idea why the man was here in the first place, or more concerning, what he knew. Colin took a long draft of his scotch before settling back in his chair. "I find I'm curious as to what I can do for you, my lord."

"Well, I've heard your name bandied about the house a time or two, and since I haven't been able to attend many functions lately, I thought I would take it upon myself to meet the prodigal son of the great Sir Frederick Tate."

"Not so much prodigal, but certainly I am the son."

"Beatrice has spoken for years about your father's masterpieces. I'm sorry for your loss."

Colin nodded his acceptance, but refrained from saying anything more. He was content to let Raleigh set the tone, so he knew better where he stood with the man. He thought of the kiss in the loft, which he later realized had played out in front of the window. Not the smartest moment in his life, even if there had been no light from within to illuminate them. God help him if Raleigh somehow learned of the kiss.

Of course, if that were the case, he probably wouldn't be sitting calmly in Colin's aunt's library, sipping his scotch.

After a moment, he sat back in his chair and angled his head, watching Colin with disconcertingly clear blue eyes. "Well, I'm quite anxious to learn more about the man who descended from a legend and is only just now emerging into the public eye. You are a baronet now, are you not?"

"Indeed. I am also a barrister in training who has lived in London for the last two years." It was more than needed to be said, but he didn't like being made to feel as though he'd been hiding under a rock somewhere, waiting for his chance at the title.

Raleigh's brow lifted in surprise. "Two years, you say? And nary a ball or party? Good God, man, however have you filled your time?"

"You'd be amazed how much time learning a trade can fill."

For some reason, Colin's slightly acerbic response raised genuine amusement in Raleigh's otherwise impassive expression. "No, actually, I wouldn't. I know full well the dedication that goes into learning a trade, and I respect any person, man or woman, who can submit themselves thusly. It can leave a man with a devil of a sore arm."

Colin raised an eyebrow. "A sore arm, my lord?"

"Yes, a sore arm. So I wonder, then, what made you decide to take the plunge into society now. I saw your father a few times over the years, by the way. He certainly seemed to fit right in."

Of course he did. He had charm, charisma, and the favor of the Prince Regent. Colin knew full well the beau monde looked at his father like some sort of plaything to be taken down from the shelf from time to time and examined. Father, on the other hand, never saw it. He genuinely thought he was part of their world and basked in the attention like an unquestioning lapdog.

Which, at this point, would have been preferable to the role Colin was currently filling in society: cliché impoverished nobleman. He took a bracing drink and met Raleigh's gaze straight-on.

"The committee for the memorial exhibit in honor of my father's work asked that I return for the event. Since I relinquished my place in the Inn for the rest of the year following my father's death, I had the time and inclination to finally 'take the plunge,' as you say." It was none of Raleigh's business that Colin's break from the Inns was indefinite, pending his ability to actually finance his final year.

"Ah. That explains why you're staying with your aunt." Setting aside his empty glass, Raleigh templed his fingers and regarded Colin, his gaze sharp. "So you've been taking your meals at the Inns these past two years, have you?"

"I have."

"The law is such an interesting animal, is it not? All those little tidbits and caveats written in over time. So much to learn."

He was getting at something—of that, Colin had no doubt. "I daresay a barrister is always learning, since the law is ever changing."

"So you are aware, then, for example, of all the interesting things I can get away with thanks to the privilege of peerage? Such a *fascinating* subject, don't you think?"

"I am aware that it does not extend to courtesy titles, which I'm assuming yours is since your father is still alive," Colin replied mildly. "And I'm also aware that the privilege extends to civil offenses, not criminal."

Raleigh smiled affably, shrugging a shoulder. "So they say. Although it is rather remarkable how one never hears of peers—or those with *courtesy* titles—finding their way to gaol."

"Should I be envious, then, since my title falls just short of peerage? So convenient to be able to set laws, then exempt oneself from them."

For the second time since they had sat down, genuine amusement crossed the earl's face. "Yes, though not so different from arguing the word of law until it bends to suit your purposes. Perhaps we have something in common, after all. Which, incidentally, brings me back to my sister."

"Oh?" The next words from Raleigh's mouth would undoubtedly be the ones he came here for in the first place.

"Your attention and your *gifts*," he said, adding special emphasis, "have made her quite happy. I simply wanted to thank you. My sister's happiness is my absolute priority in life. Anyone who hurts her will have me to answer to."

"As it should be," Colin responded, thinking of his own little sister.

"And as we've established, I have no one to answer to but me, and I tend to be *very* understanding with myself."

"Good to know."

"Well, then, lovely to meet you," he said, coming to his feet and offering a perfunctory nod. "If you're ever in the mood for sports, do seek me out at Gentleman Jackson's. As one of his longest-standing and most proficient patrons, I'm there every week, without fail."

Colin nodded, and the earl took his leave, striding from the room without a backward glance. Well, that had quite possibly been the most singular conversation of his life. Oddly enough, he didn't seem to be warning him away from Beatrice, only from hurting her. It was like asking his intentions without coming right out and actually doing so.

Finishing off the contents of his tumbler, Colin set it on the wide arm of the leather chair and leaned back. The question was, what were his intentions?

His original intentions—which, truly, were none at all—had changed in the space of a single kiss. All along he had rejected Beatrice as a wife candidate because he had absolutely nothing to offer someone of her wealth and status. But much had changed since then. In almost every instance, she had been the one to show her preference for him, not the other way around. Learning about his father, becoming part of his world through her association with Colin seemed to be of higher currency than even the loftiest title or the wealthiest coffers to her.

But all that aside, she seemed to want him. To be attracted to him almost as much as he was to her. She had kissed him, well and truly kissed him of her own volition. The desire he felt for her—and not just physically—seemed to be wholly requited.

Therefore . . . why not have intentions toward her? Why not consider her as a possible bride? Heaven knew she would bring more than enough to the table monetarily speaking. But more important than that, he could actually envision having her by his side . . . and in his bed.

He swallowed, letting the pleasure of that thought linger.

His search for a wife went from distasteful to delectable just that fast. He came to his feet, discarding the glass on a side table on his way to the escritoire. It was time he took the reins in their relationship.

Chapter Fifteen

Music was most assuredly not Beatrice's forte. In fact, it probably went hand in hand with her lack of dancing prowess. She could appreciate fine quality and exceptional playing, but it just didn't speak to her the way it did others. She did, however, have a well-developed sense of loyalty, which was why she was seated beside her mother at her friend's second recital in six months.

Situated in a middle row close to the outside edge, she refrained from nodding her head or tapping her foot as some of the others were doing, lest she betray her terrible lack of rhythm. Instead, she smiled at Sophie and her sister as they did a lovely if slightly incongruous duet. Sophie had a true talent with her oboe, hitting soft, pure notes time and again. Her older sister was as accomplished on the bassoon as Beatrice imagined anyone could be. But when the two totally opposite range instruments were pitted against each other, well, it did rather make one question the wisdom of the pairing.

At least the performance was as memorable as their mother hoped it would be, if not quite for the same reason as she had envisioned. She famously believed that the more unique the instruments, the more memorable the musician.

Poor Sophie. She had asked to have the opportunity to perform a solo, but her mother felt it would be unjustly stealing attention from her older sister. Perhaps Sarah would marry before the next musicale, and Sophie would have her chance.

Movement out of the corner of Beatrice's eye made her glance right just as a man slipped into the empty seat beside her. In the half second before she actually saw his face, the fine hairs on the back of her neck stood up at his presence, and she just knew who it would be.

Colin.

When their gazes collided, he flashed her his beautiful smile, all white teeth and masculine perfection. He lingered for the space of a breath before he nodded to Mama, then turned his attention toward the front of the room.

It was all Beatrice could do to turn her gaze back to the musicians. Even with her eyes trained steadfastly forward, she could positively *feel* him beside her. All the pent-up emotions that had been bouncing around inside of her for days came roaring back to life. The last time she had seen him, she had been wrapped in his arms, his lips pressed to hers. . . . She shifted in her seat, trying to distract herself from the direction of her thoughts.

Which, of course, was impossible.

The music seemed oddly distant as every part of her focused in on Colin. Was he as aware of her as she was of him? Did he think of their kiss as often as she did, or remember her touch as keenly as she did his? And that wasn't all she was curious about. She was dying to know what had happened when her nosy brother had called on Colin two days earlier, but Richard had remained annoyingly closemouthed, saying only that they "understood each other." What the devil was that supposed to mean?

Now, at least, she knew that whatever the under-standing, Richard had not scared poor Colin away. He could have sat in any one of the available seats around the room, but he had chosen to join her. To be near to her.

That had to be a positive sign.

She held perfectly still, looking straight ahead as if she actually saw the Wembleys and wasn't trying to master the art of peripheral vision. He'd worn another dark jacket this evening, with what appeared to be an emerald waistcoat and efficiently tied white cravat. Simple, unfussy, and attractive, just like him.

She had ascertained from Sophie yesterday that he would be here, but when the music started and he still hadn't arrived, she had stopped watching the doorway and had resigned herself to a night without him. She really should not be so giddy to have him here now.

The first hints of his fresh and clean yet perfectly masculine scent teased her senses, and she drew a long, slow, utterly indulgent breath. She was instantly put to mind of the feel of his skin beneath her fingertips, of the warmth of his breath upon her cheek, of his lips tasting hers. . . .

She drew another breath, this one trying to quiet her pounding heart. It was a wonder no one could hear it over the music. For heaven's sake, she couldn't very well go to pieces just because a man sat beside her.

Bowing her head, she focused on her clasped hands on her lap. Her heart seemed to rise with the notes of the oboe, reaching higher with each beat. Cutting a glance toward Colin, she realized that his hand was only inches away from her skirts, settled close enough that if she adjusted her position at all, she could easily close the space between them.

Not that she would do such a thing in the middle of

a musicale. Even with the lamps turned down and everyone's attention on the musicians, she'd be a fool to indulge the impulse. With a simple glance around, anyone could see if his fingers brushed against her skirts, or if her hand settled beside his, or if their fingers should somehow become entwined with one another's.

Beatrice snapped her head up, diverting her gaze from his closeness and focusing on Sophie as if her life depended on it. The next fifteen minutes were the longest of her life. Knowing that he was so close, yet being unable to speak with him, or even look at him, was a new kind of oddly sweet torment.

When Sophie's last note finally rang out, the gathering politely clapped and the girls made their curtsies. The lamps were turned up, and with anticipation burning like a torch within her belly, Beatrice stood and met Colin's smoke-colored gaze.

His expression was all that was proper, but somehow she still felt the tug of attraction between them as he offered a slight bow. "Good evening, Lady Granville, Lady Beatrice. I hope you are both as well as you look."

Mama's smile was bright and welcoming as she linked arms with Beatrice. "Yes, thank you. It's so lovely to see you here, Sir Colin. Are you a lover of music?"

"I am a lover of all forms of beauty, my lady."

If it had been Richard, the same comment would have been flirtatious and teasing and would probably have been followed up with something about how that's why he chose to sit beside them. Not Colin. As usual, his words were simple and unembellished. Becoming a barrister was a good choice for him. He had a way of speaking that invited one to trust him.

"You must have inherited that trait from your father," Beatrice said. "He could find beauty in so much, transcribing it onto the canvas for the rest of us to enjoy."

"Actually, I like to think my mother had a hand in that. She died when I was very young, but I can still remember her walking through the meadow with me, marveling at the birdsong, the warm breeze, even the shapes of the clouds. I think she would have pointed out every petal of every flower if she could have."

"What a wonderful memory to have," Mama said, her eyes full of sympathy even as she smiled softly. Looking to Beatrice, she squeezed her hand before pulling away. "Well, I do believe I'm feeling quite parched."

Colin gestured toward the refreshment table in the back. "I'd be happy to fetch you some lemonade."

"Oh, no, thank you. It will be nice to move around a bit after sitting for so long."

Well, Colin couldn't have appealed to Mama more if he tried. Bringing up a much-cherished memory of his mother and then politely offering to tend to Mama? It was little wonder she gave Beatrice an almost imperceptible wink as she walked away. Was that a good or a bad thing? On the one hand, he clearly had Mama's approval. On the other, Beatrice dreaded the thought of Mama pushing the issue between the two of them. As if Richard's involvement wasn't bad enough—she didn't need a meddling mother added to the situation.

Speaking of Richard . . . Beatrice glanced around them as casually as she could. For the most part, people had cleared out of the seating area fairly quickly, leaving them in as private a setting as they could hope for in this sort of gathering. "So, I hear you met yet another member of my family this week."

He didn't even blink an eye. "I did."

"And?"

"I appreciated the opportunity to meet another of your siblings."

Blast. He was going to make her pry, wasn't he? "Whatever did you find to talk about? I can't think of a thing that the two of you might have in common."

"Not a thing?" he responded, raising an eyebrow.

"Well, yes, *one* thing, but surely you didn't talk about me the whole time." Or did they? She really didn't like the thought of the pair of them discussing her over tea. Or, more likely, scotch.

"I was referring to the fact that we are both titled gentlemen with noteworthy fathers and an appreciation for fine spirits, but, yes, there is you, as well." His expression was completely straightforward, but she knew from the glint in his eyes that he was teasing— the cad.

"You two are about as alike as a horseshoe and a fish. I seriously doubt you sat around debating the merits of your titles."

His raven brows rose just enough to impart earnestness. "We did, actually. I was even able to use some of my fancy legal terms. I've so missed a good debate since my father died and I had to take leave of the Inn to return to Scotland to visit my family."

She sighed in resignation. He would tell her nothing about the stupid meeting, she could already tell. She'd have to make sure the next meeting was at Granville House, so she could properly eavesdrop. "Fine, fine, have your manly secrets. I've got some of my own, anyway."

"You have manly secrets?"

She chuckled and shook her head. "Not quite. But I do have one secret that *involves* a man. Does that count?"

He leaned toward her the slightest amount, but it

was enough to make her breath catch. "Only if I'm the man." His voice was so low, it felt almost like a caress, making her shiver.

"I see," she said, her voice as light as her head just then. "Well, then, perhaps you would like to join—"

"No, no," he said, interrupting her with a raise of his hand. "Doona say another word until I've said what I came here to say."

Curiosity duly piqued, she pressed her lips together and lifted a brow, encouraging him to go on.

"Lady Beatrice, would you do me the honor of accompanying me on an excursion tomorrow?"

How charmingly formal. It all sounded so official when he said it like that. "I'd be delighted. What sort of excursion did you have in mind?"

"The sort that would allow us to continue what we started."

She blinked, shocked that he would be so bold about the embrace they had shared at the studio. She was usually the one who came right out and said things, not the other way around. Something in her expression amused him, and he made a visible effort to contain the laugh she felt sure was lurking behind his studiously closed lips.

"The portrait, Lady Beatrice. I thought perhaps we could carry on with it."

The *portrait*— Yes, of course! She grinned up at him, not at all embarrassed to have mistaken his meaning. "I'd like that very much. I'm not certain, however, that I can escape to the studio again."

"Which is why I made special arrangements."

"Special arrangements?" He'd done special planning, just for her? Oh, but she liked the thought of that.

His lips turned up in pleasure, his expression somehow more intimate than a full smile. "Indeed. You may tell your family that I've invited you to the gallery to view the newly arrived portraits before the exhibit opening on Saturday. Let's say two o'clock?"

"Very well. What about my supplies?"

"Bring your drawing if you need it, but I shall take care of anything else."

She smiled, pressing her lips together as she always did. He would take care of everything, would he? Clearly he had put much thought into the outing. "Perfect. I shall see you at two o'clock."

"Excellent," he said, his eyes bright with satisfaction. "And I'm sorry to have interrupted you, but I was determined to invite you on the outing before you beat me to it."

"Under the circumstances, Sir Colin, I forgive you."

He bowed and left her then, making his way to the small group surrounding Sophie and her sister. She smoothed a calming hand down her front before heading to the refreshment table for something to drink. What exactly was in store for her tomorrow? A thousand hazy possibilities flitted through her mind, making the anticipation all that much greater.

"Good evening, Lady Beatrice. You are looking very well indeed, if I may say so."

Drat it all, she'd dropped her guard and somehow allowed Mr. Godfrey to sneak up on her. Colin was proving to be detrimental to her normal awareness, it would seem. Irritation mingled with an uncomfortable twinge of guilt as she turned and gave Mr. Godfrey a shallow bob of her head. "I hope you have enjoyed the music, Mr. Godfrey."

"Not nearly as much as the company. In the absence of dancing this evening, I was wondering if you might like to take the night air out on the terrace with me. The evening is wonderfully mild for this time of year."

Which up until that moment had been a *good* thing. But the lingering guilt of her unintentional slight in the cartoon weighed heavy on her conscience. It was just a few minutes of her time—a minor penance to assuage her guilt. Dipping her head in agreement, she said, "Certainly. Lead the way."

He extended his arm, and she rested the very tips of her fingers on the superfine wool of his jacket. He'd applied his cologne water with a heavy hand, and she turned her head away from him in an attempt to breathe unperfumed air.

"I was so glad to see you in attendance this evening, my lady. After my necessary yet regrettable early departure from the Westmoreland ball, I've quite been looking forward to stealing you away for a bit."

"I see." She didn't want to affirm or encourage him in any way.

"Especially since that Tate fellow interrupted our time together at Granville House. He does seem to hover about you like the commoner he was born to be."

She ground her teeth to keep from making any snide remarks. She really wished to survive the encounter with as little engagement between them as possible. They reached the double glass doors at the back of the room, and he ushered her through them with a bit more "assistance" than necessary over the low threshold.

The air was warm and damp, helping her to clear her head. "Oh, no, I'm afraid you've misunderstood. I'm the one hovering about him." She tilted her head, offering him a look of utter innocence. "Does that make me common? I do so love hearing about his father's work."

She suspected that if he'd had a mouthful of drink, he would have spit it out just then. "No, of course not. And I was clearly exaggerating—you've hardly seen the man. Do forgive me for bringing it up at all."

How little he knew about anything. "Of course." Beatrice lightened her touch even more, until she couldn't have sworn her gloved fingertips were even connecting with his jacket. As if sensing her thoughts, he brought his hand down on top of hers, pressing it firmly against his arm and effectively trapping her at his side.

"Do you know, Lady Beatrice, I must say that you have been a most agreeable companion this past month. I find myself quite looking forward to your presence at any of these events."

There were two things that made her eyebrows inch up her forehead in surprise. First of all, she was as *un*-agreeable as she could be without actually giving the man the cut direct. What part of her humorless smiles and flat conversation came across as positive to him? And that aside, his words were entirely too forward for her liking. "No need to exaggerate, Mr. Godfrey."

He led them to the corner farthest from the door, pausing by the balustrade and turning to face her. He did not, she noticed, free her hand. She wiggled her fingers a bit in subtle warning, but if anything, his grip tightened.

"No exaggeration, my dear. I'm sure you know, that as the son of a viscount, I am a perfectly suitable match for the daughter of a marquis."

She did *not* like where this was heading. Pulling against his hold, she scowled and said, "Unhand me, Mr. Godfrey."

"Calm yourself, Beatrice. There is no need to worry for your reputation, as there is no one here to witness our stolen moment."

Real fear trickled into her heart. Dear heavens, what was he doing? She started to struggle away from him, but he wrapped her up in an embrace before she could gain even an inch. He was much taller than her, and surprisingly strong, nearly swallowing her in his arms. "Let g—"

But she didn't even finish the word before his mouth swooped down and covered hers. She was so shocked, so appalled, that for a moment she didn't do anything at all. His iron grip held her in place while his mouth lay heavy across her lips, claiming her like some sort of animal. The stink of alcohol soured his breath, flavoring her nightmare.

In that moment of outrage, the door to the house whooshed open.

Chapter Sixteen

His instincts had been dead-on.

As Colin stepped out onto the terrace, he was greeted with exactly the scene he had feared most. Beatrice, wrapped in Godfrey's arms, his lips planted firmly over hers. Without stopping to consider the consequences, he started forward. At the sound of his footsteps, Godfrey broke the kiss and looked up, a gleam of satisfaction illuminating his dark eyes.

Beatrice scrambled backward, turning to him with widened eyes that shone with horror.

The rat bastard— Colin came at the other man with his fists flying. He might not spend his days at Gentleman Jackson's, but even a half Scot knew how to throw a bloody good punch when needed. And oh, the satisfaction he felt at seeing the man's expression go from smugness to fear in the space of a second would be worth every consequence that would await him when he was done with the bastard.

His fist connected with Godfrey's mouth with exacting precision. Not only did it wipe away all traces of the self-satisfied smirk; it made damn sure that the man wouldn't be kissing anyone for a while. The punch was angled in just the right way to bust a lip but not break any teeth—not that the man deserved any mercy from Colin.

He fell backward against the stone railing, flipping over it and into the bushes a few feet below. It would have been amusing, if Colin weren't so angry. Heaving a deep breath, he turned to Beatrice, whose features were drawn and pale. "Are you all right?"

"Y-yes. I think so." She shook her head, clearly a bit dazed. "It wasn't what it looked like."

"Yes, I know." He would have said more, but the bushes rustled as Godfrey extracted himself. After a moment of struggling, he came back to his feet, leaves sticking out of his hair as a trickle of blood dribbled down his chin and onto his once pristine cravat.

"You bastard," he grunted, slurring the words just a bit. "I'll see you bloody gaoled for that."

"I highly doubt that." Colin's voice was cool and collected, his barrister's training finally reemerging. "You surely wouldn't want the world to know that you tried to trap a woman into marriage, since clearly you couldn't procure one by her consent."

Godfrey's eyes narrowed to slits as his gaze darted in between Colin and Beatrice. "You don't have any idea what you're talking about." He yanked at the twigs embedded in his hair, tossing them angrily to the ground.

"Well, I do," Beatrice said, crossing her hands tightly over her bodice. "You forced yourself on me just now. If it had been anyone else walking through that door, we'd be betrothed by now." Her voice held such utter disgust, if he had possessed even the slightest doubt as to whether or not she had welcomed Godfrey's advances, they would have been banished.

Colin shook his head. "It wasn't supposed to be just anyone walking out to find you. I saw Mr. Jones as he watched the two of you head outside. He checked his watch three times before making a beeline for the doors. Lucky for me, Miss Sophie didn't bat an eyelash when I snagged the man on his way out the door and told him she wished to speak with him."

Beatrice's jaw dropped open in outrage as she rounded on Godfrey. "You scurrilous beast! Not only did you force yourself upon me, but you *arranged* for us to be caught?"

The bastard in question dragged the back of his hand across his bloodied chin. "I don't have to take this. You want her?" he asked Colin, his face contorted with disgust. "Fine, you can have her. She may have the best dowry of the Season, but the rest of her sure as hell isn't worth it. Good riddance."

He stormed through the garden and disappeared around the corner like the slithering jackass he was. Colin breathed a deep sigh and turned to Beatrice. She looked furious, her sparkling eyes radiating an internal fire as she clenched her jaw tight. She was a study in contrasts, like a small, vulnerable avenging angel. He laid a calming hand on her shoulder, wishing he could pull her into his arms and soothe away her upset. "I'm so sorry you had to go through that. Are you certain you are all right?"

She waved an angry hand toward the direction Godfrey had escaped. "Much better now that he's gone. For heaven's sake, he is *everything* that is wrong with society. Do you know, it wouldn't have even mattered that he forced his attentions on me? If we had been discovered, I would have been forced to marry him or suffer the brunt of society's censure. And he *knew* it." Despite the relative warmth of the air, a shiver racked her body.

"Perhaps we should go inside, where it's warmer. You've had quite a shock."

"Not so huge a shock," she murmured, stepping

toward the house. "I never liked the man. I just *knew* he was a fortune hunter."

"Yes, well, that infamous cartoon made that particular trait quite clear to most of society, I'm afraid. I don't know whether that was a good or a bad thing."

She glanced up at him, her eyes cautious. "What do you mean?"

"Well, if he had not been subjected to increased censure this week, he may not have felt the need for desperate measures. On the other hand, clearly it's a good thing that young women have been warned away from him."

Her mouth quirked sideways as she chewed the inside of her cheek. Even in her ruffled state, she was so damn lovely. Any other woman might have fallen to pieces after such a horrid experience. Not only was she not in hysterics, but she looked to be plotting her revenge.

"I see your point. Both of them. You know, I think I may plead a headache and go home."

He wanted to ask if she was really all right, but decided to let it be. She had a right to take her time to recover from such a traumatic episode.

"Of course. Shall we reschedule our plans as well?"

She gave a quick shake of her head, jostling the slightly worse for wear blond curls framing her face. "No, of course not. I can think of nothing I would like to do more." She drew a deep breath, her creamy skin rising above the embroidered bodice of her gown. "And thank you. By the time I got my wits about me well enough to inflict the defensive maneuver my brother once showed me, we likely would have been discovered."

"Glad to be of service." And he was—immensely so. And not only for her sake—though that was the brunt of it. But if he hadn't arrived in time, any hope of mak-

ing a match with her would have been dashed. It was
a thought he could hardly bear to consider. It had absolutely nothing to do with her fortune and everything to
do with . . . her.

The lead moved so forcefully against the paper, the
ominous tearing sound that rent the air was hardly a
surprise. "Blast and damn," Beatrice muttered, confident that no one would hear her curse.

She was too angry to be doing this now. She gathered up the paper between her hands, balling it up and
tossing it in the low fire burning in the grate. The problem was, she needed to do it now. Drawing the cartoon
for the next letter to the magazine while her stomach
still churned and her anger simmered was a good
thing—it would make her do what needed to be done
to prevent this sort of thing from happening to someone else.

She could write the letter later; she could carefully
redraw the cartoon later, but right then, the most important thing was capturing her emotions on the page.
No other woman should ever be forced into an unwanted betrothal because of a clever, conniving fortune
hunter.

Drawing in a deep breath, she pulled out another
sheet of paper and laid it out, picking up her pencil
once more. This time, she wasn't going to pull her
punches.

"How on earth did you arrange all this?" Beatrice
shook her head in wonder, sweeping a hand around to
encompass the remarkably clean easel, the fresh, white
canvas, the neatly arranged paints, and the selection of
brushes. It was such a fantastic display, even Rose
raised an eyebrow before taking out her book and retreating to the bench just outside the door. Yes, techni-

cally she should be in the same room with them, but
could Beatrice help it if there were no places to sit in the
small studio?

One side of Colin's mouth tipped up in a pleased
grin. "Connections. I told them I wished to have a re-
production of one of my father's paintings before it
was sent back to the owner after the exhibit. Of course,
I wouldn't dream of leaving the gallery with one of the
pieces, so they arranged for this."

"You clever, clever man. What happens if they discover your fib?"

"I'll simply say that it turned out that genius could
not be copied."

Beatrice grinned. "Well, that much is true. I suppose
we should get started right away. Mama will expect me
back in a little over an hour and a half." It was more time
than she'd expected to get, but not nearly enough for
what she wanted. "Can you lean against the window,
the way you did in the studio?"

"I am yours to command," he said, bowing before dutifully carrying out her bidding. Beatrice ignored the
gooseflesh that peppered her arms at his melodic voice.
He was absolute trouble, and she loved him for it.

After a few adjustments, he was in place, his gorgeous face bathed in half-light as he leaned casually
against the casing. Instead of angling his gaze out the
window, his stormy eyes were cut toward her, watching
her as she sketched the outline onto the canvas. She
worked quickly, trying to avoid those watchful eyes, lest
her concentration falter.

"Are you certain you are recovered from your ordeal?" His voice was soft with concern and undemand-
ing in a way that made her want to confess her plans
for her letter.

Completely imprudent, of course. The fewer people
who knew, the better. Instead, she simply nodded as

she kept her eyes on the drawing. "Quite certain. I wouldn't let a scoundrel like him ruin a day like this."

"Are you certain there isn'a some amount of Scot in your blood?"

A smile curved her lips as she outlined the angles of his jaw. "We English are made of sterner stock than you realize, I think. My sister Evie once crossed two counties on horseback with her injured arm in a sling."

"Really? Then the both of you must have the Scottish blood. You are siblings, after all."

She flicked a light sarcastic glance his way before concentrating on the two-dimensional version of the man. "And are Scottish lasses really as hearty as all that?"

"Certainly. Legend has it Gran once fought a bear with naught but a cast-iron pan, a spoon, and a bit of ribbon."

"My, that is impressive. With such stalwart females to choose from, it's little wonder you've avoided us wilting English violets."

He chuckled, managing to stay perfectly still as he did so. "I canna think of a single person who is further from being a wilting violet than you, *a stór*."

Pleasure at both his comment and the endearment slipped across her skin like a warm breeze, making her shiver in delight. Some women, perhaps even most, might have considered such a statement to be a bad thing, as if disparaging their femininity. But for Beatrice, he could hardly have offered a more pleasing compliment. "Mama would be devastated to hear you say that."

"No, I doona think so."

She paused, looking up with a raised eyebrow. "Don't you? Between us sisters, she's forever correcting our heathen selves."

He pursed his lips, as if considering this, then shook

his head. "She wants you to do well in society, but I think she's proud of you all. You can see it in her eyes every time she looks at you."

His comment made her smile. She didn't doubt it, either—no matter how much she fussed at them, Mama had always been free with her love when it came to her family—unlike many in the beau monde.

Beatrice tilted her head at the sketch on the canvas, her critical eye passing back and forth between the drawing and her subject. She sighed—she was never going to get him to look out the window as she wanted. She might as well portray him as his father had, looking directly at the artist. "I think perhaps it would be more natural if you simply looked at me. Turn your head a bit more in my direction. No, not that much. Yes, that's good."

Setting to work correcting the angle of his head, she thought of how different their upbringings had been. How different would her life have been without Mama's constant presence? Turning a critical eye toward him, she studied his expression for a moment before turning back to the sketch. "Do you miss your mother?"

"Every day," he said without hesitation. "Maybe it would be different if she had died when I was younger, but at five, my entire world revolved around her."

She didn't doubt it. If something happened to her parents, as had almost happened to Papa earlier in the year, Beatrice doubted she would ever get over the loss. "How did she die?" It was a bold, nosy question, but she couldn't seem to help herself. Her heart squeezed for the little boy in the portrait, his eyes so serious and challenging at such a young age.

"The usual," he said, his shoulder hitching up in a halfhearted shrug. "She and my brother died in child-birth."

Beatrice's breath caught—he'd lost his mother and

his brother in the same day? Her heart melted for the man, let alone the boy she'd never known. "I'm so sorry. How heartbreaking to lose them both at a time that should have been joyful." She shuddered to think of how things could have been different when Evie had Emma.

"Yes." The single word was filled with a wealth of emotions. For a moment he was quiet, doing nothing more than holding his pose. "It might have been different if my father had handled it better—not that I blame him. He loved my mother very much. When he lost her, he lost his wife, his helpmate, his son's mother, and his greatest champion."

Perhaps it was his hollow tone, or the sudden sadness weighing the corner of his lips down, but for some reason she felt as though she had hit upon a nerve. "But your father loved you, too, of course."

"He did, I think. In his own way. Just as I loved him in my own way. But growing up with a man more dedicated to his art than his family was a bit . . . demoralizing, shall we say."

She sucked in a surprised breath. Tate had always been such a paragon in her mind. Was Colin saying that he'd had more regard for painting than for his child? "But by working, he was providing for you, was he not? Perhaps that was what he worried about in the early days."

He nodded, looking down for a moment before meeting her gaze again. "Yes, though it might have been helpful if he had more sense with the commissions he was earning. It wasn't a long before I realized that if the accounts were to be paid and our bills not lost, it was up to me to see to it."

Beatrice offered him a sympathetic smile. "Is that how you came to be the responsible barrister?"

Even as her heart went out to him, she could scarcely

make herself believe that his legendary father could have such a failing. Everything she had heard about him had been in the vein of charming, affable, and eccentric. A little odd, as artists can sometimes be, but a great addition to any social event. She had been devastated that he had died just as she was to make her debut.

"I suppose one could say I spent my whole life in training."

"Did things not change when your father remarried?" She knew little about Tate's second wife, other than the fact she had died several years earlier.

"They did, actually. She was determined to get my father's life in order and to provide a good upbringing for her two children and me. But old habits die hard, I suppose. After four years alone with my father, letting go of the worry dinna come easy."

He was so sweet with her, so easy to be with, it was hard to imagine him as the stoic little boy he described. Her own childhood had been so carefree; it made her heart clench to imagine his staidness. She set down her pencil, picked up her brush, and began mixing paints on her palette. "Tell me about her children. Do you get along?"

It was the perfect question to ask to break the tension that had tightened his jaw and beetled his brow. "Very well. They are quite a bit younger than me, but they have always been sweet-tempered and good company. Although they were both terribly unhappy with me for leaving them behind in Scotland while I made my grand debut, so to speak."

"Now, that I can understand. I hated never being able to join in the fun when Evie was out in society. Ironic, really, since she would have rather been anywhere else."

He chuckled. "I think I'm with your sister on this

one. As for you, I think you would like Cora. She has always been fascinated with Father's work and would sneak up to his studio after bedtime to watch him paint sometimes. She got caught more often than not, sent to bed with a scolding, but it never stopped ~er from trying again."

Happy with the color on her palette, she took a deep breath, set the bristles against the canvas, and made her first stroke. "A girl after my own heart, apparently. And your stepbrother?"

She glanced up just in time to catch a look of disgust contort his features. "I'm so sorry. Are you on bad terms with him?"

"No, it's nothing like that. It's just that I hate that term. They are as much my brother and sister as your siblings are to you."

"Yes, of course. I didn't intend to insult you."

"No, I dinna think you did. But when half the family you have in the world is distanced by the word 'step,' it tends to become distasteful. We were raised together from when I was nine, and my life became infinitely better when they came along."

That was quite possibly the sweetest thing Beatrice had ever heard. Her heart softened toward the two children she had never even met. "I'm so glad to hear it. What is your brother's name?"

Any remaining stiffness fled completely from his shoulders. "Rhys. He's a born leader. I could easily see him running the estate, or even making his way into politics. He argues almost as well as I do," he said with a wink. "If he had gotten his way, he'd be here in London with me now. Luckily, I convinced him that Cora and Gran needed a man in the house to keep them safe."

"The same Gran who fought the bear?"

He laughed, beautiful amusement lighting his features. "The very one. A more terrifying woman, I have never known."

"I don't believe you. You positively glow when you speak of her."

"She is one of a kind. Half Scottish, half Irish, and with twice the superstition of either people. When I first saw you, her fanciful descriptions of forest nymphs immediately came to mind."

She paused midstroke, her eyes flitting to his. The sweet smile on his perfect lips made her belly do a little flip. "Forest nymph? Me?"

"Absolutely. The luminescent skin, those huge blue eyes, hair like moonbeams—it all seemed to fit."

Hair like *moonbeams*? She sincerely hoped her grin wasn't as foolish looking as it felt. She ducked her head a bit, giving more care to loading her brush with paint than absolutely necessary. "Perhaps it had something to do with me emerging from the curtains like some sort of mischievous mystical creature."

"Perhaps," he allowed, the warmth of his gaze heating her insides from clear across the room. "But I'm glad for the way we met. It was pure, in a way."

"Pure?" she echoed, knitting her brow at his choice of words as she worked on his outline.

"Neither of us knew a single thing about the other. The only thing I knew for sure was that you were beautiful and damn entertaining, and I dinna want to leave you to go meet a horde of strangers I dinna care about."

The strangest sensation bloomed in her heart, carried by each beat to the rest of her body, until she felt as though she were floating in a cool lake. She swallowed, slowly raising her gaze. The way he was looking at her, as if the rest of the world had ceased to exist and there was only the two of them, held her riveted in place. She licked her lips. "I'm glad for it as well."

"Are you, now?"

She nodded. "I don't know if I would have had the nerve to talk to you if we'd met after I learned who your father was."

"Nonsense," he said, his eyes crinkling at the corners. "You've nerve enough to do anything you set your mind to."

Perhaps he was right. But was that a good thing? Coming from his lips, it certainly seemed like it, even if many of society wouldn't agree. She thought of the letters to the magazine, biting her lip against sharing her secret with him. Yes, if anyone would approve, it would be him, but she wasn't ready to share such a secret just yet.

Feeling light and happy, she grinned. "You, Sir Colin, are a shameless flatterer. It's a wonder my head doesn't float away."

"I haven'a flattering bone in my body—just ask my siblings. I am exceedingly good at speaking the truth, however. And I'm delighted to hear you approve."

For the next half hour, Colin watched in fascination as Beatrice went about the task of committing his countenance to canvas. It was *much* more interesting to watch her work than it ever had been to watch his father. And it wasn't just because she was infinitely more attractive. No, it was more because of the joy she radiated as she worked. Father had always been so severe, determined to get it exactly the way he wanted in a way that seemed to indicate that death would be the penalty for an imperfect stroke.

Colin held perfectly still, not wanting to distract her work. He liked watching her this way. She was so at ease, as if standing in front of an easel was her natural state of being. She was strong and spirited, not at all the wilting violet, as she had put it, that one might expect from one so petite. And best of all, he affected her. He could see it, anytime he complimented her, or stood too close, or met her gaze—she felt for him as much as he did her.

Could he really be so lucky? Could the woman who was about as close to his perfect match as he could think of truly be standing right in front of him? She was clever and sweet, beautiful and talented. She had the fortune that he required, but it was not at all what he saw when he looked at her.

To him, she was simply his *stór*.

Slowly, deliberately, he straightened and began walking toward her. She glanced up, a single brow raised. "What do you think you are doing?"

"I thought to take a look at what you've done so far. A man can lean against a window only so long, my dear."

She came around the easel, standing defensively in front of it with her hand stretched out between them. "Oh no, you don't. An artist's work is not to be seen until it is done."

"Nonsense. How am I to know you are doing me justice?" He made to sidestep her, and she jumped to her left to block his way, mock outrage bringing her hands to her hips, which had the unexpected benefit of pushing up her small but perfect breasts.

"Don't even think about it. I shall never forgive you if you ignore me."

"Mmhmm, that's nice," he said, moving to step around her.

Both hands came up this time as she widened her eyes in laughing earnestness. "Sir Colin Tate, if you so much as take one more step, I'll—"

He stepped forward, bringing his chest flush against both of her palms. "You'll what?"

Beatrice's mouth fell open, her eyes darkening almost to navy. The fragrance of lilacs rose above the smell of paint, teasing him with its familiarity. She wasn't perfect, but she was perfect for *him*. He stood there, letting her feel his heart race beneath the fabric of his clothes. Letting her feel how much she affected him. Not even trying to hide the desire in his eyes.

After a moment, her arms relaxed a bit, bringing her wrists down against his body as well. Her tongue darted out, wetting her lips before she looked back up at him through her golden lashes. This close, he could see the halo of green around her pupils, flecked with a bit of gold.

He licked his own lips, waiting, wanting her to make the next move. When it came, it was much more bold than he could have hoped for. Drawing a deep breath, she slid both hands up his jacket and grabbed his lapels. His blood roared in his ears as want rushed through him, testing his willpower. His heart beat in a heavy rhythm once, twice, three times, and just when he thought she might change her mind, she tugged him hard and brought his lips to hers.

Chapter Seventeen

Good, it felt so good to have her lips pressed against his at last. It had been near torture, painting him when what she really wanted to do was kiss him. Having two of him—the living, breathing, warm-blooded Colin as well as the emerging portrait of him looking at her with those incredible eyes, seducing her without lifting a single finger or saying a single word was pure, delectable torture.

She held tight to his lapels, pulling him to her as if her life depended on it. For his part, he came willingly, slanting his lips over hers and overwhelming her every sense. She opened her mouth, eager to taste him once more, to feel the heat of his tongue slide against hers. His hands slipped around her waist, pulling her whole body against him, even as her arms remained between them.

The feel of being completely engulfed in his arms was so foreign but yet so pleasurable, even more so with the wickedness of it all. The light of the afternoon sun lay across them, heating the right side of her body while the rest of her languished in shadow. *His* shadow.

His tongue danced with hers, making her moan with the sensation that shot through her whole body at his touch and landed deep in her belly. Colin's arms slid farther down, cupping her bottom, shocking her at his boldness. She drew a deep breath through her nose, savoring the smell, the feel, the taste of him. Well, he wasn't the only one who could be bold.

Releasing his jacket, she slipped her hands up the side of his neck, and delved her bare fingers into the silk that was his hair. It was cool and soft—in perfect contrast to the rest of him.

He broke the kiss then, and she started to moan in complaint, but his lips moved across her cheek, down her neck, and explored the exposed line of her collarbone. Oh good heavens, it was an altogether different sensation from his lips against hers. She had no idea her skin could be so utterly sensitive, so perfectly alive to the touch of another person.

A wave of chills ran down her spine, raising gooseflesh on her exposed arms and making her shiver. He pulled away and smiled down at her, their faces almost too close for her to focus.

"You, my little artist, are entirely too delightful for your own good." He slipped his hands up her bare arms, lightly clasping her fingers and pulling them down. He kissed each hand in turn before releasing them.

Her mind was absolutely reeling with the shared intimacy between them. She had never thought a man could so thoroughly addle her senses—or that she would like it. A delicious thrill rolled down her body like a drop of warm honey. Lord have mercy, did she like it.

But not nearly as much as she liked *him*.

"What on earth is that ridiculous look on your face all about?"

Colin started, looking up from the law book he wasn't actually reading to see his cousin striding into the room. "Woolgathering, I suppose."

Lifting a sandy brow, John shook his head. "Don't believe you for a moment, old man. If ever a man was thinking of a female, it was you, just now."

Colin started to deny it, but came up short. Why not share with John? His cousin was as good a confidant as any in this city. "I'll concede the point."

"Well done, man," John said, slapping him on the shoulder before dropping into the chair across from him. "Who's the chit? Find a proper match, did you?"

A proper match. It was the perfect way to describe the way Colin felt about Beatrice. Especially when he thought about that last kiss. The first one had been innocent, sweet and passionate all at once. But the kiss from yesterday? He swallowed, adjusting his position just thinking about it. That was not the kind of kiss one shared with just anyone. "I did. And I'm thinking of asking for her hand."

"Good on you, my friend. Who is the lucky heiress?"

Colin clenched his jaw, rebelling at the descriptive. "It's not about her bloody money, John. She is the finest person I have met in society—male or female."

Concern clouded his cousin's eyes, and he leaned forward. "Devil take it, Colin—you didn't go and fall for a penniless woman, did you? Think of your family, man, not to mention that excessively mortgaged estate."

"No, no—she has an exceptional dowry. But Lady Beatrice is so much more than that."

Relief washed over John's face, and he sat back and chuckled. "Yes, I'll just bet she is. God, you had me going there for a moment. An exceptional dowry indeed."

Colin was fairly sure putting a fist through his cousin's face wouldn't go over well. The strength of his aversion to John's reaction was shocking. If he reacted this way to his own family, how would things go when others whispered behind their hands about the nobody baronet pursuing the powerful marquis's daughter?

"I'll not say it again, John. Her bloody dowry has nothing to do with the way I feel about her. She is a remarkable, talented woman."

"Sure, sure, if you say so. But if you'll remember, I warned you against the fair Lady Beatrice. How do you plan to handle the financial discussion with her family, should it come to that?"

Even though he'd already thought of that particular conversation, Colin's gut clenched. There were two ways to go about it. One, he could tell the whole truth and be instantly turned away. Two, he could disclose how much the estate made per annum, discuss his prospects as a barrister, and know that once the business loan was paid with the funds from the dowry, it would no longer be pertinent to the discussion, particularly with the generous amount he planned to keep in trust for Lady Beatrice.

In other words: He could lie.

He rubbed a hand over the back of his neck, working at the tension that seemed to follow him whenever he thought of his father's exceedingly unwise business decision. "Obviously I must disclose the details. I don't see that there is any way around it."

Approval lightened his cousin's expression, and he gave a crisp military nod. "Good plan. The Moores are a powerful family, despite their peculiarities. I wouldn't want to cross them."

"Agreed." Even if they weren't one of the oldest and most respected families in the *ton*, he didn't wish to disrespect the family of the woman he hoped to spend the rest of his life with.

"When do you plan to move forward?"

Nerves flickered through him before settling in the pit of his stomach. Moving forward meant asking for her hand, and that would mean a massive change in the rest of his life. "After the exhibit opening, I think.

From what I understand, most of her family will be there, so it should be an excellent opportunity to see how they interact with the *ton* en masse. I'd like to at least know what to expect of the earl and his wife."

"Sounds like a reasonable approach. Plus, Mother and I will both be there to support you, should you need it."

"Rallying the troops behind me, are we?"

John nodded, not a hint of irony in his expression. "One never knows when one will have need of reinforcements."

"Care to take a walk with me?"

Jane smiled from the doorway of Beatrice's studio. Her porcelain skin was a bit paler than usual, but she still looked utterly lovely in her lavender-trimmed morning gown. Thank goodness Bea had positioned her canvas so that it faced away from the doorway, hiding Colin's emerging visage from anyone who happened to drop by.

"I suppose a break could be nice. Are you feeling better today?"

"Much better than this morning, to be sure, but these last few days have been dreadful. I honestly can't imagine how Mama worked in the bakery when she was expecting. As much as I wish I could bake, the thought of stepping in the kitchen with all those smells . . ." She shook her head, wrinkling her nose in disgust. "But the sun is shining, and the air is crisp, and I am thinking that a walk might be just the thing."

Beatrice hid a grin as she stood and removed her apron. Jane never was one to sit still for very long. "Who's doing the baking for the orphanage, then? Surely it's not just Richard."

Jane's green eyes widened with delight. "It is! I'm so proud of him for it, too."

"Well, I haven't seen any bandages or splints, so clearly he is much improved since our lessons. I'm surprised he hasn't asked me to join him. I may have had only two baking lessons, but I remember being the better student, of the two of us." She winked as she led them into the corridor and shut the door.

"He's under strict orders from your parents not to involve you in anything remotely scandalous until after you are safely married." She rolled her eyes, leaning down to whisper, "Imagine what people would think if they knew you'd whisked your own eggs."

Beatrice almost snorted. If only they knew exactly how scandalous she had been. Getting her hands dirty in the kitchen was the least of her worries. "Ah, that explains it. All right. Just give me a moment to change. I'll meet you in the entry hall in ten minutes."

Ducking into her chambers, Beatrice rang for her maid before hurrying to the little escritoire tucked beneath the window. Opening the wide, shallow drawer, she unearthed the drawing she had spent the last few nights working on. She smoothed it out, inspecting the carefully rendered cartoon. This time there was no mistaking Godfrey. She had originally intended to create a completely different fortune hunter character, but after the horrid stunt at the musicale, he deserved to be called out and chastised for the scoundrel he was.

The swift clip of approaching footsteps echoed down the corridor—her maid was coming. Placing the letter atop the drawing, she rolled them together and tied them in a slender ribbon. A walk to Monsieur Allard's would be the perfect opportunity to hand them over. For all anyone had to know, it was simply a list of supplies she wished to have ordered.

Five minutes later, Jane and Beatrice stepped out into the sunshine and headed west. The air held a definite chill, but with the sunshine warming their faces, it was rather refreshing.

Jane sighed, deep and blissful. "Oh my, but it feels like heaven out here. I don't think I realized quite how cooped up I was feeling."

"I know what you mean. I will be quite relieved when Mama gives up and lets us return to Aylesbury. I know you and Richard love the city, but I must confess that it is not nearly so captivating as I once imagined."

"Oh, I am very much looking forward to spending Christmas at Hertford Hall. The city is home, but I've heard so much about it from all of you, especially Evie. But I wonder," she said, linking her arm through Beatrice's as they crossed the street, "if you are very certain there isn't something you will miss."

"Something? If you mean your scrumptious baked goods, yes, I shall be lost without them. Of course, until you feel better, I must do without anyhow."

Jane cut her gaze to Bea, a single delicate brow lifted. "Perhaps I should have said someone. And no, I am not referring to Richard or myself."

Colin's face immediately popped into her head, and Beatrice bit her lip against the silly smile that threatened. She looked down at the pavement, watching the swish of her skirts as she walked. "There is, actually."

"I knew it!" Jane gave her arm a little squeeze, grinning broadly. "A woman in love can always spot another."

"Love?" Beatrice squeaked. Was that the emotion that fairly exploded in her chest anytime she thought of him? Was love what made her heart race when she heard that incredible accent of his, or set eyes on the painting she was working on? She suddenly desperately wished Evie weren't so far away.

She hadn't even realized she stopped walking until Jane tugged her to the side, pulling her out of the way of pedestrians behind them. She blinked up at her sister-in-law, trying to get a handle on the rioting emotions that seemed to rob her of the ability to think rationally. "I don't know if it's *love*, per se. I mean, I do quite, quite like him. . . ." She trailed off, putting a gloved hand to her middle. Even as she said the words, she knew that they weren't nearly strong enough to describe the feelings she had whenever he was near.

"Well, I certainly didn't mean to upset you. It's just that you've been so different these past few weeks. And to hear you talk about Sir Colin, truly, you positively glow."

Lovely. Now she was some sort of incandescent lovesick fool.

"Oh, don't give me that look, Bea. For heaven's sake, love is a *good* thing. Especially when a couple is as compatible as Sir Colin and you. It makes things so much easier."

Beatrice shook her head and started forward, pulling Jane along with her. "Can we please not talk about this? Colin and I haven't even discussed courting."

"'Colin,' is it?" Jane's knowing look was altogether too much. "And I'll grant your wish, provided you answer one last question."

Cutting a suspicious look at her sister-in-law, Beatrice said, "What question is that?"

"Has he kissed you?"

"Jane!"

Two men walking past started at Beatrice's exclamation, but Jane simply smiled impassively at them until they went on their way. As if this moment could be any more mortifying.

"I'm fairly certain that is a yes, but I won't press."

They walked in silence for a few more blocks. The residential homes gave way to businesses, and the traffic around them increased. The wagon carts, horse hooves, and shouting costermongers did little to drown out the noise in her own head as she went over and over the word "love" in her mind. And the wonderful, wicked, incredible kisses she had shared with Colin.

"Yes."

Jane looked at her, confusion knitting her brow. "I beg your pardon?"

"Yes, I kissed him."

Of the two of them, Jane was the one who blushed at this. "I'm quite certain it is my duty as an old married woman to scold you. However," she said, her almond-shaped eyes crinkling at the corners, "clearly I am not one to talk. Was it wonderful?"

A wave of butterflies took flight in her belly as Beatrice lingered on the memory of their kisses. "There is not a superlative in the English language that could properly describe its wonderfulness."

"That, my dear, is quite possibly the sweetest thing I have ever heard . . . and exactly how it should be."

They reached Monsieur Allard's shop, and Beatrice led the way inside. It was ironic, really. Here she was writing a column about how to avoid bad men, and the only thing she could think of was one very good man.

Even as she smiled and greeted the Frenchman, her mind was already moving ahead. With the gallery opening at hand, and the length of Colin's stay in London unknown, perhaps it was time for them to consider what the future might hold for them.

Chapter Eighteen

There was no doubt the exhibit was already a re-sounding success, even though not even an hour had passed since the gallery doors had opened. A harp-ist set the mood, her elegant Grecian-style gown the perfect complement to the white-and-gold decor, while her surprisingly dark and moody tones fit the look of the portraits quite exactly. Where normally the noise of so many people might have been deafening, the attend-ees spoke in quiet, reverent tones as they wandered from portrait to portrait.

So far, everything was perfect.

Which did not help Colin's nerves in the least. Every time someone walked through the door, he darted a glance that way, willing the new arrival to be Beatrice. Unfortunately, his vigilance had earned him little but a few displeased looks from the people he was talking to at the time.

"I think his later works really embody his true tal-ent, don't you agree? Just look at the level of detail on Lady Danbridge's gown. I feel as though I could reach out and touch it."

Colin nodded politely to the purple-gowned woman whose name he couldn't remember. She had tight ringlets covering her head, distracting him every time she moved.

"And the sunbeams"—*bounce, swing, bounce*—"aren't they simply divine?"

This time she turned to him for confirmation of her opinion, and Colin dipped his head. "I agree completely."

In that moment, the back of his neck tingled as if someone blew across the sensitive hairs there. He turned, his eyes going straight to the doorway, where a group of newcomers ventured into the room, glancing about. His heart kicked in his chest as his gaze collided with Beatrice's. "Will you excuse me?" he murmured, not waiting for the matron's response.

He strode across the room, pulled toward Beatrice like a fish on a line. Her mouth was turned up in the suggestion of a smile, her cheeks sweetly rounded, while her sapphire gaze, with its subtle hint of emerald, sparkled in silent greeting.

She was absolute perfection.

He wanted to do nothing but stare at her all night, his sweet *stór* in her bejeweled gown, but of course that was impossible. As he drew close enough to address the family at large, he smiled. "Good evening and welcome. I'm so glad that you all could join us tonight."

"We wouldn't miss it," Lady Granville said, her regal features warm and pleasant. "I believe you have met my son, the Earl of Raleigh, but allow me to introduce to you his wife, Lady Raleigh."

The dark-haired beauty on Raleigh's arm wasn't at all what he had expected, given the way his aunt had described the former baker. Her flawless skin and bright emerald eyes were lovely, but it was the countess's grin that struck Colin most. It seemed completely pure, in no way contrived, and he found himself liking her immediately. "My lady, it is a pleasure."

"I have heard so much about you, Sir Colin. It's lovely to finally make your acquaintance."

His gaze flickered to Beatrice. Was she the one telling Lady Raleigh about him? He rather hoped so. He liked to think that she was as captivated with him as he was with her. Diplomatically, he turned his attention to the twins, who were looking about as if they'd never been to a gallery. Or perhaps it was that they had never been to a gathering like this. They had yet to debut, after all. "Lady Carolyn, Lady Jocelyn, it is a delight to see you again. I do hope you will all enjoy the exhibit. And do let me know if you would like the background on any of the portraits. I am happy to divulge all of the artist's secrets, as Lady Beatrice might have told you."

"No, actually," replied Lady Jocelyn, raising a pale brow in Beatrice's direction. "She's shared precious little about her guided tour, or any of her excursions for that matter."

Lady Granville shook her head, already looking exasperated before she'd even been there five minutes. "Now, now, a lady can't be expected to divulge all of her secrets. And she also must refrain from monopolizing her host's time. Thank you for the greeting, Sir Colin. We are most anxious to view the featured works."

With the efficiency of a captain directing his troops, the marchioness herded the family toward the first portrait, pausing only long enough to accept a glass of negus from a passing footman.

Lady Beatrice remained by his side, watching as her family merged with the crowd. "You survived," she said, a bit of mischief tugging up the corners of her mouth.

He lifted his wineglass to his lips and took an unconcerned sip. "Not so very terrifying, I assure you."

"You say that now, but you are forgetting, I think,

that you have yet to meet my father, sister, niece, and brother-in-law. When we are all in one room, then we'll see how brave you are."

"Is that an invitation?"

She pressed her lips together and lifted a slender shoulder, drawing his attention to her very kissable collarbone. "Perhaps. If you decide you are a glutton for punishment, that is."

"Any time spent in your presence could hardly be punishment."

"Oh well, yes, there is that." Her eyes sparkled with amusement.

He knew his duty was to be greeting guests and offering unique insight into the artist, but the thought of pulling himself away from her was distasteful in the extreme. Turned as he was with a view toward the entrance, he noted the arrival of a distinguished-looking gentleman in a rather resplendent naval uniform. Stepping into the gallery, the man surveyed the area as if inspecting his fleet. He was poised as if standing on deck, his feet firmly planted and his shoulders squared as if for optimum balance. Every dark hair was in place, and his boots were so well shined as to reflect the light from the chandelier above.

Colin started to point him out to ask Beatrice if she knew who the man was, but his dark eyes landed on them in that moment and his stern expression vanished. Actually, Colin realized, his gaze wasn't on them so much as it was on *her*. Colin straightened, biting the inside of his lip against a scowl as the man smiled and extended a hand as he approached.

"Lady Beatrice, how lovely to see you."

Her delight was palpable as she smiled warmly— perhaps a bit too warmly, if you asked Colin—and allowed him to kiss her gloved hand. "Captain Curry, what a wonderful surprise. I thought you were still sailing the seven seas, dutifully frightening all of England's enemies away from her shores."

"Yes, well, even the saltiest of sea captains craves a bit of dry land now and again. What a pleasure to find you here. I should have known you'd never be able to resist this particular exhibit."

They chuckled as if sharing a private joke. "I am devastated to be so predictable. I shall try harder to maintain an air of mystery in the future."

"Don't you dare—you are perfect just the way you are."

Colin's gaze bounced back and forth between them, his brows inching closer and closer together. Who was this Captain Curry, and why did he seem to be on such intimate terms with Beatrice? More important, what was it about the man that inspired the altogether foreign sensation of jealousy?

"Oh my, where are my manners?" she said, turning to include Colin in the conversation. He straightened at once, correcting his expression to its normal neutrality as she made the introductions. "Captain Edward Curry, have you met the son of the legend himself, Sir Colin Tate?"

"I don't believe I have," the older man said, sizing Colin up in one glance. "Your father was a phenomenal talent. Please accept my condolences for your loss."

Colin nodded his acceptance of the sentiment. "Thank you, sir. Tell me, how is it you and Lady Beatrice are acquainted with each other?"

"Actually," Beatrice said, smiling once again at the officer, "Captain Curry owns quite a collection of naval paintings. He is generous enough to open his home to visitors, and I just happened to visit when he was in residence this spring."

"Yes, and imagine my surprise to learn that this young lady seemed to know more about the artists than I did. We had quite a stimulating conversation that afternoon."

"And imagine *my* surprise to discover that the Pirate Gentleman was much more gentleman than pirate," she teased, shaking her head as if disappointed. "I had high hopes for a parrot and a peg leg."

"Shocking, I'm sure," Colin muttered. The thought of them sharing such "stimulating" conversations did not sit well with him. He wanted to be the one doing the stimulating when it came to Beatrice. "Well, as an art collector, you must be eager to take a look around, Captain."

"Oh, indeed you must be," Beatrice exclaimed. "It is a thousand times better than I had even imagined. And I haven't even seen the royal portrait yet."

The captain extended his arm, his eyebrows raised in question. "Shall we go see it together? I'm sure Sir Colin must have all sorts of duties that we are keeping him from."

Beatrice blinked and looked around them, as if just noticing the newcomers trickling in. "Oh, goodness, I wasn't thinking. Of course we'll allow you to get back to your duties."

"No, it's fine, really—"

"Don't be silly. I've taken up far too much of your time already." She accepted Curry's arm before turning back to Colin. "Perhaps later, when things have settled down a bit, we could discuss the newest painting."

The way she emphasized "newest" was subtle, but Colin knew she must be referring to the portrait she was painting of him. Good—he wanted her thinking of the portrait and the kisses they had shared during the sittings. And at that exact moment in time, he didn't care how juvenile such a thought might be.

He dipped his head in agreement and watched them as they headed toward the far end of the gallery, where the royal portrait was displayed. Well, that was a different experience. He couldn't remember a single other time in his life when the uncomfortable rub of jealousy had been felt quite so keenly.

Squaring his shoulders, he turned to resume his duties, only to catch Lord Raleigh's eye. The earl smiled and raised his glass, an odd toast of sorts, before turning his attention back to the Devonshire piece his wife was observing.

What was that about? Had he been watching the exchange? As private a person as Colin was, the thought rankled a bit. When he spoke with Beatrice later, he'd have to keep in mind how many curious gazes might be settled on them.

Gritting his teeth into smilelike proportions, he welcomed the older couple closest to him. He had so much he wanted to say to Beatrice, now more than ever, but first he had to get through the next few hours.

The evening was long, but one of the more pleasant Beatrice had ever spent. Surrounded by Sir Frederick's paintings, speaking with many who actually cared about art, and best of all, being so close to Colin as to be able to sneak glances all night had combined to give her a near dizzy sort of pleasure. It wasn't unlike the effect of a glass or two of champagne, making everything a little more exciting and enhancing the giddiness she felt every time her eyes landed on Colin's dark form.

Captain Curry had departed not long after Prinny's arrival, which had caused the usual hubbub. Mama had left more than an hour earlier with the twins and an exhausted Jane, but Richard volunteered to stay with her as long as she liked. She knew he was her favorite brother for a reason. Now that the royal party had moved on, only a smattering of guests remained.

With Richard engaged in a lively conversation with one of his friends from his club, Beatrice finally made her way over to where Colin stood beside Lord Northup's painting.

His smile was the perfect greeting, quiet and sincere. "At last, I find my treasure."

She would never stop loving the way her stomach flipped when his Scottish-flavored words caressed her ears. "Did you ever lose it?"

"No, I doona think as I did. Though one can never trust a treasure around a pirate."

She laughed lightly, shaking her head at him. "You're forgetting that he's more gentleman than pirate . . . and I'm your *stór*, no one else's."

She'd shocked him. Actually, she'd shocked both of them. Perhaps the negus was stronger than she realized. Not that she minded—it was rather exciting to say such naughty things in such a public place, even if her voice had been much too low for anyone but Colin to hear.

And Colin did hear it. There was no denying the sudden intake of breath or the widening of his pupils. "I doona think I've ever heard more pleasing words in my entire life," he said, keeping his tone casual even as his gaze turned to an alluring smoky gray.

"Does that make you happy, then?"

"More than I could express in a roomful of people. Especially since it so thoroughly echoes the way I feel."

Warmth bubbled up within her, spreading from her fingertips to her cheeks. Seeing him in his element tonight, surrounded by the works of his father, looked to with respect and listened to with interest, she couldn't help but feel that no one else could possibly suit her better. Her gaze dropped to his mouth, with its cupid's bow upper lip and perfectly proportioned lower. She'd studied those lips, drawn and painted them, and explored them with her own.

"Then perhaps you'd like to come by Granville House this week. I may be busy," she said, licking her own lips with sudden nervousness for what she was about to say, "but my brother should be home. I'm quite certain he'd be happy to speak to you, if you were struck by such a desire."

"Desire" was the perfect word to describe the almost molten quality of his gaze. He knew exactly what she was implying. A wave of anxiety almost made her lose her nerve, but something in that heated look made her stand her ground. He was silent for a moment, his chest rising and falling in shallow succession, before swallowing and taking a small step closer. "Beatrice, is that truly your wish?"

"Yes." The single word was breathless, raw in a way that couldn't be mistaken.

He reached forward and slid his hand beneath hers, bringing it to his lips without ever breaking eye contact. "Allow me to bid you good evening, my lady. I look forward to seeing you again *very* soon."

Chapter Nineteen

"Sir Colin Tate, my lord."

At the butler's introduction, the earl, seated in an oversized brown leather chair behind the large dark desk, came to his feet, holding a hand out to Colin.

"Come in. Come in. Have a seat, my good man. May I offer you a fine scotch?" Raleigh seemed to be in exceptionally high spirits, not at all the imposing force Colin half expected. It was a bit jarring, actually, especially given the dark and imposing quality of the study. Warm browns and rich reds filled the space from floor to ceiling, relieved only by the uncovered windows at the back of the room.

The butler shut the door behind him, and taking a fortifying breath, Colin nodded. "Yes, thank you." He settled into one of the chairs facing the massive desk, his spine rigid despite the earl's greeting. He'd waited all of a day before coming. Amazing he had lasted even that long. The night of the gallery opening, he had been debating how best to move forward.

He could have never imagined Beatrice would be the one to do the job for him. Just like that, looking up into his eyes with her fiery, intimate gaze, suggesting that he speak to her brother. It was as if she had waved a wand, granting his greatest wish.

At the credenza, Raleigh filled two crystal tumblers, then handed one to Colin before taking a seat behind the desk. Taking a hearty swig, he leaned back. "I thought I might see you here this week."

"Did you?"

"Absolutely. I have eyes, after all," he said, his lips tipped up in an easy grin. "All right then. Acting on behalf of my absentee father, allow me to ask of you, Sir Colin, what is your business here today?"

Colin's throat tightened and he cleared it, surprised at the force of his nerves. "I'm here today to request your permission, as well as your blessing, for me to ask for Lady Beatrice's hand in marriage."

"As I suspected," Raleigh said with a nod. "Well, I've never done this sort of thing before, but I assume we must first hash through all the proper financial bits and pieces. No, actually, let's do that second. First, let me say that I'm damn glad to hear of your interest. Especially since I believe we understand each other so well."

An oddly jovial threat if Colin had ever heard one. He smiled as well as he could manage and nodded in acceptance of the earl's statement. "Thank you, my lord. And, yes, it is always best to have full understanding of where another stands."

"And though Beatrice will have the final say as to the acceptance of your offer for marriage, it is my opinion that the two of you will suit quite well. Now, then," Raleigh said, setting his drink down and sitting up straight in the chair, assuming a more businesslike tone, "on with the monetary part of the arrangement. Beatrice's dowry has been set at twenty-five thousand pounds. I am aware that you have an estate in Scotland and that you are training to become a barrister. What are your prospects?"

If ever there was a loaded question. Since it probably

wasn't a good idea to start the conversation by saying, "Utterly dreadful," Colin started with the good news. "The estate is quite stable and brings in around two thousand a year. My brother and sister live there now with my grandmother. I have another year at the Inns of Court, but after that I have every expectation of pursuing a career as King's Counsel."

He went on, discussing all of his careful plans that he had spent years developing. He was concise, factual, and clearheaded, wanting to be very sure that Raleigh understood his ambition and character. Raleigh nodded every now and then, allowing him to say his piece.

And then came the part he had been dreading since he got there. Hell, he'd been dreading it since the moment he decided to come to London to find an heiress. Taking a deep, bracing breath, he dove in. "When I arrived in the city, it was with the knowledge that it was time for me to choose a bride. It never occurred to me that Lady Beatrice might be that bride. As far as I could tell, she was—is—above me in almost every way possible."

The earl cracked a smile, but didn't interrupt. Colin gathered he agreed with the sentiment. "But then I came to know her, and I discovered her to be the talented, confident, beautiful woman I had always suspected her to be. What I didn't expect was for her to find something of interest in me. But I believe that she did, and beyond that, I feel that we suit perfectly, in a way I never imagined any woman might. When I am near her, I feel like a better person for it."

His fingers wrapped around the curved wooden armrest of his chair as he willed himself to speak plainly about his situation. "Unfortunately, I did not have the luxury of choosing a wife based on compatibility and mutual affection alone. This is because my father chose to mortgage the estate against a business loan he procured in hopes of starting a successful engraving business. I was unaware of this decision until a month ago, when his creditors arrived at the estate to inform me that the loan will be due in January."

For the first time, the earl's affable facade slipped. "Cannot the business be sold to satisfy the debt?"

Heat crept up Colin's chest, a combination of lingering anger and shame. "The business failed. The property has been sold, as well as the equipment, but much of the original investment has been lost."

"How much is owed at this point?"

"Ten thousand pounds."

Raleigh's jaw clenched at the amount, and he sat back in his chair. Nothing remained of his earlier enthusiasm. "Why don't you sell the estate? I know it's not entailed, and it hasn't even been in the family for long."

"I would happily do just that, but unfortunately, my father agreed to some rather atrocious terms in his enthusiasm to get the business going. He actually signed the estate over to the creditors in trust, so that if the loan defaulted, the creditors get it all."

"Bloody hell."

If that didn't sum up the situation, Colin didn't know what did. "Yes, quite. Which brings me to my offer of marriage. Originally, I had planned to find a bride whose family would be happy to have a baronet. A business transaction of sorts: She would bring the funds necessary to release the estate, and I would be able to offer whatever good standing I have in society. What I didn't plan on was losing my heart to a lady so thoroughly without need of my very minor title."

Raleigh didn't say a word, but clearly he agreed with him. With the worst of it out, Colin sat up a little straighter, looking the man in the eye. "So here is what I propose. It was never my intention to live off of anyone's dowry. The estate's income, combined with what I'll earn when I am a barrister, is more than enough to have a comfortable life. Though I do need the ten thousand to pay off the debt, the rest of the dowry, in its entirety, shall be signed over to my wife in the marriage settlement. I also want you to know that, in addition to the forfeiture of the remaining dowry, it is my intention to gift her my father's studios, in hopes that she will continue to create her beautiful artwork."

Having said all that he'd intended, Colin closed his mouth, settled his hands in his lap, and waited. For a few moments, the only sounds in the room over the pounding of Colin's heart were the ticking of the clock and the distant rumbling of carriage wheels on the street beyond the window. The earl watched him through narrowed eyes, either deciding what to do with him or wishing him to perdition.

Probably the latter.

At last, Raleigh blew out a harsh breath. "Christ." He dragged a hand through his hair, a show of emotion that might have surprised Colin in another man but fit the unconventional earl. "Confound it all, man—why did you have to put me in such a bloody awful position?"

Colin tilted his head in confusion. Of the two of them, Colin was most definitely the one in the bad position. No man wanted to lay bare his family's failures, opening himself up for judgment and rejection. "It was never my intention to cause you difficulty."

The earl sighed with exasperation, crossing his arms over his chest and leveling his disconcertingly clear gaze on Colin. "My whole responsibility in this transaction is to look after my sister's best interest. If she thought for one second you were marrying her for her money—"

"I swear to you I am not. You've heard my plan. No

man would make such a proposal if they wished to marry for money alone."

"*I* believe you."

The statement should have been more reassuring than it was. Perhaps it was the subtle emphasis on the word "I," implying that no one else would.

"The problem is, Beatrice has it in her mind that there is no greater devil than a fortune hunter. She's been hurt in the past, as has one of her friends. I love my sister very much, but sometimes she can get a thought into her head and it can take an act of Parliament to get it out."

"You doona think she would accept me, under the circumstances?"

"I *know* she wouldn't accept you."

Bloody hell. There was no plainer answer than that. His chest ached as if the words had been knives, piercing straight through to his heart. She could never love him. How was that possible, given the strength of the feelings he had for her? And he knew that she had strong feelings for him as well. Had she not practically asked him to ask for her hand? He sat for a moment, absorbing the pain, absorbing the blow to his hopes. Had he not known all along that this was a possible—hell, even likely—outcome?

The thing was, he had foreseen rejection from her brother, but not from her. He needed to regroup, to have some time to sort out what the hell to do next. It wasn't something he could do with Raleigh's keen gaze lying heavy on him. He started to stand, but the earl held up a hand.

"Stay where you are."

In general, he didn't allow himself to be commanded by another man, but something in Raleigh's tone had him obeying.

"The reason why you have managed to put me in a

rather shit position is because I know she won't accept your suit, given the circumstances of your finances, but I also know how she feels about you."

Colin's face was completely impassive. He knew because he was concentrating every ounce of his willpower to accomplish just that. Everything inside him wanted to beg Raleigh to expound, to tell him exactly how Beatrice felt. His ribs ached with the force of emotion ricocheting beneath them. With a neutrality born from his years taking his meals at the Inn, he said, "Oh?"

"I have to say, I think you are a damn good match for her. I think you showed honor in the way you approached the subject of your finances and a clear determination to keep her best interests at heart. Most important, I've seen the two of you together."

The sly look he gave Colin left him feeling completely exposed. What had he seen? Colin prided himself on his impassive facade—never revealing anything he didn't intend to. Perhaps there was one emotion that simply couldn't be hidden: love.

Raleigh shifted back in his chair, putting one hand to his chin and tapping the other on the gleaming surface of the desk. "I want my sister to be happy, Tate. I know what I've seen, but let me leave nothing to chance. Do you love her?"

"Yes." No hesitation. None needed.

"Then I will offer you this: You may ask for her hand in marriage, but only under one condition."

Caution and prudency went straight out the window as hope flared to life once more. "Name it."

"Do not, under any circumstances, let her know about this whole mortgage business."

Colin blinked. Surely he had misheard the earl. "You wish for me to lie to her?"

"No, of course not. If she should ever say to you, 'Sir Colin, is your estate saddled with debt that can only be paid off with the use of my dowry?' then obviously you should answer truthfully."

So in other words, Raleigh wished for Colin to continue what he had been doing. Withholding the truth unless explicitly asked. The thought of it weighed heavy in his stomach, but what other choice did he have? The earl was offering him a way to be with the woman he loved and, by extension, save the estate for the family he loved.

"I don't know what to say."

"There is no need to decide anything now. I just wish for you to know this: I've never seen my sister quite so happy as when she is with you. The point is, I don't want anyone to stand in the way of her happiness—including herself. I know how miserable a person can be when they decide to act with their head instead of their heart. It's not a fate that I wish her to endure.

"From what I can tell, your financial distress is not of your making and can be fixed in short order. With any luck, Bea will be so pleased with the marriage settlement, she'll never question what happens with the ten thousand."

Coming to his feet, Colin offered the earl a curt nod. "Thank you for your time, your suggestion, and your faith in me. I can assure you it is not misguided."

Raleigh tipped his head. "I'm counting on it."

Colin turned and made his way to the door, feeling the earl's gaze on his back the entire time. Just as his fingers touched the small brass knob, the earl said, "And, Sir Colin?"

He knew that had gone too well. Turning, he lifted a questioning brow.

"If I find that you are less than sincere in any of your intentions, I don't care if I am just shy of the right of peer privilege. I *will* kill you." The threat, delivered with a calm smile, was accompanied by dead-serious blue eyes.

"Duly noted."

Chapter Twenty

If she never saw the inside of a modiste shop again, it would be too soon.

Beatrice sighed in relief when the carriage pulled to a stop in front of the black lacquer door of Granville House.

"I still think there was time to visit one more shop," Carolyn said, straightening her bonnet as they waited for the door to open.

Beatrice barely had the strength to roll her eyes. "If six shops weren't enough to find what you were looking for, I don't imagine another would make much difference. Besides, Mama would have our heads if we stayed one minute after five."

"Which makes it all the more intriguing," Jocelyn replied, flashing a devilish grin. "If five o'clock is when the gentlemen come out to play, then I'd say it's the perfect time for one to lose track of ten or fifteen minutes in a shop with an exceptionally large front window, don't you?"

The door swung open before Beatrice could properly scold her, so she settled for a brief heavenward glance, with a shake of her head thrown in for good measure. She let her sisters disembark first, waiting patiently while they gathered their reticules and skirts.

Lord, but she could already tell they were going to be trouble next Season. Half the words spoken today had been dedicated to the gentlemen at the gallery opening last night. Actually, it was more like three-quarters.

But for the first time, Beatrice had had absolutely no interest in discussing the gentlemen of the *ton*. She'd seen the other men there and had even spoken with several, but there was nothing about them that interested her any longer.

Which, in a roundabout way, explained why the day had been so tedious. She had exactly one man on her mind, and the whole time she was out, she was wondering if he would actually speak to her brother. She pressed her hand against her chest to combat the fresh wave of nerves that assailed her at the mere thought of such a thing.

She had been beyond bold by suggesting he do so, but why shouldn't she have a hand in her future? Isn't that what she had been encouraging with her letters to the magazine? For women to stop looking to others and instead take matters into their own hands?

When both girls had exited the closed carriage, she scooted to the edge, taking care to gather her skirts so they didn't trip her. With her eyes on the step, she grasped the gloved hand waiting to assist her. But instead of providing impassive support, the servant's hand returned her grasp, and she knew at once it wasn't a servant.

Colin!

Her eyes darted up, meeting his with the sort of flash one expected during a lightning storm. She braced for the thunder and felt it all through her body, through every last fiber of her being.

He was here. He was smiling unabashedly at her, and his hand was holding hers as though it were a lifeline. Had he spoken to her brother? He had to have—

otherwise he could have never been so forward, here in the open in front of her home. Her heart pounded in her chest as she allowed him to guide her to solid ground. At least it was supposed to be solid. She could have been standing on the deck of a ship at sea for all the steadiness she felt.

With her sisters looking on and them standing practically in the middle of St. James's Square, she knew she should say something. Wetting her lips, she smiled up at him, letting her fingers drag against his as she released his hold. "Good afternoon, Sir Colin."

"Good afternoon." His voice was deep and rich and as delicious as warm chocolate. "I was just leaving when your carriage pulled up. I hope you don't mind that I wished to say hello."

He was just leaving? Even in her mind, the question came out like a squeak. Then he *had* to have spoken with Richard. "Well, if you have a few moments to spare, perhaps you would join us for tea?"

Beside her, Carolyn cocked her head to the side. "But we just had tea at—"

"*Carolyn*," Beatrice interrupted, "why don't you let them know that a tray will be needed in the drawing room?"

Her sister blinked, then—bless her—nodded and went to do her bidding. Beatrice turned to Jocelyn next, whose gaze seemed to miss nothing. "Would you mind fetching Mama and inquiring if she'd like to join us?"

"Certainly. Is there anything else you'll be needing, my lady?"

Now was not the moment to be amused by her sister's cheek. Bea widened her eyes in warning at the girl, who merely chuckled before retreating into the house. In the relative privacy of the front stoop, Beatrice paused long enough to smile up at Colin, wishing she could clasp hands with him again. "You came."

He nodded, the sharp angles of his jaw softening as he looked down at her. "I did."

She wanted to say more, but Finnington had the door open and waiting. They paused to shed their coats, then walked together across the entry hall and up the grand staircase. A footman, blast the man, followed up behind them, intent on one duty or another, so she couldn't very well say more to Colin. When they reached the gold-and-cream drawing room, Beatrice drew up short.

"What is it?" Colin asked, standing just behind her, close enough for her to catch a hint of his perfect scent.

"No one's here. How odd."

He slid his hand down her arm, and she looked up to him in surprise. "Not so very odd, I think," he said, his breath warming the sensitive skin of her neck. He stepped forward, lightly pulling her into the room behind him.

Butterflies roared to life in her stomach as he turned, facing her fully and joining hands with hers. The door clicked closed behind her, and she started in surprise. Had a servant pulled it shut? "The door . . ."

"Is exactly as it should be. There are only a few times in life when such a thing is perfectly acceptable, and this just happens to be one of them. Beatrice," he said, then shook his head. "Oh, to hell with it."

He tugged her full against him, in broad daylight in her own drawing room. He wasted no time in taking advantage of the position, leaning down to press his lips fully across hers in a quick but searing kiss. "There," he said, his voice raspy as he pulled away. "I feel much better."

She grinned, happiness covering her like a warm blanket. "That makes two of us. I've wanted to do that for days. Now, Sir Colin, was there something you wanted to say?"

"Marry me, *a stór.*"

All the passion in the world, wrapped up into four little words. No flowery prose, no odes to her beauty or talk of their compatibility—just a pure, simple, perfect entreaty.

One that needed only one word in response. "Yes."

He closed his eyes, breathing a ragged breath before opening them once more. "Yes?"

She nodded. "Yes."

Without warning, he scooped her up in his arms and spun her around as though she weighed no more than a rag doll. She giggled in delight, pure joy radiating from her heart as if it were the sun itself. When he set her down again, his mouth crashed down on hers, swallowing her laughter, sharing it just as they would soon share everything.

The kiss was something different from before. It was possessive, and fierce, and fiery in a way she would like to think she could be but could never achieve without him. His hands came to either side of her face, cupping her jaw as if she were made of the most delicate of porcelains. Breaking the kiss, he pressed his forehead against hers. "Can I say something without you thinking me a complete loon?"

She closed her eyes and nodded once. He could say anything if he would continue to hold her just like this.

"I've fallen in love with you, Beatrice Moore."

Her heart skipped two full beats at the pronouncement, and she pulled away to look him in the eye. His gaze held a wealth of emotion, silvery and steely and still somehow soft.

"Thank goodness I'm not the only one," she breathed.

Colin had never heard sweeter words in his whole life. She loved him! All the worries about the dowry, Raleigh's condition, and his own misgivings seemed to melt away in an instant. Nothing in the world mattered except this: He loved Beatrice, and she loved him.

With a soft, low growl, his lips found hers again, more insistent than ever. He could feel her hammering pulse beneath his fingers, matching his own racing heartbeat. They were so close as to almost seem as one. Feeling reckless, he lifted her in his arms. She squeaked in surprise, but didn't break the kiss, instead pressing against him that much more.

He closed the distance to the sofa in three sure steps, then lowered them both to the cushions until she was square in his lap. The weight of her against his chest and thighs was intoxicating, and he had the sudden image of her naked, her honey hair cascading down her shoulders and across his bare skin.

Everything about her—her smell, her taste, her size, and even her voice—seemed custom-made to drive him mad. He wrapped both his arms fully around her, pressing her more snugly against him. She gave a breathy little moan, and he smiled against her lips.

He could make her happy. He knew it without doubt. She could have her painting and do with her money whatever she desired. They could have as many children as would suit her, and they would always, always have this perfect passion between them. Raleigh was right—there was no reason to ruin what they had for something that wouldn't even be an issue after the wedding. What mattered was that he loved her, and damned if she didn't love him as well.

An odd tapping noise broke through his muddled senses, and he paused, his lips pressed still against hers as he listened. Footsteps! Beatrice must have realized it at the exact moment he did, because she sprang from his lap as if shot from a cannon.

She shook out her skirts and tugged at the wrinkles,

desperately trying to put herself to rights. She looked charming as hell, all rumpled and red-lipped, and he couldn't help but smile. "How do I look? And good heavens, why are you looking at me like that?"

The footsteps, inordinately loud and slow, had almost reached the door. "It's all right, my love. They know that I was here to ask for your hand. I think a little kissing is to be expected."

The emotions on her face scrolled from worry, to shock, to surprise, to impish delight. He came to his feet, straightening his jacket and planting a kiss on her nose. "Clearly they are giving us ample warning as to their presence."

She grinned, shaking her head as the person outside the door jiggled the knob as if they had never worked such a contraption before. By the time the door swung open—slowly—they were standing side by side, her hand cradled in the crook of his arm.

Lady Granville looked between them, her whole face glowing with pleasure. "Well, I assume a question has been asked and answered?"

"What question?" Beatrice asked, tilting her head in wonderment.

The marchioness drew back in surprise, her gray eyes rounding. "Er, well, I—"

"I'm only teasing, Mama. Yes, a question has been asked and answered."

"And?"

Beatrice squeezed his arm, pulling them more tightly together. "The answer was a most emphatic yes."

Three feminine shouts of joy rang from the corridor, and the twins and Lady Raleigh poured into the room. There was laughter and hugs and plenty of congratulations to go around. The earl came to join in the celebrations, ringing for a celebratory round of sherry for the ladies and port for the two men.

Once everything had calmed a bit, Lady Granville settled onto the sofa and took a small sip of her drink. "Of course, we mustn't make any announcements until your father and sister have been notified."

"I can only imagine how surprised they will be," Beatrice said, her eyes dancing with happiness.

"Not so very surprised, perhaps." The marchioness grinned, her impish expression making her look years younger. "At least not your father."

"Mama," Beatrice exclaimed, her hand going to her mouth as she laughed. "What did you write him?"

"I may have mentioned that there was a certain young gentleman who had caught your interest . . . and that the gentleman in question appeared to reciprocate."

A very encouraging sign, indeed. If her mother had taken enough note to write to Granville about him, she must have seen something between them. Just as Raleigh had. The lingering uneasiness about his deception eased that much more, and he settled back into the cushions of the cream-colored sofa, silently observing as the women discussed things like flowers and gowns.

"When would you like to have the wedding, Sir Colin?"

Immediately. The sooner they were wed, the sooner he could dispatch with the circling creditors and be done with the worry of Beatrice asking about the use of the dowry. "Sooner rather than later, I would think. Perhaps in the New Year, after the celebrations of Christmas are behind us."

Chapter Twenty-one

The air was cold but not biting, the wind gentle enough to stir the multihued fallen leaves along the path, but not so much as to sting the exposed skin of Colin's face. The sun slipped out intermittently as the low clouds rolled overhead.

In other words, it was perfect. Since it wasn't raining, he could escape to Hyde Park with Beatrice without raising any eyebrows, yet it was cold enough to keep most from the grounds. Colin adjusted his hand, pressing Beatrice's fingers more firmly against his arm as they strolled along the nearly deserted banks of the Serpentine. With all the excitement surrounding the betrothal, they had had almost no time for just the two of them, and it was driving him mad.

He felt relaxed, at peace in a way he hadn't been since the moment he knew of his father's downfall. He had not only accomplished what he had set out to do, but he hadn't compromised his own heart to do so. He glanced down at Beatrice, smiling at her red-tipped nose and rosy cheeks. She was a thousand times better than he had hoped for, a million times better than he deserved. And yet she was his.

Already this morning they had talked of the future—of having their families meet for the first time, of traveling to Italy for their honeymoon in order to tour the works of the old masters, and of renting a small town house here in London as he completed his last year at Lincoln's Inn.

But there was one last thing he wanted to do just for her. "I daresay we'll have trouble finding a place with as nice a studio as you have now."

She gave a little shrug, unconcerned. "I don't mind. I can always visit Granville House to use it if I need to."

"Yes, but I thought perhaps you might wish for a place just for you. So I visited my solicitor today and had him extend the lease on Father's studio for another year."

She grinned up at him, her blue eyes putting the rippling water of the Serpentine to shame. "I was hoping you'd say that."

"You were? And here I thought it would be a surprise."

"I covet that space far too much to leave such a thing to chance. I was prepared to beg if necessary."

"Is that a fact?" he said, his eyebrows raised.

"Indeed. Fortunately for me, you saved me the trouble." She gave him a teasing wink, pleased with herself.

"Well fine, then. But in the future, I fully intend to make you work for what you want."

"Do you?" she said, raising a challenging eyebrow. "Well, do be careful, because I can very easily do the same to you."

"You think so?"

She nodded imperiously, lifting her chin as though she just knew he would be putty in her hands. He loved how irreverent she could be. He would have enough seriousness in his life with his chosen career—knowing he would come home to her every day filled a part of him that had been empty almost his whole life.

"And what if it's something you want as well? After

all, I want nothing more than to make you happy. Would you still make things difficult for me?"

"Ah, a woman's prerogative, remember? Yes, I may very well make you work for something, even if I want it as well. It's good not to always get what you want, when you want it. Wouldn't you agree?" Her grin was pure cheek.

"Oh sure, but I doona think you'd be able to follow through. A woman's prerogative is generally exactly that: to have what she wants, exactly when she wants it."

She scoffed, lifting a shoulder. "Clearly you don't know me very well if you don't think I'll follow through."

Casually, he glanced around, checking to see who might be able to see them. Few people were braving the cold, none of whom seemed to be paying them any mind.

Quickly, so as to catch her off guard, he whisked her from the path and into a copse of weeping willows. Sliding his arm from beneath her fingers until he could clasp her hand in his, he slipped between the cascading branches of the largest tree, tugging her in behind him. The tree's limbs flowed like a waterfall down to the earth, shielding them from both the elements and any prying eyes. Golden light filtered through the autumn leaves and shimmered in Beatrice's widened eyes.

"Colin!" she gasped, covering her open mouth with her hand. "What on earth are you doing?"

"Putting your theory to the test." He turned to face her fully, savoring the thrill of being well and truly alone with her. The feeling of being a little reckless, carefree even, was as intoxicating as the very best scotch. Just like the night they had met, she looked every bit the nymph in this light, as ethereal and beautiful as anything he'd ever seen.

He reached out and untied the ribbons of her bonnet, then gently pulled it away. She neither helped nor hindered; she merely watched him with the bemused expression of one unsure of what was happening, but unwilling to stop it.

Pulling his own hat off, he set them both on the ground before resituating himself directly in front of her, close enough to smell the slightest hint of lilac on the cold air. He soaked in the moment, savoring the growing desire that spread with every beat of his heart.

"There now," he said, allowing a hint of challenge to lift the corners of his lips. "Make me work for what I want."

Beatrice drew a short breath, taken aback by his command. Her heart, not yet recovered from their sudden dash, pounded that much harder at the seductive look in his eyes and the utter wickedness of being alone in a public place with him. For heaven's sake, someone could walk right by them and not even know they were there.

She licked her lips, looking up into his eyes, the same dark color as the web of branches around them. "And what is it that you want?"

"I should hope you'd know the answer to that by now, sweet Beatrice." He stepped closer still, his movements slow and deliberate. "I want nothing on earth so much as I want you."

Her eyes fluttered closed at the pleasure of his words as she exhaled. Opening them to peer up at him once more, she said, "But you already have me." Her voice was breathy, quiet.

"So you're prepared to relent, just like that?" He was teasing her, not only with his words, but with his closeness, making it hard for her to think straight.

"Of course not," she said, rallying. "I never give in."

He clasped his hands behind him and walked in a small semicircle, coming to stand just behind her. He leaned forward until his mouth was close enough to her ear that she could feel the warmth of his breath. "Prove it," he murmured, daring her to play along. "I want you to kiss me. Let me see if I can make that happen."

She loved this side of him, when the mischievousness within him outweighed the practical. She nodded, pressing her eyes closed and concentrating on the warmth of his skin mere inches from hers. Every nerve in her body seemed attuned to him, waiting for the moment he would touch her.

Only he didn't.

Instead, he slowly exhaled, stirring the fine hairs at her nape and sending hot air fanning across her neck. She shivered; she couldn't help it, even as she knew it was exactly what he wanted.

He chuckled softly, knowing he affected her. Oh no, she wasn't going to let him win that easily. Taking a deep breath, she straightened both her spine and her resolve, then tilted her head to the right, granting him better access. Challenging him.

It was madness, standing there beneath a tree in broad daylight, denying her betrothed the kiss she already wanted. The feelings he stirred within her, the heady rush of emotion and anticipation was at once so much better and far worse than simply giving in to her desire.

After a rustle of fabric behind her, she felt the warmth of his bare skin as he drew a finger down the length of her jaw. He was cheating, taking off his glove like that.

"Such beautiful skin. As pure as silk and twice as soft." Now he was using his most effective weapon— that mesmerizing accent of his.

Colin let his fingertip trail down the column of her throat and along the edge of her cashmere shawl. He pulled away, and she almost protested until his hands found her waist and slowly, inexorably, pulled her to him. When she was oh so lightly pressed against his chest, he leaned down and nuzzled the sensitive skin just below her ear.

Good heavens, she could hardly breathe and he hadn't even touched his lips to her yet.

"I love how perfectly petite you are. You fit against me as if we were molded for each other. See how well my hands fit your waist?"

Yes, she did. His touch was still feather light, though, and she longed to feel him embrace her solidly, pulling her against him.

When his lips finally touched her neck, she sucked in a lungful of air, squeezing her eyes shut against the need to turn to him, to give him her lips and have him kiss her properly. Each kiss seemed lighter than the one before, so soft he could have been trailing her finest paintbrush across her skin. Even so, she felt every one through her whole body, as if a thread wound from each spot, and each kiss, each pull of the thread made her fingers and toes curl.

It was the sweetest torture she could have ever imagined.

"I swear, *a stór*, you taste every bit as good as you smell." His whispered words were as sweet as a caress, and she bit her lip against the need to turn around.

His lips found her earlobe, a spot she had never considered anyplace of note. She was wrong. Lord have mercy, was she wrong. Of its own volition, her head tilted toward him, silently begging for more. He obliged, scraping the incredibly sensitive skin with his teeth.

And she was lost.

She turned to him, her arms wrapping around his neck as she pressed her lips hard against his. He didn't hold back, didn't torture her with any more feather-light touches. Instead, his arms went fully around her waist, pulling her to him so tightly that her feet left the ground.

She no longer felt the cold, no longer heard the birds or smelled the leaves. All there was in the world was the heat of his body, his scent, his strength, his soul.

By the time he set her down, they were both panting, leaning against each other as they tried to catch their breath.

After a moment, he sighed and smiled down at her. "Havers, lass, perhaps we should get back before I decide to whisk you away to Gretna Green and be done with it."

She didn't even try to stop the giddy grin that came to her lips. Yes, they should definitely get back, because at this rate, she might just let him.

She wasn't going to make it. Yes, Beatrice knew that she should wait to tell anyone about the betrothal until Papa and Evie had been properly notified, but she was fairly dying with the need to tell someone about it. She couldn't possibly share all that had transpired between her and Colin, but at least she could share her happiness.

Which, incidentally, was how she came to find herself being shown into Sophie's drawing room the very next day.

"Beatrice!" her friend exclaimed, her dark, curly brown hair fluttering about as she rushed to greet her. She was as bright and sunny as her lemon-colored gown, holding her hands out in greeting. "I'm so glad to see you. I should have known you'd come the moment I laid eyes on it this morning."

It? Beatrice came up short, all thoughts of her good news falling by the wayside. "Laid eyes on what?"

Sophie looked at her as if her dress were on backward. "Whatever do you mean, 'laid eyes on what?' What else? *A Proper Young Lady's Fashion Companion*, of course. You must have seen the second letter that was printed there."

How could she have possibly forgotten that it would be out today? It seemed like a lifetime ago that she had written the letter and drawn the cartoon. But, having already acted as though she had no idea what Sophie was talking about, Bea shook her head. "My copy must have been filched by my sisters. What does it say?"

Sophie gaped at her. "Truly? Do you mean I actually know something before you do? Gracious, what a red-letter day. And I can't possibly do it justice from memory. Give me just a moment and I'll go fetch it."

She hurried away, nearly knocking over a spindly little side table in her haste. Red-letter day, indeed. Biting her lip, Bea settled on the settee beside the fireplace, extending her hands to the warmth. She couldn't wait to see the next installment. She was doubly happy now that she had finished it while she was still so furious at Mr. Godfrey. With the sort of bliss currently flowing through her veins, she doubted she could have gotten across the force of her emotion on the subject.

The patter of Sophie's slippered feet on the wood floor heralded her return. "This one is quite a bit bolder than last time—just wait until you see it. There is absolutely no possible way this isn't Mr. Godfrey."

She plopped down on the cushions beside Beatrice and thrust the magazine into her waiting hands. Ignoring the letter, Bea's eyes went directly to the cartoon, which filled the entire lower half of the page. "I do believe you're right," she murmured, mainly because she could tell Sophie was waiting for her to say something.

"Of course I'm right—even a blind person could see the resemblance. Well, not a *blind* person, but certainly someone exceptionally shortsighted. His features are hardly even caricatured." She swept a finger over the perfect likeness of his hair and facial features, all of which Monsieur Allard had painstakingly transcribed in the etching.

"Indeed," Beatrice replied absently, studying the scene on the page before her. In it, two men were synchronizing their watches, all the while leering at a young woman standing nearby. The caption read, *Give me three minutes to get her alone and then pretend to stumble upon us. By the end of the night, her dowry will be as good as lining my pockets.*

"He must be absolutely livid to be represented this way. Do you think this is based on something that actually happened? Oh," Sophie exclaimed, her hand going to her mouth as her eyes widened, "do you think the author is getting revenge? How utterly scandalous!"

"I don't think it is so much revenge as the man getting what he deserved."

Sophie's brow knitted. "Isn't that revenge? I mean, if he did something truly dreadful and the victim wanted him to be made to suffer for the offense, isn't that actually the definition of revenge?"

She did have a point. "I suppose you are right. Well, if it is revenge, then I commend the author for using the experience for helping others."

Sophie grasped her arm, leaning forward as if she had the most delicious of *on-dits* to share. "Did you hear then? About Miss Briggs?"

Drat it all, had she managed to miss *two* major events? This whole betrothal business seemed to be hindering her normal vigilance. "What happened with Miss Briggs?"

"Beatrice! You're supposed to be the one who knows everything. I shan't know what to do with myself if our roles were suddenly reversed. Although, if that were the case, then wouldn't I already have known it to be so?"

"Sophie!"

"Sorry, sorry. All right, Miss Briggs. My sister— Sarah, that is; the others are much too young to have any good gossip—told me that Miss Briggs told Miss Chamberlain that she figured out from advice from the last letter that Lord Jenson was only asking the very highest dowered—is that a word? Anyway, he was asking only the ladies with the highest dowries to dance.

"Normally, she wouldn't have minded such a thing, since she freely admits that her father hopes to purchase a nice title for the family, but she had actually quite liked Lord Jenson. Better to have seen his motives now than for her to have fallen for the man only to discover he was after her purse."

"Are you telling me," Beatrice said, trying to separate the meat of the story from all of her asides, "that Miss Briggs feels that the first letter saved her from the attentions of a fortune hunter?"

Sophie nodded, her brown eyes alight with the joy of having imparted information that Beatrice hadn't already known.

"Well, isn't that nice?" A grossly underwhelming summation of how she really was feeling. She had done it! Her words had saved an heiress's heart. Instead of the mildly interested smile she offered her friend, she wanted to laugh with delight, to throw her hands up and declare victory for her fellow debutante.

"Yes, I'd say so. Heaven knows I'd never make it

married to a man who didn't love me. Not that I have to worry about a fortune hunter. It's not as though we have pockets to let, but we certainly aren't worth targeting. Not like you, you poor thing." Sophie wrinkled her nose. "You must be constantly fighting off unwanted attention."

"Well, it certainly won't be a problem after this week." She said it casually, but excitement once again sprang to life within her.

"Why ever not?"

"Because I'm getting married."

"*What?*" Sophie's already-high voice went up an entire octave. "Why didn't you tell me?" She grabbed Beatrice's hand and jumped from the settee, pulling them both to their feet without any care for decorum. Swallowing her in an impromptu hug, Sophie squeezed her before setting her away. "I don't care how dreadfully familiar that was, I'm just so happy for you I could bust. You must tell me, who is your betrothed?"

"I can't say just yet. We still are waiting until we can get word to Papa and Evie. But I am very, very pleased."

"It wouldn't happen to be a certain painter's son, would it? He was quite concerned for you at the musicale."

At the mere thought of the man, Beatrice melted a bit, her insides going all soft and warm. She lifted her shoulders, a secretive smile curving her lips. "I can neither confirm nor deny."

"Of course you can. Either nod your head for yes or shake it for no. It's quite simple, really." She looked to Beatrice with beseeching eyes, begging to be let in on the secret.

"Only under threat of death, I'm afraid. But in a few more days, all will be revealed."

"You dreadful tease, you. Very well, have your secrets. But tell me, is it a love match?"

She looked so hopeful, so invested in the romance of it all that Beatrice couldn't help but indulge her.

"As a matter of fact, it is."

"It's a damn good thing you are already betrothed."

"On that, we agree," Colin said, not even looking up as he spread marmalade over his toast. "But in general, 'Good morning' is the proper way to greet one's family."

Setting his knife down, he took a bite of his breakfast and winked at his cousin. John shook his head and dropped a magazine beside Colin's plate. "Good morning." Snagging a sweet bun from the sideboard behind them, he pulled out the chair at Colin's left and took a seat.

"Good morning to you as well," Colin replied, the good cheer of the last several days still coloring his tone. With his toast in one hand, Colin picked up the periodical with the other. "Reading ladies' magazines again, I see."

"Very funny. I find myself in awe of the brashness of this person. And the magazine itself, for that matter."

He skimmed the letter first, catching words like "fortune hunters," "preying," and "innocents." As before, the author was providing possible ways to identify a nefarious fortune hunter, the very worst villain, in the humble author's opinion. In closing, it read: *At least a highwayman robs only of possessions. A fortune hunter robs a woman of her money, her dignity, and her hopes for a contented future.*

Honestly, this woman was given to dramatics. Had she not thought to consider that some who seek fortunes do so with the best of intentions? She had no idea of the circumstances some may be faced with. She was probably some pampered heiress, sitting in her ivory tower with her jewels and morning chocolate, looking down upon all those whose lots in life were less fortunate.

"A bit extreme, I think."

"Have you gotten to the engraving yet? Then we'll talk extremes."

Raising an eyebrow, Colin turned his attention to the drawing. The lines were bolder this time, the figures more realistically portrayed. As he took in the three figures and the finely detailed background, a sliver of dread worked its way between his ribs, like the slow winding of a silken ribbon being tied into an inescapable knot. There was no mistaking Godfrey this time—he couldn't have been more plainly portrayed if he had posed for the thing.

But it was worse than that. It was the all too familiar balcony, the scene from a night he would rather forget. Synchronized watches, the hooked nose of Mr. Jones—all of it was there, as if plucked from his memory.

Or drawn by another who was there.

Beatrice. Muttering a curse, he dropped the uneaten portion of his toast on his plate and came to his feet.

"Like I said, it's a good thing you are betrothed. Someone in the *ton* is out to expose those intent on securing a well-dowered wife. I'd say you are damned fortunate, old man."

Fortunate? Colin had never felt less fortunate in his life. He had known, thanks to Raleigh, of Beatrice's clear aversion of fortune hunters, but he never imagined her revulsion was so strong as to prompt her to write the letters. "Indeed. Now, if you will excuse me, I have rather a lot to attend to today. Good day."

Her immense dislike of men like him wasn't even the whole problem. In writing this last letter, she opened herself up for Godfrey to recognize her as the author. Only three people had been privy to the scene. It wouldn't take the man long to put together which of the two of them was the disgruntled debutant.

Stuffing the magazine into his jacket, he paused long enough to collect his hat and greatcoat before heading out into the frosty November morning. It might be entirely too early in the morning for society's unwritten rules, but he hardly gave a damn. He had to see Beatrice, and he intended to do so at once.

Chapter Twenty-two

The one true advantage to Granville House over Hertford Hall was that the morning sun, on those rare cloudless days, seemed to shine through the haze over the city differently than it did in the country, creating a soft, diffused pink-tinged light that seemed to glow in Beatrice's studio.

On mornings like this, the inspiration was so heady, she could hardly seem to paint fast enough. Each stroke felt exactly right, every line just so—it was as if someone else guided her hand. She was so intent on her work, she didn't hear the quiet clip of footsteps until they were practically at her door. Turning Colin's portrait away from where it could be seen from the doorway, she slipped around toward another painting when the scratch at the door came.

When she bade them to enter, Finnington pushed open the door and dipped his head. "Pardon the interruption of your studio time, my lady, but I thought you might like to know that Sir Colin has arrived and is waiting in the drawing room."

Colin? Her eyes darted to the clock. She hadn't lost track of time—it was only eleven o'clock. "Thank you, Finnington. I'll be down in ten minutes." She waited until the door clicked shut again before yanking off her apron and scrubbing at the paint spots on her fingers. If he was here this early, it was either an exceedingly good thing or a terribly bad thing.

Eleven minutes later, with a fresh gown and tidied hair in place, she paused outside the drawing room door, drew a steadying breath to slow her pounding heartbeat, and glided into the room.

Colin stood by the window, his arms crossed as he looked out onto the square. She stopped just inside the room, watching him while he wasn't yet aware of her presence. He looked . . . striking. His black hair, glossy in the late-morning sun, was combed back from his forehead. The sharp line of his jaw was even harsher than usual, the muscles tensed. So somber and serious—exactly the way she imagined he would look in a courtroom.

He looked up suddenly, his gaze going straight to her. The sternness didn't leave altogether, but his brow relaxed considerably, and he held out a hand to her. "Good morning."

The music of his voice so early in the day was like an unexpected present, tied with a satin bow and set in her lap. She was definitely going to like waking up to him each morning.

She went to him, a slight blush heating her cheeks and a not so slight grin on her lips. "Good morning to you as well." Lifting onto her toes, she kissed him full on the lips. "To what do I owe the pleasure of your morning visit? And how can I make it happen again?"

He chuckled reluctantly, as if wanting to remain stern, but unable to do so. Good. If he was going to surprise her for a visit, she wanted it to be on good terms.

"I'd have come earlier, if I had known it was your wish. As it happens," he said, his voice reverting to Serious Colin, "I came after my breakfast was interrupted with a certain magazine being dropped on my plate."

Beatrice's enthusiasm slipped, sliding backward toward caution. "Oh?"

He reached into his jacket and extracted a rather rumpled copy of *A Proper Young Lady's Fashion Companion*. "Imagine my surprise when I opened it this morning."

His voice was soft, not at all accusing. How best to proceed? He didn't seem angry or censorious, but clearly he wasn't happy. Now that he was so close, she could see the faint lines creasing the skin surrounding his eyes. She accepted the magazine, looking over her handiwork once more. "Recognize my superior drawing skills, did you?" Her words were light and teasing even as worry tightened her throat. There was no telling what he would say.

"I recognized something, to be sure."

"Sir Godfrey?"

"Him, the background, the point of the scene." He shook his head, running a hand at the back of his neck. "Did you not consider that he would see this? He'd know in moments that it was one of the two of us, and we all know I am not the artist of my family."

Dread coiled within her, just like when she first realized that she had unintentionally drawn Mr. Godfrey in the last letter. She lifted her chin. "I don't know about that. All I know is that he had tried to ruin my life—and very nearly succeeded." The familiar fire of righteous anger sparked to life within her as she looked at the scene again. "So what if he recognizes me? If he says anything, it will only be confirming that he is a heartless fortune hunter."

"And once he sees this, do you think he will be feeling particularly rational about it?"

She put a hand to her middle to try to soothe the building turmoil. She wasn't wrong. Perhaps imprudent, but not wrong. "And will you be ashamed of me if he does?" Her chin hitched up a bit higher, an almost unconscious defense.

He looked down at her, frustration dulling his stony gaze. With a sigh, he reached for her hand, entwining his fingers with hers. "Never, *a stór*. But worry and shame are two very different things. I doona want you to be hurt if Godfrey should open his mouth."

The warmth of his touch soaked into her skin, calming her. "I'm making a difference for the ladies of the *ton*, Colin. If it can help someone avoid a similar trap, then I can handle a bit of scandal."

"A bit of scandal? Practically naming a well-liked son of a peer as a villain in a publication distributed to half the manors, halls, and mansions in England may qualify as something more than a bit."

He was very good at putting things in a way that made them sound much worse than they were. She hoped. "I still stand behind it. I'm proud of it, actually. I had hoped you might be as well."

He made no effort to hide his disbelief. "You were planning on telling me, then?"

"Yes, of course." She paused, tilting her head. "Someday, anyway." She grinned impishly, a sly, close-mouthed upturning of her lips designed to elicit at least a small smile from him.

"Someday? You mean when we're old and gray and I haven't the strength to chastise you?"

"Something like that."

Offering a very slight smile, he pulled her to him, slow but steady. "I'm fairly certain there is a statute of limitations on how long after an incident a confession holds value."

"Well, there must be some mystery between us. How else are we to keep life interesting?"

"Somehow," he said, dropping a soft, altogether too quick kiss on her upturned lips, "I doona think that will be a problem for the two of us."

"I—" She paused, a sound from below catching her attention. "What was that?" She pulled away from him, hating the loss of his warmth but too curious not to investigate the muffled noises arising from beyond the partially closed door.

"What—"

"Shh!" She put her finger to her lips, dashing on the toes of her slippers for the door. She could hear voices, both male and female, rising from the entry hall below. The echo on the marble was distorting the words, making it impossible to discern what anyone was saying— or who was saying it, for that matter.

Grasping the knob, she pulled it open and poked her head out. A servant dashed by, rushing toward the entry hall and all of the commotion below. Just as the footman descended the stairs, someone came up in the opposite direction. All at once, Beatrice recognized the blond woman ascending the last few steps, and she gasped in surprise.

"Evie!"

Beatrice hadn't been exaggerating when she had warned Colin of just how overwhelming her family could be when they were all together. Within the space of ten minutes, he went from having an intimate discussion with his betrothed to being swallowed up by the chaos of introductions to her sister, brother-in-law, niece, and, most unnerving of all, her father.

For someone who had been traveling for a day and a half, the marquis looked remarkably well put together. His graying hair was combed back from his forehead, revealing slightly tanned skin and a pair of piercing blue eyes, not so very different from Raleigh's. He exuded authority as some might wear cologne. When they had been introduced, he had eyed Colin up and down as if surmising his worth in a single glance.

Unnerving, even for someone who was studying to be subjected to exactly that sort of perusal for the rest of his career.

After five minutes of chatter, Granville had put a hand to Colin's shoulder. "Let's have a talk, shall we?"

As much as his mind conjured images of being taken to a dungeon and questioned under duress, the marquis led him to a spacious and comfortable billiards room, full of masculine details like claw-footed furniture and the distinctive scent of fine tobacco.

The marquis gestured to an impressive humidor. "Can I offer you a cheroot? Cigar?"

"A kind offer, but no, thank you." He doubted it would be a credit to him if he was coughing through the interview. His sister had weak lungs when it came to smoke and soot, so it was a habit he had never picked up.

Nodding, Granville bypassed the box and settled into one of the wide chairs, the leather creaking beneath his weight. Leaning back in the chair, he regarded Colin with a slight tilt of his head. "I imagine you expected me to lead you to the dungeon and interrogate you."

"The thought had crossed my mind. You'll be wanting to ensure your daughter's happiness, after all."

"You may be relieved to know that I trust my son implicitly. If he has deemed you a good match for Beatrice, then I will defer to his judgment. However," he said, his voice ever casual, "that doesn't mean that I don't wish to get to know my future son-in-law. How has it been, stepping into society for the first time?"

"Well enough. People seem to have respected my father and are extending a certain amount of courtesy to me."

"Courtesy or curiosity?"

Colin allowed a small grin. The man was astute. "Both, I think. Then again, I think my father was always a bit of a curiosity to the *ton*, so it stands to reason that I would be as well."

"I met him once, you know. He didn't necessarily frequent the same events we did, but he attended the Duke of Thornton's ball a year and a half ago." He gave a soft snort of amusement, shaking his head. "Damned if the man didn't turn down my attempts to hire him."

"So I've heard," Colin responded, his voice dry as winter wheat. "My father didn't possess the most prudent of souls."

"No, but it is my understanding that you do. And to be honest, I find the situation has a rather impressive irony to it."

"That is one way to look at it. I'm merely relieved you don't hold his idiosyncrasies against me." Actually, Colin was relieved about a lot of things. The marquis wasn't at all what he had been expecting.

"A man can be responsible only for his own actions. Which brings us quite neatly to you."

Here was the talk he had been waiting for. "Yes, sir. I've one more year at the Inns of Court—"

Granville's upraised hand stopped him midsentence. "I've read quite enough about your prospects, Sir Colin. What I wish to know is how you will treat my daughter and what you expect from her."

Not a question he would have ever anticipated from the Marquis of Granville. And not a question to be taken lightly. The older man watched him with keen eyes, a subtle warning that what Colin said mattered to him.

"Lady Beatrice is a remarkable woman, my lord. It is my wish to provide for her a house in which she can be comfortable, a studio in which she can paint, and a marriage in which she can be loved and honored."

"And in return you expect what from her?"

"It is my wish for her to be a contented wife, a reliable mistress of my household, and a devoted mother to our future children. She already hails from a family that values hard work, so I have no doubt she will thrive as the wife of a baronet barrister."

Granville's eyes softened the slightest bit at that compliment to his work ethic. One didn't run a thriving horse-breeding business without hard work and dedication. "I see. My daughter is accustomed to the finest things in life. Two thousand a year is a pittance compared to the wealth she was raised in."

Is that what the man thought was important to Beatrice? Colin held his ground, refusing to be cowed by Granville's blunt words. "Your daughter is accustomed to a loving family. She will be welcomed most joyfully into mine, I am certain. Her needs will always be met, and she will of course be able to spend her marriage settlement in any way she chooses. But it is my belief, sir, that so long as she has her paints, most everything in life is secondary to her."

This time the marquis actually smiled as he leaned back in his chair and templed his fingers. "It appears my son was correct. Clearly you have an understanding of what makes Beatrice happy. And only a simpleton would miss the fondness with which you speak of her. I am well aware that many of the *ton* believe love to be unnecessary to a marriage, but I couldn't disagree more. As far as I am concerned, it is the cornerstone to a happy life."

Colin blinked, working to keep the surprise from his face. Unexpected emotion welled up within him at the approval in the older man's voice. Certainly not a sentiment he was used to from his own father. "Thank you, sir. I am deeply honored to not only be gaining a wonderful wife, but to be joining your fine family as well."

As they rose and shook hands, Colin let go of the stress that had plagued him since the debt collectors showed up at his door. For a short amount of time, he would keep his secret from Beatrice, but once they were married, all would be well. He would have a wife he loved, a family he could count on, and the estate safely preserved for the next generation.

The wedding couldn't come fast enough.

"Bonjour, monsieur!"

The old man didn't even look up from his inventory as he held up a hand, more in acknowledgment than greeting. "I will be with you in just a moment." The last word was said with a hard "T," emphasizing the English version of the word.

Bent at the waist as he was, all Beatrice could see was the top of Monsieur Allard's dark cap and the tufts of white hair poking out in disarray. She walked up to the counter and peeked over at what new supplies he had just received. "Oh, I love those broad-handled new brushes."

"Broad handles for broad hands, my lady. They would rest like bricks in your fingers." Brushing off his hands, he straightened slowly, eyeing her over the rims of his spectacles. "Was there something you needed?"

It was beyond her why the man was so endearing to her. He was abrupt with her at every turn. Although, come to think of it, that might be exactly why. So many people groveled or kowtowed to a woman of her station. Monsieur Allard gave no special treatment, and his gruff manner made her like him all the more. And there was the small issue of him helping her with the engravings.

"Yes, indeed. Apparently, I have quite a fascination with shades of gray lately. I'm very nearly out of both black and white pigments."

Nodding, he turned and rifled through his stores, coming up with two small pots. "Is that all?"

"Yes, thank you."

He shook his head, wrapping up her purchase with slow but steady hands. "You do realize that footmen are very good at fetching such things."

"Remarkably, so am I," she said, not at all offended by his usual grumbling, "especially when I have good news to share. Or perhaps you may think it bad, since you soon may be deprived of my patronage."

His bushy eyebrows rose the slightest amount—a veritable outpouring of emotion for him. "Yes?"

She grinned hugely, not caring for once that her crooked front tooth was on display. "I'm getting married."

She had his attention now. "Married?"

"Indeed. And you will never guess who my betrothed is—or, rather, who his father was." She could hardly wait to tell him, a fellow artist. Normal people might appreciate what Tate had achieved, but a true artist was in awe of him. With her hands gripping the edge of the counter, she leaned forward. "Sir Frederick Tate."

Monsieur Allard's mouth opened in surprise, and his eyes blinked rapidly behind his spectacles. "The famous painter? That is . . . I mean to say . . . My lady, I don't know what to say."

"Congratulations is perfectly acceptable, I assure you," she teased, floating with happiness. It was hard to imagine how a single person could be so unaccountably fortunate.

"But . . . your letters." He shook his head, his brow

crumpled together like a discarded piece of parchment. "I do not understand."

She cocked her head. "What do the letters have to do with this? I can still write them, after the marriage." The Frenchman wasn't making a lick of sense.

"That's not what I meant. Your letters were so fiercely against the fortune hunter." He raised his shoulders to his ears, his hands spread palm up. "How could you marry a man who is *en faillite*?"

"*En faillite?*" she repeated, at a complete loss. She knew French fairly well, but the word was unfamiliar. She had no idea why he somehow seemed upset instead of elated, or at the very least mildly happy for her.

"Eh, how to say . . . ?" He shook his head, trying to recall the translation. All at once his expression cleared, and he snapped his fingers. "Bankrupt!"

Chapter Twenty-three

The word reverberated in her head like a cannon shot, echoing over and over as she stared at him with her mouth wide open. "Bankrupt?" Her voice was a ragged whisper, unfamiliar to her own ears. "Sir Colin Tate is *bankrupt*?"

Saying the words together was almost as absurd as saying Sir Colin Tate is purple, or Sir Colin Tate is Chinese. Her brain couldn't seem to reconcile them.

"Oui, mademoiselle."

The whole situation was made all the more odd by Monsieur Allard's use of his native language. He was just as unnerved as she was, especially as it became obvious she had no idea what on earth he was talking about.

"That can't be right. Monsieur, you must be mistaken."

"Perhaps," he said, rubbing a hand over the raspy afternoon stubble on his cheek. "But I do not think so. Please, my lady, sit down." He gestured to the ancient stool at the end of the counter.

She shook her head. No, this was all some mistake. She wasn't going to sit down and have a fit of vapors because it wasn't true. It couldn't be. "Explain yourself, please. Why do you think this?"

He sighed and pulled his work stool over, the legs screeching as they dragged over the old floor. Settling onto it, he leaned an elbow on the counter and studied her. "I know my business, my lady. A year ago, old Georges received an offer to work in a new engraving company in Edinburgh, headed by the great Frederick Tate himself. He wished for me to be his master engraver and to help train new recruits in the art.

"I did not wish to leave the shop, so I turned him down. My competitor, John Gotter, was hired instead. It was a decision that Gotter bitterly regrets, since not only did the business fold before it ever even really began, but the journal he worked for had already replaced him."

Beatrice held a hand over her stomach, but it did nothing to stop the turmoil. "How could this be? Why wouldn't anyone know about it?"

"Because of so much mishandling, it never actually opened. Tate's business partner ran off with much of the money from investors, venders refused to refund the cost of equipment that was never used, and voilà, there wasn't even a farthing to pay Gotter for his trouble. The word never got out because no announcements were made. It could be called a silent catastrophe."

A silent catastrophe. The perfect description for the agony of discovering the man she had pledged her life to had in fact been the exact thing she'd thought to avoid. Her blood turned to ice in her veins, making her shake in a way she could not seem to stop.

A scurrilous, duplicitous, deceitful fortune hunter.

"I'm so sorry, my lady. I see that I have brought you much pain."

She looked up to him, her gaze meeting his. Compassion and empathy reflected from within. Or was it pity? She swallowed and nodded, using every bit of willpower she possessed in the world to hold back the tears that stung the backs of her eyes, demanding to be freed. "*Merci, monsieur*," she said, her voice choked with the force of her emotions.

"Please, can I—"

"No." The word was wrenched from deep within her, from the place unwilling to hear even another word from anyone until she had a moment to think. She swallowed, lifting her chin with the effort to maintain her crumbling composure. "But thank you. I'll just see myself out."

It was all she could do to turn and walk from the store, leaving behind all of the hopes and dreams on which she had floated in. They lay like shattered china on the floor where she had stood, forever marking the loss of her innocence.

Beatrice had devised a thousand different ideas for how best to respond to Monsieur Allard's shocking news. She could burst into Colin's home—or rather, his aunt's home—demanding to know the truth. But whether it proved to be true or not, such a tactic was unlikely to result in anything good. Besides, she knew without a shadow of a doubt that there was simply no way for her to approach him with any amount of rationality right now.

She could go to her brother and insist he tell her every last detail of what transpired during the meeting he had with her betrothed. However, she was loath to bring such a thing to her brother's attention if it were false. If it were true and he knew about it, she might have to kill him, and she *really* didn't want to deal with the mess.

Of all the ideas that had come and gone during her walk home, only one seemed to make any sense.

"Ah, Benedict, there you are."

Beatrice's brother-in-law glanced up from the ledger book he was studying, one dark brow raised in a wary greeting. "Here I am. Is there something I can do for you?" No doubt he had already noted her puffy eyes and reddened nose.

Glancing behind her, she ducked into the study and eased the door closed. By some small miracle, her mother and sisters had stepped out to do some shopping while she was gone, which enabled her to come this far without being noticed by anyone other than Finnington and a handful of servants. She wasn't taking any chances with her family stumbling upon the conversation she was about to have.

"You may very well regret asking that," she said, plopping down onto the chair in front of the desk. She had made it this far without faltering by sheer will alone. "I have a very big, very important favor to ask of you."

"Name it."

That was it. Two words, so simple but perfectly sincere. She took a shuddering breath, thankful beyond reason for Evie's choice of husband. "Don't you think you should ask what it is first? I may want for you to steal the crown jewels."

He shrugged, his expression relaxed even as his dark gaze missed nothing. "If you have want of them, then I am quite certain you have a good reason for it. You are rarely given to fancy. And all that aside, without your interference, things might have gone very differently between your sister and me. Therefore, no favor could be too large."

He was so kind. A good man. Wasn't that what she had wanted in her own husband? She thought that was exactly what she had found, but apparently Beatrice in

Love was tantamount to Beatrice the Overtrusting Nit-
wit. "I know you gave up your old career years ago,
but I need for you to dust off your skills, if you please."

Both brows rose at this. "I see. In what capacity, do
you think?"

"In whatever capacity it takes to find out if I am
marrying a lying, heartless villain or not."

"Very well," he said, not missing a beat. "Is there
something in particular you would like to know, or
shall I simply prepare a general report on him?"

"Before I tell you, will you promise to keep this conversation between us?" It was asking a lot, she knew,
but she couldn't bear to drag the rest of her family into
it if by some miracle Monsieur Allard was mistaken.

"You must know I won't lie to your sister. However,
I see no reason to bring up the subject unless she should
inquire specifically."

Much the same promise she had once made him.
"Thank you, Benedict. You are the very best brother-in-
law anyone could ever hope for."

"Be sure you remember that when your sisters
marry my competitors someday," he said, offering her
a quick wink. "Now, I think perhaps you should start
at the beginning."

By the time she was back in her chambers later that
evening, she was feeling marginally better. Benedict
would find out exactly what the truth was. There could
easily be some sort of mistake, some miscommunica-
tion. Monsieur Allard was old, after all. It's possible he
had confused the facts. Wouldn't she have known of
the business venture otherwise? She was one of Sir
Frederick's most ardent admirers.

Still, as she picked at the tray of food her mother had
sent up when she had pleaded a headache, Beatrice
couldn't deny the hollowness lurking inside of her. She

would have sworn before God and man that Colin felt as strongly about her as she did him. And yet . . . how could she know? Until she heard back from Benedict and his mysterious sources, she could do little more than wait.

Chapter Twenty-four

In the week since Beatrice's entire family had taken up residence at Granville House, Colin had seen her exactly two times. Two exceedingly well-chaperoned, impossible-to-be-alone visits that had driven him near crazy with her close proximity without the benefit of a single kiss. Hardly even a touch, for that matter. He had been forced to make do with little more than fleeting eye contact and shared conversation.

Meanwhile, all he could think about was the day, only six weeks away, when she would be all his and he could whisk her away without a word of explanation to her exceedingly large and ever-present family.

A sharp scratch at the door interrupted Colin's thoughts, and he looked away from his vacant study of the coffered ceiling, blinking to focus on the here and now. "Enter."

Aunt's butler let himself into the room, his eyebrows pulled together in a look that bordered on disapproval. Colin sat up a little straighter, though it wasn't as though his boots were on the table or anything. And really, so what if they were? The man had no say in how Colin lived.

"The Lady Beatrice is here to see you, sir."

Colin came to his feet in one motion. "Lady Beatrice?" An incredibly bold move, if that was the case. Either she missed his private company as much as he did hers, or her family had finally driven her mad. He hoped it was the former, but could understand if it was the latter.

"Indeed. I've put her in the green room, and due to the highly unusual nature of the visit," he said, the disapproval dripping from his tone like tar, "I have notified her ladyship. Lady Churly is with her now."

Two things were immediately apparent to Colin. First, he really didn't care why she had decided to come see him. He was simply damn glad for it. The second was that Simmons was a bit of an arse.

Without bothering to acknowledge the man, Colin brushed past him, heading for the green room with long, swift strides. He strode into the room, immediately seeking Beatrice, anxious to see her face. She looked up at him, her bearing as regal as a queen, despite the simple and sweet white muslin gown she wore.

Something wasn't right.

He slowed, taking care to temper his expression with his aunt's keen eyes observing them both. Everything about Beatrice just seemed a little bit off. Her lips were turned down, her shoulders unusually taut. Either his aunt had said something in offense, or his betrothed was here for a reason far less pleasant than he imagined.

"There you are, Colin," Aunt Constance said, her lips tipped up in a knowing smile. "Your lovely betrothed and I were just discussing how delightful the exhibit was last month. I'm ever so glad she decided to pay us a visit."

Aunt was in full form, her fingers lined with a rainbow of gems, her heavy burgundy gown draped elegantly from her tall, willowy form, and her hair pulled back in glossy braids, which were piled on her head like a silvery crown. She looked as though she had been expecting the queen, not the young future bride of her nephew. Still, nothing about her demeanor suggested that she was anything but polite to their guest.

Colin took his time making his way to the sofa to have a seat beside Beatrice, evaluating her as a barrister would a witness during an examination. Her hands were clenched tightly in her lap, her breaths shallow. Her chin was tipped up in the way it always was when she wished she were taller. Her cheeks were flushed, rosy against the alabaster white of the rest of her skin.

But it was her eyes that gave him the greatest concern. The ever-present sparkle that always lit her eyes from within, that gorgeous fire that called to him with its life and vitality, was gone. Completely. What remained was the dull, deep blue of dried paint, flat and dimensionless.

"It was indeed a great success," he said, sliding his gaze toward his aunt. "I wonder, Aunt, if you would indulge us with a few minutes alone. With the door open, of course, but I find I'd like nothing more than a few private words with my betrothed."

It was a bold, almost rude request, but Aunt Constance was no fool. With the wealth and status of Beatrice's family, she was more than happy to indulge the two young lovers in a few minutes of time alone. She smiled and came to her feet. "I believe I have a few things to attend to. I shall return in ten minutes. And mind, the door shall stay open. We are nothing if not proper in this household."

Colin smiled his thanks, all the while clenching his jaw against the growing impatience to know what was going on. When she swept through the door, he waited until the sound of her footsteps died before he turned to Beatrice. "Tell me what's wrong."

She looked up at him, her face nearly angelic in its sweetness, framed so prettily by her golden curls. She looked at home in the green room, the emerald hues accentuating the subtle color in the center of her eyes. She didn't say anything, just looked.

A weight formed in his chest, growing larger with each tick of the tall clock behind him. He sank down onto the sofa beside her, the cushions giving beneath his weight and shifting her further toward him. "Did you know that you have the prettiest hint of green in your eyes?"

The words seemed to break the spell, and she averted her eyes to her lap. "I don't think I should have come."

"Why? I'm happy to have you here."

She half snorted, half laughed. "Of that, I have no doubt."

Colin narrowed his eyes, working to decipher the odd mood that had taken hold of his betrothed. "As you never should. I'd rather be with you above all people."

"Is that a fact? Above all people?"

"Beatrice, what has gotten hold of you? If I dinna wish to be with you more than any other person on earth, I wouldn'a have asked you to marry me."

For the first time since he'd entered the room, a spark flared in her eyes. "Well, how convenient. What a serendipitous moment to realize that you actually have some amount of affection for the woman attached to the dowry you seek."

It all came together with utter clarity in that moment. Hellfire and damnation. She knew.

"Beatrice, it's not what you think—"

"You have no idea what I'm thinking," she said, the words pushed from behind clenched teeth. "How dare you even presume—"

"I know exactly what you are thinking. You think I am marrying you for your dowry." He didn't even know how to begin to fix this. He could already see the resentment burning in her eyes, branding him a liar and a coward.

"And why," she said, her voice dangerously low, "would I think such a thing?"

Bloody hell. To say the words out loud would be to cement whatever bitterness she had ever felt for men like him. He could never recover. "I doona know, but clearly something has transpired."

"No. You do not get to take the easy way out of this. Tell me why I might ever come to the conclusion that you wished to marry me only for my money."

The future depended on what he said next. He could see it in her every shaky breath, in her flared nostrils and fisted hands. He didn't give a damn just then what her brother would say if Colin broke his promise. All he cared about was Beatrice, and not breaking her heart.

As if it weren't already too late.

"Because my family is in debt. Because it is up to me to correct the problem. Because you canna believe that a man in need of money can have a heart."

She came to her feet as if spring-loaded, staring down on him as if he were an insect on the street. "Don't you dare turn this back on me. You are the one who lied. You are the one who represented yourself as something you are not. You are the exact fortune hunter I have spent the past year trying desperately to avoid."

"Why? Because I'm not some wealthy highborn aristocrat, sitting on piles of old money? Because I have a family who depends on me to see to its well-being and I happened to be lucky enough to fall in love with the woman who has the power to correct the sins of my father?"

She jerked back as if he had slapped her. "Love? For love of money, I should think."

A rattle from outside stopped her cold, and her eyes darted to the doorway. A servant carried a tray laden with Aunt's best tea set, steam rising from the spout of the fine bone pot. Setting the tray onto the sofa table, he turned to address them, but one look at Colin's fierce expression and he promptly retreated, leaving them in icy silence.

The clock continued its relentless ticking behind him as they watched each other. "For love of *Beatrice*," he finally said, pouring his soul into her name. "For the love of an artist, and a woman, and all the things she makes me feel."

"Oh, so you'd like to talk about feelings, would you? Well, there is a subject about which I can speak with great authority. Let's talk about what it feels like to have a passing acquaintance tell me about my own betrothed's father's business failure. Let's talk about the denial, and the shock, and the inability to believe the truth of it. Let's discuss what it feels like to go to a trusted source and have him use his contacts to investigate these horrible accusations, all the while desperately hoping they'll be disproved."

Her hand went to her chest, as if she could hold together the broken pieces. "And then we can delve into exactly what it feels like to learn that, if anything, the truth was even worse than feared." She swallowed, the pain in her eyes ripping at his heart. "On second thought, I don't want to discuss anything. A fortune hunter will say anything to qualify his selfish ways. If it were any other way, you would have told me the truth before ever proposing marriage. You would have given me the opportunity to *choose*."

Colin raked a hand through his hair. The air seemed to have gotten thinner, like the highest peaks of Scotland, making it impossible to breathe. He could defend himself, tell her that her own brother had stipulated that he not reveal his financial situation, but he had more honor than that. Her brother didn't deserve to be dragged into it when all he wanted was his sister's happiness.

"I was wrong. Stupid, and selfish, and wrong. But my offer had nothing to do with money and everything to do with finding the perfect person with whom to share my life. For God's sake, you experienced our kisses—you know the fire that burns between us."

She held a hand up, leveling an accusing finger at his chest. "Don't you dare bring that up. None of it meant anything—not when it was based on lies."

"It was based on *passion*," he exclaimed, stepping closer to her, but only pushing her farther away. "It was based on what happens when two souls find each other in the world and know without a shred of doubt that they were meant for each other."

"*Everything* is thrown into doubt when secrets stand between them."

They were talking in circles, and with every circuit, he could feel her slipping away. "I'm not the only one with secrets here. Should not you have told me of your letters? To inform your future husband of an activity that could have—and still may—impact how society views us?"

Her mouth pressed into a mutinous line, her eyes narrowed to slits. "That isn't the same at all."

"Isn't it? I argue that it is. After the wedding, my family's debts will be settled for good. A short-term issue, at most. If you are revealed as the author of those scandalous letters, our standing could be impacted for years—perhaps even tainting our children."

"Tainting?" she exclaimed, backing up another step

and bumping into the table, rattling the untouched tea service. "If that is what you think of what I do—"

He didn't let her finish. He stepped forward, grabbing her hand and tugging her hard against him. Her eyes went huge, wide with shock as her breasts rose and fell against his chest with each ragged breath. "I think you are brilliant. I think you are bold, and brave, and incredibly clever. But we both know society wouldn't look at us the same way."

She didn't speak, just watched him with her fierce sapphire gaze. He held her tight against him, forcing her to feel his agitation, to witness it in his rapid breath and pounding heart. To see it in his intense gaze. After almost half a minute, she licked her lips, raising her chin in defiance. "I don't know about society, but I know all about never being able to look at someone the same way again."

"Damn it, Beatrice," he breathed, frustration building within him, like hot steam begging for release. "Doona let your stubbornness ruin what could be."

"How could I ruin what was never really there?"

That was it; he couldn't take another word. With a growl of frustration, he let go of his iron control, swooping down to claim her lips in a kiss that was searing and raw, brutally honest in its passion.

She resisted, holding herself as stiff and unyielding as a marble statue. He squeezed his eyes shut. He couldn't do it. He couldn't force her to see reason. But he *could* coax her. Gentling his kiss to the barest of touches, he released his hold on her waist and slipped his hands up to cup her jaw. He poured every ounce of the love he felt for her into the moment, worshipping her as the goddess she was.

He pressed hot kisses on her cheek, sliding his thumbs along the sensitive skin of her temple. This time he wasn't holding her to him with his arms; he was holding her to him with a sensual assault, designed to remind her of exactly what they shared, of exactly what their life together would be like.

Desire flooded his veins, drowning out every distraction except her. Her scent of lilacs, her taste of reluctance, the sound of her uneven breathing, the searing heat of her skin wherever his lips touched. In that moment, his entire world was wrapped up in the woman before him, beginning and ending with every beat of her heart.

"You must believe that my desire for you is exactly that," he breathed, his words a caress upon the curve of her cheek as he continued his sensual assault. "Please give me a chance to prove it to you."

Beatrice squeezed her eyes shut against the need to lean into him, to accept his words and give in to her body's traitorous need to be touched by him. *Persuaded* by him.

She was nearly shaking with the desire to give in, to believe his quiet words, to trust the sincerity in his voice. His lips moved across her skin, leaving tiny kisses that seemed to have a direct connection to her heart, melting her anger a little more with every one.

What if his words were true? What if he truly did feel as strongly for her as she always dreamed her husband would? A small, breathy sound escaped her lips, *without* her permission, when his mouth reached her earlobe. She fought not to indulge the shiver that begged to be released.

"Please, Beatrice," he whispered, and there was no stopping the shiver then.

Garnering every shred of willpower she possessed in the world, she pulled away from him, trying to regain some semblance of sanity. "How? How can I ever trust you now? How could you possibly prove your intentions were not what they seemed?"

The pain she saw in his stony gaze threatened to undercut her determination. Knowing he was hurting didn't make her own humiliation and pain any better. Only worse.

Much, much worse.

"I doona know," he said, shaking his head. "But I swear to you I will think of something. Just give me some time."

"No. I don't want to give you time. Prove it to me right here, now. I want this settled." The thought of walking out of this house without a solution was enough to take her breath away.

"All right—what about the marriage settlement? Over and above the amount needed to release the estate, I have allowed for every last penny to be in your control."

"Which seemed so phenomenally generous when my brother told me. But now I see it for what it is: You got what you wanted and made a token effort to divert any suspicions about your motives."

"Token?" His brow rose halfway up his forehead. "I hardly call fifteen thousand pounds *token*."

"It is if your eyes were set on the ten-thousand-pound prize." She paced away from him, her ire burning a path from her throat to her belly. Everything about this situation was wrong—it left no room for anything but suspicion and heartbreak. There was truly only one way to be absolutely sure of his motives. "Very well—you want to know what you can do? Accept none of my dowry."

The muscles worked at the corners of his jaw. "I can't do that." His words were flat. Final. "Without that money, we won't even have a place to live after we are married. And by we, I doona just mean you and me. I mean my whole family, including Cora, Rhys, and Gran."

"You see? Proving your intentions to me is impossible when the blasted money is so fundamental to the union." It was hopeless. Nothing he could do would ever take away the hollowness that filled the place in her heart once overflowing with happiness. And love. No matter how misguided, she couldn't deny how she had once felt about him.

"I'll come up with something. By the time we marry, I'll have proved myself to you."

"*If* we marry."

It was as if a steel plate slammed shut in his eyes. Hard, dull, impenetrable. "The announcement has already been made, the contracts signed."

She crossed her arms tightly in front of her chest. "I don't care. I'd rather live my life as an outcast than marry a fortune hunter."

"I could sue. Your father would be forced to pay for restitution."

"Then I guess you'll get what you wanted, won't you?" She hated the words, even as she said them. She hated the pain that flared in his eyes moments before his expression became hooded.

"How much time do I have?"

She lifted her shoulders, shaking her head at the hopelessness of his task. "I don't know. A week? A month?" What did it matter? It was an impossible task.

His nod was sharp, just like his features. "One month. And, Beatrice?"

She met his iron gaze, unable to deny him that.

"Doona give up on me yet."

Chapter Twenty-five

The sight of the austere stone house rising above the leafless trees and barren winter gardens was a relief for more reasons than simply the promise of the blessed warmth within, though after four days of traveling north in a cramped and half-frozen mail coach, he'd kill for a hot bath and a good scotch.

But that had nothing to do with the emotions seeing the house elicited within him.

He was home.

Colin pressed close to the glass, eager for the hack to reach the manor house at last. He needed his family's counsel. His success in convincing Beatrice of his true intentions would impact them every bit as much as it did him. It was why, within half an hour of her departure from his aunt's house, Colin was packed and on his way to see them.

Which meant none of them had any idea he was coming.

He didn't relax until the wheels crunched over the gravel drive, heralding his arrival. He had barely opened the door when a commotion at the house had him looking up, just in time to see Cora rushing toward the carriage, her dark wool skirts swishing around her booted feet.

"Colin! Whatever are you doing here?" Apparently she was in too great a rush to have thought to grab a hat or proper coat. Her dark hair was coiled in a neat braid atop her head, leaving her neck bare to the frigid wind. "We're all set to come to London at the end of the month for the wedding. We dinna think we'd see you before then."

He dropped to the ground, holding his hat in one hand and accepting her eager hug with the other. "I canna say I expected it either. Come. Let's get us out of the freezing wind before you catch your death."

"Oh pish. You've been gone from Scotland too long if you think this is freezing." Her brown eyes danced with excitement, making him smile for the first time in days. He had been right to come home. Together they could come up with a proper plan; he felt sure of it.

"I believe you are correct, Cora-belle."

"Colin! You mustn't call me that. I'm not a wee lass anymore."

Rhys appeared in the door then, a wide grin on his face. "Doona be daft, Cora—you've only just given up your dolls. You've years yet to be a proper woman."

Colin's smile grew larger, even as it felt oddly foreign on his lips. "Listen to your brothers, Cor—the pair of us are far from ready to see you grown."

"Oh, stop with you both. Gran was already married by the time she was my age."

The house was so warm as to be almost stifling after hours in the thin-walled coach. As his siblings continued to tease, he shed his outerwear, reveling in the familiar smell of the old house. It might not have been in their family long, but it had always smelled like home. Wood, beeswax, and lemon oil, he thought, plus something else entirely unique to the place. After hanging up his hat and coat, he herded his siblings into the main drawing room, where Gran always spent her afternoons.

As expected, she sat bundled in her favorite knitted blanket on the antique sofa that had come with the house, darning what looked to be a pair of Rhys's socks. It didn't matter that they still had a maid of all work—she'd keep her hands busy no matter how many servants attended to her. It was one of the things that made Gran, Gran.

She looked up at their noisy entry. "As I live and breathe, my dear Colin." She started to set aside her work, but he put up a hand.

"No, no, doona get up." He went to greet her, kissing both of her soft, papery cheeks. She smelled of wool and lavender, just as she always had. "I'm happy to see you looking so well."

"Havers, boy." She chuckled, her voice strong despite the rasp of age. "If ye believe that, perhaps ye should be getting yerself to the doctor's for a check of those lying eyes of yers."

"The God's honest truth, Gran. You look hale enough to tackle any bear that should wander into the drawing room."

She pursed her lips in mock severity, even as her blue eyes twinkled with delight. "Such cheek, lad." She paused, taking him in from head to boot. "And where is the lass whit keep ye in line?"

Leave it to Gran to get straight to the heart of things without even trying. "Back in London, far away from this miserable weather. Speaking of which, Cora, can you see about ordering a tea service? I'm chilled straight through to the marrow, I swear."

She nodded and set off to do his bidding, and Colin settled onto his father's favorite chair, stretching his hands to the fire burning behind the decorative iron screen. The room was huge, extending from the front of the house straight through to the back, with windows at both ends. Despite its large size, the massive stone fireplace and the low ceiling helped keep the space warm and cozy, making it the primary gathering spot in the house. Of course, Gran's knitting helped keep it homey as well, with throws and blankets draped across the comfortable, decades-old furnishings.

His brother plopped down next to Gran, linking an arm with hers. "So, if your lady love is in London, what the devil are you doing here?"

"Rhys," Colin admonished, widening his eyes at his brother. "Watch your language, please."

Gran clucked her tongue, shaking her head. "Och, I'm not going ta wither at the sound of a wee curse word. Answer the question, if ye please."

Direct as always. Colin rubbed a hand over his eyes, which felt dry and gritty after days on the road. He'd come here for their help, hadn't he? The sooner they tackled the problem, the sooner they could come up with a solution. "Let's wait for Cora, at least. I'd rather not have to hash it out twice."

"I'm here, I'm here—doona delay on my account," Cora said, hurrying through the doorway and settling on Gran's other side. His siblings towered over their adopted grandmother, but Colin had no doubt Gran could still ring a peal over their heads, if she should be so moved.

Rhys leaned over, addressing his sister. "Colin was just about to tell us what has those purple moons beneath his eyes. I think it's safe to assume it has something to do with the absent Lady Beatrice."

Cora turned her huge amber eyes on him. "Doona tell me you managed to make a muck o'things before you even walked down the aisle?"

Making a muck of things was putting it mildly. "That's a fairly accurate summary, actually."

"Cripes, man," Rhys said, his adolescent voice cracking a bit. "I knew there had to be a reason for you coming all the way here so close to the wedding, but I wouldn'a have thought it could be as bad as all that."

Gran patted his arm in disapproval. "Stop wit yer doomsayin' before ye even know tit from tat. On wit yer story, Colin. Best ta have it out all at once. Then we can chew it over and spit out the fat."

The expression almost brought a smile to Colin's lips. "It's simple enough, really. I never told Beatrice of the state of the estate before the betrothal, and her brother asked me not to do so after. I knew she disliked fortune hunters, but I had no idea she despised them quite so thoroughly."

The look of utter disgust on her face when she confronted him was something he wouldn't soon forget— if he ever did. One would have thought he was the lowliest of criminals. The lingering shame still dug beneath his skin, a dull but present sliver in his conscience. Unclenching his tightened jaw, he said, "Which may have never been a problem, if she hadn'a found out on her own. Suffice it to say, she would have just as soon seen me at the bottom of the Thames than at the front of the church."

As he spoke, the humor on his family's faces faded, each seeming to grasp the gravity of the situation. Colin could practically see his brother's mind go straight to what this news could mean for the whole family and the estate they had called home for years. "But the banns have been read, no? She canna back out now."

"The announcement has been made, the banns have been read once, and of course, the contract was signed. But all of that means nothing if she is determined to avoid marriage."

"What have ye come to us for?" Gran asked, her voice stern. "Yer bride's up in high doh, and yer in a swither as to what to do with the lass?"

"Give me some credit, Gran," Colin said, leaning

back against the firm cushions of his chair. "It is more than just the jitters. She thinks I've targeted her like some sort of military marksman, coldly lying about my every thought and emotion. She is convinced I don't love her and I used her only to get to her money."

Cora cocked her head to the side. "Dinna you?"

Oh, for the love of God. "Of course not! Dinna you read a word I wrote about her? I never once thought of her as some sort of walking dowry. As a matter of fact, I thought she was far too high above me to even consider marrying for her money."

"You doona have to bite her head off," Rhys grumbled, glaring at Colin. "We all know you went to London to marry for money."

"Yes—an heiress who might have a care to be wife to a baronet. A logical, careful marriage arrangement where both parties would be benefitted. I never intended to fall in love with the daughter of a marquis, for heaven's sake."

"Still, it was rather convenient," Cora persisted.

Colin bit the inside of his lip to keep from snapping at her. If his own family didn't believe him, how could he ever convince Beatrice? "Yes, very convenient to have nothing to offer one's bride but a paltry title and a house mired in debt. If it weren't for her near worshipful adoration of Father, I'd have nothing to give her at all."

Gran made a *tsk*ing sound, shaking her head in admonishment. "A man's love is hardly nothing, Colin. Entire countries can be made or lost for love."

He had to work not to roll his eyes. He should be lucky to make it out of this conversation without being told a fable or two. "A man's love is nothing if it is not believed, Gran. Beatrice doesn't believe there is a way to prove that my intentions were honorable and honest. I convinced her to give me a month to do just that, but short of forfeiting the dowry altogether—which I canna do—I haven'a a clue how to accomplish that."

Cora's eyes were narrowed, as if trying to work a riddle. "She wants you to prove you wanted to marry her only for her?"

"Aye."

"I think I like this lady."

"Cora," Rhys exclaimed, glaring at her over the top of Gran's head. "You're not exactly helping. She's set us about a fool's errand."

"I ken, but any woman who'd stand up for love must have a kind heart."

"No' if it means standing against your brother—or the lot of us, for that matter."

Gran put a staying hand to each of her grandchildren's arms. "Hush now, the both of ye. Colin, do ye have time to find another bride if she cries off?"

The thought was like a punch to the gut. "Not with the scandal such a thing would bring. And I doona know if I made myself clear: I love her. Regardless of anything else, I don't want to lose her for that reason alone."

His words seemed to echo in the room, and he realized he had raised his voice. Three pairs of widened eyes stared at him from the sofa, with varying levels of surprise. He had surprised himself, really, with the vehemence of his response. At that moment, the maid bustled into the room, carrying the tea service. With her eyes on the tray and the path to the table, she had no idea of the climate of the room. "Welcome home, Sir Colin," she said, her voice light and cheery. "Congratulations on yer betrothal, such bonny good news."

Setting down the tray on the long oval sofa table, she brushed off her hands and glanced up at him. Seeing Colin's expression, her smile immediately dropped.

"Beggin' yer pardon, sir—I dinna mean to interrupt anything."

Great—now he was scaring the servants. "Doona mind me, Abigail. I'm afraid the journey has exhausted me. Thank you for your sentiments, however."

She didn't look particularly convinced. Bobbing a curtsy, she retreated from the room like a bird in flight, pulling the door closed behind her.

Pinching the bridge of his nose in an effort to push back against the headache that had been plaguing him for days, he turned back to his family. "So, how does one go about proving the impossible?" He almost felt foolish for coming. What could they do for him that he hadn't already done for himself? A fresh perspective could do only so much.

"No miracles to be had whit those bags beneath yer eyes." Gran set aside her knitting and leaned forward to pour a cup of tea. Pulling a slender flask from her skirts, she splashed a healthy amount into the cup and handed it to him. "Drink up, laddie. Then ye should get a bit of a rest. Come supper, we'll think of something to help ye and yer lass."

He gave his grandmother a rueful smile. A bit of hard tea and a decent rest certainly weren't going to solve his problem, but it was a starting point. "Thank you," he murmured, taking a long sip of the brew. The hot burn as it went down had nothing to do with the temperature of the tea. It did little to unravel the hard knot in his stomach.

Pouring another cup for herself, she added a dollop of cream before settling back. "Do ye know the saying 'Whit's for ye will no' go by ye'?"

"Aye." For some reason, the moment he was with his family, the proper English yeses seemed to go right out the window. "If it's meant to happen, it will happen."

Not the most encouraging of sayings. He was a man of action, not of sitting around accepting what fate doled out. If that were the case, he sure as hell wouldn't have ridden across the whole of the British Isles in the dead of winter.

Gran set down her cup with a decisive clink. "Utter nonsense. If there's something ye want, boy, ye must strive for it. And we'll help ye—doona ye doubt, we'll think of something."

The words, spoken by an old woman who'd never even met his bride or seen them together, filled the empty void in his chest. A ghost of a smile came to his lips. "Aye, Gran, I'm counting on it."

Chapter Twenty-six

"Bea, you aren't paying even a lick of attention. This is your wedding, my dear, not mine."

Drat—now what had she missed? Beatrice looked at the two swatches of silk taffeta Evie held, the color seeming somehow faded, as if left in the sun too long. It was how everything looked to Bea these days— washed out, dull, uninspiring in the extreme. "The green, of course."

Evie's left eyebrow went up, and her hand went to her hips, the swatches adding a splash of contrast against her dark blue skirts. "They are *both* green."

"That one," she said, pointing to the swatch in Evie's right hand. "Cece should have no trouble matching the flowers to green, at least."

They had heard word from their cousin just that morning that she was planning to come to the wedding and would be bringing flowers from her greenhouse for decoration. Though Beatrice loved the idea of see- ing Cece, knowing that the wedding might not even happen had sapped all the excitement from the news.

Looking over to Madame Gisele, who hovered over the pattern books laid out all over the worktable, Evie smiled. "Madame, could you see if you have any other silks in the back?"

It was her cue to leave, and they all knew it. The older woman, who'd been eager to please them since the moment they had arrived almost an hour earlier, dipped her head. "As you wish. Pardon me, *s'il vous plaît*." With her unnaturally red hair bouncing in time with her enviable bosom, she made a quick exit, swishing the curtains closed behind her.

Turning her attention back to Beatrice, Evie dropped the swatches on the table and sat down beside her. She started to speak, but Beatrice held up a hand, silently asking for quiet. She knew a spy at work when she encountered one. Slipping over to the curtain, she cleared her throat loudly. Aha—there were the receding footsteps she was waiting for. Returning to her chair, she sank back down. "You were saying?"

Sighing, Evie shook her head. "Honestly, Bea, what has gotten into you? You had more fun planning my wedding than you've had planning your own."

A very accurate observation. Of course, Beatrice had known from the beginning that Benedict had been madly in love with her sister. There may have been a few bumps in the road, but she never doubted the intensity of their feelings—or the truth of them.

"I just wonder if—" Bea paused, struggling with the right words to say. It was difficult to admit she had been so blind, so utterly oblivious. "If I wasn't too hasty in agreeing to marry."

All exasperation and humor vanished from her sister's face. "And why would you think such a thing? I've seen the way he looks at you—as far as I could tell, it didn't seem as though things could be hasty *enough*."

Lust, pure and simple. Regardless of all else, she was attracted to him in a way she had never been to another man. More than handsome, well beyond normal—he was in a class wholly unto himself. "Attraction is hardly the same thing as love. Unfortunately, they are all too easily confused."

"Such sage, wise words from one so young," Evie said, the corners of her lips turned up. "Would you like to talk it over? I'm a dreadful listener, but for your sake I shall try."

She had intended to keep the truth of it to herself until she heard from Colin, but blast it all, she wanted an ally. She wanted someone who could look at it objectively and then side with her. At the very least, she wanted reassurance that her pain wasn't unfounded.

"He's a fortune hunter."

"A *what*?"

"A fortune hunter. One who wants nothing more than a moneyed wife so he can fill his coffers and—"

"I know what a fortune hunter is, Bea." She rolled her eyes and picked up a piece of Pomona green silk taffeta, turning it in her hands. "I simply don't believe the charge. Are you quite certain?"

"Ask your husband."

"Benedict?"

"Do you have another?" At Evie's sarcastic glare, Beatrice relented. "He did a little investigating for me to verify the truth of it."

"And what is the truth?"

"That he owes ten thousand pounds against his estate, and he didn't think to mention this to me before, you know, asking me to marry him."

Evie cringed, biting her lip. "Oh my. I suppose such a truth doesn't exactly cast his motives in the best of lights. What did he have to say for himself?"

The pain of their last conversation assailed her. The hopelessness of ever being able to trust him, of being able to believe that he truly fell for Beatrice, pulled at her belly. "The usual. He loves me; he felt that my dowry was nothing more than a happy coincidence, et cetera, et cetera."

"The devil is in the 'et cetera,' sister-mine." Her voice was soft and kind—if that didn't speak to the gravity of the situation, Beatrice didn't know what did.

"He swears he fell for me the person, not me the heiress. That we are each other's perfect match, perfectly suited in every way. And . . ." She trailed off, thinking of his searing last kiss, of the heat of his breath across her cheek, caressing her ear.

"I don't know what, exactly, you intended to say after 'and,'" Evie said, her brow raised halfway up her forehead, "but based on the heat of your very rare blush, I'm not certain I wish to know."

The warmth in Beatrice's cheeks must have been more visible than she realized. A genuine grin, what felt like the first in a week, came to her lips. "Suffice it to say, though I may doubt his motives, I can't honestly say I doubt his attraction."

"Oh good Lord in heaven, if we need to move up the wedding, you need to tell me this instant, Beatrice Eloise Moore."

She hadn't meant to burst out with horrified laughter, but she could hardly do otherwise in the face of her sister's aghast expression. "No, though it is almost worth it for me to say yes just to see my very level-headed sister have a fit of vapors."

"So glad I could provide you with such entertainment." Her straight-faced, flat-toned response made her sarcasm abundantly clear. "Now, back to the issue at hand. Without reducing me to vapors," she said, lifting a brow, "what does your heart say?"

"That he lied. That he manipulated me. That he betrayed my trust in a way that could never be fixed."

"Well. I must say, that wasn't the answer I was expecting. Why haven't you broken the contract? I know there will be scandal, but it is a lesser evil than a lifetime of misery."

She thought of his portrait, half finished in her studio. Every feature exactingly reproduced, each angle laid out with her brush with as tender a touch as her own hands upon his skin. She shook her head, swallowing back the unnamable emotion that clogged her throat. "I don't know. He asked, and I let him have a chance to somehow prove himself."

"You don't know? I don't believe that for a second. You're the one who always knows everything."

"I wish. This time around, I have been the worst of oblivious fools. When he was near, it was as though everything else in the world faded away. It was just him and me, alone in the world together. I saw only him, heard only him." Tasted him, smelled him, felt him—his presence had consumed her every sense. She still didn't know what happened to her normally astute self when he was near.

"I see," Evie said slowly, eyeing Bea with a sharpness that hadn't been there before. "You're in love."

"Was." The single word broke her heart, tearing at the hopes that she had harbored.

"*Are*. Why else would you be giving him a chance?"

The words floated in the air like Chinese lanterns, bright and optimistic, but destined to burn out and crash to the ground. Beatrice sighed and came to her feet, turning away from her sister's all too knowing gaze.

"It doesn't matter if I am or not. If he can't prove that he truly loves me for me, then there is no future for us."

Evie stood as well, coming to where Beatrice stood and slipping an arm around her. "Then let us hope," she said, compassion gentling her voice and loosening the loneliness Bea had felt since Colin left, "that he specializes in the impossible."

Blowing his hair from his forehead, Colin stood and set his hands to his hips, surveying the mes‿ before him. The studio, the bedchambers, and now the attic had been searched from top to bottom. Not surprisingly, he hadn't found any paintings. Nor chests of gold or hidden jewels, for that matter.

Bloody hell.

He blew out a frustrated breath, sending a puff of crystallized air to the attic rafters. Two hours in the freezing cold, three sneezing fits, one startled mouse, and exactly zero items of worth to show for it.

It just didn't make any bloody sense. According to his family, Father was working on a fix to their problems. God only knew what, exactly, that fix was, seeing how the studio was all but empty. Which he already knew. Shortly after the creditors showed up on the doorstep, Colin had done much the same thing, searching the house for anything of value to sell.

It shouldn't have been a surprise—he knew full well that Father hadn't taken on any new clients in the months leading to his death. And even if he had, the portrait would belong to the customer. But he had hoped against hope that Father's fix would have involved a brilliant . . . *something*. Colin didn't know what. Another portrait of one of the royals, perhaps?

It wasn't as though a normal painting would raise enough funds, after all. If Father was planning to paint them out of debt, it would have to be something so spectacular, it could bring ten thousand pounds.

Not unheard of for the old masters, but as celebrated as his father was, his pieces were not yet that valuable—particularly since they were commissioned to depict specific people.

However, as morbid as such a thought was, the fact that his father was now gone would have instantly made his paintings more valuable. Whether it would be valuable *enough* was a whole different issue—but at least it was a chance.

The resentment boiled up within him once more. Irrationally, he cursed his father beneath his breath. Colin had spent half his life cleaning up his father's messes. Irate visits from their creditors, empty cupboards and dry lamps from his father's forgetfulness to order more of what they needed. And now this. He couldn't have died, leaving things in order. It wouldn't have been his father if he had.

He wanted to rail at the man, to take him by the collar and demand to know why he had lacked all regard for Colin's comfort and well-being.

"Find anything?"

He started at the sound of his sister's voice and turned to see her framed in the narrow doorway at the top of the stairs. He must have been completely lost in his own thoughts not to have heard her come up. "All the dust you could want. My mother's out-of-date dresses. A few pieces of ugly furniture."

Cora wrinkled her nose, climbing the rest of the way up to join him. "So I'm to assume you dinna find a stash of gold tucked in the rafters?"

"I'd be halfway to London by now if that were the case."

"Honestly, I doona know what happened. Papa spent hours each day wandering the estate, and then he'd hie away in his studio for half the night. He swore that he was working on something important and that we were no' to disturb him. He even locked the door so I couldn'a sneak up. I still canna believe the studio was empty."

Not just the studio. Everything was empty. Colin's

house was empty of anything of value. His mind was empty of a way to fix it. His heart was empty of the love of his chosen bride, and unless something drastic happened in the next two days, his future would be empty of promise.

He shook his head, looking over Cora's shoulder out the small window that offered up a small, framed view of the estate. "It's ironic, isn't it?"

Cora looked up from the yellowed fabric of his mother's gowns. "What?"

"A man spends his entire career painting portraits and yet he left nothing behind of his own life. No portraits of him, or even the old landscapes showing his childhood home. None of my mother, or yours, or even Gran. There were a few of me, but that was back when he was perfecting his art, and most of those were painted over. It was almost as if he was never here at all."

Cora clearly didn't know what to make of his maudlin mood. Holding out an arm, she said, "Why doona we go have a nice cup o'tea with Gran before the pair of us catches our death up here."

Fifteen minutes later, with hot tea still warming his belly, he stood by the terrace door beside Gran. "If you were any sort of grandmother at all, you'd have the perfect plan for me to convince Beatrice of my intentions."

She chuckled, her gaze on the rippled surface of the pond. "Would that I could, lad. Sometimes, no matter our intentions, things can gang agley. We have to work whit what we have. And at the moment, we have naught but one another."

"Thanks to Father."

"Judge not lest ye be judged," she said, lifting her wrinkled brow. "I think ye forget, Colin, that yer father never set out to harm the ones he loved. Take it from an auld soul: It doesn'a do any good ta hate a man who has left this world ahint."

"On the contrary. It gives me a target for my anger. If we lose this place—"

"Then we lose this place. It's a great pile of stone, now, isn't it? The only thing that matters is that we doona lose one another. And that be including yer father's memory."

A damn sight easier said than done. It seemed that everything he ever wanted in life had been jeopardized. How could he possibly forgive his father when he was on the cusp of losing it all?

Gran put a hand to his back, rubbing it like he was a child. "I think yer forgetting who yer father truly was. So here it is: I'm prepared to give up this old gusty place if it means ye'll have yer life's love. But what I'm not willing to give up is yer fondness for yer da's memory."

"I doona know if that's still possible, Gran."

"We'll see about that." She crossed her arms, rubbing her hands back and forth over her slender arms. "Ye know, there's no better way to know a man's soul than to walk in his footsteps for a day."

Colin scrubbed a weary hand over his face. "Gran, I appreciate the thought, but I have absolutely no intention of following my father's path. In fact, I have made a point of *not* following in his footsteps for years."

"And see now where that's gotten ye, lad."

"Actually," he said, making an effort not to grind his teeth, "it got me quite far, until this mess yanked me back. Which, I feel compelled to point out, was entirely of his doing."

She clucked her tongue, shaking her head from side to side. "Ye've always been harsh where yer da's concerned. No' without reason, I ken. But have you acknowledged, lad, that ye'd have never met yer lass if it weren't for him?"

It was true, damn it. Colin dipped his head in reluctant agreement. Nothing else would have ever put him in the same room as Beatrice. And even if it had, the only reason she had given him even a moment's notice was because of her fascination with his father.

The irony was rich indeed. His father was single-handedly responsible for both Colin's love and heartache. He had simultaneously brought Beatrice to Colin and torn her from him.

Impressive, really.

"Oh, Colin, what's an old woman ta do whit ye? Go. Walk the trails leading to the west. Frederick set out every morning for the foothills, no matter the rain or chill. I think ye need a different perspective, and sometimes that's only ta be had among the forest. Ye never know when the fairies will whisper to ye."

He doubted a trek through the estate in the dead of winter was going to bring anything more than frostbite. But he had been pacing like a caged lion in the house for days. There was not a room unsearched, no cupboard unopened. He was out of ideas, out of patience, and almost out of time.

"Perhaps I will." Offering her a perfunctory kiss on her soft, wrinkled cheek, he strode to the front door, retrieved his greatcoat and hat, and set off toward the tree line where a narrow trail split the vegetation. The wind was vicious, but at least it had stopped raining last night, leaving the rocky path muddy but passable.

The cold was invigorating, clearing the muddled cobwebs from his mind. He took Gran's advice, following the path to the west, away from the small loch and toward the foothills rising upward into the mist. He used to come this way when they first moved in, a young adolescent exploring his new domain. From the rolling meadow filled with wildflowers in the spring to the old gamekeeper's cottage with its dilapidated thatched roof and river-rock chimney, to the crystal clear stream that swept through the property before dumping into the small loch not far from the house.

He might not have been born here, and he might not have even lived here for much of the past two years, but it was a part of him. It was home, more than any other place on earth. He loved it here and could scarce imagine anyone but his family calling it home.

The trail sloped up and to the left, delving deeper into the towering trees. He kept a steady pace, his boots hitting the rocky earth at an almost rhythmic pace. The bare, spindly branches extended over him in a weblike canopy, shielding him from the worst of the wind, but the bitterness of the day still chilled the exposed skin of his face.

His father had taken this walk nearly every day, Gran had said. Why? What had the land held for him? Perhaps he had been soaking it in. Enjoying the last of his time as master of the hard-won estate and the prosperity that he had earned and lost in the space of a decade and a half.

Before anyone else knew the dire state of their finances, he had already been saying good-bye.

Colin kicked a stone, sending it flying through the underbrush. A warning might have been nice. The selfishness of it all was hard to comprehend and impossible to forgive. Damn it all. This walk wasn't having the intended effect. His breath came out in abbreviated puffs, and despite the cold, sweat trickled down his back.

He was about to turn around to head back when the stone chimney of the gamekeeper's cottage came into view, its gray rock nearly blending in with the clouded skies behind it. It was probably best that he stop to rest before he soaked through his clothes and caught his death.

Slowing as he approached the tiny cabin, the barest hint of a smile lifted the corner of his lip. It looked exactly the same as it had a decade ago, with its squat walls covered in ivy and its uneven, thatched roof looking like an overgrown mop of hair. It sat right on the edge of the meadow, with a view to the mountains beyond through its two back windows. Perhaps "windows" wasn't the right word—they were just open portals, covered by sturdy shutters that swung out on ancient hinges.

He'd spent many an afternoon in the place, exploring, reading, pretending to live alone in the woods. His pulse settled as he walked up the gravel path and stomped his feet on the flagstone stoop. It was like stepping back in time, standing here again. An icy blast of wind assailed him, and he quickly lifted the latch and let himself in.

Almost instantly, he came to an abrupt stop.

He stood in the doorway, frozen in a way that had nothing to do with the frigid air buffeting his back. Breathing deeply, he looked around the dim interior. The exact essence of his father was here—the scent of linseed oils and earthy pigments, the Spartan furnishings and bare windows, the open painter's box set upon the single small table in the back of the room.

But the most significant of all was a simple easel set up beside the window near the back corner. On it a single canvas waited, tauntingly averted from where he stood.

Dear God.

Colin swallowed, his eyes riveted on the open frame of the back of the canvas. His heart beat so hard, the pounding seemed to ricochet through his head. Rioting hope propelled him forward, like sails catching wind for the first time in days. *Please, please.* He kicked the door shut behind him before rushing forward, the anticipation stealing the air from his anxious lungs. This could be it—everything he had hoped for. Everything that he had come here seeking.

Coming upon it, he paused, pressing his eyes closed. Sucking in a strangled breath, he sent up a quick prayer and stepped around the easel.

Blinking, he stared in astonishment at the sight before him, unable to fully absorb what he was seeing. It couldn't be. It couldn't possibly be. He rubbed his gloved hands over his eyes, pressing hard. Dragging in a deep breath, he opened his eyes, only to confirm what he already knew he would see.

The canvas was blank.

Chapter Twenty-seven

Colin dropped to the stool beside the easel, his body seeming to lose all rigidity in the face of the discovery. He shook his head, staring at the canvas. Nothing. Emptiness. The words described the canvas, the day, and the suddenly absent emotions within him.

Logically, he knew the anger would come later. He knew he'd fight fury as he stood in front of Beatrice and told her that all he had to offer was his word. There was no doubt he'd be consumed with resentment when he was forced to move his family to God only knew where and went begging to his aunt to sponsor his last year at the Inns of Court.

But not now.

He reached out, running his hand over the blank canvas, primed as if only moments from being used. The painter's box stood open, with brushes lined up and pig bladders full of premixed paint, everything ready to start fresh. It was as if his father had just stepped away, fully intent on returning to begin his next work.

Only . . . he hadn't. And he never would again. And despite it all, Colin missed him. He was unreliable, infuriating, and at times neglectful, but he was still Colin's father, and damn if he didn't miss him.

He bowed his head, rubbing his hands up and down the tops of his legs. He was gone, and Colin would never see his face again. Never shake his hand, or argue with him, or see him across the table at supper.

With a long, deep sigh, he came to his feet. It was too cold to linger in a place that couldn't help him, especially with the day dipping toward evening. He had taken two steps toward the door when he looked up and saw a figure. He jumped back in surprise, his body tensing as his mind ran a second behind his instincts.

His father was staring him right in the face.

Colin's heart, his lungs, his brain—all of them stopped in an instant, and then everything came roaring back to life all at once. Not his father—a *portrait* of his father. Perched on a low shelf beside the door, a large canvas leaned against the wall. He rushed toward it, soaking in the sight of his father, perfectly rendered by the man's own hand.

It was beyond incredible—it was astonishing. He stared back at Colin with the light of devilment in his eyes, so well painted as to look three-dimensional. God, it looked exactly like him. He hadn't realized just how faded his memory of his father's face was until that moment, when his angled jaw and broad brow came into sharp focus.

Despite the freezing temperatures, his blood warmed, pumped with renewed vigor through his veins. God, how he'd missed him. To see him again was like laying eyes on scotch after a month of water. The emotions assailing him were so sharp as to almost burn, searing their way through his chest and gut. All the anger, the resentment, all of the bitterness of the last eight months fell away like a broken shell.

It was several minutes before he could pull his gaze away from his father's likeness and take in the rest of the picture. Behind him, the rugged Scottish landscape rose toward the heavens, with brilliant green grasses and leaves that seemed to move in an invisible wind. Wildflowers dotted the sloping meadow, and the rocky outcrops of the base of the mountain glistened with falling water.

It was masterful.

All those years he had set aside the landscapes that had been his first love had done nothing to diminish the talent. In fact, it seemed to have grown—Father's first works didn't have nearly this level of detail. Colin knew his father had grown disenchanted with portraits lately, but he rather thought it was painting altogether. But the joy in this picture was undeniable.

The landscape was that of the view from the cottage—the land Father had been so damned pleased to own. The estate! Colin had been so caught up in the revelation of his father's only self-portrait, of seeing his face and experiencing the landscape, he had completely forgotten what the painting meant.

Freedom.

He finally had something to give to Beatrice—something of worth that could put them on equal footing. He could already imagine her delight, her joy at such a perfect gift. Mind made up, he pulled the canvas down from its shelf and started for the door. At the last moment, he doubled back and grabbed the primed canvas from the easel. Barely pausing to shut the door, he hit the trail running.

"Lady Beatrice, what a surprise."

Oh, drat and blast, where had *he* come from? Beatrice turned slowly, nodding with a brief bob of her head. "Mr. Godfrey. I didn't realize you were still in the city."

She pulled her cloak more tightly around her, a not so subtle hint that it was cold and she didn't wish to stand in the street and talk to him. She exchanged a glance with her maid, but the girl misinterpreted her silent plea and dropped back to give them privacy.

"Indeed. Is it because of the vitriol published about me in a certain magazine that you assumed I might escape to the country, or because you thought I might have given up and accepted the position my father so keenly wishes for me to take?"

Beatrice could actually feel the blood draining from her face. A very, very bold statement on his part. Good Lord, had Colin been right after all? If Godfrey knew she was the author of the letters, what, exactly, did he want with her? Despite the fact they were in the open for anyone to see, she suddenly felt extremely vulnerable.

"Neither, of course. Just that so many have already left the city for the winter."

He shook his head, looking at her as though she were a profound disappointment. "I knew it was you the moment I saw the second cartoon, you know."

At least now she knew where she stood. She stiffened her spine and lifted her chin, refusing to be intimidated by the man. "Why? Because you so thoroughly recognized yourself? If you didn't wish for the world to know of your underhanded tactics, you should have refrained from using them on me."

He chuckled, the sound colder than the December air. "And here I went to all this trouble to come up with irrefutable proof that you wrote the bloody thing, and apparently all I needed to do was ask."

"That's right. Some of us have integrity and answer truthfully when asked." It might not have been the wisest thing to say, but she wasn't about to let him think he had her cornered.

"Oh, feisty today, are we?" He smiled, a cruel stretching of his lips that was more sneer than grin.

"Well, I won't keep you. I merely wished to congratulate you on your coming nuptials."

Warning bells clanged in her head, making it impossible for her to turn and walk away. He had something more to say, something that she felt in her very marrow she did not want to hear. "Somehow I doubt that."

"Truly, I wish you both the very best." Tilting his head, he tapped the crystal handle of his rapier-thin walking stick against his chin. "I honestly thought that I would win the wager, but I underestimated the influence his father had over you. Of course, I didn't foresee his ruse after the musicale, pretending to rescue you, either." He gave a casual shrug of his shoulders. "Such is life. I did, however, find great amusement in the fact that the author of those pathetic letters fell victim to exactly what she thought to warn others about."

He looked supremely satisfied with himself, his eyes alight with mischief. She clenched her teeth, willing herself not to respond. Wager? She wouldn't believe a word he said. He was nothing if not a liar and a cheat. Still . . . how else did he know that Colin's family was up the River Tick? Disgust welled up within her, almost choking her.

Had they had a wager? Even if they hadn't, what did it matter? It was clear she would always doubt Colin's motives—always be susceptible to thinking the worst of him.

Nothing felt certain except that she had to get away from Godfrey. She started to turn, to escape from his sneering face when his parting words brought her up short.

"Enjoy your fortune hunter, my dear. You two deserve each other."

Traveling to Edinburgh had been a leisurely ride in the park compared to the trip back. Not only was Colin beyond anxious to get back to Beatrice; it was nerve-racking as hell to be transporting the painting. He doubted he would be this edgy if he were in charge of the crown jewels.

And, based on the way his family had reacted to the painting, it might as well have *been* the crown jewels. He smiled, thinking of their reaction when he arrived home with their salvation tucked beneath his arm.

"I knew yer father had ta be up to something," Gran had said, nodding as though it hadn't been months of hell wondering what would become of them. "All that walking, and nary an inch off his middle." The celebration had gone on into the wee hours of the night, all four of them gathered around the painting, holding close the precious gem that was the image of the man they loved.

The brown grass and barren trees of the countryside gave way to the sooty sky and dirty buildings of the city, his impatience nearly burning a hole through his chest with each passing landmark. He was almost there—so close to seeing Beatrice again he could almost smell the lilac and linseed oil.

Thank God it was a fairly early arrival—he actually had hope of seeing her today. He could hardly wait to see the look on her face when he presented the painting to her. It was the perfect solution. She could have something of genuine worth from him, and the painting would stay in the family, something that meant more to him now than he ever imagined it would.

To have not only a likeness of his father, but one done in his own hand, gave Colin the connection he had been missing all this time. His father hadn't just sat back and let ruin come to them. He truly had been trying to recapture his love of painting, to provide a way out of the unmitigated mess that fell upon them when the engraving business failed.

By the time the coach pulled to a halt in front of the London post office, he felt like a coiled spring, ready to explode. He made it to his aunt's street in record time, heedless of the damp chill pervading the city or the disgruntled glances from the people he rushed by.

As he vaulted up the stairs to his aunt's town house, the door opened and his cousin appeared, as impeccably groomed as ever. "Colin," he said, taking a step back in surprise. "Wasn't expecting to see you for a few more days yet." His eyes fell to the items in Colin's hands. "I say, is that what I think it is?"

There was no stopping the triumphant grin that came to his face. "Perhaps you'd best come inside with me."

John agreed readily, trailing behind as Colin rushed to the drawing room. "Simmons," he called as he passed the man, "I've a missive I will need sent momentarily."

Carefully depositing his precious cargo, he went to the writing desk tucked in the back of the room and rifled through it, unearthing paper, pen, and ink. "I must say, it has been quite an eventful fortnight," he said over his shoulder. "I can hardly wait to show you." More important, he could hardly wait to show Beatrice. He didn't care that he was chilled to the bone, hungry, and in need of a bath. He dashed off a quick note, tossed a handful of sand across it, and folded it into a neat square. By the time the thing was sealed, a footman stood waiting just inside the door. "Please, have this sent to Lady Beatrice at Granville House in St. James's Square at once."

The moment the man was gone, he turned to John. "Anything disparaging that I ever said about my father?"

"Yes?" John said, his lips already turned up in a grin. "I take it all back."

*   *   *

"I'm afraid you have not caught me in the best of moods, Sophie." Beatrice smiled wanly to her friend, patting the sofa beside her. "Though it is nice to see a friendly face."

"Oh dear—have you recently been in the presence of an *un*friendly face? Shall I seek them out and knock them over the head with my oboe? It's quite stout, and I'm rather handy with it."

Rotten mood or not, Sophie was impossible not to smile at. With her cheery daffodil gown and slightly mischievous smile—not to mention her sweet disposition—she was like walking sunshine. "Perhaps not. I should hate to get you in trouble."

"Are you quite sure? It fits rather handily inside my cloak. No one would be the wiser."

Beatrice couldn't help but chuckle at her earnest expression. "You, my friend, are a treasure." The moment the words left her mouth, her mood crashed to the floor once more. *A stór.* It was a sentiment she would probably never hear again, and if she did, there was no way to know if she could trust it.

Sophie hadn't missed her reaction. Her constant smile slipped a bit as her brow puckered in concern. "You truly are unhappy. My dear, you are to be married soon. *And* you were able to choose your husband. I think there is a law somewhere that says you must be giddy with excitement. If nothing else, think of the trousseau!"

Grabbing a biscuit from the plate left over from tea earlier, Beatrice took a bite and shook her head. "Ugh, I'd rather not. At this point, I've done little else. I've been poked, and pinned, and prodded, and fitted within an inch of my life." And she had felt like a fraud the entire time. Godfrey's damning words repeated in her head, tightening her mouth and flaring her nostrils. Of course Colin would deny the allegations, but it was yet another thing that he would be unable to prove. She bit off another huge bite of the biscuit, taking comfort in its buttery deliciousness.

"Blasphemy, I declare," Sophie said, shaking her head with great dramatic flair. "Well, fiddlesticks. In my mind, assembling a trousseau would be the most fun of all of it. I think I'll pretend we never had this conversation, thank you very much."

"I warned you I was dreadful company."

The butler's measured footsteps caught Bea's ear, and she turned to the doorway. He appeared a few seconds later, holding a silver salver. That got her attention. Generally, any correspondence would be held until after a guest had left. "What is it, Finnington?"

"A letter, my lady, sent from Sir Colin Tate. He asked that it be delivered at once and his family's footman is awaiting your response."

Colin was back? She didn't even wait for the butler to reach her before jumping up and meeting the man halfway. "Thank you, Finnington. I'll ring when I'm ready."

She waited while he nodded and headed back to his post. Sophie popped up and hurried to join her, her dark eyes sparkling like sunlit bronze. "He sent you an urgent missive? How romantic—he must miss you! Don't you think it's romantic? Oh, I wonder what he wants."

Nodding vaguely, Beatrice turned the note over in her hand, her heart racing so fast, it robbed her of her breath. If he was in town, this could mean only one of two things. Either he was willing to concede defeat, or he had found a way to prove his intentions.

A flutter of nerves started deep in her belly as she slipped a finger beneath the wax seal, almost ripping the paper in her haste. The handwriting was crisp and clean, exactly as she would have expected. As angry at the situation as she was, she hadn't expected the sudden welling of emotion as she held his words in her hands.

My dearest Beatrice,

I have returned this very day, and I must see you as soon as possible. Can you meet me at my father's studio? Ever your servant, I await your response.

Yours,
Colin

"Well? Yes, I know, it is dreadfully rude to ask, but is it a romantic letter?" Sophie put her hands to her heart, clearly already expecting it to be so.

Beatrice looked back down at the letter, reading his brief missive once more. What had happened on his journey? He seemed anxious to see her. After what the blackguard Godfrey had said, Beatrice was determined to shield her heart, but it seemed to defy her wishes. Her wildly fluttering pulse was proof enough of that.

"Not romantic, really—just matter-of-fact."

Sophie's face fell. "Oh. Well, I suppose he doesn't wish to put such sentiments in writing—I imagine many men wouldn't. But now that he's back, he wishes to see you, doesn't he? I'll bet he's thought of little else since he's been gone."

It was likely true—but what were his real intentions? For a person who prided herself on being able to read others, there could be no more frustrating or infuriating question. She refolded the paper and turned her attention to Sophie. "In fact, he does wish to see me. Today, actually."

That was all the encouragement Sophie's romantic mind needed. "See? I knew it. Of course you probably already knew it as well, knowing you. Are you going to see him?"

"That depends. Would you mind terribly if we cut short our visit?"

Grinning broadly, she gave a little wink. "Would you look at the time? I simply must be on my way. Enjoy your evening, Beatrice."

Easily said, impossible to do. Two hours later, she and her maid stood on the landing outside the studio, Bea's heart pounding so loudly, she could scarcely hear the traffic on the street below. "Rose," she said, her voice a bit unsteady, "you do realize that Sir Colin and I are betrothed?"

Her maid flushed at once, from her neck all the way to her hairline. "Yes, my lady."

"For heaven's sake, I'm not going to say or do anything untoward. I was merely going to say that we were hoping for a private conversation. That is why I said we were going out for art supplies. I don't wish for everyone to be privy to our conversation. Do you understand what I'm saying?"

"You wish for me to . . . give the pair of you some privacy?"

"Yes, that's it exactly. If you wouldn't mind reading in the back room, I would very much appreciate it." She might as well use the betrothal card while she still had it. Heaven knew where things would stand after this conversation.

"Yes, my lady."

"Thank you," she said, offering the best smile she could muster. Turning toward the door, she drew a deep, bracing breath, lifted her hand, and knocked.

Chapter Twenty-eight

Finally.

Colin exhaled the breath he had been holding since he heard quiet footsteps on the stairs, waiting for Beatrice to knock. Counting to three, he whisked open the door. God, but she was beautiful. In her own special Beatrice way, but absolutely beautiful nonetheless.

"Beatrice." He should have probably said something much more eloquent, but for the life of him he could barely breathe, let alone make a proper sentence. He wanted to snag an arm around her waist, pull her to him, and kiss her until they were both gasping for air.

"Colin," she returned, her eyes giving away nothing as to what exactly she was thinking. She turned and nodded to her maid, and the girl scurried past her, headed for the back room.

Well, that worked out rather better than he had hoped. The moment she was out of view, he turned to Beatrice, ready to do exactly what he had just imagined.

As if sensing his intention, she held up both hands. "I'm here only to talk." Even as she said the words, her gaze traveled over him, burning a path everywhere it touched. Her lips were parted, her pupils so large as to make her eyes seem fathomless. But he knew the significance of her words. She hadn't softened in his absence.

He pressed his lips together and nodded, inviting her in. She walked past him, maintaining an arm's distance between them. The air stirred around him, chilled from outside and flavored with the faintest hint of lilac. It didn't last nearly long enough as it carried past him and mixed with the warmth from the fire he'd lit when he arrived almost an hour earlier.

Her eyes flitted around the room, tripping past the easel that held the primed, blank canvas from his father's cabin—another gift for her. His gaze lingered for a second on the object hidden beneath an inconspicuous white sheet, waiting for the perfect moment to reveal it with all the pomp and circumstance due the painting that would save a marriage.

Closing the door, he turned to face her, not even trying to hide the emotion from his eyes. "I missed you." The words were quiet. Sincere.

She swallowed, accepting them without comment. She met his gaze, but with the wariness of a woman meeting a strange man on the street. Reluctance was one thing, but why the hell did she look so blasted wary? All he could think about was wrapping his arms around her and kissing her senseless, and she looked like judge and jury at a case he knew nothing about.

"Is something amiss? More than the obvious, I mean?" Damn it, now *he* was wary. He sensed something significant had shifted since he left.

Her eyes flared with the spark he knew so well, but she held the rest of herself in icy, rigid control. His stomach dropped as if he'd walked off an unexpected step. "That depends," she said, her voice too tight to be called neutral.

"On?"

She tilted her head, watching him through slightly narrowed eyes, as if trying to peer into his soul. He left himself as open as possible to her scrutiny—he had nothing to hide.

"On how well you know Mr. Godfrey, for starters."

"Mr. Godfrey?" What the hell did that jackass have to do with anything? "You've been with me both times I have encountered the man. I'd say I know him not at all, other than his status as a wastrel."

"You know he's a gambler?"

"Vaguely."

She started pacing, slowly, but with pent-up energy that bespoke agitation. "Could 'vaguely' be used to encompass something as quickly done as, say, making a wager?"

"I beg your pardon?" His impatience with this line of questioning made his voice sharper than he intended, but what the bloody hell was she getting at?

She stopped abruptly, turning to face him straight-on. "A wager. As in, did you make a wager with Mr. Godfrey?"

"Of course not! Why would you think such a fool thing?"

She was not happy with his wording, but he wasn't happy with the insinuation he was somehow colluding with Godfrey. "Because he said as much."

"And you believed *that*?" He shook his head, at a loss for what to even think, let alone say. "You couldn'a believe that I loved you, or that my intentions were toward you and not your dowry, but you believed that rat's tale? And what were you even doing talking to the man?"

Her spine went as stiff as mortar. "I didn't *believe* him—not straight out. That's why I'm asking. How else is one to know?"

"Oh, I don't know, by not thinking me some sort of

conniving scoundrel who would fraternize with a man who tried to force your hand in marrying him?" The joy of only moments earlier faded to black. Was he so bloody untrustworthy in her eyes? "And what sort of bet am I supposed to have made, exactly?"

For the first time, she looked uncomfortable, twisting her hands together. "He said you had a wager to see who could win my hand in marriage. I should point out, by the way, that he knew all about your financial situation. How would he have known that if you didn't tell him?"

He was speechless, utterly speechless. He stared at her for a good three seconds before gathering his wits enough to respond. "I never hid the truth of my situation—I merely didn't speak of it. If anyone had made serious inquiries into me, they might have stumbled across it. You did, did you not?"

"I stumbled upon it because I was going to marry you. Why on earth would he be making inquiries into you? That doesn't make any sense."

"Perhaps because you publicly shamed him, and he set out to find a way to exact revenge."

"Don't put this back on my shoulders. If you had been honest with me, I wouldn't have had reason to doubt anything about you. Now I can't help but question everything!" Her cheeks were fiercely pink. Good—then he wasn't the only one fighting against a rising tide of emotions.

"I *couldn't* tell you everything."

Her lip curled in derision. "Of course you could—you chose not to."

"I would have, but—" He slammed his mouth shut. This wasn't about her brother, damn it.

"But what?"

"Do you want the truth? Here it is: You wouldn'a have given me half a chance if you had known about the debt. You would have seen me as the enemy, no matter what."

"So you are admitting that you purposely withheld that information in a bid to secure my affection."

He growled in frustration, raking both hands through his hair. "You are so blasted blind. You doona see that a man without money can be just as fine a person as a wealthy man—or better, for that matter. You decided fortune hunters were the devil, no matter who he was. Well, you know what? That's *wrong*."

Her eyes became hooded, and she crossed her arms protectively over her chest. "You'll say anything to—"

"I'll say the truth." He stalked closer to her, forcing her to look up at him, to witness the truth of his words. "You cannot judge a man—or his passions—by his coffers. Am I a bad person for not wanting my grandmother, sister, and brother to be tossed on the streets? For wanting to preserve my father's legacy and give my siblings a future? Does being relieved that I fell in love with a woman whose dowry would save my family make me an evil person?"

He lifted a hand and trailed a finger down her cheek. She didn't move, didn't even blink. "Because, as God is my witness, I would have fallen for you either way. The difference, my dear, is that I wouldn'a have been able to marry you, were you poor."

Still she didn't move, but he heard her intake of air, saw the darkening of her eyes. He dropped his hand from her cheek, seeking instead her gloved hand. "That doesn'a mean that I would stop loving you." He tugged on the buttery kid leather, sliding it from her fingers. "It would mean that I would be miserable for the rest of my life because I would have had to sacrifice you in order to marry a woman who could save my family."

With her hand bared, he lifted it to his lips, turning it over to kiss the soft, sensitive skin of her palm. Her lips parted as his touched her, her eyes riveted on their point of contact. Finally, he was getting through to her. His gaze flitted to the painting, ready to tell her exactly what he had found in Scotland, but the moment their eye contact was broken, she yanked her hand from his grasp, taking a quick step backward.

"No, I know what you are doing," she said, taking yet another step back, putting more than just distance between them. Her walls were up, their connection of moments ago severed. "You are trained in the art of debate. Who better to convince a person of anything than a barrister? A successful barrister can make any jury believe his client's innocence—whether it is true or not."

"Beatrice—"

"No," she exclaimed, darting around the easel. "You know full well the effect you have on me. You know that you've only to touch me and my defenses are weakened. So tell me now. Please look me straight in the eye and without manipulation or exploitation of my weaknesses, tell me: Do you have any real proof of your claims?"

He stared at her, taking in the huge blue eyes that had haunted his dreams, the lips that had always been so quick to smile, and her slender frame that had fit so perfectly in his arms. He had agonized about how to prove his love to her, only now to realize the cold, harsh truth.

He couldn't.

So long as she was so damn eager to believe the worst of him, he could never truly win her over. And that wasn't the only truth reverberating around inside his skull, cracking the foundations of their relationship.

The painting had seemed like such a lifesaver—something tangible to point to and prove that he was willing to turn over his family's single most valuable possession to her. How could she doubt him?

But he knew now that it was all wrong. She would see it as a bribe—as a *manipulation* of her appreciation of his father. One look at her stricken features and glittering eyes and he just *knew* that the painting would solve nothing. If she didn't believe him on the merit of his word, on the fierceness of his passion and the strength of his affection, then no tangible object was going to change things.

And, honestly, perhaps it would have been a manipulation, however unintended. He'd been so damned happy to have something of worth to offer her, it never occurred to him that his gifts to her—the studio time, the gallery tour, the paintbrushes—may have reduced him to little more than her idol's son. At this point, how could he even know if she had any true affection for him?

His heart ached brutally, his body unable to accept what his mind was coming to realize. He shook his head slowly, breathing in the last hints of lilac. "If you doona already have the proof you need, then nothing I say will change anything."

It was exactly what she had been expecting.

So why did she feel as though she'd been kicked in the chest by one of Papa's best stallions? Beatrice clenched her jaw against the disappointment that flooded through her, washing away the last vestiges of hope.

"So . . . that's it?" The flood receded, and she was left with a huge, yawning emptiness inside her. How could she be so utterly unprepared for an eventuality that she had predicted?

He spread his hands. "The decision is in your hands, Bea. Either you trust what we have between us, or you do not." The angles of his face had never looked more severe, more harsh. More beautiful.

She closed her eyes, and immediately Godfrey's face came to mind, his sneering eyes and self-satisfied smirk as clear as if he were standing before her. Had he been so smug because she had been duped by a fortune hunter, or because he could cast doubt on an already-shaky relationship? Wreaking havoc for the point of wreaking havoc?

She pushed Godfrey from her mind only to have him replaced by Diana, the way she had looked the night she had discovered her husband's betrayal. She was shattered, broken in a way that could never be fixed by a fortune-hunting scumbag.

She opened her eyes and looked to her betrothed, helpless to know what to say. Her traitorous body sang for him, wanting nothing more than to curl up in his arms and be lost in his embrace. Her palm still burned from his kiss, a delicious, tempting heat that proved that she couldn't trust herself around him. She needed time to think, away from the siren call of his gaze. She *wanted* to believe him, but if she relented and married him and discovered he had been lying, there was no turning back.

"I don't know," she said, raising her shoulders in a helpless shrug. "There is no separating the money and the marriage. I don't want to make the wrong decision and regret it for the rest of my life."

A muscle in his cheek jumped as though he were grinding steel with his teeth. "If the answer isn'a yes, then it's a no. Period. You canna have it both ways."

"I need more time."

"What are you going to learn with more time that your heart hasn'a already told you?"

For once in her life the pieces just wouldn't fall into place for her. All of her normal powers of reason seemed to be completely abandoning her, leaving her vulnerable and unsure—two things she absolutely hated. "You can't just expect me to choose right here and now. Colin, don't be unreasonable."

He crossed his arms, his muscles flexing against the sturdy wool of his jacket. "Of the two of us, I am not the unreasonable one."

"I beg your pardon?"

"No, you don't actually. You've insulted my integrity, called into question my sincerity, and doubted the depth of my emotion for you. But the one thing you have *not* done is begged my pardon." He stalked to the door and pulled it open. "So, I doona see the point of us hashing this out again and again."

"Colin—"

"No," he said with a decisive sweep of his hand. "I have put everything on the table for you, and you canna even see your way to accepting the sentiment, let alone returning it."

She pressed her lips together, frustration and anger boiling up. She had every right to be cautious—they had agreed that he was the one who had to prove himself. "Who are you to judge me—"

"Your betrothed, remember?"

The statement fell flat on the floor between them, stopping the argument dead in its tracks.

"As if could I forget."

Colin's flint-colored eyes ignited, and he took a step back as if physically attacked. She hadn't intended the bitterness burning in her battered heart to so vividly color her words, but she couldn't take it back now.

"I see." He scrubbed a weary hand over his face. "Well, I guess we know where you stand now."

Panic welled up within her, but she refused to speak when she couldn't be at all sure of what she would say.

If only she had employed the tactic before she opened her mouth last time.

"Fine. I canna force you to see reason, clearly. Just know that if you wish for the marriage contract to be broken, then you'll have to be the one to do it. As much as I doona wish to be yoked to a wife who finds my every word suspicious, I won't open myself up to legal ramifications."

Her stomach pitched like a storm-tossed ship. How had things come to this? But in that moment, something else occurred to her. If she broke the betrothal, then he would be entitled to sue for the promised dowry. Blast it all, she would drive herself mad, second-guessing herself like this. She had to talk to someone; otherwise she'd have herself tied up in knots in no time.

She had to get out of there, the sooner the better. "Rose," she called, her voice shaking the tiniest bit. The maid quickly appeared, her book in her hand. "We're leaving."

She had thought Colin's features couldn't grow any harder, but before her eyes he seemed to turn to stone. His eyes frosted over, and he stared straight ahead as if she weren't even in the room.

Beatrice motioned for her maid to go ahead of her; then, straightening her spine, she headed for the door, steeling herself to pass by him. She could have stopped. She could have wrapped her arms around him and begged his pardon.

But she didn't.

Instead, she pushed forward, each tap of her boots on the wood stairs underscoring the chasm opening up between them. She had either just made the best decision in her life . . . or the absolute worst.

Chapter Twenty-nine

Five days.

It had been five torturous days of misery, where Beatrice had done nothing but second-guess herself. But no matter how she looked at it, it always came back to trust. Once compromised, things could never be the same. Naïveté couldn't be reclaimed; innocence could never be rebuilt.

And she had yet to tell a soul about her decision. Her parents and younger sisters had returned to the country, and Evie and Benedict were spending some time with his brother before the rest of them returned home next week. With so much of her family out of touch, she wasn't prepared to make an announcement that drastic in the form of a letter. No, when they all returned to the Hall for Christmas, she would do it then. In the scheme of things, a couple of weeks really didn't matter. Colin knew the truth, and that's what counted at that point.

A sound caught her attention, and she put down her useless paintbrush and looked to the door. The footsteps were long-strided and sure—Benedict was here.

Seconds later, he appeared in the doorway. "Do you have a moment?"

It was not the greeting of a man simply visiting family. His features were neutral, his tone bordering on official. Beatrice came around from the unused easel and pulled off her apron. "Yes, of course, Benedict. I wasn't expecting to see you here. Is something the matter?"

"That depends on how you interpret the information I come bearing."

Well, that certainly didn't put one at ease. "Come, have a seat," she said, gesturing to the old sofa. The morning sun poured into the studio, warming the space far better than even a fire would. That had been a good thing, a few moments ago. Now, a prickle of concern combined with her heavy winter morning gown, making her sweat.

"I could certainly use some good news, Benedict."

He smiled, his dimple creasing his left cheek. "I can see that. Unfortunately, I have no idea whether you will like or dislike the information I come bearing, but I decided you should have it nonetheless."

"My, that does sound serious. All right, then, let's hear it." She braced herself, completely uncertain of what he could possibly have to tell her. If it was bad news, she was not opposed to boarding the next ship to France for an extended sojourn. Five or so years ought to do it.

"I received a missive today from one of my contacts who I had requested help from last month. There is to be an announcement in tomorrow's paper, but select private invitations have already been issued." Benedict leaned forward, rubbing his hands together. "Evidently, a single portrait is to go to auction next week. Sir Frederick Tate's final masterpiece."

Beatrice's mouth dropped in utter astonishment. He could have just as well said Rembrandt was in town. "A final masterpiece? Does Colin know?"

"Colin is the one who is to sell it."

The words were like a blow to the chest. "How could

that be? He never . . ." She trailed off, unable to comprehend the enormity of the situation. He'd never said a word. She thought back to their meeting, which he had so eagerly arranged the moment he had returned. Was there a significance to them meeting in his father's studio?

"From what I gather, it is a previously unknown work, discovered at the estate during his recent visit." He leveled his chocolate gaze on her, taking in her reaction. "There are bound to be questions about why he would choose to sell the work."

She nodded slowly. Of course there would be. Everyone would think the estate was in trouble—why else would a man sell his newly deceased father's last piece? But in that moment, it didn't matter to her. The whole world could think he was a penniless fortune hunter, for all she cared.

Because in that moment, in a sudden, blinding flash of clarity, she knew better.

He had every right to sue if she backed out of the betrothal. He would win, too. She had no case—and more than that, she was quite certain every detail of the settlement had been attended to in order to be certain it was legally binding.

He could ruin her. He could take his rightful settlement, and he could restore his estate. He could choose some sweet bride—a thought that had Beatrice balling her fists into the fabric of her skirts—and move on with his life.

But he wouldn't.

Her mind reeled, dashing back and forth between their many conversations about Sir Frederick. About how difficult their relationship had been, about how hard things had been. Yet whenever he looked at one of his father's paintings, his face lit up. She knew he mourned the fact that not a single one had remained with his family, save the four in his aunt's collection, which probably belonged to her late husband's estate, anyway.

Yet here was a previously undiscovered painting, and instead of keeping the piece and exploiting the money from her dowry, he was taking the last thing he had from his father and he was sacrificing it. Giving it up, lost to the highest bidder. Tears welled in her eyes, an outward manifestation of the emotion overwhelming her on the inside. Of all the tangled feelings balled up in her belly, there were but two exploding in her heart.

Incredible love and burning regret.

The surge of love was indescribable, filling her chest to near bursting. Her mind finally accepted what her body and soul had believed since the moment she laid eyes on him in the empty portrait hall. Since they had danced in the gallery, since he'd presented her with the paintbrushes, since his lips had touched hers.

Oh, but the regret was just as strong.

Why had she forced him away? Putting him through hell, making him chase after the impossible only to turn her back on him? She had been so wrong. Horribly, wretchedly, terribly wrong. How could she ever set this right?

Concern darkened Benedict's eyes and creased his brow. "Are you quite all right, Bea? Should I send for someone? Your maid perhaps?"

"Yes." He started to rise, and she waved a staying hand. "No. I mean, I'm all right." Warm, wet tears spilled down her cheeks, and he raised a doubtful eyebrow. "No, I swear to it. I am well. But on second thought, you can find someone for me."

"Yes?" He was on his feet, ready for action. Poor man—he imparts simple news to his sister-in-law and ends up with a watering pot on his hands.

She drew a deep breath, swiping away the moisture

from her face. She was not a crier—she was a doer. And she had something she had to do. "Richard. Please, tell Richard that I need to speak with him at once."

"I have a most unusual request."

"Excellent," Richard said, leaning back in his desk chair with a wink. "It wouldn't be any fun if it were usual."

Beatrice paused in her pacing to smile at her brother. "I'm so glad you think so. Because I need to borrow ten thousand pounds."

Richard, who had been balancing on the two back legs of his chair, wheeled his arms as he very nearly fell backward. He overcompensated, slamming the two front legs onto the floor with an echoing bang.

"Good Lord, don't tease like that. You almost made me fall flat on my arse." He resituated himself, sitting more properly in the chair this time.

"Oh, no, not teasing. Although, technically, I don't wish to borrow money so much as I wish to have a portion of my dowry now."

"I'm afraid the paint pigment dust must have finally done in your brain, Bea. Shall I order some biscuits and a cup of tea to supply you with some much-needed sugar?"

Leaning on the back of the chair in front of her, she shook her head. "My brain is in perfect working order, though I admit I have been rather stupid these past few weeks."

"Perhaps you should get to the point, Bea. I'm feeling a bit lost."

"Oh, good idea." Stepping around the chair, she sat and crossed her arms, facing her brother and all of his cautious glory. He was completely incongruous with the space, his gorgeous blue jacket sticking out among the dark wood of the furniture and walls. To Beatrice, he looked exactly like the bull's-eye in the center of a target. "Let's start in the middle and then work our way backward and forward, shall we?"

Richard's eyebrow went up. "Convoluted, but I think I can keep up. Carry on."

"Several weeks ago, I learned I was betrothed to a fortune hunter." As shocking statements went, it was a darn good one, if she did say so herself.

Richard's eyes widened, and he leaned back in his chair, one hand rubbing his chin. "I . . . see."

"Well, I did not—before that moment, that is. I was shocked, furious, humiliated—basically every negative emotion you can imagine. I confronted Colin, at which time he confessed the truth of the allegations, though he did proclaim his love for me.

"As you can imagine, it was not enough. Not nearly enough. After such deception, I couldn't marry a man like that. He begged for a chance to prove himself, and I agreed to let him try. An impossible task, but I couldn't deny that I loved him—or at least thought I loved him—and so I was willing to see what he could come up with."

Richard said nothing, simply watching and listening as if a blond-headed statue.

"So let's move forward to five days ago. Colin returned, we fought, and the engagement was called off."

"*What?*"

Beatrice smiled sweetly. "No interruptions until the end, if you please."

He nodded, though she was fairly certain she heard his teeth grind.

"Thank you. Now, let us back up. Apparently, while Colin was in Scotland, he somehow discovered an unknown painting from his father. I believe it was his intention to reveal this to me the night he returned, but I, in all my indignant glory, made it clear the trust between us was destroyed and I could never truly have faith in him again."

Beatrice stood, resuming her pacing, her footfalls silent on the thick rug. "At this point, I fully expected him to sue for the dowry owed to him in the marriage contract. It was worth it to me, however—I'd rather be ruined and dowryless than marry a fortune hunter. So imagine my astonishment when I learned this very day that he had put up the newfound treasure for auction.

"Now, why would he do such a thing? He has won whether I marry him or not. He is a barrister, so I have absolutely no doubt that the marriage contract is iron-clad, carefully and meticulously created to the benefit and protection of both parties involved.

"And then it came to me—because he really does love me. Oh the joy! Except for the minor detail of me effectively renouncing his suit, of course. As I sat there, exulting in my grand fortune, it hit me." She stopped, turning to face her brother with both hands on her hips.

When she didn't say anything more, just stood there eyeing her brother, he finally raised his hands, palms out. "Yes?"

"The contract was ironclad."

"Yes, you said that."

"Which means you had to have known about his finances."

He exhaled as though he'd been holding his breath for days. "Indeed."

"*Indeed?*" she exclaimed, stalking forward to brace herself with both arms on the desk. "I've suffered the worst anguish over a deception that you already knew about, and all you have to say is 'indeed'?"

It took almost all her willpower not to sweep her hand across his paper-covered desk, throwing a proper fit. She would have trusted her brother with her life, and as casually as a cruel-hearted sinner, he had betrayed her in the worst possible way.

He leaned forward, meeting her gaze head-on. "If you had come to me with any of this, *any* of it, I would have told you everything. But none of us had any idea you were anything more than moody about the fact that your betrothed had gone away. We thought you were *missing* him, for God's sake."

"Why, Richard? Why did you do it in the first place?"

"To protect you from yourself, Bea. Any idiot with half a brain could see how much you were in love with the man. Man to man, I believed he loved you, trusted not only his words but his actions when he signed over the bulk of the dowry to a trust for you."

Pushing away from the desk, she whirled and resumed her pacing. As much as it was a dagger to the heart to admit it, he was right, for the most part. Still, he was her brother, and he should have been honest. "Right. Well, I made a fine mess of everything by declaring that I could never really trust him. At that point, whatever trust he had in me was well and truly crushed.

"And that," she said, spreading her arms, "is where the ten thousand pounds comes in."

Chapter Thirty

The gathered crowd was a surprise, considering the time of year. Apparently, a once-in-a-lifetime opportunity really meant something to the art world.

Sitting in the back of the room, Colin kept from making direct eye contact with anyone. He didn't wish to see the speculation in anyone's eyes. They might all be glad for the circumstance that propelled him to sell the last and most remarkable portrait his father had ever created, but that didn't keep them from judging.

Evidently, he was a man others found it easy to judge. For God's sake, the woman he loved would rather live as a social outcast than be married to him. She had yet to make the split official, but he knew when he was beat. No matter how devastated he was, he couldn't afford to sit back and do nothing. His family's well-being came first, and that meant selling the painting to save the estate. Suing Beatrice's family would never, ever be an option, so here he was, cloistered in a large, overwarm room filled with men coveting his only tangible link to his father.

He glanced back to the portrait, hoping to soak in his father's likeness for the last time. He hadn't bothered to do so the last time they had parted. Who would have known that he would never see the man alive again? So instead he memorized the portrait. At least it was static—he could better remember the painting he had spent weeks staring at than the man he had casually glimpsed his whole life.

Mr. Christie, the auction house owner, walked into the room and headed to the small podium. With his gray hair and fastidiously neat grooming, he might have looked unassuming, but the moment he spoke, he commanded attention. "Good afternoon, gentlemen. As you know, today's auction is for the sale of a single portrait, notable as the final painting ever completed by the late Sir Frederick Tate and the only known self-portrait."

Colin put his head down, squeezing his eyes closed. If he could live without his mother, his father, and even his betrothed, then he could damn well live without the painting.

"Now, may I have an opening bid please at one hundred pounds?"

His gut clenched. It was a long, long way to ten thousand pounds from here.

A hand lifted in the front. "One hundred pounds."

"We are started, gentlemen, at one hundred pounds. May I have two hundred? Excellent, now three?"

"Three hundred." Lord Northup's man, if Colin wasn't mistaken

"We are at three, can I have four hundred. Yes? Now five?"

A wealthy landowner raised his hand, though his name eluded Colin at that moment. Drake, was it? Derby?

Mr. Christie nodded. "Very good—we have five. Can we have six, please? There's six and now seven? Seven hundred pounds."

Northup's agent raised his hand again, just as another solicitor said, "Eight hundred."

"Eight in the room, how about nine? There's nine, now one thousand pounds? One thousand?" Mr. Christie paused, and Colin's eyes darted to the gathered men. For God's sake, it had to go for more than a thousand pounds.

At last a hand slipped up, the landowner again.

A nod from the auctioneer.

Colin blew out a pent-up breath and bowed his head again. Around him, the numbers climbed as the men continued to bid. He lifted his gaze, tuning out the drone of Mr. Christie's voice as he focused on his father's face again.

His father had come through for him. When he needed him most, his father hadn't let him down. Even if it wasn't enough in the end, he had truly tried.

"We have six thousand. Who will give me seven? Can I have seven thousand—Yes, thank you, Mr. Smith. Seven, now eight, seven thousand, now waiting for eight? Can I have eight, please? Who will give me eight?"

Colin leaned forward in his seat, willing the stakes to be raised. Seven thousand wasn't good enough. It was a huge amount of money, more than the estate made in two years, but it didn't hold water against the debt owed.

Mr. Christie pressed on, his eyes scanning back and forth over the room. "We have seven now, can I have seven thousand five hundred? Seven thousand five hundred for a piece of history? Yes, excellent, seven five from Mr. Darcy.

"Going now to eight thousand. At seven thousand five hundred now, only need five hundred more." He kept on with his monotonous litany, sweeping his eyes over the room, pointing to former bidders. Each time, they gave a shake of their head.

Damn it all—the painting was worth so much more

than that. He knew it was a rotten time of year to move forward with the auction, but time was of the essence. If it wasn't going to hit ten, he'd lose the estate anyway, so what was the point? It would buy them time and comfort, but in that moment, he wanted nothing more than to yank the portrait from its place of honor and walk away, keeping his father close to him in a way he never had in life.

"Now's your chance, gentlemen. Don't let five hundred pounds get in the way of you and this extraordinary painting. Seven thousand five hundred now, only need five hundred more. Can I have five hundred more, just eight thousand."

Nothing. Not a sound, not a movement, just the smiling profile of Mr. Darcy, clearly pleased to be winning.

"Fair warning, gentlemen. It will go at seven five. Fair warning. I need to hear five hundred more. Going once . . ."

No, not going! Colin gritted his teeth, holding on to the bottom of his chair to keep from coming to his feet and making a fool of himself.

"Going twice . . ." Christie made one last sweep of the room, then lifted his knocker to seal the deal with a single slam on the desk.

"Ten thousand pounds."

A low gasp echoed through the room as men turned in their seats, looking toward the back door. Colin jerked around, unable to believe the turn of events. A nondescript man in an understated brown jacket and with neatly cropped hair stood just inside the door. Colin had never seen the man in his life—he was quite certain—but he very nearly leapt to his feet to kiss the man.

A ripple of low conversation buzzed through the room, and Mr. Christie cleared his throat. "Ten thousand pounds. Mr. Darcy, do you want to bid ten thousand five hundred?" The man gave his head a decidedly firm shake. "Very well, fair warning at ten, ten, ten. . . . *Sold*, to the man in the back for ten thousand pounds."

The strike of the knocker rang through the room, a bullet through the heart of Colin's nightmare. He pressed his eyes closed for a brief moment, long enough to give thanks for the incredible turn of events. His financial worries were over.

He expected a rush of happiness, a joy born of the surge of relief filling his veins and setting his mind at ease. But there was none. Though the release of stress and worry was profound, there was no accompanying excitement, no elation.

He had what he had set out to attain since the moment he learned of the estate's debt, yet it didn't matter like it should have. How could it? His finances might be safe, but his heart had been lost.

A new awareness swept through him and he sat up straight. Well, he was free now, was he not? He was a fortune hunter no more, the proof of which would likely be in the papers by week's end. To hell with what Beatrice said. To hell with playing by her rules.

He had proof now, and by God he intended to let her know. Coming to his feet, he headed to the front of the room, where Mr. Christie was finishing up. "Thank you, sir. I trust you can handle the rest of the transaction from here?"

The man grinned, pleasure at the coup written all over his face. "Indeed, sir. And thank you for trusting us with this incredible item. It was a privilege."

Colin gave a perfunctory nod, accepting the praise. "Thank you. Now, if you will excuse me, I have some very important business to attend to." With one last look at the portrait of his father, he turned and strode from the room.

*   *   *

Colin was out of breath and thoroughly disheveled by the time he arrived in front of the black lacquered door of Granville House. He bent over, sucking in a lungful of frigid air just as the front door opened. The butler looked down at him, showing no reaction whatsoever to seeing a doubled-over gentleman on his front stoop. Extending a folded white piece of paper, he said, "For you, sir."

And then he shut the door.

What the hell? Standing up straight, he turned the paper over in his hand. There were no markings of any kind, just a small dollop of red sealing wax holding it closed. Wasting no time, he ripped open the paper. His brow furrowed in surprise. There were no words, merely a sketch of a wide arching window with indistinct rooftops beyond.

Nothing more, but it was enough.

Colin's feet were moving before he even stuffed the drawing in his pocket. For whatever reason, Beatrice wished for him to go to his father's studio, and he didn't wish to waste even a single moment.

He hurried down the street, dodging pedestrians and darting across the street between carriages and carts. The studio was only a few blocks away, but with anticipation powering through his veins like a drug, it had never seemed farther.

It wasn't until he reached the building and headed up the stairs that it occurred to him that she could just want to officially end the betrothal. Well, today he was a free man, no longer a fortune hunter, and he planned to fight for what he wanted.

He didn't even pause at the landing. The knob turned easily in his hand and he strode inside, his gaze seeking nothing but Beatrice's face.

She stood beside the window, her eyes sparkling in the late-afternoon sun. Her gaze was made all the more brilliant by the gorgeous Eton blue of her gown, the perfect marriage for the blues and greens of her eyes. She stood straight and as tall as her petite frame would allow, her blond curls piled on her head for an extra bit of height.

He didn't say a word, just slammed the door behind him and walked straight toward her. She opened her mouth to say something, but he wasn't about to let her words get in the way of things now. He didn't stop until his body was pressed firmly against hers and his hands were cupping either side of her jaw. Not allowing even a second for her to protest, he captured her mouth with his, taking full advantage of her open mouth.

He poured every ounce of him into his kiss, pulling her against him as his tongue delved into her mouth. He had expected her to fight, or resist, or even remain stock-still, but she didn't do any of these. Instead, she wrapped her arms around his neck and kissed him with just as much passion as he did her.

Heat shot through his body at her response, and he half groaned, half growled as he backed her up against the wall. She gave a breathy little moan, unleashing whatever restraint existed within him. There was no gentleness between them, just raw passion that sent waves of sensation to every nerve ending in his body. He pressed hard against her, cursing the winter clothes that hid her skin from him.

The kiss was more all consuming than he ever imagined a kiss could be, connecting them in a way that went beyond the physical. She was his, damn it. She was meant for him and he for her.

At last he pulled away, but he didn't give up control. His gaze burned into hers as he jerked the buttons of his greatcoat open. "I love you, Beatrice Moore." He was still panting from the kiss as he tugged off the coat and tossed it to the floor. "You can keep your blasted money, every last penny." He wrenched off his gloves, letting them fall to the ground without notice. "I want you to be my wife. *You*, not some bloody dowry."

Her eyes were wide, her pupils huge as she watched him, her chest heaving just as much as his. He put a bare hand to the exposed skin of her chest and nearly closed his eyes at the explosion of sensation the touch caused. "Do you feel that? That is passion, pure and simple."

With his other hand, he lifted her gloved fingers to his own chest, pressing hard. "And do you feel that? My heart beats for you, Beatrice, just as yours pounds for me. You canna hide that, or deny the truth of it."

He drew in a deep breath, making his chest rise with her hand still upon it. "Do you feel that? I breathe for you. I can live without you, Bea, but I doona *want* to. Everything in my life is better when you are near. I thought I could walk away, let you have what you so obviously wanted, but I've changed my mind. I'll still do it, but not without a fight."

He gathered both her hands in his, twining their fingers together. "Now, I'll ask you one more time. Beatrice Eloise Moore, will you—"

"No, don't say it."

His heart plummeted to the pit of his stomach. Damn it all. After all of this—

"Not yet, anyway."

He jerked his gaze up to meet hers. She didn't look away, didn't flinch at all. Instead, she gave his fingers a little squeeze.

"First, I have something I need to say."

"All right," he said, his voice gruff. Hope was the cruelest of all torture devices. He hoped to God Beatrice wasn't stringing him along.

"There's no easy way to say this, so I think it's best

if I just be as honest as possible." She drew in a breath and licked her lips. "I, Beatrice Moore, am a complete and total imbecile."

His mouth dropped open in a caricature of himself. "I beg your pardon?"

"No," she said fiercely, fire coming to her eyes. "I beg *your* pardon. Humbly, meekly, I ask your forgiveness for being so incredibly blind. For not trusting you, or the bond between us. For taking so long to realize how very wrong I was. You deserve more than that, and I hope that you can forgive me."

Forgive her? The relief was so acute, it was almost painful, like a limb that had gone to sleep and was roaring back to life with pins and needles. He looked down at her, hardly able to contain the joy that seemed to inhabit every part of him. "Are you finished?"

For the first time, she looked truly uncertain. With her brow coming together in a little vee, she nodded.

"In that case, Beatrice Eloise Moore, will you still marry me?"

She laughed, squeezing his hands tightly. "For heaven's sake, don't do that to me!"

"Is that a yes?"

"Aye," she said in a teasing Scottish accent. She wrapped their joined hands around his back and tugged him flat against her. "And now that I've found my *stór*, I vow to never, ever let him go."

Epilogue

"They love you."

"I definitely wouldn't go that far." Beatrice peered over Colin's shoulder to where his grandmother was conversing with Mama over a cup of tea. The older woman looked up, catching Beatrice's stolen glimpse. Inwardly cringing, she smiled serenely before ducking back behind him. "I think your gran is still suspicious as to why I didn't love you unconditionally instead of sending you on a fool's errand."

"Good question, actually," he murmured, seeming to enjoy her discomfort a bit too much. "Why was that?"

She smacked his arm lightly, rounding her eyes at him. "Oh no, I forbid you to mention that little lapse in judgment ever again." She didn't know why he thought it was so adorable—his word—that she was so discomfited around his family. Attempting to make a good impression on people that were predisposed to dislike a person was more than a little daunting.

"Very well. Shall I mention all the things I'd like to do with you in less than a fortnight, when we are married?"

"Colin," she admonished, glancing around the room even though she knew full well that no one else could hear them as they strolled around the perimeter, especially with Carolyn playing the pianoforte in the adjoining room.

"Is that a yes? Let's see. First I shall unbutton—"

"Oh, good Lord in heaven, shush!" She didn't care if no one else could hear him. *She* could hear him, and it was already bringing a blush to her face. It was one thing to think such things, but to speak of it with one's grandmother fifteen feet away was another thing entirely.

"I do so love seeing you blush. I almost never have the pleasure." His hand covered hers where it rested on his arm, giving it a little squeeze. "I shall endeavor to make it happen more often."

The music came to an end, and both families paused in their conversation to applaud. Beatrice snuck a glance at the clock on the mantel. It was almost time. "Come. Let's go have a seat on the sofa. I have a bit of a surprise for you."

"For me? Well, I do like the sound of that. Have you finally come to your senses and decided to elope with me to Scotland to get this wedding over and done with?"

"Not a chance. No, this is a little something I planned to give to you when I had you come to me in your father's studio, but your—eagerness, shall we call it?—" she said with a mischievous lift of her brow, "told me it wasn't quite the right time. But now, with your family here with mine, is perfect, I think."

Behind her, the clock struck five, and Finnington appeared in the doorway, right on time. Disengaging her hand from Colin's arm, she motioned for him to have a seat on the sofa beside his grandmother.

"If I could have your attention for a moment, there is something that I would like to share with you all on this special occasion of our families coming together for the first time." She looked to Colin, smiling in earnest.

"Sir Frederick is the entire reason that we met, and I am forever grateful to him for bringing you to me. And now, as my betrothal gift to you—and your family, for that matter—I'd like very much to bring him to you."

On cue, two footmen came into the room, carrying a framed canvas covered by a sheet. Colin watched it with interest, then turned his charcoal gaze back to her. "Is this what's become of the portrait you painted for me?" He smiled broadly, softening the angles of his face. "I told you to use your own techniques, not his."

She bit her lip and shook her head, suddenly swamped with unexpected butterflies. His portrait was completed. In fact, she had finished just this week, signing the mainly black, white, and gray painting with a crimson kiss in the bottom corner. But that was for later—this was for his whole family. His siblings watched her with curious gazes, while Gran eyed her with a spark lighting her whole face. Did she suspect?

A third footman set up a small easel, and the others set their bundle on it before retreating. "I'm sorry to say it's not that painting, but I'm hoping this one will be infinitely more dear."

Watching her soon-to-be family, she grasped the edge of the sheet and drew a deep breath. Her life with them wouldn't begin when she exchanged her vows, but when she lifted the sheet, returning to them all that they had sacrificed because of her stubbornness. She caught Colin's eye and basked in the love and joy held in his gaze. With her heart bursting with excitement, she counted down to the rest of her life.

Five, four, three, two . . .

And don't miss the next book in
Erin Knightley's Sealed with a Kiss series,
coming from Signet Eclipse in June!
Read on for a special preview.

Hell and damnation, was he to have no peace at all? Hugh Danby, the new and exceedingly reluctant Baron Cadgwith, pressed the heels of his hands into his eye sockets, pushing back against the fresh pounding that the godforsaken noise next door had reawakened.

"Go to Bath," his sister-in-law had said. "It's practically deserted in the summer. Think of the peace and quiet you'll have."

Bloody hogwash. This torture was about as far from peace as one could get. Not that he blamed Felicity; clearly the news of the first annual Summer Serenade in Somerset festival hadn't made it to their tiny little corner of England when she offered her seemingly useful suggestion. Still, he'd love to get his hands on the person who thought it was a good idea to organize the damn thing.

He tugged the pillow from the empty spot beside him and crammed it over his head, trying to muffle the jaunty pianoforte music filtering through the shared wall of his bedchamber. The notes were high and fast, like a foal prancing in a springtime meadow. Or, more aptly, a foal prancing on his eardrums.

There was no hope for it. There would be no more sleep for him now.

Tossing the useless pillow, he rolled to his side, bracing himself for the wave of nausea that always greeted him on mornings like this. Ah, there it was. He gritted his teeth until it passed, then dragged himself up into a sitting position and glanced about the room.

The curtains were closed tight, but the afternoon sunlight still forced its way around the edges, causing a white-hot seam that felt as if it burned straight through his retinas. He squinted and looked away, focusing instead on the dark burgundy-and-brown Aubusson rug on the floor. His clothes were still scattered in a trail leading to the bed, and several empty glasses lined his nightstand.

Ah, thank God—not *all* were empty.

He reached for the one still holding a good finger of liquid and brought it to his nose. Brandy. With a shrug, he drained the glass, squeezing his eyes against the burn.

Still the music, if one could call it that, continued. Must the blasted pianoforte player have such a love affair with brain-cracking high notes? Though he'd yet to meet the neighbors who occupied the adjoining town house, he knew without question she was a female. No self-respecting male would have the time, inclination, or enthusiasm to play such musical drivel.

Setting the tumbler back down on the nightstand, he scrubbed both hands over his face, willing the alcohol to deaden the pounding in his brain. The notes grew louder and faster, rising to a crescendo that could surely be heard all the way home in Cadgwith, some two hundred miles away.

And then . . . *blessed silence.*

He closed his eyes and breathed out a long breath. The hush settled over him like a balm, quieting the ache and lowering his blood pressure. Thank God. He'd rather walk barefoot through glass than—

The music roared back to life, pounding the nails back into his skull with the relentlessness of waves pounding a beach at high tide. *Damn it all to hell.* Grimacing, he tossed aside the counterpane and came to his feet, ignoring the violent protest of his head. Reaching for his clothes, he yanked them on with enough force to rip the seams, had they been of any lesser quality.

It was bloody well time he met his neighbors.

Freedom in D Minor.

Charity Effington grinned at the words she had scrawled at the top of the rumpled foolscap, above the torrent of hastily drawn notes that danced up and down the static five-lined staff.

The title could not be more perfect.

Sighing with contentment, she set down her pencil on the burled oak surface of her pianoforte and stretched. Whenever she had days like this, when the music seemed to pour from her soul like water from an upturned pitcher, her shoulders and back inevitably paid the price.

She unfurled her fingers, reaching toward the unlit chandelier that hung above her. The room was almost too warm, with sunlight pouring through the sheers that covered the wide windows facing the private gardens behind the house, but she didn't mind. She'd much rather be here in the stifling heat than up north with her parents and their stifling expectations.

And Grandmama couldn't have chosen a more perfect town house to rent. With soaring ceilings, airy rooms, and generous windows lining both the front and back—not to mention the gorgeous pianoforte she now sat at—it was a wonderful little musical retreat.

Exactly what Charity needed after the awfulness of the last Season.

Dropping her hands to the keys once more, she closed her eyes and purged all thoughts of that particular topic from her mind. It was never good for creativity to focus on stressful topics. Exhaling, she stretched her fingers over the cool ivory keys, finding her way by touch.

Bliss. The pianoforte was perfectly tuned, the notes floating through the air like wisps of steam curling from the Baths. Light and airy, the music reflected the joy filling her every pore. Freedom.

Free from her mother and her relentless matchmaking. Free from the gossip that seemed to follow her like a fog. Free from all the strict rules every young lady must abide by during the Season.

The notes rose higher as her right hand swept up the scale, tapping the keys with the quickness of a flitting hummingbird. Her left hand provided counterbalance with low, smooth notes that anchored the song.

A sudden noise from the doorway startled her from her trance, abruptly stopping the flow of music and engulfing the room in an echoing silence. Jeffers, Grandmama's ancient butler, stood in the doorway, his stooped shoulders oddly rigid.

"I do beg your pardon, Miss Effington. Lady Effington requests your presence in the drawing room."

Now? Just when she was truly finding her stride? But Charity wasn't about to make the woman wait— not after she had single-handedly saved Charity from a summer of tedium in Durham with her disgruntled parents. "Thank you, Jeffers," she said, coming to her feet.

She headed down the stairs, humming the beginning of her new creation. Her steps were in time with the music in her mind, which had her moving light and fast on her feet. The town house was medium sized, with more than enough room for the two of them and the four servants Grandmama had brought, so it only took her a minute to reach the spacious drawing room from the music room.

Breezing through the doorway with a ready smile on her face, Charity came up short when the person before her was most definitely *not* her four-foot-eleven silver-haired grandmother.

Mercy!

She only just managed to contain her squeak of surprise at the sight of the tall, lanky man standing in the middle of the room, his rumpled dark clothes in stark contrast to the cheery soft blues and golds of the immaculate drawing room. She swallowed, working to keep her expression passive as her mind raced to figure out who on earth the man was.

Charity had never seen him before—of that, she was absolutely sure. It would be impossible to forget the distinctive scars crisscrossing his left temple and disappearing into his dark blond hair. One of the puckered white lines cut through his eyebrow, dividing it neatly in half before ending perilously close to one of his vividly green—and terribly bloodshot—eyes.

He was watching her unflinchingly, accepting her inspection. Or perhaps he was simply indifferent to it. It was . . . disconcerting.

"There you are," Grandmama said, snapping Charity's attention away from the stranger. Sitting primly at her usual spot on the overstuffed sofa centered in the room, her grandmother offered Charity a soft smile. "Charity, Lord Cadgwith has kindly come over to introduce himself. He is to be our neighbor for the summer."

Kindly? Charity couldn't help her raised eyebrow. The man had come over without invitation or introduction, and Grandmama had actually allowed it?

Correctly interpreting Charity's reaction, the older woman chuckled, clasping her hands over the black fabric of her skirts. "Yes, I realize we are not strictly adhering to the rules, but it is summer, is it not? Exceptions can be made, especially when the good baron overheard your playing and so wished to meet the musician." Her gray eyes sparkled as she smiled at the man.

It was all Charity could do not to gape at the woman. Yes, no one was more proud of Charity's playing than her grandmother, but this was beyond the pale. Good gracious, if Mama and Papa knew how much Grandmama's formally strict nature had been changed by her extended illness, they never would have allowed Charity to accompany her to Bath without them.

The baron bowed, the movement crisp despite his slightly disheveled appearance. "A pleasure to make your acquaintance, Miss Effington," he said, his voice low and a little raspy like the low register of a flute.

Despite the perfectly proper greeting, something about him seemed a little untamed. Must be the scars, the origin of which she couldn't help but wonder about. War wounds? A carriage accident? A duel? Setting aside her curiosity, she arranged her lips in a polite smile. "And you as well, Lord Cadgwith. Are you here for the festival?"

"Please don't mumble, my dear," Grandmama cut in, her whispered reprimand loud and clear. Charity cringed—the older woman insisted that her hearing was fine, and that any problem in understanding laid in the enunciation of those around her.

"Yes, ma'am," she responded in elevated, carefully pronounced tones. "Lord Cadgwith, are you here for the festival?" Heat stole up her cheeks, despite her effort to keep the blush at bay. She had never liked standing out—when away from her pianoforte, of course—and practically shouting in the presence of their neighbor was beyond awkward. One would think she'd have come to terms with the easy blushes to which her pale, freckled skin lent itself—but knowing her cheeks were warming only made her blush that much more violently.

It certainly didn't help that he was by far the most attractive man to ever stand in her drawing room, scars or no. She swallowed against the unexpected rush of butterflies that flitted through her.

For his part, Lord Cadgwith did not look amused. "No, actually. I had no knowledge of the event until my arrival." He made the effort to speak in a way that Grandmama could hear, his dark, deep voice carrying easily through the room. A man used to being heard, she guessed. A military man, perhaps?

"Well, what a happy surprise it must have been when you arrived," her grandmother said, smiling easily. "Charity is planning to audition for the Tuesday Evening Musicale series later this afternoon. There are a limited number of slots, but I have no doubt our Charity will earn a place."

And . . . more blushing. Charity gritted her teeth as she smiled demurely at her grandmother. Music was the one thing for which Charity had no need for false modesty, but sharing her plans with the virtual stranger standing in their drawing room felt oddly invasive. "I'm sure Lord Cadgwith isn't interested in my playing, Grandmama."

"On the contrary," he said, his voice rough but loud enough to carry. "It is, after all, your music that prompted me to visit in the first place."

Her mouth fell open in a little "Oh" of surprise before she got her wits about her. Still, pleasure, warm and fizzy, poured through her. Her music had called this incredibly handsome man to her? Not her looks (such as they were), not her father's station, not curiosity from the gossipmongers. No, he had sought her out because her playing touched him. Pride mingled with pleasure, bringing an irrepressible grin to her lips.

Grandmama beamed, her shrewd gaze flitting back and forth between them. "Well, I do hope you'll stay for tea, my lord."

His smile was oddly sharp. "Unfortunately, I must be off. I just wanted to introduce myself after being serenaded this morning. Lady Effington, thank you for your indulgence of my whim."

Lady Effington nodded as regally as the queen, pleasure clear in the pink tinge of the normally papery white skin of her cheeks.

He turned to face Charity, his green eyes meeting hers levelly. "Miss Effington," he said, lowering his voice to a much more intimate tone as he bent his head in acknowledgment, "do please have a care for your captive audience in the adjoining town houses, and keep the infernal racket to a minimum."

Because she was lost in the vivid dark green of his eyes, it took a moment for his words to sink in. She blinked several times in quick succession, trying to make sense of his gentle tone and bitingly rude words. He couldn't possibly have just said . . . "I beg your pardon?"

"Pardon granted. Good day, Miss Effington."

And just like that, the baron turned on his heel and strode from the room. It was then that she caught the fleeting hint of spirits in his wake, faint but unmistakable. A few seconds later, the sound of the front door opening and closing reached her burning ears. Of all the insufferable, boorish, rude—

"My goodness, but he was a delightful young man." Grandmama's sweet voice broke through Charity's fury, just before she was about to explode. The older woman looked so happy, so utterly pleased with the encounter, that Charity forced herself to bite her tongue. It wouldn't do to upset her—after all, she was only just now recovering from her illness. The currish baron wasn't worth the strife it would cause.

Forcing a brittle smile to her lips, she nodded. "Mmhmm. And you know what? I think I'll go play an extra-enthusiastic composition just for him."

With that, she marched from the room directly back to her pianoforte bench. The baron could have been pleasant. He could have kindly asked her to play more quietly or perhaps less frequently. But, no, he had chosen to go about it in the most uncivilized, humiliating way possible. It was his decision to throw down the gauntlet as though they were enemies instead of neighbors.

She plopped down on her bench with a complete lack of elegance and paused only long enough to lace her hands together and stretch out her muscles. Then she spread her fingers out over the keys and smiled.

This, Lord Cadgwith, means war.

ALSO AVAILABLE FROM

ERIN KNIGHTLEY

MORE THAN A STRANGER

A Sealed with a Kiss Novel

When his family abandoned him at Eton,
Benedict Hastings found an ally in his best friend's sister,
Evelyn, with whom he began a heartfelt correspondence.
Years later, Benedict has seen his share of betrayal, but
when treachery hits close to home, he turns to his old
friend for safe haven, and finds Evelyn is no longer the
demure young girl he remembered—but a woman who
sets his heart racing...

**"This sweet treat of a romance will entrance
you with its delicious humor, dollop of suspense,
and delectable characters."**
—*New York Times* bestselling author Sabrina Jeffries

Available wherever books are sold or at
penguin.com

facebook.com/LoveAlwaysBooks